I0628380

Also from Indigo Sea Press
Novels by Bud Fussell

Scoundrel
Shepherds
Redemption?
Mixed Emotions
Whirlwind

indigoseapress.com

Serendipity

By

Bud Fussell

Sepia Books
Published by Indigo Sea Press
Winston-Salem

Sepia Books
Indigo Sea Press
302 Ricks Drive
Winston-Salem, NC 27103

This book is a work of fiction. Names, characters, locations and events are either a product of the author's imagination, fictitious or used fictitiously. Any resemblance to any event, locale or person, living or dead, is purely coincidental.

First Sepia Books edition published
December, 2015
Sepia Books, Moon Sailor and all production design are trademarks of Indigo Sea Press, used under license.

For information regarding bulk purchases of this book, digital purchase and special discounts, please contact the publisher at
indigoseapress.com

Cover design by Pan Morelli

Manufactured in the United States of America
ISBN 978-1-63066-207-3

CHAPTER ONE

The days immediately following graduation were truly lazy days for the Shepherd twins. Johnny was going to leave for the army in about six weeks, and Jimmy was counting on getting to leave for some baseball city in four or five weeks; he wouldn't be sure until after the Major League Baseball Draft on June fifth, sixth, and seventh. He couldn't get the thought out of his mind, though, that he had decided against playing professional football. He was more than likely going to be drafted by one of the teams that had invited him to the NFL Combine and to Pro Day. He thought, *what if I don't get drafted by a baseball team, and I passed up the opportunity to play football. Man, that would be a bummer. I guess I'll just have to keep praying about it; God knows what I'm supposed to do, and I'll just have to remember that.*

Monty wasn't going to make them work with that short of a time before they had to leave, but it bothered him a little to see them just lying around the pool, doing nothing, while he worked himself silly. One day, after they had been home for a few days and were soaking up the sun at the pool, Joan went out to be with them for a little while. After she had been out there a few minutes, Jimmy said, "Mom, since Johnny and I will be leaving pretty soon, why don't we all go to Florida for a few days?"

"I'd like to, but I don't know if your Dad can get off. He has been so busy, but I'll ask him. I'd like to go, too. You guys haven't been since the house was remodeled, have you?"

"No ma'am, but I'd sure like to see it. I hear it's really pretty and huge."

"It is. It doesn't even look like the same place; it's beautiful. Do you want just us to go or do you want to take somebody with you?"

Johnny chimed in and said, "I want to take Analisa, and Mom, how would it be if you invited Mr. and Mrs. Davis to go with us? They're really nice and fun to be around, and I think you and Dad would enjoy being with them. I feel sure they would love to go."

"Okay, but let me talk to your Dad first. We have to find out if we can even go. If he says we can and says we can invite the Davises, then I'll call Nancy tonight."

"Thanks, Mom."

"Why don't we make this a large, family vacation," Jimmy asked. Let's ask Sue and Bobby and their parents, you want to? We always enjoy them."

Joan asked, "When do you want to go?"

Jimmy said, "The sooner the better."

"Okay, I'll call your Dad."

Joan got up and went into the house and picked up the phone. "Hello, Connie, is my husband busy?

Connie replied, "Never too busy to talk to you. Hold on just a second."

Monty picked up on the first ring, "This is Monty."

Joan said, "I must be connected to the wrong person. I was calling the person known as *Mr. Wonderful.*"

"This is Mr. Wonderful. What can I do for you?"

"Are you sure? You don't sound like him."

"Well take my word for it. This is the true Mr. W.. How can I help you?"

"Well, your family wants to go to Florida, and I told them I would call Mr. Wonderful to see if we could go. What do you think?"

"I think it's a fantastic idea. When do you want to go?"

"Just as soon as we can."

"How does Saturday sound?"

"It sounds perfect."

"Okay, make your plans and I'll have the plane ready."

"One more thing, Mr. Wonderful; your sons want to take some people, and I told them I'd ask."

"What people?"

"Johnny wants to take Analisa, of course, but he also wants to take her parents. Jimmy wants Sue, Bobby, Ben and Liz. What do you think?"

"I think it would be fun. I'd like to get to know Nancy and Brad a little better. Set it up."

"Okay. I'll see you tonight."

"Bye."

On Saturday morning, everyone was at the airport in time for the planned ten o'clock takeoff. This was the first time Brad and Nancy had seen the Shepherd plane, and Brad, especially, was blown away by the beauty of the Gulfstream Four. While he was marveling at the

Gulfstream, Nancy nudged him and pointed to the 707 parked just down the way. That really impressed him. In a few minutes, Mike Taylor, the pilot, came to the door and invited everyone to come aboard. Monty was still inside the terminal, but came out in time to board right after Joan. Everyone picked a seat, and in a couple of minutes, Mike started the engines, and they taxied out the runway to the spot where they would begin their run to takeoff.

Monty took time to speak to everyone before they took off and singled out Brad and Nancy. He told the couple, "I'm glad y'all could make it. The weatherman says it should be pretty all next week, so we should have a great time. I'm going to the back and sit down until we takeoff, and I'll see you after the seat-belt light goes out."

The flight only took a little over an hour, and they landed a few minutes after eleven. Monty had a car, but it was at the house, so he rented a nine-passenger van and also hailed a cab to take everybody to the house. He was going to keep the van until they got ready to go back home, so if they wanted to go somewhere they could. With the car, there should be plenty of transportation available.

As soon as they unloaded the vehicles and took their luggage to where they would be sleeping, Joan said, "If sandwiches are okay with everybody for lunch, I'm going to run over to Winn-Dixie and grab a few things."

Liz said, "I'll go with you."

Nancy was in another part of the house and didn't hear Joan say she was going, so she and Brad stuck close to Monty, and he gave them a tour of the house and grounds. Joan and Liz weren't gone too long, and when they got back, Joan, with help from Liz, spread out just about anything anybody would want in cold cuts. All the young folks had already changed and gone to the beach, so they had to be called. Everyone ate their fill and the young people gulped theirs down so they could get back down to the water; two or three of them taking a handful of sandwiches or cookies or something else with them.

When the older adults finished and Joan was cleaning up the kitchen, Monty suggested they all get their suits on and go to the beach. He yelled out the door to Jimmy and Johnny and told them to come to the storage building and get some umbrellas and chairs. In a few minutes everyone was either sitting or lying in the sun or sitting in the shade under one of the nice umbrellas that Joan and Monty had.

Monty sat close to Brad in order to talk and get better acquainted. After they had agreed that the weather was just about perfect, Brad said, "Monty, this is a beautiful place. I bet you all really enjoy it, don't you?"

"Yes we do. This was my parents' place until my Dad died, and actually it still belongs to my Mother, but since I'm an only child now, I'm able to act as if it's mine. We just recently completed an extensive renovation on the house. After Dad died, Joan and I thought we might sell it and buy something, somewhere else. We looked at a lot of places and while we found some outstanding homes, we could never find a piece of property like we have here, so we decided to just add on to this house and stay here."

Just then, Joan and the other ladies decided to take a walk down the beach, and they left Brad and Monty alone to talk.

Monty resumed where he left off. "Our property is exactly five acres; six hundred and sixty feet of beach front by three hundred and something deep. There are just not many properties like this available anymore, and we're thankful to have it.

"The house has always been a nice house, but Joan and I have decided that this is where we will retire, and we wanted a larger, nicer place to live in permanently, so we enlarged it."

Brad asked, "How big was it before you enlarged it?"

"It was large enough I guess, but it didn't seem like it. It had four bedrooms and four baths. We added another four bedrooms and four baths and enlarged the kitchen to where it's probably too large, but Joan likes it and that's what counts. We also added the pool, which was probably overkill, but we like the fresh water."

"Well, you've got a wonderful place here, and Nancy and I really appreciate you inviting us. I don't think I've ever been to a place that was quite as nice."

"Thank you, Brad."

Then, Brad asked, "Tell me about your airplane, Monty. That Gulfstream is a honey, and before we left Chattanooga, did I see a large airliner with Shepherd on it?"

"Yeah, you did."

"I'd like to hear about 'em if you'd like to tell me."

"I'll be glad to tell you about them."

"My Grandfather started Shepherd Apparel years ago, and when he retired, he turned the business over to my Dad. He had made the company very successful, but Dad wanted it to become larger and even more successful, so he decide to go international. He had been talking to a German gentleman named Ulrich Steen before my Grandfather retired and when he retired, Ulrich and Dad got together. He already had a large sales agency in place in Germany, and they covered a large part of Europe as well. He and his sales staff took on our line and almost instantly, it grew to an amazing point.

"Soon, he expanded into London and the rest of Great Britain, and Dad was having to travel over there about every three weeks. You travel, Brad, so you know all the hassles of flying commercial. As the company grew larger, Dad felt like he was spending more time in airports than he was flying or with his customers, so one day he decided to buy a plane. His first plane was a beautiful, customized DC-8 that had belonged to an Arab Sheikh, and it took much of the stress off of him. A few years later, when the DC-8 was getting quite a bit of age on it, he found the 707 that you saw at Lovell Field. Dad had two heart attacks, and after the second one, he turned the business over to me.

"God has been extremely good to me and has let me take the company to heights that no one would have ever imagined. In addition to Europe, we're now in Israel, South America, Canada, Japan, and South Korea. We have to get to all these places on a regular basis, and it's next to impossible with just one plane, so we bought the Gulfstream for domestic and Canadian flights, leaving the 707 to make the longer trips. Someone said, one time, that the two planes looked like a *vulgar display of wealth*, and I can understand how some people might get that idea, but if they just knew how important they were to our business I don't think they would think that anymore."

Just then, Jimmy and Johnny slipped up behind Monty and grabbed him; one on his right side and one on his left. They had every intention of throwing him in the ocean, but he was stronger than they thought, and they were unsuccessful in their attempt. That pretty much ended Brad and Monty's conversation. In a little while the ladies came back from their walk and told about the things they had seen. Apparently they had discussed dinner during their walk and had decided that they would go out to eat since it was the first night, and they didn't have groceries for a large dinner. Joan had only bought lunch food, earlier.

At dinner, Analisa sat between Joan and Johnny and sometime during the meal Joan overheard Johnny say, "Not tonight; maybe we can tell them tomorrow or the next day." Being an inquisitive mother, she had to almost bite her lip to keep from asking what they were talking about, but she used constraint and didn't say anything. As she and Monty were getting ready for bed, later, she mentioned to Monty what she heard. "What do you think they're going to tell us? I'll bet they're going to tell us that they're going to get married. What do you think?"

Monty replied, "I have no idea. Whatever it is, I'm sure they'll tell us when they're ready."

"Aren't you the least bit curious about what it is?"

"No, and you shouldn't be either. Now get changed and let's go to bed."

Joan didn't say anything else, but Monty could hear her mumbling to herself, *I'll bet they're going to get married. How're they going to do that? Johnny has* ***to go to the army.***

Every day at the beach starts virtually the same way; get up, have some coffee and maybe a bite of something to eat, get your stuff and go to the beach. The next day at Monty's was no different. While they were all sitting around, trying to get some of the good morning sun, Brad said to Jimmy, "Jimmy, I haven't had a chance to congratulate you on your making All America. That's a huge accomplishment. What's next?"

"Thanks, Mr. Davis. I had a real good year, but making the big team was just luck. There were a lot of players better than me that didn't make it. The Major League Draft is coming up next week and I'm hoping to get drafted."

"Have any teams contacted you yet."

"Yes sir, I've been contacted by Atlanta, Baltimore and St. Louis. I'd love to go to Atlanta, but when I think of playing for a team where Stan Musial played, I think I would like to go to St. Louis. Then, thinking of playing third base where Brooks Robinson and Cal Ripkin, Jr. played makes me want to go to Baltimore. I guess if I'm lucky enough to get drafted by any of those three it will be a blessing."

"Well, I'll keep my fingers crossed for you."

"Thanks, Mr. Davis."

"Since we may be family one day, how about calling me Brad?"

"Okay Brad."

The rest of that day went just as expected; lie on the beach, take walks, snack throughout the day, play Rook or some other game after dark, and then go to bed. Not a word from Johnny and Analisa.

Then, on Monday afternoon, while everybody was together on the beach, Johnny said, "Can I please have everyone's attention for a minute?" Joan thought, *Uh-oh, here it comes.*

Johnny said, with a slight tremble in his voice, "All of you know that Analisa and I have been going together for a long time, and now we want to take it to the next level; we want to get married. Mom, I know you're going to say, "Why don't you wait until you get out of the service," but we don't want to wait any longer. We have thought through this and have decided to marry before I leave. I have to report to Fort Benning on July first and after some initial indoctrination, I can move into a house better known as family quarters, and Analisa can join me there. We can live our normal lives the same as if we lived in Chattanooga.

"We want a small wedding; in fact, all of you guys will be the only ones at the wedding, except for maybe Grandmother, Margaret and Shirley. We may invite a couple more of our closest friends, but you guys will be the main ones there. We ask for your blessings and want you to know we love all of you dearly."

Silence: the only sound was from the waves splashing on the beach. Not one of the group said anything until Jimmy piped up and said, "Well, I think that's great. I've been wondering when I was going to get a sister-in-law," and he got up and went over to Analisa and gave her a kiss on the cheek. He pulled her up, out of her chair, and gave her a hug. Then, he pulled Johnny up from his chair and gave him a big hug. Since I'm the oldest and smartest, this should be me, but you outdid me on this, didn't you, Bro."

Jimmy's words and action seemed to spur conversation and action from some of the others. Monty was the first one to get up and tell Analisa that he had been looking forward to the time that she would become his daughter. He also gave her a kiss on the cheek. Brad followed by shaking Johnny's hand and telling him how proud he would be to have him as a son-in-law. Both mothers lagged behind, but as soon as Brad said what he did to Johnny they got up and went to the couple and hugged them both. Joan told each of them that she loved them as did Nancy. The announcement seemed to trigger something inside Joan and Nancy that said *we need to get home; there's a lot of work to do.*

When Joan said something to Monty about leaving Florida early, Monty said, "Nonsense; you heard what they said. It's going to be a small wedding. All we have to do is show up. You and Nancy should just relax.

The rest of the week was enjoyable. After Johnny's and Analisa's announcement, the pressure was off of them, and they joined the others in fun at the beach.

On Friday, Monty called Mike Taylor and told him to be at their airport at noon, Monday and to have food on board for lunch. The time came too quickly for everyone except Joan and Nancy. They wanted to get home to do things for the wedding; they weren't sure exactly what, but they needed to get there. Monday would be May twenty sixth, and it was Memorial Day. They went down on the seventeenth, so they had been in Florida for ten days. By Monday Monty was beginning to get a little antsy, feeling guilty about missing so much work. The group got to the airport a little after eleven, and by the time they unloaded the taxi, and Monty turned in the van, it was approaching eleven-thirty. They sat down by the large window-wall and in just a few minutes someone said, "Here comes our ride."

The Gulfstream was one beautiful sight. The wheels touched down so softly, it looked as if they had landed on a feather pillow. Mike taxied over to where the group would board, and after he did what he was supposed to do on the ground, they took off for Chattanooga. After they had reached altitude, Johnny got up for something, and when he did, Jimmy went over and sat in Johnny's seat next to Analisa. When Johnny came back and saw Jimmy in his seat, he didn't say a word; he just went over and sat down in another seat. After a few minutes like that, Jimmy got up and told Johnny to come on back and sit in his seat. Jimmy had hoped to get a rise out of him, but it didn't work.

On the way home, Jimmy sat in a seat close to both Brad and Monty, and Brad couldn't resist asking questions about the upcoming baseball draft. "Well, Jimmy, I guess in a couple of weeks you'll be a professional baseball player."

"I hope so."

"You said you had been contacted by St. Louis, Baltimore, and Atlanta. Deep down, which one do you hope takes you?"

"I guess I hope Atlanta takes me. I've been a Braves fan all my life, but either of the other two wouldn't be bad, either.

After the Gulfstream landed in Chattanooga, and everyone deplaned, Brad thanked Monty and Joan for a wonderful vacation and made it plain that he and Nancy would like to see more of them. He also made a point of wishing Jimmy good luck in the draft and asked him to let him know who drafted him and where he was going. The farewells lasted a few more minutes and then everyone got into their cars and went home. Analisa even went home with her mother and daddy.

That afternoon, after talking to Analisa on the phone, Johnny told Jimmy, "Hey, Bro. Analisa and I are going to a movie tonight. Why don't you call Shirley Batson, and y'all go with us? Analisa talked to Shirley a little while ago and she said she would like to go. You want to?"

"Yeah, I'll go. I'm as jittery as a pregnant nun about to meet the Pope. Maybe a movie will calm me down a little."

"Why are you so jittery?"

"Because the draft is in ten days, and my whole future is involved, you dork."

"Well, calm down. It won't do you any good to worry about it."

"Yeah, right. You're not the least bit nervous about getting married and going to the army, are you?"

"Well, that's different."

The ten days seemed like an eternity, and since Jimmy was at home with nothing to do but think, he was beginning to get nervous. Johnny was also getting nervous because he and Analisa would be getting married in only two weeks. He wasn't sure if he was more nervous about getting married or leaving for the army.

He was going to ask Monty if it would be alright if he and Analisa went back to his Florida house for their honeymoon. They were going to have to watch their pennies, at least until he started getting paid by the army. Hopefully, when he got settled in Columbus, and Analisa got down there with him, she could find a job, too, but that would be at least two, and maybe three months. He had had the equivalent of basic training when he was in college, but the training he would have to go through in order to be a Ranger was going to take quite a bit more time. He had wanted to be a Green Beret, but when he talked to his ROTC instructor he found out that one can't even apply to be a Green Beret until after they've been in the army for at least three years, and then the training lasts four years. Ranger School was nowhere near as hard, but it was said to be ten times harder than regular basic training, with much emphasis placed on the physical part, but he had kept in good shape, so maybe it wouldn't be too bad.

Finally, June fifth arrived; day one of the forty-round Major League

Draft, and Jimmy was as nervous as a cat in a roomful of rockers. Matt Hawks had called the night before to let him know that he was still on the Braves' radar. Jack Woods also called from the Cardinals. Jimmy thought, on the morning of the draft, that Baltimore must not have been interested any longer, since they didn't call. He had all sorts of thoughts going through his mind and wasn't sure about any of them; he would just have to wait and see. He said a short prayer. He told God, *Father, please let the best thing happen in the draft. I would like to play for any of the teams that have called me, but Lord, you know what's best, and I'm turning it over to you to handle for me, Thank you in advance for your decision, and I'm making this prayer in Jesus' name. Amen.*

At twelve-thirty on June fifth, the phone rang and Jimmy ran to it and answered. "Hello."

"Hello, Jim; Matthew Hawks. How ya doing?

"I'm fine, thank you. How are you?"

"I'm good, thank you. Well, you and your Dad were right; four years of playing college ball increased your demand. I'm happy to tell you that the Braves selected you in the third round this morning."

"Really?" Do you know where I'll be going?"

"It looks like you're going to our Double-A team in Pearl, Mississippi. Do you have a problem going to Mississippi?"

"No sir. I'd like to go to Mississippi. When do I go?"

"Probably in just a few days. There are several things that have to be done first. Is your Dad still going to act as your agent? We have to negotiate a contract for you, and as your agent, he'll be the one we will negotiate with."

"We haven't talked about it, but I feel sure he will. He's in Brazil right now, and I think he's coming back Sunday and should be here all next week. My brother is getting married on the fourteenth, so I'm sure he'll be here until after the wedding. Maybe we can all get together sometime next week, if that would be alright."

"Maybe it will. At this point, we're in a big rush. Our starting third-baseman at Pearl pulled a hamstring the other day and will be out for several weeks, and our number two third-baseman is not doing as well as we would like, so you're going to be thrown into the fire just as soon as you get down there. In college you were a pretty cool customer, and I just hope you're as cool in the pros. This is the fifth, and the fourteenth is a full week and a half away. I don't know what our manager is going to say about your taking so long to get there. He's a pretty no-nonsense guy, and I'll have to ask him."

Jimmy bowed his back and stood up to the Braves guy, saying, "Mr. Hawks, my brother and I are identical twins, and we're very close. His wedding is really important to him and to me. Now, when I get to Pearl, I'm going to work my tail off, and try to do whatever I can to help the team win ball games. I don't want to sound arrogant or smart alec, but I'm not going to miss his wedding. If your manager refuses to let me stay here long enough to attend my brother's big day, then maybe the Braves is not where I'm supposed to be. I've talked to two other teams, and maybe one of them is where I should go."

Matthew seemed a little shocked at the way Jimmy stood up to him and said, "Hold on there partner. Don't get your feathers ruffled. I'm sure we can work it out. I just wanted to emphasize how important it is to get to Pearl as soon as possible. Calm down, and we'll get it worked out, okay?"

A smile came to the corner of Jimmy's mouth and he said, "Okay."

Matthew said, "Do you think you and your Dad can meet with me on Monday?"

"I feel sure we can, but I don't know his schedule. Brazil is on the same time as we are, so let me call him when he's had time to finish working, and I'll call you. Will that be alright?"

"That's perfect. Do you still have my number? If not, I'll give it to you; do you have a pen and paper?"

"Yes sir. I'm ready," and Matthew gave him his number.

As soon as he hung up he called Connie, Monty's secretary, at Shepherd Apparel. "Hello, Connie, this is Jimmy Shepherd."

Hello Jimmy, how are you?"

"I'm fine, thank you. Listen Connie, will you be talking to my Dad today?"

"I don't know, Jimmy. If I do, do you want me to give him a message?"

"I really need to talk to him. Do you think you can call him and tell him to call me?"

"I'll try. When he makes these trips, he stays pretty busy, but I'll try. I may have to leave word and have him call you when he gets the message. Will that be alright?"

"Yeah, that'll be okay, but I hope you can get in touch with him."

"Maybe I can reach him. It's lunch time, so they might be in the office. Let me see what I can do."

"Okay. Thanks, Connie."

She must have been successful because Monty called in about ten minutes. "Hi, Jimmy. Do you have a problem?"

"No sir; just the opposite. The Braves drafted me in the third round. Whatta ya think about that?"

"I think that's wonderful. That's what you've been hoping and praying for, isn't it?"

"Yes sir, it is. Listen, Dad, Matthew Hawks would like to meet with us Monday. Can we do that?"

"Where does he want to meet?"

"I didn't ask him. I guess here."

"Well, you can tell him we can meet Monday as long as it's in Chattanooga, but I don't have time to go to Atlanta."

"Thanks, Dad. I knew you'd come through. Love ya, bye."

When he hung up from talking to Monty, he called Matthew Hawks and told him they could meet Monday as long as it was in Chattanooga. Matthew said that that was the plan all along, and they set eleven o'clock at Monty's house as the time and place to meet.

On Monday, Jimmy got up wide-eyed and full of energy. Monty had gone to the office early and told Joan he would be back in plenty of time for their meeting. Johnny hung around to see how the meeting would go, plus he wanted to meet Matthew Hawks. Monty came in about a quarter to eleven, and Matthew got there about five 'til. When he rang the doorbell, Johnny was the closest to the door, so he answered it. When he opened the door, Matthew said, "Good morning, Jim. Are you ready to become a Brave?"

"I'm Johnny," Johnny told him."

"Oh, I'm sorry. You guys look so much alike."

"Come in," Johnny said, and he led him into the den where Jimmy and Monty were waiting for him.

When he got into the den, he told what happened at the door, and Jimmy said, "When you've been around for a while, you won't have any trouble telling us apart. I'm the good-looking one."

Matthew said, "Well, I think you're both good-looking, and I'm not going to get in the middle of this."

As soon as the banter was over, Monty stepped forward, held out his hand and said, "Matthew, I'm Monty Shepherd."

They shook hands and sat down. Three or four minutes of unimportant small-talk went on until Monty said, "Matthew, are you here to give my boy a million dollar signing bonus?"

Evading the question, "Well, becoming a Brave is like getting a million dollars to a lot of young men," he answered.

The minute they began to talk about baseball, Johnny got up and excused himself to let them talk in private. Monty was a pretty strong negotiator and was able to get Jimmy a very handsome signing bonus. The fact that he went so high in the draft played a large part in the amount he got. They also talked about Jimmy staying home until after Johnny's wedding, and it was agreed that he could wait and leave for Pearl on Monday, after the wedding on Saturday.

CHAPTER TWO

Johnny and Analisa had been trying to find a romantic place to have the wedding, and after looking at several places and thinking about several others, they finally decided on the spot at Chickamauga Lake where Monty proposed to Joan years ago. It was a pretty place, and knowing that Monty and Joan had become engaged there made it even more romantic.

Johnny had had a terrible time trying to figure out who he wanted to be his best man. He was so close to both his Dad and brother that he agonized over the decision, and finally, after talking to Monty about it, he chose Jimmy. Analisa picked Shirley Batson as her maid of honor, and other than the preacher, that was the entire wedding party.

In attendance were Johnny's parents, his brother and sister, Analisa's parents, Ben and Liz Shepherd, and Sue and Bobby Joyner. Thil, Johnny's grandmother, and her friend Margaret were there, also. Analisa and Johnny wanted a small wedding, and that is what they got. The wedding party and attendees totaled fourteen people. The two mothers were disappointed that it wasn't larger, but Monty and Brad were happy with it as most fathers would be.

The ceremony was simple, with no music or special vows. When it was over and Johnny kissed his bride, everyone milled around for a few minutes, hugging and kissing the newlyweds, and then everybody went to Monty's and Joan's for refreshments, including a beautiful little cake.

Monty had given his permission for the couple to go to his place in Florida, and in a generous gesture, he was having the company's Gulfstream fly them down. About the only thing he didn't do was to pay for a cab from the airport to the house, and he probably just forgot that. As Johnny and Analisa were getting ready for Jimmy to take them to the airport, Monty called them aside, into the kitchen.

He told Analisa, "Analisa Honey, I can't tell you how proud I am to have you as my daughter-in-law. I love you and hope you're going to have a wonderful life as a part of the Shepherd family."

He then turned to Johnny and said, "Son, you've got a good woman here. Love her and take good care of her, and there's no reason why you two can't be as happy as your mother and I have been for the last twenty something years. I hope you all have a great time in Florida. I checked the Weather Channel, and it shows beautiful weather for the next week. I'll have the plane come down to pick you up next Sunday, and I'll see you Sunday afternoon."

As they were turning to leave, he reached into his pocket and said, "Here, son. Take this and don't be afraid to take your bride to some of those good restaurants down there," and he handed him five one-hundred dollar bills.

"Thank you so much, Dad. I really appreciate this," and he hugged him and said, "I love you, Dad."

Monty responded with, "I love you, too. You two have a great time."

The three of them returned to the dining room where everyone was ready to see them off. After hugs and kisses all around, Jimmy and the newlyweds went out and got into Monty's car because it had more room than Jimmy's Mustang.

At the airport, Jimmy and Johnny had a hard time saying good bye. The three stood with their arms tightly around each other. The twins had always been together and had never been apart for more than two or three days at a time, but now, Jimmy was going in one direction to play baseball, and Johnny was going in another to become a soldier. Neither knew when he would see the other again. They promised to call each other every day or two, but that wasn't the same. In a few minutes Mike Taylor came to the plane's door and asked, "Are you kids ready to take off?" And that ended their embrace. As they parted, all three had tears in their eyes. Jimmy stood where he was until Johnny and Analisa got inside the plane and then went into the terminal and watched it take off.

He had never felt as lonely as he did on the way home, but when he got there, everyone except the preacher and Margaret were still there, and the atmosphere was still cheerful and upbeat. He wasn't in the mood to be around a bunch of people, but he told himself that he had to snap out of it because he had *big doins* coming up Monday.

Matthew Hawks met Jimmy at the Atlanta airport Monday morning when he was changing planes for Jackson. He wanted to give him some papers to give to Tom Buckley, the Mississippi Braves manager, and to also wish him luck. He reassured him about his ability and tried to bolster his confidence a little. Jimmy didn't need much bolstering because he had always been confident in his ability. The worst part of the trip was having to go to a strange place where he knew absolutely no one, and he wondered what it was going to be like when he took to the field the first time.

He would soon find out because it was only a couple of hours after he arrived in Pearl that he had to get into his work-out clothes and hit the field for pre-game practice. His infield coach was introducing him to the other members of the team, and when he came to a guy named Burr Sawyers, who was the catcher, Burr said, “Well, it looks like we’ve got another pretty-boy here. Can you play baseball, pretty-boy?”

Jimmy stopped smiling, looked Burr straight in the eye and said, “I don’t know. I think I can, but we’ll see, won’t we?” Burr didn’t respond to that.

The time was one-thirty, and the game wasn’t until seven o’clock, so Jimmy had time to get the kinks out after his trip, and he wanted to be really loose by the time the game started, if for no other reason than to impress Burr Sawyers. He had been told that he was starting that night, and he really wanted to be on his game, especially since it was his first game as a professional.

The Mississippi Braves had contracted with a large apartment complex for apartments for the players, and Jimmy moved into one of them. When he entered it he looked around and was not very happy with what he saw. It was a furnished apartment, but it had only the bare necessities. The living room had a sofa and two chairs with one end table and a lamp and an overhead light. The kitchen had a refrigerator and stove and a small microwave that sat on the counter. It also had a chrome trimmed wood-grain formica top table with four chairs trimmed in chrome The one bedroom had a double bed, a bedside table, and a chest of drawers. A mirror hung alone on the wall next to the chest of drawers with a light hanging from the ceiling. The bathroom was complete with a toilet, tub and shower combination, and a sink. He thought, *Man, having to live in a place like this will make you work extra hard to get to TRIPLE-A. This place is a disaster.*

After he put all his clothes away, he stretched out on the bed and took what he called a *power-nap.* He felt better after the nap, and it was getting close to time to go to the stadium to warm up for the game. When he got to the stadium, he went into the dressing room to get his uniform on. They had given him number thirteen, and he was thrilled with that because that was Alex Rodriguez’ number. He took batting practice first, then infield practice, and in a few minutes he felt ready to play. The closer it got to game time the more butterflies he had.

About ten 'til seven, both teams lined up on the baselines for the national anthem. Jimmy tried to sing with the music, but the butterflies were all the way up almost in his throat, and it didn't help that they were playing the Chattanooga Lookouts; a team that he had grown up watching all his life at home.

After the anthem, the Braves went to their bench and got their gloves while the managers met at home plate for their handshake. Since the game was being played at the Braves' field, they, as the home team, gave their opponents the first *at bat.* After the managers' handshake and conference at home plate the umpire shouted, "PLAY BALL," and the game was ready to start.

The first player up for the Lookouts was a left-hander, and after a one-two count he grounded out to the first baseman. The next batter flied out to short right field, and the third batter was a left-hander who the infield coach had told Jimmy during the pre-game drills was a really good hitter. The butterflies had died down some during the first two batters, but now, with this guy up to bat, they were returning. Jimmy said silently, *"Father; if this ball comes to me, please don't let me bobble it or make a bad play,*" and the Lord answered his prayer because the guy swung at a high, inside pitch, and the ball zipped down to third base where Jimmy was waiting for it. He didn't even have to take a step. He caught the ball and fired it over to first for the third out.

Manager Tom Buckley had put Jimmy in seventh position in the batting order, and while Jimmy didn't like being down that far in the lineup he understood because he hadn't established a track record yet. The Lookouts got the Braves three up and three down in the first inning, and Jimmy didn't get to bat. In the top of the second, two ground balls were hit to him, and he was successful in fielding them and throwing the batters out.

When the Braves went to bat in the bottom of the second inning, Jimmy was fourth down in the order, and he hoped at least one of the three ahead of him would get on base so he could get to bat. The first batter walked, and Jimmy began feeling anxious because he was sure to get a bat. The second man struck out, and the third batter hit a short fly over second base for a single. Then it was Jimmy's turn at bat. He said a short prayer as he walked to the plate and got ready for the first pitch. Strike one; he didn't swing at it. He stepped out of the batter's box and thought, *This guy is not any faster than the ones I faced in college. I think I can hit him.* He stepped back in the box, and the second pitch was low and down the middle; just the kind he liked. He stepped into it and swung the bat, and he could feel the sweet contact as the bat came in contact with the ball. He knew he had hit it good as he took off for first, and when he looked at the ball, it was clearing the right-field fence. A home run the first time he went to bat as a professional. He knocked in the two runners on base and the Braves led three to nothing. Burr Sawyers was one of the runners that he brought in, and when they made eye contact, Jimmy just smiled.

As the game went on Jimmy got one more hit; a double, and went two for four for the night. Tom Buckley went into the locker room after the game and heaped praise on him for his play as a rookie playing his first game. Some of the other guys also complimented him on his play. As he was getting ready to leave for his apartment, the short stop; a boy by the name of Jerry Simpson caught up with him and asked if he would like to go grab a sandwich and a Coke. He said L.T. Reeves, the first baseman, was going, and they would like to have him go with them. Jimmy accepted the invitation and the three of them went to the Steak N Shake and had burgers and shakes. Jerry and L.T. made him feel at home, and he could see that he was going to enjoy being in Pearl.

The Braves went on and swept the Lookouts in a four game series with Jimmy getting seven hits with no errors. Next, they went to Birmingham and played the Birmingham Barons three games. Jimmy got five hits in that series. Still, no errors. Then, on to Huntsville to play the Huntsville Stars four games. The Stars couldn't stop him; he hit an incredible five-hundred against them, including a home run, making his batting average for his first three series and unbelievable four-thirty-one. Next, they were going to Chattanooga to play the Lookouts another four game series, and Jimmy couldn't wait to get there, so he could see his Mom and Dad.

Always before, when he would call home, he would call Johnny, too. Now, Johnny was gone. He left on the first of July for Fort Benning, and since he was going into training for the Rangers, Jimmy didn't know whether or not they would let him have his cell phone. He had tried to call several times, but there was no answer. He had left messages two or three times, but Johnny never called him back, so he assumed he was not able to have it.

When Johnny arrived at Fort Benning, he learned that getting to be a Ranger was a lot harder than he thought it would be. He found out that over fifty percent of the soldiers starting Ranger School washed out, and that sixty percent of that group washed out within the first four days. As near as he could find out, Ranger Training lasted sixty one days.

Johnny had thought the training he received when he went out for football at Tennessee Tech was hard, but what he had to go through in Ranger School made that very tame. He was having to go through long, hard physical training. Everywhere they went, they had to run. They had to make miles of marches with heavy backpacks and a gun. One of Johnny's favorite parts was Airborne School. He was very apprehensive before his first jump, but after the first one he could hardly wait to jump again. Airborne training was very important because when the Rangers went into a war zone, most of the time they parachuted in, and many times it was at night.

It was rumored that when they got back into camp, they would be able to live in regular quarters and resume normal training activities. Johnny hoped that would mean he could soon bring Analisa to be with him. He was dying to talk to her and to Jimmy. He didn't know this for sure because he began to hear about the ones who pass the Darby Phase, which was what he was doing, and next he had to move on to the Mountain Phase. After the Mountain Phase would be the Florida Phase, and after the Florida Phase came graduation from Ranger School.

Finally; Graduation day, and he would get to see Analisa and his Mom and Dad. He was very proud of himself because nearly one hundred men began Ranger School with him, and only forty two finished. Monty was proud of him, too. He had made such an impression on his superiors during Ranger School that he was being promoted to First Lieutenant. With the promotion came more responsibility and a little higher status as well as more pay.

The Graduates were all getting three-day passes, and rather than go somewhere, Analisa wanted to just stay in Columbus, so Monty booked two rooms at the Holiday Inn, where the four of them had a grand time. They ate at a burger joint Friday night because Johnny was sick of MRE's, and that was what he wanted. While they were eating, Monty asked him if he had talked to Jimmy, and he said, "No, it's been hard to find any time to use the phone during Ranger training, and what time I had, I used to call Analisa. I did try to call him a couple of times, but didn't get an answer."

"Well, your brother is tearing it up at Pearl. He started the game just a few hours after he got there, and hit a home-run his first time at bat. His hitting and fielding have been superb since he got there, and I just hope they keep letting him play."

"If he's doing that good, why wouldn't they?"

"Because the first string third baseman has been on the disabled list, and is probably about ready to come back."

"Well, if he's doing that good, they may just keep him in there. That happens lots of times in professional ball, not just in baseball, but other sports as well. I'll try to call him tonight or tomorrow."

On Saturday, Analisa and Johnny spent a large part of the day trying to decide whether to live in family housing on the base or try to find an affordable apartment off the base. After a tiresome search in Columbus without finding anything they liked, they decided to just live on the base. The places available at Fort Benning were, for the most part, just as nice as most of the apartments they had seen in town, although there was a waiting list. Even though most of them looked a lot alike, there were subtle differences in them, and Johnny and Analisa found one they liked a lot, and Johnny said he would try to get it. The *Shepherd* luck was still intact. Even though there was a waiting list for on-base housing, when Johnny went to see the Housing Director, she was so impressed with him that she *thought* the apartment he wanted was available, and proceeded to set it up for him. Analisa wondered if they would still have been able to get the apartment if she had gone with him to apply because he was a good-looking dude in his uniform and tan beret.

Joan and Monty wanted to leave them alone, so they found some shopping malls, and Joan had a good time. She wore Monty out, and they went back to the hotel around three o'clock, and Monty turned on a baseball game and immediately went to sleep.

The newlyweds returned to the hotel around four thirty, exhausted from all the apartment hunting. Johnny called Joan when they got there, and Joan told him that they wanted to treat them to dinner that night. She said Monty had asked someone at the hotel about nice places, and someone told him about a really nice place called *A Touch of Elegance.* It sounded nice and that's where they would go unless there were objections. There were none, so they had plenty of time to rest before they went. It turned out to be a great place, although pricey, and they stored it in their memory for a future time.

The next morning, Analisa wanted to pick up a newspaper so she could peruse the want-ads to try and find a job. She had never worked, but she took some classes in college that were a help to her resume. According to her professors, she was well qualified to be a computer programmer, even though she had no experience. Monty always read the Sunday paper, so when he finished his, he gave it to her. They all enjoyed a nice breakfast together, and didn't have anything in particular planned for the day. Johnny had to be back at the base at 6 o'clock, so Monty called Mike and told him to be at the Columbus airport at five.

It's always hard when loved ones have to part, and this time was no different. It was heartbreaking for Joan and Monty to leave their son. Analisa had a hard time leaving, but not nearly as hard as Monty and Joan because she would be back the following weekend to move with Johnny into their apartment. They stood around the plane as long as they could, but Mike's flight plan called for takeoff at a certain time, and they were nearing that time. Monty made the first move by hugging Johnny and shaking his hand and saying, "I'll see you son. I'm very proud of you and hope you'll be careful. You'll be fine when Analisa gets back down here, and I know you'll be very happy. Keep in touch with your Mom and me. Now that we all have cell phones, it shouldn't be a problem to call real often, and please call your brother. I'm gonna go now, Son. I love you, and if you need anything, be sure to call me."

"I will. I love you, too."

Joan was the next one to hug and kiss him. She put her arms around him, and with tears in her eyes she said, "I love you, Darling. I'm going to miss you. Please stay in touch, will you?"

"Yes ma'am, I will. I love you."

Finally, Analisa said goodbye. Knowing that she would be back in a week made it much easier on her, but she still hugged him very tight and said, "I love you."

Transportation all weekend had been by rental car, and Monty had to turn it in when they got to the airport. Since Johnny didn't have his car down there yet and wanted to go to the airport with them, Monty paid for a cab to take him to Fort Benning from the airport.

The Shepherd plane lifted off at five-thirty, and Johnny returned to Fort Benning to begin his new career.

CHAPTER THREE

Meanwhile, over in Pearl, the Mississippi Braves were preparing to go to Chattanooga for a four game series with the Lookouts. Even though the Braves number one third baseman was off the Disabled List, Jimmy had been playing so good, and hitting like crazy, they were leaving him in the number one spot. He absolutely could not wait to get to Chattanooga because that was where he grew up. He would get to see his parents and hopefully play before many of his friends. He just prayed that he would play good and not embarrass himself. Normally, the team all stays together when they make a road trip, but since Jimmy was from Chattanooga, and his parents lived there, Tom Buckley gave permission for him to stay at Monty's during the trip. Jimmy hesitated asking, but he asked Tom if it would be possible for Jerry Simpson to stay at his parents' also, and Tom said he could.

The series went well for the Braves and for Jimmy. He had a large cheering squad at the stadium to watch him play, and he didn't disappoint them. He went two for four in the first game, one for four in the second, three for four in the third, and two for three in the fourth. He hit one homerun and one triple. The Braves won three of four games in the series, and Monty could hardly contain himself while he watched Jimmy play.

Joan and Monty thought they would have some of Jimmy's friends in while he was in town, and they all had a very good time. Everyone seemed to like Jerry and he acted as if he liked them, especially Sissy Watson.

Jimmy had to leave the morning after the series was over, and Joan and Monty had to once more bid farewell to one of their children. Telling Jimmy goodbye wasn't quite as hard as saying goodbye to Johnny, because Jimmy wasn't going to have to possibly go a dangerous place, and he would, hopefully, be back in the fall, but it was still hard. He had left his car at home when he first left, but now he wanted it and he and Jerry drove it back to Pearl. It was a little over two-hundred miles and only took about three and a half hours to drive it.

When they pulled out of the driveway, Monty looked at Joan and said, "Sugar-Babe, the crowd at our house is getting smaller, isn't it?"

"It sure is, and I don't like it."

"Well, you will just have to concentrate on doing girly things with Mary Ann until she goes back to school."

"I know, if I can ever find her. She's either at Betsy's or Sue's or Shirley's the biggest part of the time, but maybe we can do some things."

"Monty, how about you and I going somewhere together? No children, no friends, nobody but you and me."

"Do you mean like a second honeymoon?"

"Well, yes, if that's what you want to call it. I just want to be somewhere with only you. Whatta ya say?"

"Where do you want to go?"

"I don't care. It could be St. Elmo as long as it's just you and me."

"I think we can find somewhere a little farther away than St. Elmo. I hear Cabo San Lucas is nice."

"Cabo San Lucas; are you kidding?"

"Why not? You've spent most of your life raising two fine young men and one fine, beautiful young woman, and I think you need to be rewarded. If you'd rather go somewhere besides Cabo, tell me and we'll go there. It's your choice."

"I've heard about Cabo San Lucas all my life and what a wonderful place it is. If you're willing to take me there, I'm sure willing to go."

"Okay. Call Mom and see if Mary Ann can stay with her while we're gone, and we'll start making plans. And oh yeah, you need to talk to Mary Ann about it, too. Just don't make her think we're not considering her on these decisions."

Joan did just what Monty told her not to. She called Thil and asked her if Mary Ann could stay with her for a few days, and Thil was thrilled at the idea, but when she talked to Mary Ann that night, it was a different story.

Mary Ann let her know that she didn't need a babysitter. She said, "I'm twenty years old and I'm plenty old enough to stay by myself. Even though I love Grandmother dearly and might go over and stay with her some, I don't appreciate having arrangements made for me like I'm a child. After all, I'm about to begin my third year of college, and I don't have to stay with anyone for nine months out of the year. I just hope you remember this, Mom. I've gotta go. Bye."

Joan stood there, stunned. Mary Ann had never talked to her like that, and before Mary Ann could get to the back door, Joan called out to her, “Mary Ann, wait a minute.”

Mary Ann turned around and said. "What?”

Joan walked over to her and said, “I’m sorry, Honey. I guess I still look at you as my little girl. Of course you don’t have to stay with your Grandmother. You’re plenty old enough to stay wherever you want to, but it would be nice if you would stay with her some. She was thrilled when I told her we were going out of town and would like for you to stay with her, so think about it, will you?”

“Mary Ann hugged her mother and said, “Of course I’ll stay with her some. I’m sorry I snapped at you. I love you.”

As soon as Monty had had time to get to his office, Joan picked up the phone and called him. When he answered, Joan said, “Monty. I’ve changed my mind.”

“About what?”

“About going somewhere with just you and me. I’ve decided that I want to take Mary Ann.”

“What brought that on?”

“I just think we’ve neglected Mary Ann in favor of the boys for a long time, and it won’t be too much longer until she’s gone too, and I’d just like to give her some special attention and TLC.”

“What does she say about going with us?”

“I haven’t talked to her about it yet. I wanted to talk to you first. What do you think?”

“It’s fine with me. This trip was your idea, so whatever you want to do with it is okay.”

“I knew you’d say that. I’ll see you tonight. I love you.”

Mary Ann came back in a couple of hours, and Joan didn’t waste any time talking to her about the trip. “Honey, your Dad and I are thinking about going to Cabo San Lucas for a few days and were hoping. you would like to go with us. I’ve heard that it’s a wonderful place to go; there’s so much to do when you get there.”

“Why do you want me to go all of a sudden? Is it because I said I didn’t want to stay at Grandmother’s? If that’s the reason, then no, I don’t want to go.”

“No, no, Honey, that’s not the reason. We have been so wrapped up in your brothers’ college graduations, and their leaving the nest to go to, who knows where, that we want to spend some time with just you. I’m sure you have probably felt neglected from time to time, and we don’t ever want you to feel that we've neglected you, so what do you say? Will you go with us?"

"Well, I've heard Cabo is a cool place. Can I take a friend?"

"If you want to. Who do you want to take?"

"I'd like to take Betsy. You know, she's just about my oldest friend, and I have to leave for school in a few weeks, and we'll be separated again, so what do you think about her?"

"Betsy's fine. By the way, where is she going to school? I haven't seen her in a long time."

"She goes to UTC. I was hoping she would go to Tech with Shirley and me, but she said it was a lot less expensive to stay here. That way, she doesn't have to pay for room and board and other things that cost money when you go out of town. I'll go and call her now; when are we going?"

"I'll have to talk to your Daddy; maybe this coming weekend. Tell her you'll have to call her."

"How long will we be gone?"

"I'll have to talk to your Daddy about that, too. I would guess about four or five days, and oh yeah, tell her it won't cost her anything except for things that she might want to buy while she's down there. Does she have a passport? She'll have to have one."

"I don't know. I'll ask her."

Mary Ann called Betsy, and she was thrilled to death by the invitation. She had a passport from when she and her parents went to the Caribbean a few years ago, so everything was all set. The next Saturday the four of them flew to Cabo and checked into the beautiful Sheraton Hacienda hotel where Monty had booked a lovely two-bedroom suite for four nights plus a single room for Mike. None of the four except Mike were fishermen, but Monty booked a charter boat for Tuesday, and they all went fishing and everybody caught some fish; Betsy caught a nice sailfish.

After a fun-filled three days and four nights they went back to Chattanooga. Monty told Joan that he didn't need to take any more trips for a while; that he had neglected his work too much lately.

Soon, all was back to normal; Mary Ann was back at Tennessee Tech as was Bobby and Sue Joyner. Jimmy and Johnny were pretty much settled in, and they called Monty and Joan at least twice a week and sometimes three. On Johnny's last call, he said that they were told they were going to be activated and likely deployed within the next couple of months, and that alarmed them terribly, especially Joan.

They continued on with their lives as if nothing was wrong, but at the same time they knew the army wouldn't say anything about being activated unless there was something to it. Football season had rolled around again, and as usual, Monty bought season tickets. Since his boys weren't playing any longer, he and Joan didn't feel required to be at every game the way they used to be, but they didn't miss many. The games and the association with friends each week helped with their burden about Johnny leaving.

Monty was still in strong demand as a speaker at various Fellowship of Christian Athletes functions, and the current season was no exception. It seemed to him that a new tradition had been born over the last few years; He would speak at Tennessee Tech on Homecoming weekend and then go to Memphis State a couple of weeks later.

Part of that started several years ago when he and Joan met their good friends, Barry, Allen, and Mark and their wives at Homecoming. It was an unforgettable weekend with all six of their friends accepting Jesus. Since that weekend, at least one of the three would go to Chattanooga and go to Memphis with Monty. Sometimes, all three would show up, and talk about a strong, winning team for Jesus; when all four were there, it was amazing.

The Lord's work, along with Monty's work at Shepherd Apparel, not to mention his work with Wauhatchie Farms was spreading him so thin, he hardly had time to think about the possibility of Johnny's deployment, but Joan was a different story. She didn't work and was at home most of the time, so she had ample time to think about it.

One day, at work, after seeing how depressed she was the night before, he began calling her friends. He called Liz, Nancy Davis, his mother, Thil, and two or three others and explained the situation to each of them and asked if they would stop by and see her or invite her to lunch or maybe an afternoon of shopping or anything else they could think of that would get her mind off of Johnny. That worked pretty well because soon she was so busy she hardly had time to do anything but socialize, and Monty, pleased with the way things were turning out for her thought, *what kind of monster have I created?*

October, 2 Months later

Baseball season was winding down, and Jimmy's parents were

looking forward to him coming home, however, on one of his calls home, he told Monty that Jerry Simpson and L. T. Reeves and a couple of other guys on the team had formed a band and had invited him to be a part of it. He said that Jerry had a friend who was an agent, and he was able to get their band a gig in Hattiesburg, and he told Monty he was going to play guitar in it and wouldn't be home after the season.

That stunned Joan and Monty, and they were very disappointed, and to top that off, Johnny called two days later and said he was being deployed in three weeks.

"Where are you going?" Monty asked.

"They haven't told us, Dad, but that's the way the Rangers work. They send you somewhere in the world and you or your family don't know where you're going. I hope they'll tell us before we leave. I hate to leave Analisa down here not knowing where I am, but it may happen. I'm supposed to get a week off before we go, so I'll be home to see you guys in a couple of weeks. Analisa is going to try to get off so she can come with me, but I don't know if she can or not. The company she works for is pretty strict."

"How long will you be gone? Did they tell you that?" Monty asked.

"No sir, they didn't tell us, but usually the Rangers are only deployed for three months at a time; not twelve months like other branches of the service."

"Well, that's one thing we can be thankful for."

"I know, and I'll be alright, Dad."

"Has no information been leaked about where you're going?"

"Not really, but there have been rumors that we may be going to Iraq. You know, things are starting to heat up over there."

Two weeks later Johnny and Analisa started out for Chattanooga. Analisa had not been feeling well for a couple of weeks, and Johnny had to stop twice for her to throw-up, but they finally got there. They had talked on the way and decided that since both sets of parents lived in Chattanooga Analisa would spend the time at home with Brad and Nancy, and Johnny would stay with Joan and Monty. They arrived home late Saturday morning, and didn't have to go back until the following Sunday, giving them nine days, less six hours travel time.

Joan couldn't do enough for Johnny while he was there, and she nearly smothered him to death. Finally, Monty stepped in and told her to back off a little. She didn't appreciate it, but she did ease up some.

On Tuesday night she and Monty had Nancy, Brad, and Analisa over for dinner, and they all seemed to have a really nice time, except Analisa wasn't feeling well. Johnny just thought she had caught some kind of bug. Deployment wasn't talked about; rather most of the conversation was about how Analisa and Johnny were getting along in their new married life, their apartment, and how Analisa was doing with her new job. They talked some about Jimmy, and how he was having such a good year. They talked about everything; trying to keep off the subject of the deployment.

Brad and Nancy brought Analisa over to Monty's Sunday morning to keep Johnny from having to drive any more than necessary. Columbus was a little over three hours from Chattanooga, and Johnny wanted to get home before dark, so they left around noon. At that time of the year it got dark around six-thirty, so they were in good shape for their estimated time of arrival. The goodbyes were emotional, but maybe not quite as sad as when they first left for the army. Almost as soon as they got out of sight of Monty's house, the couple was back to normal when it came to their demeanor. Both of them had enjoyed seeing their parents, but the down moods of their mothers took a lot away from their enjoyment. They arrived at the gate of Fort Benning at three-thirty, and there was still time to watch some football and relax before having to start another week the next day.

The intensity which the Rangers were going through the following week was unlike anything Johnny had seen since he had been there. Equipment was being inspected and organized, and weaponry was being brought out, checked, and cleaned. Everything about the Rangers was always serious business, but Johnny could tell by the senior officers' demeanor that something out of the ordinary was about to happen. Whenever he would ask somebody that he thought he could trust about what was going on, he would always get the same answer; "I don't know" or "They haven't told us anything," or "You'd better ask the C.O. because I don't know anything." After a few of these answers Johnny decided to keep his mouth shut and just wait until he was told something.

Work on the equipment was done in the mornings, and in the afternoons they had classes about how to handle a variety of scenarios. Senior officers were always present at the classes, but the main presentations were done, usually, by a *battle-tested* first sergeant or the Sergeant-Major or someone like that.

When the work was finished on Friday afternoon, the 75th was told to have a restful weekend and be back for roll-call at the airfield terminal at 5 A.M. Monday morning and to bring their toothbrush because they would be taking a trip and wouldn't be back for a while. Some of the guys asked questions about where were they going and how long would they be gone, but they didn't get any satisfactory answers. The Commanding Officer was the one presiding, and making an attempt to be cute he said, "It's going to be a surprise, but I can tell you this; you won't be back for about three months."

One soldier asked, "Can we take our cell phones?"

"Affirmative, but at some point we will collect them from you, and that reminds me; before you come Monday, tape your name on your phone, so you can identify it when it's returned to you."

Analisa got up when Johnny did and drove him to the airfield right there at Fort Benning. They arrived at four-forty-five, and there were already several people there. Johnny was pleasantly surprised to see a group of commercial airline planes because he thought they had to be more comfortable than the planes the army used for them to make their parachute jumps.

He looked around for his best buddy, Pat Shumate, but didn't see him. Pat was a second lieutenant, and he and Johnny went through Ranger School together. They had become close friends, and Analisa was beginning to get close with Pat's wife, Amanda. At two minutes 'til five Pat and Amanda showed up. When the C.O. saw then he said, "You're cutting it kind of close, aren't you, Shumate. I thought maybe you didn't want to go to the party."

"Yes sir; sorry sir."

In a few minutes the loud speaker announced, "Thirty minutes until boarding. Repeat; thirty minutes until boarding."

Analisa grabbed Johnny and put her arms around him and was prepared to hold on to him for the full thirty minutes, but Johnny couldn't stay in that position. The thirty minutes passed in a flash, and Johnny kissed Analisa and walked to his plane. He turned around and she was crying, and that made him cry, too. He blew her a kiss and walked up the steps to the inside of the plane. He was lucky enough to find an aisle seat, and Pat got the aisle seat next to him. On commercial airlines the seats are so close an aisle seat is just about the only place where a passenger can stretch their legs.

Johnny and Pat strained their necks and saw Amanda and Analisa standing on the tarmac with their arms around each other, crying. Someone outside must have told them to move back from the plane because as soon as they did the engines started. Soon, they were airborne, and most of the guys found something to talk about other than leaving home and wondering where they were going.

****

Before Analisa even got out of the airport, she had to go to the ladies' room and throw up. She felt so bad. Amanda told her she needed to go to the doctor, but she refused. Amanda wouldn't take "No" for an answer and insisted she go see what was wrong, since she had been feeling bad for so long. Finally, Analisa consented and called for an appointment when she got home. She felt so bad she didn't go to work. When she told the lady at the doctor's office how bad she felt and that she had been sick for a long time, the lady checked her book and told her to come in at two-fifteen, and they would work her in.

She called Amanda and said she would really like for her to go to the doctor with her, and Amanda went gladly. They were both happy to have company since their husbands had just left. The doctor took her pretty quick after she got there, and it didn't take him long to diagnose her problem. He said, smiling, "Mrs. Shepherd, I have good news and bad news; the bad news first. You will probably still feel bad and throw up for a little while yet. The good news is, it looks like you're about to become a mommy." She said, "Pregnant? I can't be pregnant. My husband just left this morning for who knows where. I can't be pregnant."

The doctor asked, "How long will your husband be gone?"

"For about three months."

"Well, you'll have plenty of time to carry this baby before he comes home. It looks as if you're just barely eight weeks, so there should be no problem."

When Analisa thought about what he said she settled down and told him, "You're right, Doctor. I guess I've been feeling sorry for myself because my husband was just deployed and this took me by total surprise. Now that I think about it, I'm thrilled to have a baby, and my husband will be, too. I'm sorry I sounded like I don't want the baby; I do, very much. Thank you, Doctor."

When she returned to the waiting room, she told Amanda what the doctor said, and they both hugged and danced a little jig. Amanda said they should go somewhere for dinner and celebrate the good news, and Analisa agreed. Both ladies had taken the day off from work; Amanda, because of Pat's deployment, and Analisa because she felt so bad in addition to Johnny's leaving. That gave them a chance to spend the afternoon together. Analisa had a *sinking* spell at one point, so they went to Amanda's so she could lie down. She slept for about an hour, and when she woke up she seemed refreshed and feeling better. She asked Amanda, "Are we still going somewhere to eat?"

"If you want to. Do you feel like it?"

"Yeah, I feel a whole lot better. Where would you like to go?"

"I don't know. Do you have any suggestions?"

"Have you ever been to the Epic? It's really good."

"No, I haven't been there, but I'll take your word for it. Let's go there."

They freshened up and left for the Epic restaurant. While they were eating, the conversation went to questions about when they would get to talk to their husbands. Analisa said she hoped it wouldn't be long because she wanted to tell Johnny about the baby, and Amanda said she wanted to talk to Pat because she just wanted to talk to him.

The two had become good friends because their husbands were such good friends, and while they were sitting there, they tried to lay out some semblance of plans for regular contact, so neither would be so lonesome. They agreed to talk every day and to see each other as much as possible. Amanda had parked her car at Analisa's so when they left the restaurant they rode together so Amanda could get her car. When they reached Analisa's, they said how much they enjoyed the day, then they hugged and Amanda got into her car and went home. Analisa went inside her apartment and changed into her pajamas and came back into the living room and stared at the telephone, praying that it would ring, but her prayer wasn't answered, and after a while, she turned the lights out and went to bed.

****

Before long their Commanding Officer got on the intercom and announced, "Men, we are on our way to Frankfort, Germany. Our flying time will be twelve hours from now. We will have a two hour layover in Frankfort, and then proceed to our second stop, which will be Kuwait City. The flying time to Kuwait City will be six and a half hours from Frankfort. We will spend the night in Kuwait City before going on to our final destination."

One of the soldiers asked, "What is our final destination, Colonel?"

"Our first, final destination will be the Baghdad airport, where we will remain, temporarily, then, parts of the unit will be deployed to other locations to handle certain situations."

The plane finally landed; almost twenty-four hours after it left Fort Benning. They were to stay three nights in Kuwait City before going to the Baghdad airport. The nights were free, so they were able to walk around and get away from the tight structure for a while.

CHAPTER FOUR

When the day arrived for them to go into Iraq, there was a C-130 plane plus two Chinook helicopters there to transport them. "C" company, under the command of Captain William Easton was assigned space on the C-130 for the two and a half hour flight. Johnny was the First Lieutenant in command of the second platoon, "C" Company. Before they landed, the Company Commander told them to be at a meeting at fifteen-hundred hours (three o'clock) in the assembly hall. Someone would be there to direct them to where the assembly hall was located. When they landed, there was a soldier with a clipboard there to assign everyone sleeping quarters and to give them directions. To Johnny's surprise, most of the beds were located in semi-trailers with two people to a trailer, and many of the toilets were porta-potties. Johnny had requested ahead of time that he and Pat Shumate be roommates, and the request was granted. That would work out well because Pat was Johnny's assistant in command of the second platoon. The men in the second platoon had given Johnny the nick name "El-Tee", a reference to his rank.

The assembly hall was a rejuvenated hangar away from the bustle of the main part of the airport. The United States had erected walls, installed air conditioning and other things to keep it from being just an airplane hangar. They had also built a large, separate room where they made a nice internet café for the troops to use.

Captain Easton called the meeting to order promptly at fifteen hundred hours and wasted no time getting to why they were there. "As most of you know, an organization known as Al-Qaida has owned up to the events of 9-1-1, and they've let the world know that they intend to destroy everything and everybody that is not Islamic. That is why we're here, men. You are, at this minute, sitting in the middle of Al-Qaida's homeland, and the headquarters of President Saddam Hussein. It's up to us to nip this situation in the bud, and that's why we're here.

"Word has reached us that a group of insurgents has been causing trouble in the city of Ramadi and the mayor of Ramadi has asked for our help, and we're going to oblige him. Tomorrow, "C" Company will travel to Ramadi to take care of the problem. Immediately following this meeting, I want to see all "C" Company platoon leaders right here. All you Rangers be prepared to leave here at o-six-hundred in the morning. We will drive to Ramadi instead of flying, and the driving time is approximately one hour and twenty-five minutes. Take all your battle gear since we don't know what we are going to encounter when we get there."

When the platoon leaders met, they were given detailed maps of Ramadi with all the major buildings marked. The government buildings were marked in red while other buildings were marked in a variety of colors, depending on their importance. The mission the next day was to liberate the seat of the city government from Al-Qaida insurgents.

Heavy trucks and Humvees made up the convoy the next morning heading toward Ramadi. Since Johnny and Pat were officers they got to ride in a Humvee. On the way to Ramadi, Pat asked Johnny, "Where do you suppose they came up with the name Humvee? It must stand for something."

"You got me. I have no idea," Johnny answered.

The sergeant driving the vehicle turned and said, "It stands for High Mobility Multipurpose Wheeled Vehicle, Sir."

"Man, where did you learn that, Sergeant?"

"I used to be in the motor pool before I transferred to the Rangers, Sir, and I learned it there."

"Well, I'm glad they call it Humvee instead of all that other, aren't you?"

"Yes Sir, I sure am."

"What's your name, Soldier?" Johnny asked.

"My name is Tony Owens, Sir."

"Where are you from, Tony?"

"I'm from Baxter, Kentucky, Sir."

"Why did you join the army, Tony?"

"Well, Sir, if you've ever been to Baxter and Harlan County you will know why I enlisted. Baxter is in the heart of coal country, and there is little else to do to make a living, and if you do manage to earn a living it's hard, and there's no money. Unless you come from money, which I don't, it's a hard life, so I joined the Army to improve my circumstances."

"How long have you been in?"

"If I make it through this deployment, February will be six years."

"Are you planning to make a career out of the Army?"

"I don't know, Sir. I'm thinking about it."

"Are you married?"

"Yes Sir. My wife makes pretty good working at Collins Apparel Company up in Opelika, and with both our incomes, we do pretty good, but you never know what's going to happen."

"You sure don't. I'm from Chattanooga, and right now I wish I was there. This Al-Qaida bunch has screwed up everything."

From the back seat Pat said, "I know. I guess we'll just have to take care of the situation while we're over here, so we can get back to normal."

All at once the convoy came to a sudden halt. Johnny said, "I wonder what's going on."

At that moment a sergeant approached them front the front of the convoy and said, "They spotted an IED up front, and they're taking care of it. Be alert because we don't know who might be concealed next to the road as we go by."

Johnny asked, "How much farther to Ramadi?"

"It's approximately fifty kilometers, Sir. From here on in to Ramadi, it's very dangerous, so keep your eyes open. This IED is away from town a little more than normal, and that's an indication that the terrorists are ready for us. Most of the time IED's are concentrated more in the heavier populated areas."

In a couple of minutes they heard the explosion as the ordnance handling experts detonated the IED, and immediately the convoy began to move again.

Each squad knew exactly where to go and what to do when they got there provided they weren't distracted by the enemy, so when they rolled into the city of Ramadi, the platoon spread out and went about carrying out their jobs. The advanced planning was very good because Ramadi was a city of about two-hundred thousand, and they went right to their intended destination.

Johnny led his men to what could be called *City Hall,* and everybody acted with extreme caution. As they approached the front entrance, someone from just inside the gate threw the gate open and opened fire. Fortunately, they missed everybody, but Johnny's men didn't. Three of his men returned fire and dispatched one of the terrorist while two others ran away. When they approached the main building, they were met with sniper fire with the same results. Snipers, zero; Rangers, two. The rest of the terrorists disappeared and didn't show back up the rest of the day.

After the brief firefight, the Mayor of Ramadi along with some of his associates came out of hiding and greeted Johnny and his men, thanking them for what they did.

When they were pretty sure that the insurgents were gone, and the city officials felt they were once again safe, "C" Company left to go back to the Baghdad airport around four o'clock. Not knowing what the road would be like after dark, the C.O. said they should get back while they still had some daylight.

If there could be such a thing as a somber, yet good mood, that would probably best describe the platoon on the way back to Baghdad. Somber fit well because they had killed three people, even though the three were the enemy who had tried to kill them, and good because they had made it through their first mission without any casualties and were on their way back to relative safety, although nowhere in Iraq was safe.

On the way back, Johnny asked Pat, "Pat, how do you feel after being a part of a fight where three men were killed?"

"I don't know. I don't think it has sunk in yet. I'm just thankful it wasn't any of our guys. What about you?"

"I don't know, either. There wasn't time to think about it when it was happening, and now that it's over I just thank God that I'm still alive. How about you, Tony?"

"Sir, I'm really thankful to be alive. I don't know if you realize it or not, but I was one of the guys that the terrorist's encountered when they threw the gate open when we first got there, and I think my bullet was the one that killed the first one. Remember that guy throwing the gate open and us killing him? I can't describe the feeling."

Johnny said, "Yeah, I remember. Good job, Tony."

After a period of silence, Pat asked Johnny, "John, do think we might be able to call home tonight? I sure would like to talk to Amanda."

"Maybe; I'd like to talk to Analisa, too. She hasn't been feeling well lately, and I told her I thought she should go to the doctor. We'll look into it when we get back. We'll have to figure out the time to call because we're eight hours ahead of Columbus, and we don't want to waste any calls in case they're not at home. What time does Amanda get home from work?"

"Usually around five-thirty."

"Analisa gets home about the same time. Man, that means if we wait 'til they get home to call, we will have to wait 'til two or two-thirty in the morning."

"I can call Amanda at work. Can you call Analisa?"

"I don't know. I've never called her at work, but I'm going to tell her to explain the circumstances to her boss and see if they will permit her to take my calls. They probably will, but I think I'm gonna stay up tonight and try to talk to her."

When they all got back to Baghdad it was chow time. Johnny and Pat went to eat, and then they went to their quarters and lay down to take a nap. They set their alarm for one-thirty, and when it went off, they got up and went to the telephones. Even at that time of the morning they had to stand in line before they could get a telephone. Finally, two phones came open at the same time, and they both grabbed them and placed their calls to Columbus.

Analisa's phone rang three times before she answered, and Johnny was beginning to think she wasn't at home. Finally, on the fourth ring, she answered, "Hello."

"Hi, Darling. What are you doing?"

Analisa screamed, Johnny, is that you? I didn't think you would be calling. I'm so glad to hear from you. Where are you?"

"I can't tell you, honey."

Is it bad where you are?"

"No, it's okay. How are you feeling? I've been worried about you. Did you go to the doctor?"

"Yeah, I went yesterday."

"What did he say?"

"He said he had good news and bad news. The bad news is I'm probably going to continue feeling bad for a few more weeks."

"Did he say what's wrong with you?"

"Well, that's what the good news is?"

"What do you mean? I don't understand. What's the good news?"

"Johnny, we're going to have a baby. Can you believe that?"

"Really? That's great. When?"

"I'm only eight weeks now, so it will be after you get home."

Johnny held the phone away from his face and yelled at Pat. "Hey Pat; we're pregnant," then resumed his conversation with Analisa.

"That's wonderful, Honey. Did you call Mom and Dad?"

"Yeah, I called them last night, and they are thrilled. They're worried about you, Johnny. Can you call them?"

"Yeah, I'll call them when we hang up. Anybody heard from Jimmy? Is he actually playing guitar in a band?"

"He is, and apparently he's real good, according to people who have heard him."

Johnny talked a few minutes longer, and noticed a line forming behind him. "Analisa, Honey, there are several guys behind me wanting to use the phone, so I'm going to hang up and let another guy call his wife. I'll call you again whenever I can, and oh, would you call Mom and Dad and tell them I called and I'll call them soon. We don't have a mission tomorrow, so maybe I can call then, but tell them not to worry if I don't call. I may not have access to a telephone. I love you, Baby, and I'm thrilled that we're going to be parents. I can't wait until he or she is born. You take care, and I'll call you again just as soon as I can. Bye." He waited until Pat hung up, and they walked together back to their quarters.

Pat said, "Well, tell me about the pregnancy. Amanda told me a little because she went to the doctor with Analisa, but didn't go into any detail."

"Well, it was a total surprise. We had talked about having children, but not right now. We were going to wait until I got another promotion or two and maybe go to a base where we could settle down for a few years, but I guess God had different plans for us. She said the doctor told her that she is just barely eight weeks, so I should be home in plenty of time before the baby is born. The doctor told her that she would probably feel bad for a few more weeks, but she's relieved that the reason she feels so bad is because she's pregnant rather than some serious illness."

Johnny's platoon didn't have a mission the next day, so he got to sleep a little later than usual, and that helped to make up for not getting into bed until so late. He took advantage of the day by calling Analisa again as well as his Mom and Dad. Joan was bowled over when she answered the phone, and it was Johnny. "You sound like you're here in town," she said. Where are you, Johnny?"

"Mom, you know I can't tell you that, but I'm all right, okay?"

"I wish you would come home."

"Me too, Mom, but it won't be too much longer. Listen, I'm going to hang up and call Dad before the phones get too busy, and I can't talk. I love you, Mom, and I'll call you again real soon. Bye."

When he called Monty, Monty was just as glad to hear from him as Joan was, and they talked for about ten minutes. At one point, Monty asked if he was ready to come home and go to work at Shepherd Apparel yet, and Johnny responded, "Not yet, Dad. Dad, I need to hang up now and let some of these other guys use the phone, but I'll call you again in a day or so. I love you, Dad," and he hung up.

For the next month or so, Johnny's platoon went on a mission just about every other night. Some were pretty much routine with nothing out of the ordinary happening, but some of them were pretty scary. They had become good at spotting roadside bombs, but they never did get good at distinguishing the good guys from the bad guys. Everybody looked alike, so they couldn't trust anyone for fear that the very one to whom they let their guard down would kill them. That had happened more than once.

One day, about six weeks into his deployment, Johnny's platoon had the morning off after a pretty hard mission the day before. As he usually did on his days-off, he called Analisa and his parents and then just killed time for a large part of the day, but at lunch, an announcement was made that there would be a called meeting of all platoon leaders and assistant platoon leaders at 1500 hours (3 P.M.).

CHAPTER FIVE

At the meeting the C.O. explained, "Men, four weeks ago, an American convoy was ambushed in the city of Fallujah. You might have heard about it. Eleven brave Americans were killed, and nine were captured. Last week, after three weeks in captivity, eight of the soldiers were rescued, however, there is one still in captivity, and our mission tomorrow will be to rescue that soldier. His name is Brandon Palmer. This will be a chance for us to do what Rangers do best.

"On July 3, a convoy of the Army's 408th Maintenance Company and the 2nd Combat Support Battalion elements, led by a Humvee driven by Larry Poston, made a wrong turn and were ambushed near Sulaymaniya, a major crossing point between the Baranan Mountain in the south and the Tasluja Hills in the west. The convoy was supposed to detour around the town and instead turned directly into it, eventually running into an ambush. Apparently, they took more than one wrong turn. The convoy came under attack by enemy fire. The Humvee in which Palmer was riding was hit by a rocket-propelled grenade, and it crashed into a building. Palmer was severely injured."

Johnny asked, "Captain, didn't they have a GPS? I don't understand how they could have made two wrong turns if they had one."

"They could have had one, John. Some military vehicles have them, but they don't work too well out here. Maps of the area lack the detail required to properly navigate through tight city streets. That is probably why they made more than one wrong turn.

"Palmer, then a supply clerk with the 408th Maintenance Company from Fort Bliss, Texas was wounded and captured by Iraqi forces. He was initially listed as missing in action. Eleven other soldiers in the company were killed in the ambush. Nine others were captured and subsequently rescued twenty-one days later. Palmer's best friend, Larry Poston, received a serious head wound and died in an Iraqi civilian hospital.

"After some time in the custody of the Iraqi army regiment that had captured him, Palmer was taken to a hospital in Sulaymaniyah. The hospital staff, including two doctors said they shielded Palmer from Iraqi military and government agents who were using the hospital as a base for military operations.

"Yesterday, we were tipped off as to Palmer's whereabouts by an Iraqi, who said he had been tortured and injured, but was still alive. The Iraqi is a young lawyer, named, let me see; I've got it written down. His name is Muhammed Gaber al Hakim, and the United States has agreed to grant him and his family refugee status if his information is truthful and the rescue is successful. By the way, Hakim's wife is a nurse at the hospital where Palmer is supposed to be.

"We'll find out tomorrow night how accurate our information is because our mission is to go to Sulaymaniyah to rescue Palmer."

Johnny asked, "Captain, did you say tomorrow night?"

"Yes, tomorrow night. There are going to be a lot people involved in this rescue. There will be elements from two Marine Battalions as well as members from the Navy Seals under the command of the U.S. Army. All those people will create a diversionary attack, besieging nearby Iraqi irregulars to draw them away from the hospital in Sulaymaniyah. Meanwhile, an element from the U.S. Army Special Forces, Air Force Para-rescuemen, Army Rangers, and Delta Force will launch a nighttime raid on the hospital. Our goal is to retrieve Palmer and the bodies of several other American soldiers."

Johnny asked, "Sir, how will we travel? It seems to me that it would be risky traveling by Humvees at night."

"You're right, John. We'll be traveling by Chinook helicopters. It's a little more than two hundred and sixty-five kilometers, so ground travel would not be wise, besides, we need to get in and out quickly."

The following night, all the participants in the raid gathered for the mission. For some reason, nighttime missions seemed to be more risky than daytime missions, and as the men prepared to board the helicopters, there was not much talking. Everyone was serious minded and quiet.

The Chinook took almost an hour to fly the one hundred and sixty-five mile trip, landing in the parking lot at the hospital. Expecting at least some resistance, there was none; all the Iraqi resistors had left. The only people there were doctors and nurses, and the Special Operations Forces gathered them all into groups at gunpoint until they could be identified as hospital staff. Special Operations Forces are trained to expect the worst and move quickly, initially treating each person they encounter as a possible threat.

After they were satisfied the hospital staff was who they said they were, the doctors told them that the Iraqi military had left the hospital the day before. Some of the staff led the Americans to the room where Brandon Palmer was located with a broken arm, a broken leg, and a dislocated ankle. Palmer was rolled outside on a gurney and put into one of the Chinooks while the rescuers searched for any other survivors.

Eleven bodies were recovered from a shallow graveside and two from the morgue. Following forensic identification, eight were identified as fellow members of his company, including Larry Poston. All the bodies were put into a Chinook, and after a few more hours with nothing else found, the forces boarded the helicopters and returned to the Baghdad airport.

The sun was coming up when they landed in Baghdad, and Johnny asked Pat, “Are you hungry?”

“I’m starved. Let’s go get some breakfast before we crash. Do you want to?”

“Absolutely, I’m starved, too.”

Pat and Johnny must not have been the only ones that were hungry because when they got to the mess hall, there was already a crowd. They both ate a big breakfast and went to their quarters and went to bed.

Fighting was beginning to step up a notch in the cities circling Baghdad. Iraqis were conducting mortar attacks on the Baghdad airport with regularity, and the roads were getting to the critical stage because of an increase in roadside bombs. Each mission had become something to dread by nearly every soldier, and Johnny had acquired something that he didn’t want; a premonition that something bad was going to happen.

According to what Johnny considered to be a reliable source, his Ranger unit would not be staying at the airport very much more. Instead, they would be going on multi-day missions, and would be sleeping where they would be fighting. His source suggested he call home because they probably wouldn’t be there after that day. Johnny heard this at lunch one day, and when he heard it, he took it to heart and called Analisa as well as Joan and Monty. He still couldn’t tell them where he was, but he was able to tell them that he would be on multiple missions and would not be back to his quarters for an undetermined amount of time. He doubted if there would be telephones where he would be going.

Analisa and Joan both cried when Johnny told them that on his calls to them, and that brought tears to his eyes as well. That day, in addition to Analisa and his parents, he called Brad and Nancy Davis, and they were thrilled to hear from him, although his call was a shock. As he did when he hung up from the others, he told the Davises that he loved them. Pat was waiting on him when he got off the phone, and they walked to their quarters together.

At breakfast the next morning, an announcement came over the speakers telling "C" Company to meet at ten-hundred hours at the Assembly Hall. Johnny looked at Pat and said, "I wonder what that's all about."

At ten-hundred hours (10 o'clock) Captain Easton addressed the men of "C" Company. "Men, we've been called to go on a mission that may take four or five days, and it promises to be pretty dangerous so you'll have to be very careful. The mission is to rout the Iraqis from the Majnoon oil field and to hold it until all hostilities are ended in that area. We will land in the town of Basra, and partner up with units from the Navy Seals and Special Operations Forces. After the rendezvous with the Seals and Special Forces, we will then go to the oil fields, a distance of about sixty kilometers (thirty-five miles) from Basra. If all goes according to schedule, we should reach Majnoon just as the sun rises. We will camouflage our vehicles and then seize what we call Objective Gus and insure the fields aren't rigged to be blown. The enemy situation stated the fields were heavily guarded with one to two hundred enemy personnel, numerous armored vehicles including T-55 Battle tanks and in excess of fifty anti-aircraft artillery pieces."

When new Intelligence was received, within three hours the commander worked on a plan. He designated different groups to do certain things. First platoon mission was to clear the inside of the field and allow our breachers to confirm the field was not in danger of being blown up. The plan was completed as the sun began to set, and they departed from Basra for the sixty kilometer trip to Operation Gus. Getting near, Johnny told the platoon, "Okay, Men, we're almost there so be careful and let's show these terror-types what a U.S. Army Ranger can do when he's ticked off." He directed some of his men to do certain things, and then told the first squad, "You fellows come with me; we're going up that small hill with an M-240 machine gun, and we're going to clear a building on the left-hand side of the road."

The platoon cautiously approached the hill, and when they reached the building, everyone had gone, causing Johnny to realize the apparent complexity of the mission. When they reached the top of the hill, there was not one building, but twelve large buildings. He had the M-240 moved to the roof of the building to cover the platoon's movement, then, he began alternating the two squads between the buildings across the objective. Everything was still pretty quiet at that point. Once they cleared the far side of the hill to allow heavy guns to secure the southern flank, he called for all the vehicles to move up. About that time when the second squad moved across a twenty-five meter open area to a huge concrete mural of Saddam Hussein was when everything got crazy.

All at once the lip of the hill opened up with small arms, machine gun and rocket-propelled grenade (RPG) fire. Apparently, the Iraqis had moved out of the buildings to survivability positions at the base of the hill. Further out, more than twelve different mortar tubes began engaging the hill. Amazingly, at that point, no one had been hurt.

The platoon immediately returned fire and began what turned out to be a five-hour battle. As the fight continued into the morning light, it continued to show more and more problems.

As the day continued, the enemy forces would consolidate in groups of fifty to one-hundred approximately six to eight kilometers from Johnny's location. "C" company used 120mm mortars to prevent their consolidation. They would then disburse and come at the Rangers in human waves of ten to fifteen personnel.

The fight lasted through the night, and at one point an enemy machine-gun began firing at Ranger positions, seriously wounding two in Johnny's platoon. Somehow, the enemy was able to get back to one of the buildings and set the gun up. It pretty much had Johnny's platoon pinned down when he made a decision; he would go out, himself, and take out the machine-gun. He called Pat over to his position and told him what he was going to do. Pat pleaded with him not to do it, but Johnny out-ranked him and said he was going. "Tell your men to cover me, and I'll be back in a few minutes," and with that he slipped out of his position and began crawling toward the machine-gun. His platoon opened fire on the enemy and was answered by heavy machine-gun fire. Johnny thought, *I probably shouldn't have done this, but I have to take out that gun to save my men.*

Bullets started hitting the ground all around him, and he prayed, *What have I got myself into? I don't know if I can make it or not, but I've got to try. Lord, please help me. We're fighting a bunch of fanatics that won't listen to reason, and I pray that you will help us. Help me now, Father. I'm in a mess, and unless you help me, I don't think I'll come through it. Father, I don't want to die, especially now that we are going to have a baby, but Lord, you know what's best, so I'm placing my life in your hands. Thank you for your blessings, Lord, and I make this prayer in Jesus' name. Amen.*

Johnny was able to crawl to within hand-grenade range, and he threw one right on the machine-gun nest. The grenade exploded as it hit, killing the personnel operating the gun. Johnny turned around and began crawling back to his position when a sniper bullet hit him in the neck, just above the Kevlar vest that he was wearing.

His soldiers saw the flash from the sniper's gun, and nearly every one of them opened fire on the guy, killing him instantly. Not only did the medics rush to Johnny, but the entire platoon as well. One of the medics called a medevac helicopter to take him back.

When Pat reached him and saw how serious the wound was, he knelt down beside him and asked, "Bro, why did you do this? You're in charge of this bunch, and they depend on you. Why did you do it?"

Johnny, with his eyes closed, barely audible, answered, "I felt like I needed to do it. Is everyone alright?"

Then, Pat went out to the sniper's position to find the sniper, who was already dead. When he found him he emptied his gun into his already lifeless body, calling him every name he could think of. After he shot the guy and started to walk away, suddenly, he turned around and went back to his body, took out his U.S. Marine Corps knife with the eight inch blade and beheaded him. He then stood up and said, "I hope you think it was worth it, Mohammed. You won't do this again will you, you sorry piece of crap?"

Johnny was barely alive when the medics carried him back to their position, and shortly the helicopter arrived to pick him up, and the battle continued for another two days. After Johnny was shot, the Rangers fought with more resolve and finally routed the Iraqis from the oil fields.

When the unit returned to Baghdad airport, Pat went to find Johnny, but was told that they had carried him to Landstuhl Regional Medical Center in Germany where he could get the proper care.

CHAPTER SIX

Analisa had just gotten home from work when the doorbell rang. She went to the door, and before she opened it she looked out the small window adjacent to the door and saw two cars parked out front that had United States Army painted on the side. Her heart sank as she opened the door to two soldiers dressed in Class A dress uniforms. One had a gold Major's insignia on his collar, and she noticed the other wore a Chaplain's insignia.

Speaking softly, the Major asked, "Are you Mrs. John Shepherd?"

Analisa responded, "Yes, I am."

"Mrs. Shepherd, my name is Major Jeffrey Scott. I serve with the United States Rangers' Seventy-fifth regiment, and this is Chaplain John McGee. I have an important message from the Secretary of the Army. May we come in?"

Analisa pushed the storm door open wider and said, "Yes, come in."

When the two soldiers were inside, Major Scott asked Analisa, "Mrs. Shepherd, would you like to sit down?"

Analisa took a seat in what she considered to be Johnny's recliner, and Major Scott said, "Mrs. Shepherd, the Secretary of the Army has asked me to express his deep regret for the loss of your husband, First Lieutenant John Shepherd, who was killed by enemy fire while courageously fighting terrorism in the country of Iraq."

Analisa went to pieces. She squalled and got out of the chair and put her arms around Chaplain McGee, and he put his arms around her. After crying for a few minutes in Chaplain McGee's embrace, she tearfully said, "He can't be dead. There's got to be some mistake. We're going to have a baby, and he has to be here." Then, she began squalling again. In those few moments, she was too upset to notice, but Major Scott and Captain McGee both had tears in their eyes.

After a few more minutes of getting used to the shock, Major Scott said, "Mrs. Shepherd, my assignment is to be here with you and to provide you with help in any and all areas. Is there anything that Captain McGee or I can do for you right now?"

"No, thank you. I need to call my parents and Johnny's parents to tell them what happened. Excuse me."

She picked up the phone and dialed her parents' number. Nancy answered. Crying again, she said, "Mother, Johnny was killed."

Nancy said, "What did you say?"

"I said, "Johnny was killed."

"Oh, my goodness. I'm so sorry, Darling. What happened?"

"I don't know. Two officers just came to tell me, and I wanted you to know."

"Do Monty and Joan know?"

"I'm going to call them when we hang up."

"Honey, your Dad is out of town and not scheduled to be back until day after tomorrow. Let me hang up and call him. I know he'll want to come home immediately, and we'll come down there just as soon as he gets here. Okay? Do you have anyone who can stay with you?"

"I'm going to call Amanda. I'm sure she will want to come."

"Okay, Darling; let me get off of here so you can call Joan and Monty. I'll call you as soon as I talk to your Dad and let you know when we will be there."

When she hung up, she told the officers that she was going to call her husband's parents, and they nodded and said to take her time.

Unbeknownst to Analisa, a Captain Stephen Ward was simultaneously telling Monty and Joan the same thing that Major Scott told her, so they already knew when she called them.

Joan and Monty were pitiful when they were told. Joan screamed and collapsed. Monty was always the strong one; *Mr. Macho*, but when he found out his boy was dead, he lost it. He got out of his chair and went to Joan's and pulled her up, and they embraced for several minutes, crying; Joan un-controlling.

After that initial shock and crying session, Monty wiped his eyes, looked at Joan and said, "Joanie, the Lord gives and the Lord takes away. We've got to understand that Johnny is with Him now. Do you believe that?"

"Yes, I believe it, but it's still hard, Monty."

"I know it is, and it's killing me, but I've got to remember that or I'll go crazy. Honey, why don't you call Analisa back and I'll try to get in touch with Jimmy and Mary Ann, and I'll have to go tell Mom, too."

When he had made the calls, he called Mike Taylor, his Gulfstream pilot and told him about Johnny and told him to prepare to go to Columbus the next morning. He called Tom Ratcliff, also, and told him about Johnny, and told him to have Connie announce it to all the plants the next morning, and he didn't know when he would be back to work.

The rest of the evening would be taken up calling relatives and friends to give them the news about Johnny. Meanwhile, at Fort Benning, Amanda had made it to Analisa's, and she was a terrific comfort to her. Around nine or nine-thirty the trauma had done its' work on her, and she closed her eyes to go to sleep, however, Major Scott interrupted her before she got to sleep and said, "Mrs. Shepherd, I'm going to leave you now so you can rest. My assignment is to do for you whatever you need for as long as it takes, and I'll be back in the morning. We'll talk then about arrangements and other things. All right?"

"Okay, Major Scott. Thank you for your concern and your help. I'll see you in the morning." Before he left, the phone rang, and it was Nancy, Analisa's mother. "Analisa, how are you doing, Darling?"

"I'm doing okay, Mother."

"Honey, the reason I called is to tell you that your Daddy and I will be there at nine o'clock in the morning with Monty and Joan. We're coming on the Shepherd plane. I won't keep you; I just wanted to tell you that. I hope you rest well, and we'll see you in the morning."

As soon as they hung up, Analisa said, "Major Scott, that was my mother, and she and my daddy and Johnny's parents will be down here at nine o'clock in the morning. Do you think you could have someone meet them at the airport and bring them here?"

"Of course, Mrs. Shepherd. Do you know which airline they are coming on?"

"No airline. They will be on Johnny's Dad's plane. It will have Shepherd Apparel painted on the side. If you will do that for me, I will appreciate it."

"It will be my pleasure, Mrs. Shepherd. I'm going to let you rest now. I hope you sleep well. Good night."

The next morning, Major Scott met the Shepherd plane when it arrived in Columbus. He had requisitioned a van so there would be room for everybody. After his expressions of sympathy to both sets of parents, they went to Analisa's apartment.

She and Amanda were in the kitchen having coffee when the van drove up, and she went into the living room to meet everybody. She wasn't crying until she saw her mother, and then everybody cried. Major Scott even had tears in his eyes.

Major Scott was a tremendous help to the families as they got into discussing how things could and would be handled. He told them that the body would arrive at Dover Air Force Base in Delaware when it reached the United States, and he wanted to know where they would like for it to be taken from there. Monty and Brad had talked about that on the plane, and they thought if Analisa agreed, they would have the funeral at the United States National Cemetery in Chattanooga. They told that to Major Scott, and he thought that was a good choice, and Analisa agreed. Major Scott made a lot of notes during the conversation so nothing would be overlooked later.

He asked, "Mrs. Shepherd, would you like to go to Dover and be there when your husband's body arrives?"

She looked at Brad and asked. "What do you think, Daddy?"

Brad looked at Monty and asked him the same question, and Monty said, "I don't think we need to go to Dover. If they are going to take Johnny to Chattanooga, we can be there when he arrives. Is that alright with you, Analisa?"

"I guess so. You and Daddy know best."

The balance of the day was filled with making plans; both for the funeral and for Analisa after the funeral. Analisa had already decided to move off the base, but to stay in Columbus for the unforeseeable future. She had a good job with insurance, and she would need the insurance when the baby was born.

Three days later, a C-130 Army transport plane landed at Dover Air Force Base with the bodies of Johnny and three others. Major Scott had made arrangements to have Johnny's body taken to Chattanooga to be buried at the National Cemetery there, so after all the paperwork and red-tape was cleared, the body was taken to the Wilmington-Philadelphia Regional Airport in New Castle and put on a Delta flight.

Analisa had gone home with her parents so everybody was at the airport to meet the plane when it landed at Lovell Field. Major Scott had arranged for six Army Reserve soldiers to be there to take the casket off the plane and put it in the funeral-home hearse where it was taken to the Chattanooga Funeral Home to await friends and relatives at a formal visitation to be held the next night.

A news reporter had received word that Johnny's body would be arriving so naturally, he had a film crew at the airport, and he talked to some of the friends who had come out. When the news came on that afternoon, and people saw the plane and heard the interviews, the funeral home was jammed that night. They didn't wait on the formal visitation the next night; they wanted to be there right then. Monty and Joan were there as was Analisa and her parents, and due to the large crowd, it was impossible for them to grieve in private. At one point, Monty went to the funeral home office and asked the manager if it would be possible for the family to come back the next afternoon and have some privacy, and the manager agreed to the request.

The next day went relatively well. The private time spent in the afternoon and the visitation that night meant a lot to the family. Monty and Joan knew that Johnny was special, but when so many people shared their experiences with him, they were, indeed, proud.

At the funeral the next day, Rev. Doug Luffman, Monty's pastor and the pastor who helped guide Johnny and Jimmy in their early lives, did the main eulogy, then. turned the podium over to the Military Chaplain assigned to conduct the funeral. Most of the people attending had never seen a true military funeral, and they were impressed by the honor guard that participated.

The Chaplain also conducted the graveside service, and at one point, seven members of the United States Army raised and fired their rifles three times for a twenty-one gun salute, then just over the crest of a small hill from the gravesite a bugler played Taps while a final salute was given. Needless to say, there wasn't a dry eye in the entire crowd.

Immediately after Taps, six honor guards, acting as pallbearers, removed the flag from the casket and in a very strict manner meticulously folded it twelve times and presented it to Analisa, with the straight edge of the flag facing her. As he presented the flag, he said in a soft voice, "On behalf of the President of the United States, the United States Army, and a grateful nation, please accept this flag as a symbol of our appreciation for your loved one's honorable and faithful service."

That ended the service and afterwards, several members of the crowd stayed around and talked to Analisa, Monty, Joan, and Jimmy, who was having a rough time. Nobody left Mary Ann out of the conversation, but since Jimmy was Johnny's twin brother, more attention was given to him.

CHAPTER SEVEN

Analisa stayed in Chattanooga until Sunday, and then, Nancy went home with her to stay for a few days until she felt comfortable staying by herself again. While Nancy was with her, Analisa wanted to look for an apartment because she wanted to move out of Fort Benning, so they spent quite a bit of time doing that. Amanda and Pat lived in a very nice apartment and Analisa thought she would like to have one in their complex, so they went over there to look, among other places. Analisa was going to be off from work that whole week, and it allowed them to accomplish a lot.

After looking at several apartments, they went to the complex where Amanda lived and as luck would have it, there was a vacancy, and Analisa just loved it. They went back down to the manager's office and talked about it, and before they left, Analisa had rented a new apartment. She called Amanda at work and told her about it, and Amanda was thrilled. Nancy thought she was doing well enough to get by on her own, so she went home the following Sunday, and Analisa went back to work on Monday.

At every turn, Major Scott was there to help with all the details, such as insurance, changing joint things, such as bank accounts, from joint to individual, and taking Johnny's name off the car title. When she found the apartment she wanted, he even looked after the move and took care of all the expenses. The move didn't cost her anything; the government paid for it.

****

Before Mary Ann, Sue and Bobby left to go back to school on Monday, after the funeral, Monty told Bobby, "Bobby, this week is not the right time for me, but I'd like to talk to you sometime. When are you coming back home?"

"I don't know; I don't have any plans, but if you want me to, I can come back any time. Would next weekend be all right?"

"Yeah, that sounds good. If you can come back, that would be great."

Bobby left for school the next morning and wondered all week what

Monty wanted to talk to him about that was important enough for him to come all the way back from Cookeville, but he reasoned that whatever it was, he was glad to do it, because without Monty he wouldn't be able to be in college.

Also, on Monday morning, Jimmy had to leave to go back. He got up and had coffee with Monty and Joan and told them how much he hated to leave, and Joan asked, "Then why don't you just stay home? Baseball doesn't start for another three or four months. Stay with us, Honey."

"I can't, Mom. I've made a commitment to the other members of the group, and you and Dad have always taught me to honor my word. Maybe one day soon, things will work out so I can come home, but right now, I'm committed to them."

Monty chimed in; "Son, you're doing the right thing, but if you're really interested in getting out of the group and coming home. I think we can probably work something out to where you won't be going back on your word to them. Shepherd Apparel could sure use you. What do you say?"

"Let me think about it, Dad, but today I've got to go. Okay? I love you both so very much," and he got up and hugged and kissed both of them and left.

Bobby left Cookeville after his last class on Friday and drove to Chattanooga. When he got home he called Monty. "Hey, Uncle Monty, this is Bobby. I just got home and wanted to see when you want to talk to me."

"Hi, Bobby. I'm going to be in my office in the morning. Could you come out there, say, around ten o'clock?"

"Yes sir. I'll be there. I'll see you in the morning."

The next morning, Bobby arrived at Shepherd Apparel a little before ten and walked into the reception area. He could hear Monty talking to somebody down the hall, and he could tell he wasn't in his office, so he stood in the doorway of the hall, waiting on Monty to see him. In about five minutes Monty came out of an office down past where his office was located, and when he saw Bobby he said, "Good morning, Bobby. Come on back."

When Bobby got into Monty's office, Monty had him sit in one of the nice, upholstered chairs, and he sat in another one. He asked, "How was school this week?"

"It was okay; I had a hard time getting my mind on my subjects, but yesterday and Thursday were better."

"Good, I know it must have been hard on you the way it has been on the rest of us, but as they say, "Life must go on." Bobby, ever since you came into all of our lives I've looked on you as one of the family. Now that you're a senior at Tech, have you thought very much about what you want to do after you graduate?"

"Yes sir, I've thought some about it, but I can't seem to come up with anything that excites me very much. They're having a thing at school next week where a lot of companies will be there to talk to any of us who want to talk to them about jobs, and I plan to go to that. I like accounting a lot, and I would also like to be a salesman for a big company, but I hear those jobs are really hard to find."

"You're right about that. The large companies that have good products have waiting lists to get sales jobs with them. Some sales jobs are actually handed down from father to son. It's interesting that you would say that you would like to get into sales because that's why I wanted to talk to you. Do you think you might be interested in coming with Shepherd Apparel when you graduate?"

"Are you serious? I'd give anything to come to work here. Are you talking about sales?"

"Yes I am. We don't actually have anything right now, but we're always looking for the right young people to come in, learn the business the Shepherd way, and then move into more responsible jobs. Have you met Jeff Ellis or Bryce Coleman by any chance?"

"No sir, I don't think I have."

"Well, they both came out of the Don Shepherd Scholarship program, and when they got out of college, they came to work here, and now, they have big jobs, and they're making very good money. Bobby, since you're like my third son, I'd like to give you the opportunity to come with us and see if you would like to make Shepherd Apparel a career.

"When Jimmy and Johnny were at home, I guess I just took it for granted that they would come into the company, but you know how that's turned out. Johnny's gone forever, and Jimmy might as well be because between playing baseball and playing music, it doesn't look as if he will ever want to come back. I continually pray that he will, and hopefully he will someday, but in the meantime, I've got to make sure that if and when I retire that there will be capable people in here to take the company forward. I don't expect you to give me an answer right now; think about it, and we'll talk again the next time you come home."

"Uncle Monty, I don't have to think about it. I never did want to ask for any favors or anything because of how good you have been to Sue and I, but this is more than I could ever dream of. If you want me, the answer is yes."

"That's good. Now you won't need to go to go to that job fair, will you? Let me ask you something else, Bobby; you and Jimmy used to be very close. Do you ever hear from him?"

"No sir. When I saw him at the funeral was the first time I have seen him in a long time. He used to call every now and then, but it's been quite a while since I've talked to him. I wish he'd call sometime because you're right; we were very close. He became almost like my brother."

When Bobby and Monty finished, Bobby thanked him again and left for home at Wauhatchie Farms. Monty began to go over some reports when the phone rang. "Hello."

It was Joan. "Hi Sweetheart; Nancy just called and said Analisa came in late last night, and she wanted to know if we would all like to come over to their house for a cookout tonight. They're going to have burgers and dogs."

"Tell her yeah, we'd like to come."

The night was chilly, and when Joan, Mary Ann, and Monty got to the Davises Nancy had made some spiced cider and offered them a cup. "Boy, this hits the spot, Nancy," Monty said, and about that time, Analisa came into the room. After the initial hugs, Joan asked, "How're you feeling? Feeling any better?"

"Yes, Ma'am; I seem to be a little better each day. Maybe in another week or so I'll be over this darned morning sickness."

Brad was outside watching the grill, and Monty went out and joined him after speaking to Analisa. "Hey, Monty, how are you doing?"

"Good, Brad. Are you doing okay?"

"Yeah, I'm okay, I guess. I've been doing so much traveling, I'm about worn out, and with trying to help Analisa long distance, I'm about ready for a break."

"Joan and I have been concerned about her. Is she still planning to stay in Columbus?"

"Yeah, at least until after the baby's born. She doesn't have any choice, Monty. She has to have insurance. Babies cost a lot more now than they did when you and I were born, so she's locked in down there for several more months, and then, after the baby is born it will have to have insurance, too.

"Now that she's alone, she would like to come home, but it doesn't look like it's in the cards for that to happen. I'm thankful that she has Amanda, but Pat will be home in two or three weeks, and as you well know, you never know what will happen when the Rangers are involved. I wish it was so she could come, but we'll just have to make the best of a bad situation."

Nancy yelled out the back door; "How are those burgers coming? You've got four hungry women in here ready to eat."

"They're just about ready. Give me five more minutes."

Brad took the burgers, dogs, and six very appetizing ears of corn off the grill, and he and Monty went into the house to sit down to a feast. Before they ate, Brad asked Monty to ask the blessing, and then, they all began filling their plates.

All through dinner everyone was involved in conversation except Analisa, and she was very quiet. Mary Ann tried to talk to her, but she only spoke when asked a question or felt the need to same something. After several attempts, Mary Ann quit trying.

After dinner, the women cleaned up the kitchen and then joined Brad and Monty in the den. Since Analisa and the soon-to-be born baby were the center of attention, naturally, most of the conversation was directed toward her.

Once, when Nancy said something about wishing she could come home instead of being alone in Columbus, she began to cry, and got up and left the room. Nancy got up and went after her, and in a few minutes, they were back in the den. Analisa apologized and said, "I'm sorry. I guess I'm not feeling as well as I thought I did."

Monty had been waiting on the right time to bring it up, and that little episode showed it was the right time. After she had calmed down a little more, he asked, "Analisa, what would you do if you were able to come back before the baby's born?"

"I guess I'd dance a jig."

Nancy said, "I'd dance one, too."

Then Monty did a *typical Monty* thing. "You're a computer programmer aren't you, Honey?"

"Yes sir."

Do you like that kind of work?"

"I didn't know if I would like it before I got my job, but, yes sir, I really like it."

"How do you think you would like to be a computer programmer at Shepherd Apparel?"

"I would love it, but you know I can't leave Columbus because of the insurance. Being at Shepherd Apparel would be an absolute dream."

Then Monty said, "Well, let's suppose for a minute that you were able to come back and go to work at Shepherd Apparel with no insurance coverage on the pregnancy, but you knew someone who would take the place of your insurance. Do you think you would be interested in something like that?"

"I don't understand."

At that time, Brad chimed in and said, smiling,"Just say yes, Baby."

Monty continued, "Analisa, what I'm trying to say is if you want to come home and go to work for us, I'll be your insurance. I'll take care of all your expenses when the baby is born, and you won't have to worry about it. You can work until you feel you can't work any longer, and you will still get paid the same as you would if you were working. After the baby is born, you can have a reasonable amount of time off before going back to work, and you will still get paid. Would something like that interest you?"

Once again, Analisa burst into tears, and she got up and ran to Monty, threw her arms around him and said, "Thank you so much. I can't believe this is happening to me," and she sat in his lap and continued to hug and thank him.

Across the room, Nancy was also crying, and she had moved over and sat in Brad's lap while she cried. Joan was just sitting there, and when she looked at Nancy and Brad, she saw tears in Brad's eyes. She thought to herself, *this husband of mine; he's wonderful. Lord, thank you so much for letting me be married to such a wonderful man.*

When the crying was over, they began to work out the plans. It was decided that Nancy would go back home with her to help work out some of the details, and Analisa would work out a two-week notice at her company, if they wanted her to.

For the rest of the evening Analisa was like a new person; happy and smiling and talking. Nancy and Brad were in a really upbeat mood and very thankful to Monty for his love and generosity. Nancy asked if they would like to play some Rook, and Joan said she would love to, so Brad set up the card table, Nancy got the cards, and they played two or three games before Monty said it was time for them to go home. As they were leaving, Brad, Nancy, and Analisa all told Monty again how thrilled they were for his enabling Analisa to come home to have the baby, and they all gave him a hug, including Brad.

SIX MONTHS LATER

The phone at Monty's house rang at about four-thirty a.m., and when Joan answered, Nancy said, "Joan, it's time. We're leaving right now for the hospital, and we thought you guys would want to come, too."

Joan said, "Absolutely; we'll meet you there." She told Monty it was time to go, and he got up. He told her they should drive both cars because he would probably go to work from the hospital, so they got ready and took off for Erlanger to meet their first grandchild.

When they reached the hospital, the doctor told them that she was not ready yet, and it would probably be a few more hours. Since it was just a little past five, Brad said he would like a cup of coffee, and Joan said she would like one, too, so he and Monty went downstairs to the all-night snack bar and bought four large cups along with the sweetener and creamer and took it back up to the waiting room.

While they were drinking their coffee, Monty asked Nancy, "What do you think the baby will be?"

Nancy said, "I think it's going to be a little girl," and Joan said, "I think it will be a girl, too. She's carrying it high, and they say that's a sign of a girl."

Brad said, "Well, you're both wrong. I think it will be a boy," and Monty said, "I'm with you, Brad. I think it will be a little boy as well,"

At eight-twenty-three, a healthy seven pound fifteen ounce boy greeted the world, and everyone was elated. After they cleaned him up and did their routine checks, they brought him to Analisa's room to see his mother and to meet his grandparents. Of course, Nancy and Joan had to hold him immediately while Brad and Monty stood by and watched. After a few minutes, Joan handed him to Monty, and in a couple of minutes Monty gave him to Brad, then, Nancy took him once more and handed him down to Analisa, who was very proud and thankful for such a pretty, healthy boy.

After she had held him for a little while, she said, "I'm going to name him John David Shepherd, Jr. after his father." Then she broke down and cried and said to no one in particular, “Johnny, you should be here, but since you can’t be, I hope you’re able to see him, and that you’re happy for us.”

Analisa and the baby stayed in the hospital all that day and went home to Brad and Nancy’s the next day. Joan came up with all kinds of excuses to go see little Johnny every day for the next few weeks and then slowed up a little.

When the baby was about two months old, Analisa thought she should go back to work, so she worked it out for Nancy to keep him two days a week and Joan two days. The fifth day, he would go to childcare at Shepherd Apparel.

A couple of weeks after she went back to work, she thought she should get her own place to live, so she began looking for apartments on the weekends, and it wasn’t long before she found what she thought would be good for her and the baby. She took her mother and Joan to see it, and they agreed that it was nice, and she should lease it.

She and Johnny had bought furniture when they rented their apartment in Columbus, and when she moved back to Chattanooga she had it put in storage. She could get it out and would more than likely have enough without having to buy any more. Monty told her that he would have some men who worked at Shepherd Apparel move her on the following Saturday, using one of the company trucks; so hopefully, her life would soon begin to get back to normal.

For the next several months little Johnny grew by leaps and bounds, and Analisa settled into her computer job at Shepherd Apparel. One day, when Monty was having coffee in the break-room Charlotte Morris, Analisa’s supervisor, asked if she could sit down at the table with him. He, of course, said she could, and when she was seated she said, “Monty, I just want to tell you that your daughter-in-law is a real asset to the computer department. She can already do things that seasoned veteran computer programmers have a hard time with. I know how careful you are when it comes to not showing any partiality to relatives in your employ, but I want to go on record saying Analisa is ready for a promotion. She hasn’t been here as long as some of the other people in the department, but she’s the one who deserves the promotion. I wanted to tell you this in case you hear grumbling.

****

When Analisa came to work the next morning, she went to Monty's office and said, "Monty, Daddy's been transferred and they have to move within the next month. Isn't that awful?"

"Where are they going, Honey?"

"To Atlanta, and I'm just sick."

"Well, it shouldn't be too bad. Atlanta's only a couple of hours away, and you can see them on weekends whenever you want to. It shouldn't be much different than the way it is now, should it? You work all week, and there are probably some weekends when you don't see them now, aren't there?"

"Yeah, I guess you're right. Thank you, Monty."

CHAPTER EIGHT

Jimmy had been moved up from the Double-A Pearl Braves to the Triple-A Gwinnett Braves, and there was a good chance that he would move on up to the Atlanta Braves in another year. His play at third base was plenty good enough to play in Atlanta, but they had a good third baseman, so they decided to keep him in the minors to get more experience. Atlanta's third baseman was thirty-four years old, and he was planning to retire at the end of the following season, opening the door for Jimmy.

His other career, playing in a band at county fairs, night clubs, and an occasional stadium was very strong, but something about it just wasn't right. He didn't know he could sing until the band leader sort of drafted him into helping out by singing backup one night. They found that he had a terrific voice and from that night on he was a solo singer. A week or so after his first attempt at singing, he began to be the featured singer on at least two songs each night, but he was not a happy camper. The types of places where they played were what his Granddaddy called *dens of iniquity,* and he thought of his upbringing every time he went on stage. He knew that his Dad was a very wise man, and he thought he would talk to him the next time he went home.

The band had become so popular that they were in demand nearly every week, and that meant if they had two gigs a week, the other days were taken up practicing and traveling. Part of their popularity was due to three of the members being professional baseball players. He didn't know when he would be able get to Chattanooga, but he would definitely go the first time he had a break. The rest of the winter was booked up, and he wasn't able to get home except for two days at Christmas.

Spring training was due to start in mid-February, and Jimmy thought he would give everything he had to baseball in the upcoming season and maybe not start back with the band after the season was over. Jerry Simpson and L. T. Reeves had not been moved up to Gwinnett, so they were still in Pearl, and that would make it easier for him to quit the band. All the Braves teams would be together at spring training, so he would talk to them about it if he got the chance, but the way things worked out he didn't have to.

Four weeks remained before spring training, and the band was booked solid, as usual. Something had been bothering Jimmy for a while, but he kept up a front when entertaining until one night in Little Rock. They were playing at a popular night club, and all seemed well until it was time for Jimmy's first solo. He stepped forward and began his song when during the second verse he abruptly quit singing and walked off the stage and out of the club.

The other band members were stunned as was the audience. The group picked up on the next song and went on as if nothing had happened. Jimmy, however, went back to where he was staying, got his stuff together, checked out, and headed toward Chattanooga.

When spring training began, Jimmy was chomping at the bit to get started. He had kept in good shape during the off-season, even though he was busy playing music nearly every night, and it felt good to walk out on the field during practice. The season opened in Durham, North Carolina with the Durham Bulls. Gwinnett lost four to two, but Jimmy was able to get two hits and score one of the two runs. The Braves split the series two to two.

Jimmy was feeling better than he had for a long time, and his play showed it. He was having a great year. Since Gwinnett County, or Lawrenceville, was only two hours from Chattanooga, Monty, Joan, and some of their other friends could go watch him play whenever they had home games. Since Brad and Nancy had moved to Atlanta, Brad went to watch him fairly often because Lawrenceville was a suburb of Atlanta.

Jimmy's first season with the Gwinnett Braves was turning out to be his best since becoming a professional, but as the old saying goes; all good things must come to an end. On August twenty-first, the Braves were in Syracuse playing the Syracuse Chiefs when the unthinkable happened. Jimmy had walked, and the next batter had doubled, sending him to third base. The next batter hit a slow grounder to the short stop, and Jimmy took off for home. He knew the play was going to be close, so he slid, and when he did he felt something snap in his ankle. The pain was excruciating, and he couldn't get up. His teammates and manager rushed to him, and they could see that he was in a bad way. A stretcher was brought out, and he was taken to a hospital where they x-rayed and found that his Achilles tendon was torn.

Since it was August and the season would be over in a month, he was through for the year. If that was not bad enough the doctor told him that there was other damage to his ankle besides the Achilles, and it was doubtful that he could play baseball again.

Two games remained in the series with Syracuse, meaning Jimmy would have to stay there for another two days before going home, then, there was the flight home plus the slow ride from Atlanta to Chattanooga. He thought about it and asked his manager if he could call his Dad to come to Syracuse to get him. He got permission and called Shepherd Apparel. When the operator answered he asked to speak to Monty.

"May I ask whose calling?"

"It's Jimmy."

"Jimmy? What's your last name, Jimmy?"

"It's Shepherd. You must be new."

"I am. Are you related to Mr. Shepherd?"

"A little; I'm his son."

"Oh! Just a minute, Jimmy; I'll ring his office."

After a couple of rings, Monty picked up. "Jimmy? What's up, Son?"

"Dad, I've hurt my leg and might not be able to play baseball again. I'm in Syracuse, New York, and I was hoping you might be able to send your plane to pick me up. We have two more games up here, then, the flight to Atlanta, and then the trip home. Do you think you could help me out?"

"What did you do to your leg, break it?"

"No sir. I tore my Achilles tendon, and the doctor said there is more damage than that."

"Ouch! That's a tough injury. Where are you? Is there a number where I can reach you?"

"I'm at the team's hotel, and the number is 315-555-8900."

"Okay. Let me see if I can get in touch with Mike Taylor. I'll see when he can be up there, and I'll call you back. Are you in a lot of pain?"

"No sir. They gave me some pain medicine at the hospital and some pills to take when it starts hurting."

"Okay, let me get off from here and try to find Mike. I'm sorry you got hurt, but I sure am glad you're coming home"

"Thanks, Dad."

Monty hung up and called the airport to try and reach Mike Taylor. When he reached him he told him what had happened and that he wanted him to go to Syracuse. He needed the flying time so he could tell Jimmy when he called him back. Mike said it would be about forty-five minutes before he could takeoff, and then it would take approximately two and a half hours to get there.

He called Jimmy and told him, "Jimmy, I just hung up from Mike Taylor, and it looks as if it will be around nine or nine-fifteen before he can get there. Can you get to the airport?"

"Yes sir; I think so. I can get some of the guys to help me."

"Okay, do that, and your mother and I will be at the airport to meet you around midnight."

Joan and Monty were really happy to see him when he arrived in Chattanooga. Monty got on the plane and helped him off after the plane stopped, and that gave Joan a chance to play like she was doing for her little boy once again.

When they got to Monty's, they sat down in the den, and Joan pulled an ottoman over for Jimmy to rest his leg on. Before long, Monty asked him, "Son, what are your plans now?"

"I'm not sure, Dad. I might just stay here if I can't play ball again, but I'm not going to give up yet. I'm going to call my manager and see if I can see one of the Braves' doctors. Those guys are used to treating all kinds of injuries."

"I thought you said the doctor in Syracuse said it's doubtful that you can play again."

"He did, but he may not know as much as the doctor that the Braves have."

"Isn't he the team doctor in Syracuse?"

"Yes sir, he is, but Dad, I've got to explore all the possibilities. It was implied that I would be moving up to the big show next year, and I hate to end my career on an injury. I've worked really hard for four years, and this just can't be the end of the road."

"Well, let's just say that the Braves' doctor concurs with the Syracuse doctor, what are you prepared to do?"

"I don't know, Dad; I'll just have to see. I might stay here."

"Are you going to resume your music after the baseball season is over?"

"No sir. I'm through with that, too."

"What happened?"

"It's a long story, Dad. I was planning to come home and talk to you about it when this Achilles thing happened, and this sort of made up my mind for me."

Monty said, "Tell you what; let's talk about it in the morning. It's after one o'clock, and I'm beat. Can you manage with those crutches?"

"Yes sir. I can make it. Good night."

"Good night, Son. It's good to have you home."

****

The next morning when the family was at the breakfast table, Monty said to Jimmy, "Son, last night you said we would talk about why you're not going back to your music.

Do you want to talk about it now?"

"Yes sir, I guess."

"Tell me what happened."

"Dad, ever since we were little kids you and Mom taught us right from wrong. You taught us the consequences of hanging with the wrong crowd and the rewards that come from being with good people. You know how much I love to play the guitar, and when the guys invited me to play what you call professionally, I jumped at the chance. Jerry Simpson and L.T. Reeves were friends of mine and hopefully still are, but things started to get out of hand as far as I was concerned. When we first started, we played at weddings, picnics, family reunions, and a couple of county fairs, and we had a great time. Then, after our first year, a fellow by the name of Josh Lewis came to hear us one night at a festival in Vicksburg, and after we finished that night, he asked if he could meet with us the next morning.

"We met him for breakfast, and he told us he would like to represent us and be our agent. He convinced us that we could make a lot of money, and since we weren't making that much playing ball we agreed to let him represent us. He started booking us in night clubs that weren't anything more than just honky-tonks, and the type of people that went to those places were not the type of people that I was raised to associate with.

"Apparently we were pretty good because the crowds would get bigger every night, and some nights the girls would nearly drag us off the stage. It was a wild life, and I thought it was a great life at first. Then, one night, we were playing a club in Mobile, and there was a couple sitting down front. The guy was very obnoxious, and his girl reminded me of Sue Joyner; sweet and innocent. The guy was gulping down drinks and hitting on every girl that walked his way, and you could tell that she wished she was somewhere else. I looked down one time, and it looked as if she was crying. Then, I thought of your and Mom's teachings, and I wanted to go down from the stage and rescue her. That was the first time it happened to that extent. There were always mis-matched couples in those places, but that one girl really got to me.

"Then, right before this last season, we were playing in Baton Rouge in front of a really big crowd when I spotted another couple just like the one in Mobile, only the guy was more obnoxious, and the girl looked sweeter. We had played our first set, and I tried to get the couple out of my mind before we had to do the second set, but when we came back out and started playing, that guy was making so much noise, it was hard to play, and a bouncer went over and told him to quieten down The next song was one where I had a solo and the guy was quiet, but while I was singing, I looked into her eyes, and when I saw the hurt and the misery she was going through, I couldn't take it any longer. I knew that she was probably raised the same way I was; she just went out with the wrong guy, and there was no one there to help her. Her date was getting wasted, and there's no telling what happened after they left the club.

"After two verses of my song, I abruptly quit singing. I unplugged my guitar from the amplifier, put it under my arm and left the stage. As I passed L.T., I looked at him and said, "I'm sorry, L.T., and I haven't seen any of them since that night. I guess you just raised me the right way."

When he finished telling about his exit from the band, Joan got up from her place, went over to him, put her arms around his shoulder and squeezed. She said, "I love you, and I'm really glad you're home."

Monty said, "Son, I'm touched, and I'm flattered that our teachings have stayed with you. You never know what will happen with your children. All you can do is teach what you think is the correct way and turn it over to God to take it from there.

"Now, let's change the subject for a minute. If you do stay here, do you think you might want to come into the company? I need you, Son, and you would be crazy not to do it. One day, you can take over the whole thing, and right now, we're doing over two billion dollars in sales."

"Did you say two billion with a B?"

"That's right. With a B."

"What would I be doing if I came in?"

"You would be learning the business. I'd like to put you on the fast-track so you can take over the reins of the company after I'm gone. By the way; did I tell you that Bobby Joyner is working with us now?"

"No sir, you didn't. How's Bobby doing? I'd like to see him sometime."

"Bobby's doing fine. He's working in the accounting department, and I'm sure he'd like to see you, too. When he's in town you can come by and see him sometime."

"Dad, my car is in Lawrenceville. Do you think I get an appointment with Dr. Switzer, in Atlanta, someone can go with me so I can bring my car back?"

"I'm sure they can. Why don't you ask Mary Ann? It would thrill her to death to do something for her big brother."

"You didn't answer me when I asked you about coming into the company; what do you think?"

"I think I'd like to, but Dad, I'd like to take some time off before I start. I've been going non-stop for three or four years, and I'd like to rest for a little while. I've saved a little money and don't have to do anything for a while, and I would just like to have some time to do what I want to. I've been thinking about doing something with the property in Sale Creek that Granddaddy left me. Would that be all right with you?"

Monty paused- and then said, "I suppose it will have to be. Let's do this; it's the end of July now, so suppose you take off the month of August and start at Shepherd Apparel on September first. That will give you more than a month. What do you say?"

"Dad, I was thinking about more than just a month. I was thinking about several months, but we'll see."

Monty had sort of a sour look on his face when Jimmy told him that but didn't say anything, and then, changing the subject he said, "You didn't answer me when I suggested you ask Mary Ann to go to Atlanta with you."

"I know; how about it, Sis?"

"Yeah, I'd like to go to Atlanta, and I'd like to see the Braves' office. When do you want to go?"

"I don't know. Let me call and see if I can get an appointment with Dr. Switzer, and then I can tell you."

Joan said, "You should go by the childcare center when you can and meet your little nephew. He's a cutie."

"Where's the childcare center?"

"Right there at Shepherd Apparel. They have a childcare center, now. I guess you didn't know. You ought to go see him. He has your and his daddy's eyes."

That afternoon he called Darrell Parker, the manager of the Gwinnett Braves, and asked if he would mind getting him an appointment with Dr. Switzer. Darrell said he would, and later called him back and said Dr. Switzer would see him the next morning at eleven o'clock. Jimmy asked him to hold while he asked Mary Ann if she could go at that time. When she said she could, he asked Darrell to please set up the appointment.

Jimmy knew where Dr. Switzer's office was because he had taken one of his teammates there one time. He and Mary Ann arrived at his office a little before eleven, and Dr. Switzer didn't see him until almost eleven-thirty. Jimmy went in with high hopes, but came out depressed. Dr. Switzer told him the same thing the doctor in Syracuse had told him. As he came out he saw Mary Ann, and he went over to her and tearfully put his arms around her. He said, "The doctor said my baseball career is over. I just knew he would say I could play again, but he didn't." They stood there in the doctor's waiting room, embracing as Jimmy wept, and the other patients wondered what was going on.

In a couple of minutes he composed himself, and they left the doctor's office. His car was parked at his apartment close to the ball field so they went there after making a stop at the Gwinnett Braves office. They both went in, and Jimmy introduced Mary Ann to Darrell. He told Darrell what the doctor had said, and Darrell was very sympathetic because Jimmy was his man. Soon, Jimmy got up and shook Darrell's hand and told him how much he enjoyed playing for him and said he was going to keep working his leg in hopes of overcoming his injury. Darrell said, "Atta boy, Jim; keep working at it, and if you get it restored, call me because I need you"

They left Darrell's office and went by his apartment. He went to get his car, and forgot he had clothes and several other things there that he had to get, so he and Mary Ann were there a lot longer than expected. By the time they got everything out of the apartment, there were two cars almost filled up. Due to his injury and having to walk on crutches, it fell Mary Ann's lot to do most of the carrying to the cars.

Finally, they got everything and headed to Chattanooga. By that time it was a little past mid-afternoon, and I-285 was bumper-to-bumper as usual, but they eventually made it to I-75 North, and from there on, it was smooth sailing.

They were tired when they got to Monty's, and after they unloaded the cars, they sat down in the den, and it wasn't long before they were sound asleep. About a half-hour later, Monty came in from work, and in another half-hour, Joan called everybody to supper.

While they were at the table, Jimmy filled Monty in on the day's activities and said, "Dad, it looks like I'm going to be around for a while. In a little bit he asked, "Has anybody been to my place at Sale Creek lately?"

"I don't think anybody has been up there since you left."

"Man! I hate that. I'll bet it's grown up and run down in that length of time. I should have left some money so you could get somebody to keep it mowed. Granddaddy had bought quite a bit of lumber before I left; I wonder if it's still there? I think I'll go up there tomorrow and look around. Wanna go with me, Mary Ann?"

"Sure, I'd like to go."

Jimmy was right; the Sale Creek property definitely showed that no one had been there for a while. Before he left, his granddaddy, David, had planned to build the boathouse first with a bedroom in it so he could stay up there occasionally while working on the place, and that was what Jimmy wanted to see first. He picked up a heavy stick, in case he came upon a snake on the way down to the water, and fortunately he didn't have to use it. He still had his key on his key ring from the time before he left, and he unlocked the door, and he and Mary Ann went in. Years of being unused and closed up had done a toll on the atmosphere of the boathouse, but as far as he could tell, all the furniture was still in good shape, except for mildew on the mattresses.

David had planned to make the boathouse as livable as possible, so in addition to a large room that was considered a living/bedroom combination; he added a bathroom and a small, mobile-home size stove. It even had running water. A well had been drilled before David died and before Jimmy left. Later, water pipes were run from the pump to the bathroom and kitchen area in the boathouse, and hopefully, all that had to be done to get it usable was to get the electric power turned on.

Everything was real musty, and Mary Ann suggested they go to the store and buy some deodorizing spray as well as some disinfectant and come back the next day and whip the place in shape so that's what they did.

The next morning they took all kinds of sprays and soaps and rags, and before they left that afternoon the bedroom and bathroom in the boathouse looked like new. The mattresses had become too musty and damp to use, so Jimmy told Mary Ann he would get new ones when they left, and he asked her to help him pick them out,

The two of them went back the next day for the third day in a row. The mattresses were to be delivered, and the old ones picked up, but in the meantime, while they waited, they went back to where David had planned the house and visualized what it would look like. Mary Ann wanted to be a part of it, and Jimmy was happy to have her.

Later, the truck brought the new mattresses and picked up the old ones, and getting those old mattresses out automatically made the place smell better. Jimmy sat on one bed and Mary Ann sat on another and they talked. Jimmy said, "Sis, when I get over this leg problem I think I'm going to work on this place and move up here. I can live in the boathouse until the house is finished."

"Jimmy, you can't live here."

"Why not? It'll be fun."

The day ended too soon, and they went back to Monty's. At dinner Joan asked Jimmy, "Did you get out to see little Johnny today?"

"No Ma'am. Maybe I can go tomorrow."

CHAPTER NINE

Three days later, Analisa called Joan, crying, and said, "Joan, can I come over?"

"Of course you can; what's wrong?"

"Mother called a little while ago and said she had just gotten back from the doctor's office. When I asked her why she went to the doctor, she said that she had been feeling bad for a while and went to the doctor last week. She went back Monday of this week for some tests, and she went this morning to get the results. Joan, she has stage three cancer and has to take chemo."

"Darling, I'm so sorry, but maybe they can take care of it with the treatments."

"Joan, I feel like I need to go down there and take care of her. Daddy has to work, and he can't give up his job to look after her. What do you think?"

"You're going to have to do what you think is necessary, and you may be right. Your Mom is going to need someone with her."

"I hate to leave my job. I really do like it, and everybody is so nice to me, but I just don't see any other way. I don't mean to burden you with my problems, but you're the only one I have up here that I can turn to."

"You're not burdening me. You're family, and families stick together. Have you told Monty yet?"

"No, not yet. I think I should tell Charlotte, my supervisor, first, and then I'm going into his office to see him. I may need a shoulder to cry on."

"He has broad ones, so don't be afraid to do it."

After she hung up, since she just talked to her, instead of going to Joan's, she went to talk to Charlotte, and then she went to Monty's office.

When he saw her, he said, "Hey, Gal, what's up?"

"Monty, could I talk to you for a minute"

"You know you can. Do you have a problem?"

"I don't, Monty, but my Mother does. She called me a little while ago and said the doctor told her she has cancer. Its stage three, and I think I need to go to Atlanta and take care of her. Daddy can't quit work to look after her, and she can't be by herself, so it looks like I'm elected. I don't want to quit, Monty, but I don't see any other way. I love you and Joan and really hate to leave, but you understand, don't you?"

"Of course I understand. Come here and let me give you a big hug."

She walked around his desk and hugged him. She began to cry, and he assured her that God would take care of things and spoke other comforting words to help her.

He asked, "When do you plan to leave?"

"I haven't thought that far yet. I need to get down there just as quickly as I can, but I've got to do something with my furniture, and I don't know if my landlord will let me out of my lease or not. He may make me pay until the lease is up. I feel like I need to give you a two week notice before I leave here, and there is so much to think about, I don't know when I will be able to move."

"Analisa, Honey, you know Joan and I are here to help you in any way, and we can help on some of these things. Don't worry about a two week notice; I'll talk to Charlotte, and I'm sure she can get things handled in your absence. Do you think you will want to put your furniture in storage? If you do, I'll have some of my people move your stuff on one of our trucks, so don't worry about that. Why don't you talk to your landlord today or tomorrow to see what he says?"

Over the next couple of days, she was able to get everything worked out to leave. Her landlord agreed to terminate her lease early because he had someone else that wanted the apartment.

She moved into her parents' house later that same week and Brad and Nancy were not only thrilled to have her and Johnny with them; they were relieved by the thought of having her there to help her mother through her ordeal and playing with Johnny would be good therapy.

Doctors were able to stabilize Nancy's cancer for a while, but two years later, it got worse, and she passed away a little over three years after being diagnosed.

Joan and Monty, Mary Ann and Jimmy drove to Atlanta for the funeral, and Analisa really was thankful for their support. Brad was a mess over the loss of Nancy, and he certainly couldn't help Analisa with her mourning. Nancy had a sister, who came for the service, and she wanted to help, but it wasn't the same as Monty and Joan. Joan could see that their one-day visit was not going to be enough, and she spoke to Monty about it.

She told him that she wanted to stay a few days, and if she did, could he come get her when she was ready to go home. He thought it was a good idea, so she talked to Analisa about it, and she was very relieved that they would do that for her.

Friends had brought food to Brad's Church, and they had a veritable feast after the burial. Then, before Monty and the kids went home, they went back to Brad's for a while. By that time, Brad was doing a little better. It was as if the trauma had been lifted off him when Nancy was buried.

During the conversations, Joan asked Analisa, "Honey, what are you going to do now; stay in Atlanta or move back to Chattanooga?"

"I'm not sure yet. Daddy and I talked about it last night, and he says I should go back."

Brad interjected," I think I will sell the house and move into a condominium. You know, I travel a lot, and leaving Analisa here by herself doesn't seem like a good idea, so I suggested she move back. Of course she has little Johnny, but I think he, too, will be better off in Chattanooga.

Monty asked, "When do you think you might move?"

"I don't know. I want to stay here at least until the house is sold, and Daddy is in a condo. It all depends on how quick the house sells, and the way real estate is selling in this area, it shouldn't be too long."

Monty, Jimmy, and Mary Ann stayed until after dinner and then returned to Chattanooga, but before they left, each one of them gave Analisa a hug and offered to be there for her if she needed anything.

Joan stayed for another week, and during one of the many calls between her and Monty, she said she was ready to come home. That was on Friday, and Monty drove down to pick her up on Saturday.

The following week Brad contacted a realtor about selling his house, and within two weeks it was sold. He had found a nice condo and moved into it about a week later. That cleared the way for Analisa to move, and the next week Monty sent a truck to get her things. She didn't have that much; most of what she had to move was little Johnny's things; his bed and so forth.

As soon as the truck left, she got the things she was going to carry herself and went to Chattanooga. Joan had invited her to stay with them until she decided where to go and what to do. She cleared out one of the upstairs bedrooms and made room for Johnny's bed and other furniture. He was almost eight years old, and his bed was a youth bed. He could have slept in one of the beds already in the house, but he liked his bed, and Joan wanted him to have it the way grandmothers do when spoiling their grandchildren.

Analisa didn't look for a job immediately after moving. She wanted some time to decide what she would be doing from then on. She was going to receive some insurance money from a policy they had on Johnny plus there was supposed to be an insurance policy that the government furnished. The money wouldn't be enough to keep her up for too very long, but it would buy her some time until she could decide what to do. Since she was so very close to Joan and Monty, she secretly hoped that she could stay with them for a long time. She and Mary Ann were really good buddies, and she thought it would be neat if she could become part of their household.

That worked for a while, but pretty soon she figured out that it would be best if she found her own place. One home can't have but one matriarch, and Joan was definitely the matriarch of the Monty Shepherd household, and that didn't mean Analisa had to leave; it just meant that she would have to continue in a subordinate role if she stayed there. That created sort of a dilemma for her. She was ready to leave, but she didn't have a job, and she couldn't leave without having one.

One evening, after she had thought about leaving, she approached Monty after he came in from work, and asked him if he thought there would be any way that she could get back on at Shepherd Apparel. She told him what she was thinking about, and he seemed pleased that she was ready to go to work. He promised that he would talk to Charlotte Morris the next day to see if they had anything in the computer section.

She told Joan about her talk with Monty, and Joan offered to help her find an apartment. As luck would have it, her old job at Shepherd Apparel was open, and she and Joan found the ideal apartment; a beautiful town-house about two miles from Monty and Joan.

She started working the following Monday, and moved into her new apartment two weeks later; after she had a payday. Since the apartment was not very far from Monty and Joan's house, they could see one another very often.

Joan encouraged her to start back playing music at the Burger and Shake and said she and Monty would keep Johnny while she was gone, and she accepted the invitation and began playing with them again a few nights later.

CHAPTER TEN

Even though Jimmy had told his dad that he wanted to wait a few months before starting to work, Monty began planning for his arrival. He wanted to work him into every job in the huge Shepherd Apparel Company, so he would start him in sales, working and traveling with Bryce Coleman. Their business was so widespread then, that it was necessary to have someone in the air nearly every week instead of every other week.

It looked as if the additional countries that they were going into were going to require another airplane, and that was something Monty had been putting off for quite a while. His old buddy, Ted Moser, had retired, and he hesitated going to another broker, so he called Ted's company and they put him through to a fellow named Gene Garland who would turn out to be every bit as good as Ted was.

Gene and Monty made an appointment for the next day to discuss what Monty wanted and needed. In the past, when David wanted a particular kind of plane, Ted would always find one, so Monty was just assuming that Gene could do the same.

When they sat down together the next day, and all the small talk was completed, Gene asked Monty what kind of plane he was looking for, and Monty couldn't tell him. All he could do was tell him what he needed and Gene had to figure out what kind of plane it would take.

"Monty, the 707 like you have is an exceptional airplane, but the 707 is getting awfully old to think about buying and getting years of use out of. I would recommend a McDonnell Douglas MD-11 for what you're wanting. It's a wide-body plane with a glass cockpit, and that allows you to have a two-man crew instead of the three-man crew like you have. All the glass lets you eliminate the flight engineer. Its range is seventy-two hundred and forty nautical miles or in layman's terms, almost eight-thousand statute miles. In looking at Ted Moser's notes, that's more than you need, unless you've added other places in the world that are farther away."

"Well, we've added other places, but eight-thousand miles is probably far enough." Smiling, he said, "If we have to go farther than that I guess we can stop and refuel somewhere, can't we? Do you have any MD-11's available?"

"As a matter of fact, we do. I believe your 707 was once owned by a Sheik and tricked out to suit him. Well, we have an MD-11 that's about as far the other way as you can get."

"What do you mean?"

"Monty, the plane I'm thinking of is stripped on the interior. It used to be a freighter, so if you are willing to buy the plane the way it is, I can cut you a great deal, and you can have it customized the way you want it. The airplane saw very little use and has been in storage for the last few years, so it's a great deal if you're willing to do something like that."

"Where would I get customizing something like that done?"

"There's a company in Greensboro, North Carolina that does that, and they do beautiful work. I wouldn't be at all surprised if they did your 707."

"Well, what are we talking about, cost-wise, between doing something like you're talking about and buying one already fixed up?"

"I'm almost sure that you can buy the plane and have it customized to your specifications, unless you go completely overboard, a whole lot cheaper than buying one the other way. I'd like for you to at least take a look at it."

"Where is it?"

"It's in Dallas. If you can go look at it, we'll fly you out there."

"Could I take my wife?"

"Absolutely; when do you want to go?"

"I think I could go sometime next week."

"Okay; let me see if I can put a flight crew together, and I'll get back to you. I don't see any problem; it's just that we have a limited number of pilots, and sometimes when we want them for a particular time, they are tied up with another customer. I'll call you in the morning."

Monty said, "Tell me a little more about this plane. Is it larger than the 707?"

"Yes, it's quite a bit longer and much wider. Your 707 is called a narrow body, and the MD-11 is called a wide-body. For instance; your bedroom in the 707 is about eleven feet wide. In the MD-11 it will be about nineteen feet. This plane is large enough to actually give you a bedroom-suite if that's what you want. It's also plenty big enough to give you an office. That way, you won't have to put your papers in your lap when trying to work during flight. There are a lot of advantages to doing something like that if you're willing to do it."

Monty said, "I don't know anything about designing an interior for an airplane. Who would I get to do that?"

"The company in Greensboro has people that do that, and they can help you. Just tell them what you want, and they'll take it from there."

"You're a good salesman, Gene. You've got me excited. I guess the next thing is to see the plane and try to work out some kind of price with you. From the looks of that car you drove up in, getting a good price from you may not be too easy."

"I think you're going to be surprised. Okay, Monty, I'll go now and set things up for you and your wife to see the plane. I'll call you in the morning and reconfirm everything if that's all right."

"That will be fine. I'm glad I got to meet you, Gene. I'll talk to you tomorrow."

After the meeting, Monty called Joan and told her they would be going to Dallas next week to look at an airplane. "I think I'll see if Jimmy would like to go. When you see him, have him call me, will you?"

"Just a minute; he's here. I'll call him."

"Hi, Dad; what's cooking?"

"Hi, Son; I was just telling your mother that I'm going to Dallas next week to look at an airplane, and I wanted to know if she wanted to go, and then, I thought you might want to go with us. Would you like to?"

"Yes sir; you bet I would. What are you going to see?"

"A McDonnell Douglas MD-11."

"An MD-11? Wow! That's the ultimate, isn't it?"

"I hear that it's a nice plane. I don't know which day we'll go yet, but I'll let you know."

Gene called the next morning and said next Monday would be good, if it was good for Monty. Monty said it was a good time, so they set it up.

He, Joan, and Jimmy met Gene at the airport Monday morning, and they took off for Dallas. Monty cautioned Joan not to have any opinions when she saw the plane. "Why?" she asked.

"Because the interior has been stripped. If I decide to buy it, I'll have to have the interior customized the way I want it. It may cost too much, but I want to see it anyway. If I don't buy this one, I'll probably buy one just like it, if I can find one."

Jimmy asked, "Dad, why are you looking for an MD-11 over something else?"

"One reason is because it's so much larger than our 707. The master bedroom on an MD-11 is almost twice the size of the 707's. Another reason is because of the range. It can go almost eight thousand miles without refueling."

Gene interjected, "It has a much smoother ride than the 707, too."

Joan said, "I'm dying to see it, even if it is stripped."

Pretty soon, they began their descent into Love Field, where the plane they were to look at was parked. When they landed, there was a golf cart type vehicle there to take them to the MD-11. When the plane was used as a freighter, there were seats up front to accommodate a few passengers, such as company officials and people like that. Monty liked what he saw and told Gene he wanted to ride in it. Those seats came in handy because they were able to ride in comfort on their test-flight.

Jimmy asked, "What do you think, Dad?"

"I don't know yet. Do you like it?"

"Yes sir. I really do."

"Well, that's good because if I buy it, this will be your home on a lot of trips."

"Really? Well, if that's the case, if you buy it, and I'm going to be traveling in it, can I make suggestions of some of the things to put in it?"

"Such as?"

"I don't know, but I'm sure if I think about it a little, there will be some things I would like to have."

"Let me buy it first, and then, we'll see. What do you think about it, Mama?"

"It rides nice, and it's big, but I can't visualize what it will look like if you have it customized. I'm sure I'll like it. It's so big. How big did you say the master bedroom would be?"

"Almost twice the size as the one on the 707."

"That will be nice."

Completing the test-flight, they took the golf cart back to their Gulfstream and took off for Chattanooga. On the way, Gene made Monty such a good deal that he thought he couldn't afford not to buy it, unless the interior refurbishing was going to run so high that he couldn't afford it.

"Do you know anybody at the place in Greensboro that you can talk to?"

"Not really. I've talked to their chief designer, a fellow named Alex something, a couple of times, but I can't say I know him."

"When we get home, why don't you give him a call and tell him what we're looking at, and see if he will give you some sort of a ball-park figure on the customizing. I know he won't be able to give you a price, but if they do a lot of that kind of thing, he should be able to give you an idea."

"Okay, I'll call him. Are you leaning toward buying the plane?"

"Yeah, if the total cost isn't too high. That's why I want you to call that guy. How long do you think it will take to get it done?"

"I really don't know. I would guess around two or three months."

When they landed at Lovell Field, it was four o'clock, and Monty, again, wanted to know if Gene would call Alex that afternoon. They went to Monty's office and Gene made the call. Fortunately, Alex was in, and he wanted answers to a lot of questions. Gene didn't know how Monty wanted the plane and neither did Monty, so they just guessed at some of the questions, but Alex obviously had enough information to give a *guestimate*.

Monty really did want the plane, so he asked God to lead him in the right direction, and to let him buy it, if it was His will.

It must have been His will, because the next morning, after praying about it, Monty called Gene and told him he was going to buy the plane. When he got off the phone from Gene, he called Alex, the customizing guy in Greensboro and set up a time to go there and look at pictures of other planes they had done. He would go over there, Thursday, and he would take Joan and Jimmy with him there, also.

When they left Greensboro, it looked as if Monty and Shepherd Apparel were the new owners of a customized MD-11 airplane, and he couldn't wait to get it.

On the way home, Monty sat next to Jimmy, and he talked about Jimmy's coming into the company. "Son, I guess you heard; it's not definite yet, but it looks like we're going to add Italy to the list of countries that Shepherd Apparel is going into? You heard about that, didn't you?"

"No sir, this is the first I've heard of it."

"Well, we adding it, and I think I'll let you develop it."

"Me? Develop it?"

"I wouldn't have the foggiest idea where to start."

"I know, and you're starting so late, I'm going to put you on the fast track and hope you can learn as you go. When I came to work at the company, my Dad put me in the cutting department, spreading cloth, then, he put me in the pattern department, learning how to make patterns, and then, into sales. In other words, I had to learn how everything was done before I got into a higher position. I'm going to start you in a higher position, and then have you learn how everything is done when you're in town and in the plant. It's not going to be easy, but you're smart enough to do it, and I really need somebody to take charge of Italy. Are you game?"

"You bet I am. Just point me in the right direction, and I'll take it from there."

"It won't be that easy, but you will be pointed in the right direction. Are you still not ready to come to work?"

"No sir, but Dad, it won't be much longer. I'm kinda thinking Labor Day."

"Well, we talked about September first earlier, and you said you wanted to wait several months after that. I guess you changed your mind, and I'm glad you did."

Soon, they touched down in Chattanooga, and they got into Monty's car and went home, after they stopped at the Krystal and got a sack full of hamburgers and French fries.

****

Late one afternoon, Jimmy went to the little community business section not too far from Monty's. He went to Bolton's Barber Shop to get a haircut, but Mr. Bolton had died since he was last there, so in Mr. Bolton's absence he got Ray Berrier to cut his hair. While he was in the barber chair, he decided to go down the street to the Dinner Party for supper when Ray finished.

After he got his haircut and was on his way down the street he ran into several people that he knew, and they all wanted to know about his baseball career. Not many of the locals knew about his music career, so baseball was what he talked about most. He had killed about an hour talking, and he was getting hungry. About a hundred yards from the Dinner Party, a fellow named Hal Long staggered up to him and asked for some money. He was very drunk, and Jimmy said, "Mr. Long, it's me; Jimmy Shepherd. I'm a friend of your son, Randy."

With glazed over eyes, he slurred out again, "Can you let me have some money for something to eat?"

Jimmy said, "Come on, Mr. Long, and I'll buy you something to eat," but Hal refused and staggered on down the street. Jimmy watched him, and at the end of the block he turned and went into the old Willard house. The Willard house was said to be haunted, and it had been vacant for years.

Mary Ann was working part-time at the Burger and Shake Snack Bar, and she had told him they play music in the back two or three times a week. Jimmy had to pass by there on the way to his car, and he decided to go in; not only to see Mary Ann, but to listen and maybe sit in on some music. Four or five of the business people in the community would get together and play. None of them were professional musicians; they just enjoyed playing music. "Hi Jimmy, want something to eat?" Mary Ann asked.

"No, thank you. I just filled up over at the Dinner Party. Is there going to be music tonight?"

"Yeah, they're getting ready to start."

"Who plays, Mary Ann?"

"Well, there's Bill Mason. You know, he's a preacher now."

"Bill Mason, a preacher?"

"That's right, and we're dating."

"You're dating a preacher? That's great, Sis."

Mary Ann continued, "Besides Bill, there are Homer Matthews, Jack Crissman, Eddie Phillips, and our own Analisa Shepherd."

"Did you say Analisa? What does she play?"

"Guitar, and she's good. She can play the piano, too."

"Well, I'll be dog. Analisa; I haven't seen her since I got home. Is she back there tonight?"

"Yeah, go back and say hello to everybody."

"Thanks, I will."

Before he could get to the back where they played, he heard them start up. He stopped for a moment to listen before he went on back, and they sounded good. It wasn't exactly country, and it wasn't exactly pop, and Jimmy didn't know exactly what it was, but he liked it.

When he got back there everyone seemed very happy to see him, except for maybe Analisa. She was nice, but didn't have much to say the way the others did, and he was puzzled by her reception. As soon as all the *hellos* were over, they asked him to sit in with them. One of the guys had an extra guitar, so he took them up on their invitation. He sat in with them for a little while, and then said he had to go. He was invited to come back the next time, and he said that maybe he would. He couldn't get the thought out of his mind about Analisa's cool reception, though.

He was happy to get back home, and he decided to try to make regular visits on music nights, so one night, a couple of nights later, he went by. That time, he took his own guitar and sat in with the group. Analisa was much friendlier that night than the first time he was there, and that made him feel better. After about an hour, they were getting ready to fold it up for the night, and they heard thunder outside. Everybody but Jimmy hurried to their cars to beat the storm. Jimmy stayed a few minutes to spend a little time with Mary Ann before he left.

When he got to the front of the restaurant, he could see through the large windows that it was storming outside. It was dark by then, and the lightning was illuminating the sky. All at once there was a loud *boom*, and someone said that lightning must have struck something close by. Jimmy had parked about a half-block up the street, and he decided to make a run for his car. He reasoned that he could only get wet one time, so he took off.

The rain was letting up a little by then, and when he got almost to the car he looked up and saw flames coming out of the Willard house. He thought, *that's what that loud boom was. Lightning struck the house. Oh my gosh, Mr. Long is in there.*

When he saw the flames coming out of the roof, he ran up and then crossed the street and into the Willard house. The flames were getting larger and larger, and he didn't know if he would be able to find Hal or not, but he had to try. The smoke was now thick, and it was hard to breathe, so he took out his handkerchief and held it over his mouth and nose to act as a filter. He began yelling Hal's name and going from room to room until finally, he saw him lying on the floor. He was passed out and didn't know anything was happening.

Jimmy grabbed his arm and pulled him up and struggled to get him out. He told him to put his left arm around his shoulder, and Jimmy put his right arm around his waist. Hal was absolutely no help, but Jimmy managed to eventually get him outside. When they were a safe distance away from the flames, Jimmy laid him down on the grass. Between his overabundance of liquor and the large amount of smoke that he had breathed in, he was in bad shape.

By that time, the fire trucks had arrived and began to try and put out the fire. Jimmy was hailed as a hero, but he brushed off the praise as the EMT's put Hal into the ambulance. When the ambulance reached the hospital, they admitted him. Jimmy had followed and the Emergency Room doctor told him they would probably keep Hal three of four days.

When Jimmy finally got home, he explained to everyone what he had been doing, and they all were in awe of what he had done, especially Johnny. He looked over at Analisa, and she was giving him a look that said, *I really admire you, Big Boy.* He put that look in his memory bank and would recall it ever so often.

Every day, Jimmy went by to check on Hal, and on the fourth day, while he was in his room, one of the doctors came in and said he could go home. Hal looked at him with a strange look on his face because he didn't have a home to go to, but Jimmy said, "Thank you, Doctor. We'll be glad to get home, won't we, Hal?"

That afternoon, after all the paperwork was done, a nurse came into the room pushing a wheelchair and said, "All right, Mr. Long, your chariot awaits. You can blow this joint and let your son, here, take you home," and just as he had said to the doctor, Jimmy said, "We'll be glad to get home, won't we, Dad?"

Hal continued to sit in the wheelchair with a funny look on his face and said nothing. Jimmy left him with the nurse while he went after his car, and when he got back, Hal stood up and took a couple of steps toward the car. Helping him into the car and fastening his seatbelt, Jimmy said, "I've got a surprise for you. You're a carpenter, aren't you?"

"I used to be, but it's been a long time since I picked up a hammer. I did framing, mostly, and just a little bit of finishing work. You know; cabinets and things like that. Why do you ask?"

"Because I think you need some outdoor activities, and I've got just the thing for you. We're going to a place where there won't be any temptations, and you can get back to being a carpenter again. By the way, where's Randy now? I haven't seen him since we got out of high school; is he okay?"

"I don't know where he is. After I left his mother, he refused to have anything else to do with me. He told me he didn't ever want to see me again, and he shut me out of his life."

"I'm sorry, Hal; I didn't know."

"What's this surprise you said you had? Why are we going up Dayton Boulevard?"

"Because that's where the surprise is. We'll be there in ten or fifteen minutes."

In a few minutes they passed a sign that read *Sale Creek*, and about a mile later, Jimmy turned off the highway and drove to where his sixty acres was located. He pulled into the property and stopped the car. "Here we are," he proudly announced, and Hal asked, "We're where?"

"This is the place that's going to help you get rid of some of those demons. Can you cook?"

Hal thought, *that's about the stupidest question anybody has ever asked me,* but he answered, "A little; why?"

Jimmy said, "C'mon, let's take a little walk."

He led him down the slope to the boathouse and unlocked it. "C'mon in, I want you to see this."

Hal walked in and looked all around. It was different from any boathouse he had ever seen. Not only did it have a bedroom, bathroom, and kitchen, it had a very unique air conditioning system.

The air conditioning was actually very simple. There was a large four-foot square grate in the middle of the floor, and there was a large exhaust fan installed up about two-thirds of the height of the rear wall. When the fan was turned on it drew air up through the grate from the water and exhausted it out through the wall. Even in the hottest weather, when the fan was running, the interior of the boathouse remained relatively cool.

He and Hal talked quite a bit about the unusual idea, and Jimmy thought, *Granddaddy, I knew you were smart, but this is ingenious. I knew this was in here, but I didn't think about how clever it is 'til just now when I was showing it to Hal.*

After they finished looking at the boathouse, Jimmy led Hal back up the slope to where he planned to have the house. While they went over Jimmy's vision of the place, he said, "Hal, all of this is the surprise. I would like for you to help me build the house. I'm not a builder, but you are, and I need your help. In fact; I think we need each other's help. I have just put new mattresses in the boathouse, and that's where I'm living, temporarily. I'd like to invite you to stay with me while you're working on the house. You said you can cook a little, and I can cook a little, so we should be able to get by.

"I won't be living up here too much longer because I have to go to work for my Dad at his business, but even when I leave, you can stay, and I really hope you will."

Hal told Jimmy, "Son, I appreciate what you're trying to do, but I don't think I can do what you want."

And Jimmy replied, "I think you can. Hal, this is the perfect opportunity for you to begin straightening your life out. Do you know anybody else that would be willing to help you?"

"No, I don't. I guess you're right. You know, it will be good to get a hammer back in my hand again. I love working with wood, and after talking with you, I'm kind of anxious to get started."

"Great. Tell you what; we'll run down to Soddy-Daisy and get something to eat for supper. In the morning, we'll go to Chattanooga and get groceries, and we'll buy you a hammer and anything else you need to start. I don't know how far this lumber that my Granddaddy bought will go, but when it's gone, we'll get some more. How about looking over the lumber, and maybe jot down an inventory, so we'll know where we are. I have some sketches that he made, and you can go over them. There aren't any blueprints; just these sketches. Do you think you can use them?"

"Yeah, I can use them," and after looking them over, he said, "Your Granddaddy was a pretty good architect and draftsman."

"He was a good everything, Hal."

The first night at the boathouse was different, to say the least. Jimmy was used to sleeping in rooms with other guys, because he had to do that when he played baseball and went on road trips. Hal, on the other hand was used to curling up somewhere with a bottle, by himself, until he passed out. If Jimmy had his way, those nights were over.

The next morning, they fixed coffee, and then got in the pick-up and went to Chattanooga. On the way they stopped at the Southern Restaurant and ate breakfast, and then went to Home Depot to pick up some lumber; tools, levels, nails, and whatever else Hal said they needed. After they got everything they needed they went to the Red Food Store and loaded up on groceries. The fridge at the boathouse was not large, so they had to be careful and not buy too many things that had to be refrigerated. Soon, they had everything and headed back up to Sale Creek.

After unloading, Jimmy started Hal on some very preliminary jobs and left him for most of the day, while he went back to Chattanooga.

CHAPTER ELEVEN

He rode by a Little League baseball field not too far from Monty's house and thought he could, at least, watch a little baseball. When he walked over to the bleachers to take a seat, he saw Analisa sitting there, so he went over and sat down beside her. "What are you doing here at a baseball field?" he asked.

"I'm here with Johnny," she replied.

"Really? I didn't know he was playing ball."

"He wants to play so bad, but I'm afraid he's not very good. He can catch and throw really well, but he just can't seem to hit the ball."

Just as she said that, she nodded toward home plate and Johnny was up to bat. He swung at three straight pitches and didn't touch a one of them. He slammed his bat against the ground and stormed back to the dugout, mad as an old wet hen.

"You know, we can fix that," Jimmy said.

"Really? How?"

Before he could answer, Johnny took time out from practice to see his Uncle Jim. "Hi, Uncle Jim; what are you doing out here?"

Jimmy told a little white lie and said, "I came out to see you. That was a real good catch you made in the outfield. It looks to me like you're going to be a good ball player."

"I probably won't be because I can't hit the ball."

"Do you know why you can't?"

"No, I swing at the ball, but I never hit it. I think I'll just quit."

"Whoa, hold on there. A Shepherd never quits at anything. What if I help you?"

"Will you, Uncle Jim?"

"You bet I will. How about this afternoon after practice is over?"

"Oh boy; can I Mom?"

Analisa said, "I don't know; I need to get back to wait on the washing machine repair man."

"Aw Mom."

Jimmy said, "Leave him, and I'll bring him home."

"I don't know."

Before she could say anything else, Johnny said, "Please Mom, please."

Jimmy said, "Why don't you? We can work on that hitting. I'll get him home early."

"All right, if you're sure it's not too much trouble."

"It's no trouble at all; we'll both enjoy it."

"All right Johnny, get back out there, and I'll see you after practice."

"Oh boy. Thank you Uncle Jim," and he ran back out on the field with a smile on his face from ear to ear.

Jimmy knew Johnny's coach, and he asked him to leave some balls with him, and he would bring them to him when he finished. The coach was glad to do it because Johnny was a good fielder, and he wanted him to improve with his hitting, and he knew if anybody could help him it would be Jimmy.

At the end of practice Johnny came running over to Jimmy and said he was ready. Jimmy reassured Analisa that he would bring him home, and she left.

On her way home, she thought how much Johnny adored Jimmy, and she decided to try and be more understanding; after all, it wasn't Jimmy's fault that Johnny got killed. She suddenly realized that she had not been fair to blame him.

When all the players and coaches had left the ball field, Jimmy and Johnny began Johnny's batting lesson. Before a ball was thrown, Jimmy showed Johnny a baseball and all the things on it that were normally overlooked by most people.

"Okay, what do you see on this ball?"

"I see red stitches."

"What else?"

"I see the word Spalding and some little words."

"Anything else?"

"No sir."

"Okay, when you're up to bat and the pitcher throws the ball, what do you see?"

"What do you mean? I just see the ball."

"Do you see the stitches or the name Spalding?"

"No sir."

"Well, you need to look for them. If you look for those things it will help you keep your eye on the ball, and that's what you have to do if you're going to hit it. Now, let's hit a few and see how you do when you keep your eye on the ball."

Jimmy had Johnny stand at the plate, and after he checked his stance he threw the ball over the plate. Johnny swung and connected with the ball, and it went into center field. Jimmy looked at Johnny with a big smile, and Johnny smiled back. He threw another ball, and Johnny smacked it to the outfield, too. Johnny was just beside himself after hitting the ball the way he did, and Jimmy was very pleased. He began to pitch the ball faster, and Johnny kept hitting them. They threw and batted for a good while and decided it was time to go home.

Johnny talked non-stop all the way home, and when they reached Analisa's town house, he said, "Uncle Jim, come in with me while I tell my mom about how good I hit the ball, will you?"

Jimmy agreed to go in, and Johnny ran ahead of him and into the house yelling, "Mom, I'm home. Come here for a minute; I wanna tell you something."

Analisa was just signing the repair order for the washing machine when they came in. When Johnny yelled for her, she came into the room from the kitchen and said, "Boy, you sound excited. What happened?"

"Mom, Uncle Jim showed me how to hit the baseball, and I hit it almost every time, and they were good hits, too; weren't they Uncle Jim."

"They sure were. This guy's going to be a slugger, Mom."

Johnny said, "I think I'll go call Sonny. He's been teasing me about striking out all the time," and he went into the other room, but before he left completely, he turned around and said, "Thanks, Uncle Jim."

In a minute he came back into the room where Analisa and Jimmy were and asked, "Mom, can I go over to Sonny's? We're gonna play ball out in his yard."

"I guess, but dinner will be ready before too long, so don't be gone past five-thirty."

He said, "Thanks again, Uncle Jim," and he ran out of the house.

After Johnny had gone, Analisa said to Jimmy, "I've just made a fresh pot of coffee. Would you like to have some?"

"I thought I smelled coffee; yeah, I'd love a cup."

They went into the kitchen, and after she poured them a cup they sat down at the table. "Well, tell me about this miracle that you performed with my son. I've never seen him so excited."

"No miracle; just a basic principle that was apparently overlooked by the coaches. If he will remember what I told him, I think he will start hitting. Boy, this is good coffee."

"Want another cup?"

"No, thanks. I'd like one, but I've got to get these baseballs back to Coach Brown, and then I've got to get back up to Sale Creek. Hal has been up there all day by himself, and I need to take him something to eat. Thanks, anyway."

Before Jimmy got up to leave, Analisa put her hand on his and said, "Thank you for helping Johnny. He idolizes you. You're perfection in his eyes."

Noticing her tender touch on his hand, he said, "No thanks is necessary. He's part of the family, and I want to do as much as I can for him. He's a good kid. I forgot to ask him when his next game is. Do you know?"

Moving her hand away, she said, "They play on Tuesdays and Fridays. I hope you will be able to go to some of them."

"Long after she removed her hand from his, he remembered the tender touch and said, "Well, I had better go. Hal will be starved if I don't get up there pretty soon. Tell Johnny to remember what I taught him when he goes to practice next time."

"Okay; I will. Bye."

On the way to Sale Creek, Johnny thought, *I can't figure this out; when I first saw her at the Burger and Shake, she was very cool toward me, but today, she was a different person. It was only a touch on the hand, but to me, it seemed like something special. I won't forget it. Maybe I should start spending more time with Johnny. After all, he's my twin brother's kid, and I'm sure he needs a father-figure in his life. Who better than his Dad's twin to do that?*

Soon, he delivered the baseballs to Ron Brown and stopped at the Kentucky Fry to pick up some dinner for himself and Hal. When he reached the land at Sale Creek he and Hal sat down and ate the food he brought, and then, he said he was going to the grocery store to buy a few things they forgot before so they could fix breakfast, lunch, and even dinner, if they wanted to. The boathouse was that well equipped.

The next morning, he and Hal fixed breakfast, and Jimmy wanted to make sure Hal would be okay if he was gone all day. One of his college buddies invited him to play golf, and he didn't want to be gone too long if he thought Hal might not be all right. When he talked to Joan the day before, she had asked him to eat dinner with them that night, and he wanted to if Hal was okay.

He finished his golf game around three o'clock and decided to go to Monty and Joan's house to rest before dinner. While he was there, he remembered his guitar and went to his room and got it. He went out by the pool and sat in one of the plush easy-chairs and picked the guitar until he dozed off. Joan woke him up around five-thirty and told him his Dad would be home soon in case he wanted to be up when he got there. He stretched and sighed and said, "Thanks, Mom. Yeah, I want to be up when Dad comes in."

Joan fixed a wonderful dinner, and Jimmy absolutely stuffed himself. He told Joan how good it was and stayed and talked to Monty for a while, and then, the back door opened, and Johnny and Analisa came in. Analisa was dropping Johnny off while she went to the Burger and Shake to play music. When she saw Jimmy, she asked, "Why don't you come join us tonight?"

"Thanks, I think I will. Mom, do you mind if I skip out early? It's a lot of fun playing with those guys."

"I don't mind. Go ahead and have fun."

Johnny asked, "Uncle Jim, are you going to come back here when you're through playing?"

"I think I am; why?"

"No reason; I just thought we might talk a little baseball."

"Well, let me see what I can do. I'll see you later."

Jimmy invited Analisa to ride with him, but she said she would just drive her car. Since they were both coming back to Monty's later, it only made sense to drive one car, but since she declined his offer and didn't invite him to ride with her, they drove two cars.

All the others were there when they arrived and had been warming up. Jimmy and Analisa unpacked their guitars, checked them for tuning, and warmed up with them. In a couple of minutes they began to play number one on the list. Over time, the group had played many songs; some they liked and some they didn't like, so they made a list of the ones they liked and played the same ones time after time.

Jimmy suggested they try some new ones that he knew, and he would teach them to 'em. A couple of the members hesitated because they knew the ones on the list so well, but finally agreed to try the new ones. Jimmy only gave them one to start, and after they went through it a couple of times, they found out that they liked it and they put it on their list.

After about an hour or an hour and a half, Analisa and Jimmy went back to Monty's. Jimmy had planned to stay there all night, but Analisa just went by to pick up Johnny. When Johnny saw Jimmy come in he went to him and didn't want to go home. Analisa said, "Come on Johnny, we have to go."

"Aw, Mom, do we have to? I want to talk to Uncle Jim some."

"Yes, we have to go, so get your things,"

"Why do we have to go, Mom. There's no school or anything tomorrow. Can't we stay for just a little while?"

"We just need to go. I've had a busy day, and I'm ready to get out of these clothes and into my pajamas and robe. Now, get your things."

Seeing the disappointment in Johnny's eyes, she said to Jimmy, "If you would like to come over to our place, I'll make a pot of coffee, and while I change, you guys can talk."

"Oh Boy, will you Uncle Jim?"

Analisa looked at Jimmy and said, "Really, I'd like for you to. After I change, I'll have a cup with you, and you can see what it would mean to my little rascal here."

"Okay, if you're sure."

"Mom, can I ride with Uncle Jim?"

"I guess; if he doesn't mind."

"I don't mind at all. Come on slugger."

Jimmy and Johnny followed Analisa to her townhouse, and the whole way Johnny talked. When they got inside, Analisa went into the kitchen and made a pot of coffee. After she did that, she excused herself and went upstairs to change her clothes. When she came back down, Johnny and Jimmy were in deep conversation with Jimmy showing him stances to use when batting.

By the time Analisa got back downstairs the coffee was ready, and she asked Jimmy if he was ready for some. He excused himself from Johnny and told him to go practice what he had just shown him. He sat down at the table with his coffee and Analisa joined him. They talked about Johnny's baseball, her work, and Johnny's daddy, and she teared up when she talked about him. When she became emotional, Jimmy's eyes watered, too.

In a little bit, Johnny came back into the kitchen and said, "Uncle Jim, I think I've got it now. "

"Okay, great. Just keep working on it and we'll see how well you do in your game tomorrow night. You do play tomorrow night, don't you?"

"Yeah, and you're going to be there, aren't you."

"I wouldn't miss it."

Analisa said. "Okay, Babe Ruth, it's bedtime. Tell Uncle Jim goodnight."

"Aw Mom, do I have to?"

"Yes, now go on."

Jimmy said, "Go on up and get ready for bed, and if your mother doesn't mind, I'll come up and see you before I leave in a few minutes."

"Okay, I'm going. Don't forget to come up."

"I'll be there," and when he finished his coffee, he told Analisa, "Well, this has been nice, but I guess I had better go. By the way; you make a great cup of coffee."

"Thanks. Don't forget to go up and tell Johnny goodbye."

When he got up to Johnny's room, he wished him good-luck in the game the next night and asked, "Do you think you remember what I told you about looking for the stuff on the baseball?"

"Yeah, I remember."

"That's good. Remember it tomorrow night, and I'll bet you will get a hit. Don't worry if you strike out. Everybody does that some. Just keep in your mind what you're supposed to do, and everything will be fine. I've got to go now. Sleep well, and I'll be watching you tomorrow night. Good night, Pal."

When he got downstairs, Analisa offered him another cup of coffee, but he told her, "No, thanks, I've got to go. I told Hal I would be at the farm to spend the night, tonight, and he's probably wondering where I am. I'll see you tomorrow night at the game. Thanks again for the coffee."

She walked him to the door, and when he reached for the knob, she put her hand on his forearm and said, "Jimmy, thank you for what you're doing for Johnny. You're his hero, and I appreciate it." The whole time she was talking, her hand remained on his arm.

He had a hard time concentrating on what she was saying because of her hand, but he managed to say, "You don't have to thank me. He's my little partner; he has my blood in him and I want to help him all I can. I guess I had better go. I'll see you tomorrow night. Good night."

Hal had been busy trying to get things organized so the building could begin in an efficient manner. When Jimmy got there that night, Hal had strung a cord from the cabin site down to the boathouse and had put three light bulbs on it so anyone walking down there at night wouldn't have to feel their way. Hal seemed glad to see Jimmy when he came in, and he appreciated the fact that he was pleased with the lights. It was decided that they would go to Home Depot the next day and buy some real outdoor lights and make a nice walkway in place of the cord and three light bulbs. Jimmy also decided to pick up a TV and antenna when they went to town the next day. Their radio did a good job, but when somebody is alone at night in a boathouse on a remote part of the lake, a TV would provide more company. The pair made some other plans for the next few days, and in a little while, they went to bed.

Shoney's in Red Bank was where Hal wanted to go for breakfast the next morning, and they both pigged out on the large breakfast buffet. Afterwards, they went to Home Depot, bought what they needed and returned to Sale Creek.

Hal had his work cut out for the day because the kind of lights they bought was going to require that a trench be dug the entire distance to the boathouse for the cable-filled conduit to rest in. Then, every ten feet, a light fixture would be installed, and of course, each would have to be wired. The distance was a little over two-hundred feet, so it was going to be a pretty good job. They both thought it would be worth it, though.

Jimmy had thought he would spend the night with his parents that night, so he and Hal figured out two days' work before he left for Chattanooga. He didn't want to leave Hal by himself too much, but he was doing so well, he thought it would be all right. That day made almost three weeks since he had had a drink, and he thought that just maybe, he was on his way to overcoming the alcohol demons.

He planned to investigate how one got hooked up with AA when he got to town and was going to encourage Hal to join. On his way to town he began to have second thoughts about encouraging him to join because if he was able to find a meeting in Red Bank, it would mean driving over twenty miles each way. If Red Bank didn't have any meetings, and he had to go to Chattanooga, then it would be almost thirty miles each way, and he didn't know if he was ready to commit to something like that. Then, he got to thinking; *I've got to do it. I'm the one that has pretty much taken over his day to day activities, and so far I've been able to help him. I can't just drop him or fail to help him overcome his problem, so I guess I'll just have to bite the bullet and do whatever I have to do to save this individual. Maybe, if I do this God will be pleased with me; I know Dad will be.*

Jimmy didn't have any concrete plans for the day. He just wanted to see some of his friends; maybe have lunch with one or two of them and then go to his parents' for dinner. He promised Johnny that he would go to his ball game, and he could hardly wait for that, but first, he had to see about getting information on Alcoholics Anonymous for Hal.

Things went as planned and he was able to get the information he wanted for him. He went to Monty's and Joan's around four-thirty and had a nice visit with his Mom before his Dad got home.

Since it was such a beautiful day, Joan fixed fried chicken and all the trimmings and they ate by the pool. Monty wanted to know if Jimmy knew yet when he would be ready to start work at the company, but he said he wasn't ready yet, but it shouldn't be much longer. When they finished eating, he asked, "Did you all know that Johnny has a ball game tonight? I'm gonna go, and why don't you all go with me?"

Monty said, "I wish I could, but I've got to get ready for a meeting in the morning," and Joan said, "I guess I'll wait and go one night when your Dad can go."

"Okay, Mom. If you don't mind, I'm going to excuse myself and go on out to the ball field. I've been working with Johnny on a couple of things, and I want to be sure he remembers what I taught him. The chicken and everything was delicious. Listen, don't lock the door; I'm going to stay here tonight, okay?"

"Okay, Darling. I wish you would stay here every night."

"Maybe I will before long, but right now I feel like I need to be at the farm with Hal until he can overcome his problem."

CHAPTER TWELVE

The T-Ball game was still going on when he got to the ball field, but it was nearly over, and that gave him a chance to get with Johnny for a couple of minutes before his game started.

When he got close to where Johnny was, Johnny saw him and said, "Hey Uncle Jim, I'm glad you came tonight. We're going to clobber those guys."

"I like your confidence. Do you remember what I taught you?"

"Yes sir. I got Timmy to throw the ball for me this afternoon, and I hit it good. I practiced my stance, too."

"Good boy. I'll be in the stands watching you. Have a good game."

Johnny was batting seventh, and didn't get to bat in the first inning. He was up second in the second inning. The first batter walked, and Johnny came to the plate with a man on base.

The first pitch was a ball. The second was a called strike, making the count one and one. The third pitch was right over the plate. Johnny took a healthy cut and knocked the ball deep into right field for a double, scoring the man ahead of him. That was the first time he had ever hit a ball for extra bases, and the smile on his face as he stood on second base was priceless. He was able to get two more hits, and his team won eight to five.

In the stands, every time Johnny would hit the ball or do something good in the field, Analisa would grab Jimmy's arm, and each time she did it, it stirred up feelings in him.

When the game was over, Johnny ran over to the stands where Jimmy and Analisa were sitting and ran up the steps to where they were. He was so excited. "Did you see me hit the ball, Uncle Jim? I did just what you told me."

"It worked, didn't it, Pal?"

"Yeah, it really did. Are you coming to my house?"

"Well, I don't know. I hadn't thought about it. I'm supposed to stay with Mimi and Granddad tonight."

"Come to my house first, PLEASE."

"Your mother probably has something else to do."

"You don't do you Mom? Say you don't and Uncle Jim can come over."

"It's fine with me if he would like to come."

"Please Uncle Jim."

"Okay, I'll come for a little while if your Mother will fix a pot of that good coffee."

"Will you Mom?"

"Yeah. I'll fix some."

"She made some cookies last night, and you can have some with your coffee."

Smiling, he said, "Boy, I can't wait for that."

When they reached Analisa's, she went in to put on the coffee, and then, she told Johnny to go up and get his pajamas on.

"Aw Mom, do I have to? Uncle Jim's here."

Johnny, it's nine-thirty, and your bedtime is ten o'clock. You can come back down for a while, and then, maybe Uncle Jim will come up to your room before he leaves.

He was back downstairs before the coffee finished brewing, and he could not get close enough to Jimmy.

Analisa came into the room, smiling, and she asked, "Are you ready for that cup of coffee yet?"

"I sure am."

She brought it into the living room where they were sitting and handed him a mug. He was sitting on the sofa, and Johnny was sitting in the recliner, so Analisa sat on the sofa next to Jimmy while they drank and talked. Not much was said about the ball game; rather the subject of Jimmy's brother, Johnny, came up. It was not a serious conversation, but one telling of some of the funny things Johnny did when he was alive.

Analisa got up and went into the kitchen and returned with the coffee pot and gave Jimmy a refill. Then, she told Johnny it was bedtime, and of, course, he argued about it, but Jimmy told him to go on up and say his prayers and brush his teeth because he had to leave in a few minutes, and he would come up to his room before he left. Johnny got up and went upstairs, leaving Jimmy and Analisa alone. She told Jimmy, "I really do appreciate the attention you're giving Johnny. It means a lot to him; and to me. I'm finding out how hard it is to try to raise a child without a father, and I can't tell you how much it means to have you in our lives."

"Look, I'm just happy that I can be included. Now, I guess I had better get upstairs before my partner goes to sleep."

"There's no chance of that. You told him you were coming, and he will stay awake 'til morning waiting on you."

"Okay. I won't keep him up long." He put his coffee mug down and went up the stairs to Johnny's room.

"Hey, Slugger, about ready for bed?"

"Not really. Uncle Jim, you and my Mother were talking about my Daddy before I came upstairs. Will you tell me about him?"

"Your Dad was the best brother anybody ever had, and he was my best friend. We did everything together. He could do anything, and he was always helping somebody do something."

"Did he play baseball?"

"Did he play baseball? He was the best shortstop you ever saw. He almost got drafted into professional baseball straight out of high school, but he decided to go to college and get his education instead."

"Did you play, too?"

"Yeah, we played together. He played shortstop, and I played third base."

"Uncle Jim, I wish I could do some of the things he did. If I could do some of those things, I would know how he felt."

"Well, you be thinking about some of the things you would like to do, and maybe we can do some of them."

"Okay, I will."

"Listen, Buddy, I've gotta go. I'm going to spend the night at my Dad's, and I've got to go up to the farm early in the morning."

"Why do you have to go to the farm; what farm?"

"I have a small farm at a place called Sale Creek. It's on the lake, and I'm building a cabin with help from a friend of mine. You ought to get your Mom to bring you up there sometime when I'm there."

"Will you be there all day tomorrow?"

"As far as I know."

"I'll see if I can get her to come tomorrow; she's off tomorrow."

"Okay, Buddy; I'll see you. Good night."

"Good night, Uncle Jim."

As he was getting ready to go down the steps, he heard some beautiful guitar music coming from downstairs. He stood there for a moment, listening, and loved what he was hearing. When he got down there, Analisa was playing her guitar. He commented on the song and said he had never heard it before.

"I wrote it, "she said.

"Man! You have talent that I didn't know about. When did you write it?"

She said, "I wrote it for Johnny."

"I bet he liked it a lot."

"He never heard it. I wrote it after he left for Iraq."

"Wow! He would have loved it. Analisa, you should make a tape and let people hear it. You might even be able to get it recorded."

"I don't think so. I'd rather just keep it private for Johnny and me; and you. There's some coffee left. Want a cup?"

"Only if you'll play that song again."

"Alright, I'll play it."

She got up and went into the kitchen and brought him some in the mug he had already used. Then, she picked up her guitar and played the song again. Jimmy sat there with his eyes closed, enjoying the music.

When she finished, Jimmy put his cup down and said, "I had better go. I've got an early morning tomorrow."

"Why, what are you going to do?"

"I'm building a cabin up at the farm, and I have a friend helping me. He's staying up there at night, and I've got to go work with him in the morning. You ought to come up there and see what we're doing. The boathouse is already finished, and that's where we're staying at night."

Puzzled, she asked, "In the boathouse? What are you doing, sleeping in a boat?"

Jimmy laughed and said, "No, Miss Smartie, we have living quarters in there. You just need to come see it. I've got to go now. Thanks for the coffee."

"No, thank you for coming. I'm going to take you up on your invitation. Don't be surprised if you see us drive up tomorrow."

"Do you remember where it is?"

"I think so."

"Okay, good night."

As he was leaving, he turned around and said, "I hope you can come tomorrow."

She waved and went into the house.

The next morning, Jimmy was up and getting ready to leave when Monty came downstairs. "You're up early. Where are you headed?"

"I'm going to the farm. Hal stayed by himself last night, and I want to get up there to make sure everything is alright. He has three weeks under his belt now, and it looks as if he might have turned the corner. I'm trying to keep him busy so his mind will be on building and not drinking."

"I admire what you're doing, Son. I just hope you're successful."

"Me too. Well, I had better go. See ya, Dad."

Jimmy doubted that Hal had fixed anything to eat, so he stopped at Hardees and picked up some biscuits; one for him and two for Hal. He knew there would be coffee, so he didn't pick up any. When he arrived at the farm, Hal was already up and at the cabin site. When Jimmy pulled in, he put his hammer down and pulled over two saw-horses to act as chairs. Hal already had coffee in his mug, so Jimmy went down to the boathouse and got him some, then, went back up the hill and sat down and ate his biscuit.

Hal said they were ready to start building the floor, and he showed Jimmy what he needed to do. When David had had the footings poured, he had brick-masons come up and build a concrete block foundation, and that was what the guys began with.

David had wanted the cabin to be steady and strong so he ordered two-by-twelves for the floor joists. Hal did some preliminary figuring and then got Jimmy to help him with the first joist. Normally, before a house is built, and the footings and foundation are built, the house looks small, but not this house. When they finally measured the foundation before they put in any joists, it measured seventy-eight feet long by thirty feet wide, making a total of twenty-three hundred and forty square feet. That didn't include an eight foot porch running the length of the house on the lake side and a smaller porch on the front. Up until Hal did his preliminary figuring and comparing the foundation to David's drawing, he didn't realize just how big this place was going to be. This was not going to be a cabin; it was going to be a large house and would have twenty-three-hundred square feet plus the porches.

After they had put down a few floor joists and taken a break, Hal told Jimmy, "Son, I appreciate what you're trying to do for me, but like I told you before, I don't think I can do this. I didn't realize the job was going to be so big. It would take me two years or more to build something like this by myself."

Jimmy asked, "Well, do you think you can get it framed?"

"Oh yeah, I can frame it, and I can put the roof on."

"Can you put the windows in?"

"Yeah, I can do that."

"Is that all you can do?"

"Basically, yes. There may be a few more things that I can do, but you would be better off getting someone else to do the drywall and flooring. I'll work with you as much as I can, but Jim, you will be much better off getting a contractor."

"I'll tell you what. You stay and do what you think you can do, and when you reach the point where you think you can't do any more, then tell me, and I'll think about getting a contractor. How does that sound?"

"That sounds good. I just don't want to hold you up because I know you're anxious to get it finished so you can move in."

"That's where you're wrong. I may never move in. More than likely, this house will be a family weekend place, where we can come and fish and boat and just be here to get away from things, and there's no hurry to get it finished, so just relax and take your time. I don't care how long it takes. I just want to be able to help you."

They worked hard the rest of the morning, and about eleven-thirty, they heard a car coming up the driveway. In a minute a car appeared and it was Analisa and Johnny. She pulled in behind Jimmy's pickup and they got out. Jimmy walked up to where they were and said, "Well, You said you were coming. I don't know why you guys came out here in the boondocks, but I'm sure glad you are? C'mon, let me show you around."

First, he led them to where Hal was working and introduced them to him. Next, they walked down the path to the boathouse to see what he had been talking about when he told her it had living quarters, and that that was where he and Hal slept. Johnny thought it was the coolest place he ever saw, and Analisa was amazed at the comforts it had. Johnny went outside to throw some rocks in the water, leaving his Mom and Jimmy in the boathouse. She had sat down on Jimmy's bed, and he sat down on Hal's while they talked, and she told him that she had brought their lunch if they wanted some.

Jimmy said, "Analisa, you're the one. I can't believe you did that. Let's go back up the hill and see what you brought." When they got to her car she had brought tuna sandwiches, pimento cheese sandwiches, regular and barbeque chips, and a huge jug of iced tea. To top it off, she brought a large tin filled with brownies. She even brought a tablecloth. Hal pulled a couple of saw horses over and laid a piece of plywood on them, making a table. Jimmy helped her spread the tablecloth, and then, they spread the food. There were no chairs, but there were stacks of lumber, and they sat on them. Analisa looked around, and Johnny wasn't there; he was still down by the lake. She called him, and he soon joined everybody for lunch.

When they were through eating, Hal told Jimmy, "I'm going to go down to the boathouse for a few minutes. Johnny, do you want to go with me?"

"Yes sir."

"C'mon, then, let's go. I'll be back in a few minutes, Jim."

Jimmy knew Hal didn't have anything he had to do at the boathouse. He just wanted to clear the way for the two of them to be alone. He didn't know why because there was nothing going on between them except for their love for Johnny, but it was good to be at the lake with her. He said, "Gal, I appreciate your coming up here, and I really appreciate the excellent lunch. Hal or I will neither one be able to work this afternoon because we'll be too sleepy."

"I'm glad you enjoyed it I almost never got it finished for Johnny asking me how much longer would it be before we left to come up here. I can't explain just how much he loves and adores you. After about another half hour, she said, "I guess we had better go. I have some errands to run before it gets too late," and she called Johnny.

When Johnny got up there and she told him they had to go, he said, "Aw Mom, do we have to go now? Mr. Long was showing me how to catch night crawlers."

Jimmy interrupted and told Analisa, "Why don't you leave him up here with me this afternoon?"

"Are you sure?"

"Yeah, we'll put him to work, and when we finish, I'll bring him home. I'm going to stay at Mom's and Dad's again tonight."

"Well, if you're sure."

Johnny said, "Oh Boy," and he ran back down to the boathouse where Hal was.

Jimmy walked Analisa to her car and opened the door for her. Before she got in, she put her arms around him and gave him a hug. He hugged her back, and while they were embraced, she said, "I just want to tell you again how much it means to Johnny and to me for all that you're doing," and she gave him a kiss on the cheek.

Jimmy was stunned. He had always liked Analisa from the time his brother, Johnny, began dating her, and then, when she became his sister-in-law, the bond grew stronger, but there were never any romantic thoughts about her on his part. But now that Johnny is gone, things are different. Her putting her hand on his and holding it there and then grabbing his arm at her house and not turning loose started him to thinking. Now, with this hug, he didn't know what to think. This was not just a polite little hug. It was a sure-enough serious hug, and a kiss on the cheek; and he enjoyed it a lot.

On her way back to Chattanooga, Analisa was glowing after the hug by Jimmy, and she had some time to think since she was by herself. She thought, *That was fun. Jimmy is a good guy, and I can see why Johnny loves him so much. I believe I could too, if everything were to work out just right. When I hugged him, and he hugged me back; that was a thrill. I think I'll cook dinner for him one night before long and see what happens. Boy! That was fun.*

Johnny had a great time spending the afternoon with his Uncle Jim, and around four o'clock, Jim said they had to go home, much to Johnny's disappointment. As they were going down the highway, Johnny started again on how much he wished he could feel some of the things his Dad felt when he was alive.

As Johnny talked, Jimmy remembered how much his brother loved Stock Car Racing, and he thought, *I might be able to show him something he will enjoy. I read about something they have at some of the race tracks where fans can drive and ride in race cars. I bet he would love to do that. Maybe I can surprise him.*

Johnny's steady talking was pretty much tuned out by Jimmy's thoughts, and it wasn't long before they reached home. Getting out of the car, Johnny said, Thank you Uncle Jim. I had a real good time. Will I see you tomorrow?"

"I don't know, Pal. I'm going to be at your Granddad's and Mimi's, tomorrow, and after Church, I may just lie around the pool. Tell your Mom to bring you over, and I'll dunk you in the pool."

"Yeah, right. You'll be the one who gets dunked. I'll see if Mom will bring me. I hope she will. Bye, Uncle Jim."

Sunday was a beautiful day, and all was well with the world. After Church, Joan, Monty, Mary Ann and Jimmy went home where Joan spread out sandwich fixings after they changed out of their Church clothes. Then, each fixed themselves a sandwich and some leftover potato salad and went outside to the pool.

Jimmy told Monty about how the lake house was coming along, and how proud he was of Hal for staying sober for almost a month and how easy it seemed to be for him to do it. He told Monty how big the house was going to be and what a surprise it was because his Granddaddy always talked about a cabin; and that was not going to be a cabin. He said he had a little money put back, but there was no way he could finish the house without getting a loan, and he didn't know if he could get a loan without having a job, at which time, Monty said, "I know a company that's looking for a young man to learn the business, and I understand it pays a good wage. Why don't you look into it?"

"Thanks, Dad. I'm about ready to do that. As I said before, maybe around Labor Day would be a good time."

Before the conversation could go on, Bill Mason came by to see Mary Ann, and about ten minutes later, Analisa and Johnny came over. Joan offered all of them something to eat, but they said they ate before they came.

Johnny wanted his Uncle Jim to go into the pool with him, and when they got in the water, Johnny tried to dunk Jimmy, but it backfired; Jimmy dunked him. They had a good time in the water, and then, Jimmy said he wanted to get out and lay in the sun.

Analisa pulled a chaise over next to him and lay down beside him. Monty asked Bill if they had many in Church that morning, and Bill said, "Yes sir, we had a good crowd," and Monty said, "That's good. I'm going to have to come visit with you some Sunday."

Bill said, "That would be awesome. Why don't you come speak one Sunday?"

"I don't know about that, but I would like to visit with you, sometime."

Mary Ann told them, "I'm going to start going to Bill's Church. Bill, why don't you tell everybody about the benefit show that's coming up?"

Bill told them about some of his Church-members coming up with the idea of having a show to raise money to help with the cost of a new educational building. So far, they didn't have anybody booked to entertain except the group that plays in the back of the Burger and Shake, but he hoped they would find some others pretty soon. If they didn't find some other entertainment, they might have to forget about having the show. The whole time he was talking, Mary Ann was giving Jimmy the eye.

While they were lying there, Analisa asked Jimmy softly, "What are you going to do later on this afternoon?"

"I don't know. I haven't thought about it. Why?"

"I thought you might want to come over. Johnny is going to one of his friends, and I hate to be alone. I could use the company."

"Okay, I'll come over. What time?"

"How about six o'clock? Johnny's going to eat pizza at this friend's, and maybe you and I could go somewhere and get something."

"That sounds like a plan. I'll see you at six."

The rest of the afternoon was truly a lazy Sunday afternoon. Everybody there took a nap at one time or the other, and the gathering began to break up around five o'clock. Analisa and Johnny were the first to leave, then, Bill left. He told Mary Ann that he would be back around seven to pick her up, and Analisa told Jimmy she would see him in a little while. It wasn't long before Joan and Monty got up and went inside, leaving Mary Ann and Jimmy by the pool.

As soon as they got inside, Mary Ann said to Jimmy, "Big Brother, Analisa's really got her eye on you."

"What do you mean by that?"

"I mean she has her eye on you; she likes you."

"I like her, too."

"I don't mean a casual *like;* I mean a serious *like.*

"Bull! We like each other, but not in a serious way. I don't know where you get that."

"Okay, Mr. Naïve. I believe if she could have her way, she would like to become Mrs. James Shepherd."

CHAPTER THIRTEEN

"Mary Ann, you're crazy."

"We'll see. By the way, I told the entertainment group that you would be glad to play in the show."

"WHAT? Without asking me first? I said when I walked off the stage as a professional that I would never get back on a stage, so you just call your little group and tell them that I am not going to play."

"Jimmy, you've got to."

"No, I don't. Just call them."

"I can't believe this. Won't you reconsider?"

"No, I won't."

Mary Ann got up and stormed into the house and up to her room. Jimmy was upset that she had obligated him without his permission, and he got up and went inside. He went to his room and got out of his swimsuit and into some clothes. It was quarter of six, so he told Joan goodbye and left for Analisa's. She had already taken Johnny to his friend's house, and she was home alone. He rang the doorbell, and she came to the door. Jimmy asked, "Are you ready to go?"

"Yeah, where are we going?"

"I don't know. I thought you had somewhere in mind."

"No, I don't have anywhere in mind. Go where you want to go; surprise me."

"Okay, I hope you like barbeque."

"I do. That sounds good."

They went out on Highway 58 and ate at Sweeney's, and it was outstanding. Jimmy was very quiet, and finally, Analisa said, "I never have been out here. The barbecue's good, isn't it?"

"It's the best. When they had finished, Jimmy asked, "What do you want to do now?"

"I don't care. We can go back to my house if you want to."

"That sounds good. I really don't care about doing anything tonight."

"Is something wrong?"

"No, everything's alright. I'm just not in the mood to do anything tonight."

They drove back to Analisa's and went in. Jimmy sat down on the sofa, while Analisa went into the kitchen for something. When she came back into the room, she sat in a recliner across from him. He was very quiet with not much to say.

In a few minutes, Analisa asked, “Would you like to have something to drink?”

“No thanks.”

“Well, how about some coffee and some brownies?”

“Brownies? Yeah, I’ll have some.”

She got up and went back into the kitchen and put on a pot of coffee, and while it was brewing, she came back into where Jimmy was sitting and sat on the sofa next to him. As he sat there in near silence, she asked. ”A penny for your thoughts,” and he said, “Oh nothing, Ana. It’s just something between Mary Ann and me.”

“Oh, is there something I can help you with?”

“No, not really.”

“Well, would you like to talk about it? You know, you and Mary Ann are both friends, and I’d like to help if I could.”

“It’s nothing important.”

“Well, if it isn’t important, then you shouldn’t mind telling me. Now tell me what’s bothering you.”

Alright, I’ll tell you, Miss Nosey. Did you ever hear about me walking off the stage when I quit playing professionally?”

“I heard about it, but I didn’t hear any of the details.”

“When I walked off that stage that night, I told myself that I would never get back on one again, but my little sister is messing with my decision. She said that there is going to be a fund raiser for Bill’s Church, and she told them I would play without asking me. I told her no, and she and others are trying to make me feel guilty, and it just burns me up. I’m sorry to take it out on you, but I guess I’m still steaming from my conversation with Mary Ann. This is probably something pretty petty, but getting back on stage is a big deal for me, even though it’s for a good cause and in a small setting.”

“I knew Mary Ann was going to ask you, but I didn’t know all this. I understand your frustrations, but I wish you would reconsider. Our whole group is going to play, and with you in it, we could knock it out of the park.”

Aggravated, he said, “Not you, too. I’ve gotta go,” and he stood up to leave.

Analisa said, "Sit back down, Mr. Touchy. I made a pot of coffee for you, and I'm warming up brownies, and you're not leaving here until you've had some of both. Now just sit yourself back down."

Stunned by her forcefulness he sat back down, and when he looked into her stern face, he smiled and almost laughed out loud. He said, "Yes Ma'am."

"That's better," she said, "Now calm down, and we'll get this worked out, okay? Are you ready for some coffee?"

"Yeah, I'm ready."

She went into the kitchen and returned with a mug of coffee and two brownies on a plate. She said, "Here, now sweeten up, Big Boy." Then, she went back in the kitchen and returned with a mug and a brownie for herself and sat on the sofa with him, even closer than before.

Jimmy relaxed, and the subject of baseball came up, and how much Johnny had improved since he showed him how to hit. They talked for a while longer and Jimmy said, "I had better be going. Thanks for the coffee and brownies. Do you have to go after Johnny?"

"No, they're bringing him home. They're going to watch a movie after they eat pizza."

He got up and went toward the door and Analisa was with him, step for step. Turning to her, he said, "Tell Johnny that I'll try to come to one of his games next week, and to remember what I told him."

He turned all the way around, and she was standing almost nose to nose in front of him. She said, "Why don't you come back over and tell him yourself," and then, her nose was just about one inch from his. He wanted to kiss her so badly he could hardly stand it, but he held back. Analisa, on the other hand, didn't kiss him on the lips, but she did lean up and kiss him on the cheek, with a kiss that was more than just a smack. It lasted about three seconds.

Jimmy thought he had better get out of there before things got out of hand, so he leaned over and gave her a smack on the cheek and said, "I'll talk to you. Bye."

"Bye. I had fun."

After his visit with Analisa, he changed his mind about playing in the charity event, and when he got home, he told Mary Ann, and she was very happy about his decision. She asked him if he had had a good time with Analisa, and he said he did. She made several remarks about her having her eye on him, and she smiled with every remark. Then, she said, “By the way, I told Analisa that I would sit with Johnny whenever your group plays. I don’t have to work late anymore. Then, she added with a mischievous look, “And that should give you all more time together.”

“Stop it,” then he smiled and said, “I know she appreciates it.”

****

Hal was not supposed to have worked the day before, since it was Sunday, but when Jimmy got to the farm, he had finished putting in the floor joists and had begun to lay plywood for the sub-floor. When Jimmy asked why he had worked, Sunday, he said that it was lonesome up there by himself, and he had to keep busy, or else, he was afraid the demons might return.

“I’m sorry I left you by yourself,” Jimmy said, but you handled everything real well, and I’m proud of you.”

“Jim, it’s not your place to have to look after me, but I appreciate what you’re trying to do. I’ve been sober for about a month now, and I think I can make it on my own, don’t you?”

“I think it’s too soon, Hal. A month is nothing in the scheme of things, and I think you’re doing really well, but I also think you need some help and maybe a support group to stand behind you. When I was in town the other day, I made some inquiries about Alcoholics Anonymous. Are you familiar with them?”

“Yeah, but I’m not interested in that.”

“Why, Hal?”

“Because from what I hear, all you do is go to meetings and listen to people stand up and tell you what a drunk they are. I’m just not interested in something like that.”

“If I take you to one of their meetings, would you go in and see what it’s like?”

“I don’t think so, Jim. I’ll make it on my own. I’ve got my mind right, now, and I can continue like I’m doing, but thanks, anyway.”

“Okay, but my offer will stand. I just hate to see you fall off the wagon after the progress you’ve made. Now, I’m not going to be able to stay up here at night much longer, and I don’t want to leave you by yourself.”

Why? Where are you going?”

"I'm not going anywhere, but I've got to start to work right after Labor Day, and I'll be staying with my parents until I can find a place of my own."

"I wish I could find myself a job, but nobody wants to hire a drunk."

"Tell you what, Hal. Give this one more month up here, and then, if you think you're ready to move back into society, I'll help you find a job. It'll be hard, though, because you don't have anywhere to live, you don't have a car to get you around, and you don't have any money. I'm going to pay you for working up here, but that won't last long. How about giving it another month? Whatta ya say?"

"I don't know. Let me think about it overnight, and I'll let you know tomorrow. Are you going to stay tonight?"

"Well, actually, I won't be able to stay overnight until Wednesday night, but I'll be here every day. I'm playing in a little group on Monday nights, and tomorrow night I have to go to Johnny's ball game. Is that a problem for you."

"No; no problem. I just wondered."

"Let me ask you something about the house; if you decide to stay and work on it for another month, how far along do you think you will be?"

"Will you be helping?"

"Probably at least half the time."

"If you help me, we should get the framing done and possibly have it under cover."

"That would be great if we could have the roof on before winter. I'll make it a point to be here as much as I can.

"Before we get started this morning, are you hungry?"

"Yes, I am."

"Well c'mon, let's go down to Soddy-Daisy and get something to eat, and then we'll go to the grocery store. Men can't work on empty stomachs, can they?"

They piled into Jimmy's Mustang and went to a family restaurant that Jimmy knew and ate until they couldn't eat any more; then, they went across the street to the Red Food Store and loaded up on groceries. In fact; they completely filled up the back seat and floor of the car.

Having filled their bellies and bought enough food to last more than a week, they headed back to the farm, ready to put in a hard day's work.

After they put up the groceries, they went to the bathroom and lost most of the coffee they had drunk at the restaurant. Then, they began putting plywood down, over the floor joists. More than twenty-three-hundred and forty square feet was a large area, but with both men working non-stop, they were able to finish around five o'clock that afternoon.

They were very tired when they quit work for the day, and they went down to the lake by the boathouse and sat down, looking at the water. Hal said, "Do you know what would be good, Jim?"

"What?"

"Some good, fresh fish, and we have all we need swimming by right now, but we don't have anything to catch them with. Do you have any fishing equipment?"

"No, but if you're interested in fishing, I'll bring some rods and reels and other stuff. I think my Granddaddy had some, and I'll go over to his house when I get home and see if I can find it. Have you ever fished before?"

"Oh yeah; before the bottle got a hold on me I used to do a lot of things, and fishing was one of my favorite past times. I used to have a lot of equipment, but I don't have any idea what happened to it. I wish I had it. Jim, when you're looking for some things, a minnow bucket and three or four dozen minnows would be good to have. There are some tree-tops in the water right up there, and they may be holding some Crappie. If you've ever eaten Crappie, you know they are the best of all the fish to eat."

"Okay, I'll see if I can find the stuff, and I'll bring you some minnows in the morning. Listen, in the morning fix a pot of coffee, and I'll stop in Soddy-Daisy and pick up some breakfast for us. Is there anything else I need to bring?"

"We could use another tape measure."

"Okay. Anything else?"

"I think that covers it. Oh, some night crawlers. We need some night crawlers."

"Well, I'm going to leave it with you. I hope to get to my parents' house before I go to the Burger and Shake. I'll see you in the morning."

"Okay. Have a good night."

"You, too. Bye."

Joan and Monty were having dinner when he got there, and Joan said, "Sit down, Darling, and I'll get you a plate."

"No thanks, Mom. The group is playing tonight, and I'll just grab something at the Burger and Shake."

Monty asked, "Son, are you still on track to start work right after Labor Day?"

"Yes sir. As far as I know right now, I'll be there the day after."

"How's the house coming?"

"Real good. We finished the sub-floor this afternoon, and we'll start framing the walls in the morning. Did I tell you how big it's going to be?"

"Yeah, you said it was going to have over two-thousand square feet. What are you going to do with a house that large all the way up in Sale Creek?"

"Well, first of all, I didn't know it was going to be that large. Granddaddy drew the plans before he died, and we have just followed what he drew. Dad, I want to have Hal do as much as he will do, but he's not a finish carpenter, so when he gets the framing done and the roof on, I don't know what else he'll be able to do. At some point, I'm going to have a General Contractor come in and finish the house. I want it to be nice enough to where we can all enjoy it on the weekends, and maybe you and Mom will want to go up there and spend some time.

"Analisa took Johnny up there the other day and he just loved it. I'd like for him to be able to enjoy it after it's finished. He loves the water, so it's made to order for him."

Just then, Mary Ann excused herself from the table and said, "I've got to get over to Analisa's. I'm baby-sitting tonight. Are you going to play, Jimmy?"

"Yep. I just stopped by here on the way. I had to come get my guitar and some other things."

Mary Ann said, "I've got to go. Bye Mom, bye Dad. Jimmy, are you going to Analisa's after you all finish playing?"

"I hadn't planned to, why?"

"There's going to be a disappointed little boy if you don't."

"Really? Well, maybe I'll stop by for a few minutes."

As he was getting ready to leave, Monty said, "Jimmy, Bobby Joyner is getting ready to sit for his CPA exam, and you need to pray for him."

"Really? Yeah, I'll pray for him. He should do well as a CPA, but I thought he was in sales."

"Well, that was the plan, but his heart is in accounting, and I didn't want to make him make a career in something he might regret later on, so we talked about it, and I found a place for him in the accounting department. You know, his degree is in accounting."

"I didn't know that. Well, I've gotta go. Bye."

Jimmy was the last to arrive, and while he was opening the case to remove his guitar, he asked, "Have you all thought much about this charity show that we're going to be in?"

There was a little mumbling, but no one indicated that they had thought about it.

"Well, let me ask you this; are we going to play the same old songs we play every time we get together, or do you think it would be good if we learned how to play some new ones. I, for one, think it would be good to do some new songs, and I brought a few to show you, if you're interested in them."

Bill Mason said, "I'd like to hear what you brought. I'm like you, Jimmy; I think we need to learn some new tunes or else we're going to soon get tired of the same old stuff and lose interest in playing."

When Bill said that, the others all agreed, so Jimmy pulled out the music for one of the new ones he said he brought and played and sang some of it.

Jack Crissman said, when he had finished, "That sounds really good, Jimmy. Let's hear what else you've got."

Jimmy did one more and then said they should learn those before getting overwhelmed by a whole load of new music, so that's what they did. They worked on those two for a while and then went to their old *standbys* to finish the session.

CHAPTER FOURTEEN

Afterwards, when they were packing up, Analisa came over and asked Jimmy, "Are you going to come by tonight?"

"Well, I hadn't planned to until Mary Ann said that Johnny would be disappointed if I didn't, so I guess I will for a few minutes. I don't want Johnny to be disappointed."

Looking at him with a big smile, she said, "Johnny's not the only one who would be disappointed."

"I guess that cinches it. We can't have two people disappointed now, can we?"

In anticipation of Jimmy's possible visit, Analisa had told Johnny that he could stay up until he had a chance to see his Uncle Jimmy. When he walked in, and Johnny saw him, he jumped up and went to Jimmy and put his arms around his waist.

At the same time, Analisa went into the kitchen and put on a pot of coffee, and Mary Ann said she was leaving. She told Analisa that it was a pleasure sitting with Johnny.

They all talked for a while, and soon, Analisa told Johnny to go up and get his PJ's on. She told him that he could come back down for just a few minutes, but it was already past his bedtime. Johnny obeyed and ran up the stairs to hurry and change so he could come back.

Soon, the coffee was ready, and Analisa brought two mugs into the living room and sat down on the sofa next to Jimmy. About the same time, Johnny came back downstairs, and the first thing he asked was, "Uncle Jim, are you coming to my game tomorrow night?"

"I wouldn't miss it," he said.

Johnny said, "This is the last week. Our last game is Friday. Are you going to come to that one, too?"

"I plan to."

"Good. I can play better when you're there."

"You can? Why?"

"I don't know; I just can. I guess it's because you remind me of the things I was doing wrong."

"I don't know if that's right or not, but don't worry; I'll be there, okay?"

"Okay."

In a few minutes, Analisa said, "Okay, Mickey Mantle, its bed time. Tell Uncle Jim good night."

"Aw Mom, okay. Good night, Uncle Jim. I'll see you tomorrow night."

"Don't forget what I showed you."

"I won't. Good night."

As soon as he got up, Analisa asked, "Would you like to have another cup?"

"Yes, I would, thank you."

When she came back into the room, she had a cup for Jimmy, but not one for her, and Jimmy said, "Ana, before you sit down, get your guitar, will you?"

She said, "Okay, why; are you going to play something?"

"No, but you are. How about playing that song you wrote? It's such a beautiful melody, I'd like to see if we could put some equally beautiful words to it, if you would like to."

"I'd love to. Do you want me to play it now?"

"Yes, please."

She played the song, and when she finished, he said, "Now, tell me what you were thinking when you wrote that."

"I don't really know what I was thinking. Johnny had just been deployed, and I guess I was feeling pretty sorry for myself. I started strumming, and soon, a melody began to form, and then, every time I would sit down with the guitar, that same melody was there, so I intentionally started playing the melody, and it evolved into what it is now."

"Have you ever thought about putting words to it?"

"No; not really."

"I may have some ideas. Play about eight bars and then stop."

She did as he said, and he wrote something on a sheet of paper. He told her to play another eight bars, and when she did, he wrote some more. For the next hour, it was play a little bit, then write; play a little bit, then write. They didn't finish it that night, but they came awfully close to it.

Jimmy said, "Goll-ee, I've got to go. I promised Hal that I would try to find some of my Granddaddy's fishing stuff and take it to him tomorrow, so I've got to run. I had a good time, and maybe we can finish the song next time. Good night."

Analisa got up when he did and walked him to the door. She asked, why don't you come over tomorrow night and maybe we can finish it? Do you like spaghetti?"

"I love spaghetti."

"Come about six, and I'll fix some spaghetti, then we can work on the song."

"That's a date. I'll be here."

She took his hand, looked up into his face, and gave him a short kiss on the lips. "Good night," she said.

It was dawning on Jimmy that he really cared for her and couldn't wait until he could come back and see her again, but at the same time, he thought, *what am I doing? She's my brother's wife. I can't be romantic with her, but then, she's a widow, now, and isn't tied to anyone any more than I am. And Johnny; boy, I love that kid, and he loves me. Lord, is this what you have planned for me? If it is, then I will do everything in my power to please you.*

Just as soon as he got home, he went over to his Grandmother's and went into the garage to look for his Granddaddy's fishing stuff. It wasn't hard to find. His Granddaddy had been a well-organized individual, and his rods and reels were on racks next to his tackle boxes, and next to the tackle boxes sat a minnow bucket. He grabbed it all and took it home, thinking he would go through it and decide on what he needed later. He was tired. It had been a long day, but at the same time, he was on a little high from Analisa's kiss.

Jimmy stopped at a tackle store the next morning and bought four dozen minnows, and it threw him late. When he finally got to the farm, Hal was waiting on him. He was on his third cup of coffee and chomping at the bit for something to eat. Jimmy didn't just bring a biscuit; he stopped at the little family restaurant in Soddy-Daisy and bought two full breakfasts with bacon, eggs, grits, and biscuits. The restaurant put the breakfasts in Styrofoam containers, so they were still hot when Jimmy got there.

While they were eating, Hal told him that he had been looking at David's drawing, and he felt that a couple of the windows needed to be relocated. He gave his reasons to Jimmy, and they changed the drawing to show the new locations for the windows.

After breakfast, they went up to the house and got ready to build the first wall. Jimmy had failed to get another tape measure, so they had to get by with just the one that they had. Hal had hoped that Jimmy could measure and saw, and he could put the studs together. They did pretty well, but Hal kept having to borrow the tape measure.

At lunchtime Hal took two of the rods and reels and rigged up lines. He didn't try to fish, but he said he was going to when they finished work that afternoon.

By mid-afternoon, the two carpenters had the first wall framed and standing up. They hoped the second one would not take so long, since they were familiar with what to do. Hal took the single tape measure and measured out where the studs would go on the board that would act as the plate. They knocked off about four o'clock, and Jimmy told Hal that he had hoped to stay up there that night, but something had come up, and he had to go back to Chattanooga. He told him he would see him the next morning and would bring breakfast.

Hal told him to not forget a tape measure, and Jimmy said he would stop and get one on the way home.

On the drive from Sale Creek to Chattanooga, he had time to do some thinking, and he thought that he hadn't talked to Darrell Parker for a while, and he should call him and see how the Gwinnett Braves are doing. He kept up with them through the sports section in the paper, but he missed seeing all the guys every day, so when he got home he called Darrell.

"Jim, how are you, boy?"

"I'm fine, Darrell. How are you?"

"Real good. The team's doing good. Have you seen the standings lately?"

"Yeah, I keep up with you guys. I really miss being there."

"We miss you too, Jim. How's that leg?"

"It's doing pretty good, Darrell, but I don't think I'm going to be able to play on it anymore. It looks like the doctor was right."

"I'm sorry to hear that. We could use your glove and bat, but we were pretty sure what the situation was going to be when you left, weren't we?"

"Yeah, but it doesn't make it any easier."

"I know. Listen, what are you going to be doing next Wednesday?"

"I don't know of anything. Why?"

"Well we have a day off, and some of the guys are going down to the

Atlanta Motor Speedway and take a ride in a Nascar car. Why don't you come and go with us?"

"Gosh, that sounds like a lot of fun. Look, I've got this eight year old nephew that I'm very close to. Do you think I could bring him? I've been thinking about doing this very thing."

"Sure. He would get a thrill out of it. You can drive the car, yourself, or you can have one of the real drivers drive it for you, and you can ride. I'm told that they get up to about a hundred and forty miles an hour."

"That's wild. I'll plan on coming, and I'll bring Johnny with me."

"Johnny? He's your brother, isn't he?"

"I had a twin brother, Johnny, but he was killed in Iraq. The Johnny I'm bringing with me is his boy."

"I'm sorry to hear that, Man."

"Thanks, but we're all doing okay now. I'm spending a lot of time with Johnny, and I've tried to show him how to hit a baseball. Believe it or not, he responded to my coaching and turned into a pretty good little hitter. You all need to keep your eye on him. He'll be ready for you in another twelve or fourteen years."

"I'll keep him in mind. So you think you'll come down next week?"

"Yeah, for sure. Give me the time and all the details, and I'll see you Wednesday."

Darrell filled him in on the details, and Jimmy hung up. He thought to himself, *Johnny would love to do that. His Dad was a dyed in the wool Nascar fan, and he wants to know some of the things he felt, and this is perfect. I'll surprise him. Surely Analisa will let him go. I'll let him think he's going with me to the Braves office to meet some of the players, but I won't tell him about the Nascar thing.*

When he got to Monty's house, he grabbed his guitar and notes he had made the night before and headed to Analisa's. He couldn't wait to tie into that spaghetti, and even though he didn't want to admit it, he couldn't wait to see her.

She hadn't been home from work too long before he got there, so the food was not quite ready. That gave him a chance to visit with her for a little while because Johnny was down the street playing, and he welcomed that opportunity. He used the time to mention the trip to Atlanta, and to ask her permission for Johnny to go, which she gladly gave.

Soon, dinner was ready, and Analisa went outside and called Johnny to come home. She and Jimmy sat down at the table while Johnny washed his hands, and when he had finished, he sat down. Analisa asked him to say the blessing, and when he was through, they all ate.

After just a few bites, Jimmy said, "Ana, this is delicious. I thought Mom could make the best spaghetti in the world, but I believe this is just as good as hers. In fact; it tastes a lot like hers. Man, its good."

"Well, it should. This is your Mom's recipe."

There was plenty of daylight left, so when Johnny finished eating, he asked if he could be excused and went back down the street where they were playing baseball. Jimmy helped with the dishes, and then, he and Analisa went into the living room where their guitars were.

Jimmy hadn't had time to work on the song since he left the night before, so they picked up where they left off. Before long, he had a full set of lyrics written, and he sang them to her, and she thought they were wonderful. He told her that she was his inspiration for the song, at which time she went over and gave him a short kiss on the lips. When she kissed him, he said, "If that's what happens every time I write a song, then I'm going to write some more."

He stayed and tweaked the lyrics some, and in a little while, Analisa said, "I made some cookies before I went to work this morning; want some?"

"Yeah, that sounds good."

"Want some coffee to go with them?"

"What are you trying to do, spoil me? Yeah, I'd love to have some coffee."

She fixed a pot of coffee, and while they waited for it to finish brewing Johnny came in and sat on the sofa next to Jimmy. When she brought the coffee in, she handed a cup to Jimmy and started to sit in the recliner, but Johnny got up and said, "Mom, let me sit there, and you sit over here next to Uncle Jim." She smiled at Jimmy and did as Johnny wished and sat down next to him.

In a few minutes, Jimmy asked, "Johnny, how would you like to go down to Atlanta with me next week to the Braves office. There will probably be several players there."

"Are you serious? Go to the Atlanta Braves office? You bet I would like to go."

"Hold on a minute there, Padna. It's not the Atlanta Braves; it's the Gwinnett Braves. They're the Atlanta Braves' Triple A team. They're the team that I used to play for. Now, do you still want to go?"

Every bit as enthusiastic, he said, "Man, yeah. I want to go."

"Alright then. We'll make a day of it."

When Jimmy finished his coffee and cookies he said he had to go and got up to leave. Johnny asked, "Uncle Jim, why do you have to go so early?"

"Because I've got a hard day ahead of me tomorrow, and I need to get a good night's sleep."

"Will we see you tomorrow night?"

"No, I'm afraid not. I'm going to stay at the lake tomorrow night, but I'll see you at the game Friday."

"Oh, alright, but I wish you could come back tomorrow,"

"Sorry, Pal, but you don't need me here every night, anyway."

"Oh yes I do. I need you here every night."

Jimmy just looked at him and smiled, and he looked at Analisa and winked.

Overnight, Hal had decided that instead of framing the second wall next, they would frame the foyer, and that would give the first wall extra strength in case there was a bad storm. The three walls of the foyer were the equivalent of one of the main walls, so it looked as if it would be Friday before the second wall was done.

Jimmy remembered to pick up a tape measure, so when he arrived at the farm, he showed it to Hal before he gave him his breakfast. While they were eating, Hal told him about his plan for the foyer. Finishing up, he told Jimmy, "Come over here a minute."

He got up and Hal led him to a little cut-out in the bank of the lake and picked up a stringer full of fish. Most of them were Blue Gills or Bream, but there was one Largemouth Bass and one nice Crappie. He proudly announced that "This is supper, if you'll go to the store and get some cornmeal and vegetable oil."

"Good deal. Yeah, I'll go as soon as we quit work this afternoon. Be thinking of anything else that you need, and I'll pick it up at the same time.

It was a good day, and they were able to get the whole foyer framed in. Since there had to be openings for three doors, it took longer than it would for just a straight wall.

Hal cleaned the fish while Jimmy went to the store that afternoon. When the fish were cleaned, he peeled some potatoes for French fries.

Jimmy came in with the cornmeal and oil, and when he was at the store, he bought some Cole slaw at the deli. Hal immediately poured oil in a skillet and put the potatoes in to cook. While the fries were cooking, he dredged the fish in the cornmeal, and when he thought it was time, he put several pieces in another skillet. Soon, dinner was ready and they sat down to a feast.

Not only did they have a good day framing, Friday, they framed both end walls of the house, leaving only the back undone. They hoped to finish that on Saturday.

Jimmy was tired when they knocked off, and he realized he still had to go to a ball game, so he hurriedly told Hal he would see him the next morning and rushed to his parents' house to take a shower and change clothes. Johnny and Analisa were already at the ball field when he got there, and he went down to the fence to make sure Johnny saw him. Then, he went up into the bleachers and sat next to Analisa.

Johnny had been moved up to fifth in the batting order due to his improved hitting, and every time he got up to bat, Analisa would grab Jimmy's arm. Every touch sent a thrill through him, and he hated to see the game end, but like all things good, it had to.

After the game, he went home with Johnny and Analisa and had some of Analisa's good coffee, and that time, she had baked a cake to go with it. He commented that she was going to have him so spoiled that he didn't know what he would do when he didn't have ball games to attend. She put her hand on his and said, "You don't ever have to have an excuse to come over here. You're welcome any time, isn't he, Johnny?"

The three of them watched TV for a little while, and soon, Jimmy said he had to go, but Johnny begged him to stay for just a few more minutes. He did, but not for too long. He was already tired and ready for bed, and it seemed like the more he thought about the next day, the more tired he got.

Before he left, he told Johnny, "We're still on for next Wednesday aren't we, Partner?"

"Yeah, and I can't wait."

"Great, we need to leave pretty early, so I'll pick you up at eight o'clock. Is that too early?"

"No. We can leave earlier than that if you want to."

"No. Eight o'clock will be fine. I'll see you then."

"Won't I see you before then?"

"I don't know. I'm going to be at the lake working about all the time. He turned to leave, then, he turned around and said. "Here's an idea; looking at Analisa until he got her eye, he told Johnny, tomorrow's Saturday and your Mom is off from work. Why don't I leave you some money, and y'all stop at the Kentucky fry and pick up some chicken and come up to the lake, and we'll have a picnic."

"Oh Boy. Can we Mom?"

"I guess we can do that, if your Uncle Jim's not too busy."

Jim handed her a twenty and asked, "Will that be enough? Maybe not; here, take another ten. We've got to feed Hal, you know."

"This should be plenty. What do you want besides chicken?"

"I don't know. You decide. How about potato salad?"

"Okay, I'll take care of it."

Jimmy turned once more to leave and Analisa said to Johnny, "Okay, Buster, Uncle Jim's leaving, and it's time you got your PJ's on. Tell Uncle Jim bye."

"Good bye, Uncle Jim. I'll see you tomorrow. I love you."

Stunned by what he said, Jimmy replied, "I love you too."

Analisa walked him the few steps to the door and grabbed his hand. He turned toward her and she put her arms around him and said, "Thank you."

"Thank you for what?"

"Thank you for being such an important part of Johnny's life. You heard what he told you, didn't you?"

"Yeah, I heard it, and it tears me up."

"Jimmy, I don't know if you know it or not, but you're a very important part of my life, too." She pulled him down to her face height and hugged him, putting her cheek against his."

He thought that since he was the big athlete and a macho man that had control of everything, he was fooled. The last two minutes brought tears to his eyes, and he didn't have any defense. He rode home thinking about Johnny telling him he loved him, and just as important, if not more so, was what Analisa said to him. He thought, *when she said that I was an important part of her life, I should have told her that she was an important part of mine, too. I don't know where this is leading, but I know one thing; I don't want to mess up.*

On the way to the lake the next morning, he was thinking about how the next day was Sunday, and Hal wouldn't have anything to do, so before he stopped to get their breakfast, he went to the bait and tackle store and bought two tubs of Night crawlers and four dozen more minnows. That should occupy him for quite a while, he thought.

Hal took care of the minnows while Jimmy unpacked the food, and then they sat down to a huge breakfast. They were planning to frame in the fourth wall that day, and that would make the house look as if it was a house. Not wasting any time, they ate quickly, cleaned up their mess and started to work. The second tape measure really helped with the efficiency.

About eleven-thirty, they heard a car coming up the driveway, and in a couple of minutes Analisa's Impala appeared. She pulled up to the rear of Jimmy's truck, and as soon as she stopped, Johnny got out and ran down to where Jimmy was working. Jimmy stopped and went up to meet Analisa as she walked down to the house. It was sort of rough terrain, so he took her hand and helped her until she stepped up on the floor. Even though they were no longer walking, she held onto his hand.

About noon, or a little after, Analisa pulled out a tablecloth and spread their lunch out on a sheet of plywood. She had brought some iced tea, and it really hit the spot with the chicken and potato salad. They visited until about one o'clock, and Analisa said they should go. Jimmy didn't argue because he wanted to finish that fourth wall before they quit for the weekend.

He walked her and Johnny to the car, and Johnny hugged him and said he would see him Wednesday and got into the car. Jimmy and Analisa stood nose to nose and Analisa said, "So, are we really not going to see you until next Wednesday?"

"It looks that way, and I won't see you Wednesday, unless it's late Wednesday night."

"Well, I'm going to get out of here so you can get back to work. Have a good weekend. Bye."

She and Johnny left, and Hal and Jimmy really *turned it on* the rest of the day and finished the fourth wall about five o'clock. Jimmy told Hal that he would see him early Monday morning and left.

The days just crept by and Wednesday finally arrived. Jimmy was right on time when he picked up Johnny. Analisa had already left for work, so they didn't get to see each other.

On the way to Lawrenceville, they talked about everything from video games to baseball. Around Cartersville, which was about half-way,

Jimmy said, “Do you like surprises?”

And Johnny responded with, “Yeah, I like surprises. Do you have one? What is it?”

“If I tell you, it won’t be a surprise, will it?”

“Does it have something to do with the Atlanta Braves?”

“No.”

“Are we going to Six Flags?”

“No.”

“What is it Uncle Jim?”

“I’m not going to tell you until later, but it’s something you should like. You’re always wanting to know how your Dad felt about things, and the surprise is something that he would really love.”

“Please, Uncle Jim, tell me.”

“Can’t do it.”

Jimmy wished that he had not said anything about a surprise because Johnny nearly worried the life out of him trying to find out what it was.

CHAPTER FIFTEEN

It was close to ten o'clock when they rolled into the parking lot at the Gwinnett Braves Baseball Club. They got out and went inside, and Jimmy spoke to the receptionist and told her he wanted to see Darrell. He introduced Johnny to her, and in a couple of minutes, Darrell came out. "Jim, it's great to see you," and he gave him a big hug. Then, he asked, "Is this the ball player you were telling me about?"

"Yeah, it is. This is Johnny. Johnny, this is Darrell Parker. Darrell is the manager of the Gwinnett Braves."

Darrell asked Jimmy, "Did you tell Johnny what we're going to do today?"

"No, I just told him that he was going to get a surprise."

"A surprise, hunh? C'mon back to my office. The other guys should be here any minute, and then, we'll take off."

Johnny asked, "Where are we going, Uncle Jim?"

"I'll tell you when the other guys get here. It's a surprise."

"Aw Man, that's not fair. Then, he spotted a lot of pictures and trophies and baseballs and bats and many other things in Darrell' office that interested him. In a minute, he said, "Uncle Jim, here's a picture of you."

"I know."

Soon, the others arrived and it was like a reunion when they saw Jimmy. He had been an important part of their lives when he was still playing, and they thought a lot of him. They talked for a few minutes, and then, Darrell asked, "Are you characters ready to go?"

Johnny whispered, "Where are we going?"

"Okay. Here's the surprise; you like Nascar, don't you?"

"Yes sir. I love it. Jeff Gordon is my favorite driver."

"Well, we're going down to the Atlanta Motor Speedway. They have a thing called the Racing Experience, and you can either drive one of the cars or ride with a professional driver. Of course, you're too young to drive, but if you would like to ride in one, you can."

"Boy, Uncle Jim, this is the best surprise ever. Did you say my Dad liked Nascar?"

"He was eat up with it. He would have loved to do something like this, and that's why I thought you would like it. Do you want to ride with a professional driver or would you rather ride with me?"

"Do you mean you're going to drive one of the cars?"

"I thought I would. This is pretty expensive, so I'm just going to do the three laps. I think that's plenty."

Johnny said, "Cool."

The three-lap deal cost over a hundred dollars, and some of the others cost three, four, and five hundred dollars.

Counting Johnny, there were seven of them, and all the others, except one, took the more expensive rides, and that one did what Jimmy was going to do.

Before the guys could get into the cars, they had to go through a pretty detailed instruction session. It covered the basics of driving a race car, and after the instructions, they were ready to drive. Jimmy and Johnny were third, and just getting into the suits and helmets and gloves was an experience in itself. Finally, they were ready. Johnny didn't act nervous at all, but Jimmy had a slight case of butterflies.

He started the engine, and it came on with a roar. When he put it in gear, the feeling of its power was absolutely awesome. He eased it down pit road at about forty-five miles an hour, and then they were on the race track. Jimmy gradually gave the car gas, and it responded with no hesitation whatsoever. He got it up to one-hundred-twenty miles an hour on the first lap and gave it more gas when he started the second lap. Midway through the second lap, they were going a hundred and forty miles an hour, and into the first turn on the third lap, when something happened.

All at once, the car began to shimmy. The right front fender looked as though it was quite a bit lower than the left fender, and suddenly, they began to spin. In a matter of just a few seconds, THUD; they hit the wall with the right front of the car.

Johnny was hurt. In a matter of just one or two minutes, an emergency vehicle was there. Jimmy was shaken up, but it looked as if Johnny had broken his collarbone. The ambulance took them both to Grady Hospital in Atlanta, where they checked Jimmy out and released him, but they admitted Johnny. He did, in fact, have a broken collarbone, and they wanted to keep him overnight.

Darrell followed the ambulance to the hospital and stayed with Jimmy until he saw that he was alright. "Did you see what happened, Darrell?"

"I saw you spin and crash, but I didn't know why it happened until one of the crew members said the right front tire blew out, and that was why you spun out."

"Oh, so it wasn't my faulty driving."

"No, it was the tire's fault."

Jimmy would rather have taken a beating than to have to call Analisa and tell her about Johnny, but he knew he had to do it. He called Shepherd Apparel and asked to speak to Analisa Shepherd. The operator rang the computer department number and Charlotte Morris answered. "Who is this," Jimmy asked.

"This is Charlotte Morris; may I help you?"

"Charlotte, this is Jimmy Shepherd, and I need to talk to Analisa please."

"Jimmy, she's not here. She went over to Chattanooga State this morning to take a refresher on a program that she's using. Can someone else help you?"

"Charlotte, here's what I need you to do. Call Chattanooga State or go over there if you have to, but Analisa needs to be told that her son was in an accident and broke his collarbone and is in Grady Hospital in Atlanta, he's in room four-twenty-four. Tell her it's not serious. Now, would you transfer me to my Dad, please?"

"Hello, Monty Shepherd."

"Hi Dad."

"Jimmy, hi. What's up?"

"Dad, something has happened, and I don't know how to handle it. I brought Johnny down here to surprise him with something that I thought he would really like because he has said several times that he would like to know how his Dad felt when he did things. Well, you know how much Johnny loved racing, so I thought it would be really neat if little Johnny could ride in a race car, and he was thrilled with the thought.

"Dad, I called Darrell at the Gwinnett Braves office last week to just say hello, and he said that he and some of the guys were going to the Atlanta Motor Speedway to this Racing Experience thing that they have. He invited me and said I could bring Johnny, so we came down today, and I drove a race car, and Johnny rode with me. We got up to a hundred and forty miles an hour, and everything was enjoyable until a tire blew out, and we hit the wall, and it broke Johnny's collarbone.

"I wasn't able to get in touch with Analisa, so I told Charlotte Morris to find her and tell her what happened. I'm at the hospital now, and I hope you can find Analisa and tell her what happened. He's at Grady Hospital in room four-twenty-four."

"Are you hurt?"

"No sir. I was a little shaken, but I'm alright. I'm just worried about Analisa."

"Okay, let me see what I can do."

"Thanks, Dad."

In about two hours, Analisa arrived at the hospital, and charged over to the nurse's station. She was frantic and Jimmy saw her and went over to her. When she saw him – SMACK-, she slapped him in the face as hard as she could and said, "From now on, you stay away from me and my boy," and she went down the hall to Johnny's room.

Jimmy tried to reason with her, but she said, "Get out of my sight," and wouldn't talk to him, so he went into the waiting room and sat down, trying to figure out what to do next.

He didn't know it, but Monty arrived just about the time he went into the waiting room, and after asking directions, he made his way down to Johnny's room. As he approached the room he could hear Johnny talking loudly, so he stopped outside the open door. Analisa was sitting with her back to the door, and Johnny was pleading with his mother, saying, "Mom, please don't be mad at Uncle Jim. He was just trying to help me see and feel what my Dad saw and felt. It wasn't his fault that we wrecked. A tire blew out. Please, please Mom, don't be mad at Uncle Jim."

At that, Monty went into the room to see how he was and to see how Analisa was doing as well. It didn't appear that there was anything too serious, and they had told Johnny that he could go home the next day, so Monty felt a sense of relief. He stayed and visited a while longer and offered to stay until the next day to bring Johnny home, but Analisa didn't want him to. She said she would stay with him all night, and then, they would go home the next day.

As he was leaving, he passed the waiting room and saw Jimmy sitting in there with his head in his hands, so he went in. Jimmy got up and said, "Hi Dad, are you going to see Johnny?"

"I've already seen him, and he appears to be alright. Why are you sitting in here?"

"Because Analisa won't let me near them."

"Well, I think she'll cool off." Then, he looked into Jimmy's eyes with an ultra-serious look and said, “Jimmy, you did wrong. There’s no doubt about it, you did wrong, but whether you know it or not, you are carrying the weight of a young boys love and you should do everything that you can to honor that love.”

Both men were silent for a minute, then Monty broke the silence. “What are you going to do now?”

“I don’t know; I guess I’ll go home.”

They went to the parking lot, and since Darrell had driven Jimmy’s car to the hospital, he had to look for it. At last, he found it, and he and Monty got on I-75 and headed toward Chattanooga; Monty in front and Jimmy in back.

On the way, Jimmy was depressed and deep in thought. *I don’t understand why everybody thinks I did such a bad thing. I don’t think it was bad; I was just trying to do something good for Johnny. Analisa has no call to feel that way. She knows how much I love Johnny, and if she refuses to let me see him anymore, I’m not going to be a happy camper. Maybe I’ll join back up with the band and leave. I don’t want to hang around if I can’t see him, and I’ve got to admit I’d hate not getting to see Ana anymore. She and I have gotten pretty close, and I secretly thought something might develop there, but oh well, what’s done is done, and there’s nothing I can do about it now.*

It was after dark when they got home. Monty said he was hungry, but Jimmy had lost his appetite and went to his room. He thought, *I’ve got to do something or else I’ll go crazy. I haven’t talked to Bobby in a long time. I think I’ll call him.*

He dialed Liz and Ben’s number and when Liz answered, he said, “Hi, Aunt Liz, this is Jimmy. Can I speak to Bobby, please?”

“Jimmy, has it been so long since you left that you don’t know Bobby doesn’t live here anymore? He has an apartment over on Mountain Creek Road. Do you want his number?”

“Yes ma’am, if you don’t mind.”

She gave him the number, and then said, “If you can’t reach him, keep trying. He has a girlfriend now, and he’s spending a lot of time with her, so keep calling. I know he’d like to hear from you. You two used to be almost like brothers, and Jimmy, Ben and I would like to see you, too. Why don’t you come out and see us sometime?”

“Thanks, Aunt Liz. I will. I miss seeing you, too. Thanks for Bobby’s number.”

As soon as he hung up, he dialed Bobby's number. After four rings, "Hello."

"Bobby, it's Jimmy. What are you doing?"

"I'm working my butt off trying to get ready for a CPA exam that I'm going to sit for on the twenty-fifth. Man, it's good to hear from you. I heard a while back that you were back in town, and I kept thinking you would call, but you never did. Where are you now?"

"I'm at Mom and Dad's."

"Well, go get in your car and come over here. We've got a lot of catching up to do."

"I thought you were busy."

"I am, but I'm not that busy. Come over here. There's someone I want you to meet."

"Aunt Liz said you have a girlfriend. Is that who you want me to meet?"

"Yeah, it is."

Then, acting the clown, Jimmy asked, "Is she fat, Bobby?"

Bobby chuckled and said, "No."

Then Jimmy asked, "Does she have all of her teeth?"

Chuckling a little more, Bobby said, "Yes."

"My last question is, does she have a wart on her nose?"

Laughing by now, Bobby said, "Absolutely not. Now get yourself over here. I want to see you."

"He gave Jimmy the address, and Jimmy got in his car and headed that way. When he got there, Bobby gave him a big hug the minute he opened the door. "You old rascal, come in here; I want you meet somebody."

They moved through the foyer into the living room, and there sat one of the most beautiful young women Jimmy had ever seen. Bobby introduced her as Marilyn Shockley, and she and Jimmy shook hands. Smiling, Jimmy said, "Bobby, she's not fat like you said."

Marilyn had a funny look on her face, and Bobby said, "You had better watch out or you're going to get me in trouble."

Jimmy saw the look on her face and said, "Marilyn, I was just kidding. He didn't say you're fat. I just had to do that to him."

Bobby went over to her and put his right arm around her waist and said, speaking to no one in particular, "Even if she were fat, I'd still love her."

Jimmy thought, *Wow! Love? This must be serious.*

Bobby wanted to know everything Jimmy had been doing, and then, Jimmy said, "Dad told me that you're going to sit for the CPA exam. Man, I'm impressed. Did you say you're taking it on the twenty-fifth?"

"Yeah, and that's not long from now. I'm only going to take the first part that day."

"How many parts are there?"

"Four, and the first part that I'm going to take lasts four hours."

"Do all four parts take that long?"

"Two of them do, and two of them last three hours."

"What if you fail a part?"

"I'll have to take it over again. I've got to pass all four parts in eighteen months or I'll have to start all over."

"Well, good luck. I know you'll do well. Marilyn, this guy has succeeded in everything that he's ever tried to do. You have found a winner here."

Bobby said, "Monty tells me that you're going to come into the business after Labor Day; Is that right?"

"Those were the plans, but I'm not sure right now. Something happened this morning that may have changed everything."

"Really? What happened?"

"You knew that Analisa had a baby after Johnny got killed, didn't you?"

"Yeah, I knew that."

"Well, she named him Johnny after his Dad, and I've become very close to him. I've also become very close to Analisa and have wondered what our relationship may lead to. I really love Johnny, and I'm not absolutely sure what my feelings toward Analisa are, but I know I miss her bad when I'm not around her.

"Now here's my problem: I took Johnny to the Atlanta Motor Speedway this morning, and he and I took a three lap ride in one of the race cars. On the third lap, a tire blew, and we crashed into the wall. It broke Johnny's collarbone, and when Analisa got to the hospital to see him, she was livid. She slapped me and told me not to come around her little boy anymore. I attempted to reason with her, but she told me to get out of her sight, and that's where we are."

Bobby said, "That's a tough one. Don't you think she'll cool down?"

"I would like to think so, but you would have to have been there and witnessed the scene to know just how mad she was. I'm thinking seriously about leaving and rejoining my band."

"Jimmy. You don't want to do that. It will break Monty's heart if you don't come into Shepherd Apparel. You don't have to be around him long before he starts talking about it. He wanted you to join the company when you signed with the Braves, and it really disappointed him when you didn't."

"I don't know, Bobby. Since Analisa works there, I would have to see her a lot, and I don't know how that would be, knowing how she feels about me."

"Jimmy, I'm going to ask you what Monty's going to ask you when you tell him this, and that's, have you prayed about it?"

"Bobby, do you know I have not, but you can bet your boots that I will. Thanks for reminding me. Now, let's get onto a lighter subject. You're working at Shepherd Apparel now aren't you?"

"Yes, and I love it. The way your Dad treats everyone, I don't know why anyone would ever want to leave there."

"How is Sue? I'd sure like to see her."

"She's fine. She's working on her Masters and wants to teach when she finishes. She feels led to teach abused children."

"She's got a leg up on that subject, hasn't she?"

"You're right about that."

"Look Bobby, I'm going to get out of here and let you get back to studying. I just needed someone to talk to, and I thought of you. I hope you *ace* that test, and I'll talk to you again real soon."

"I hope you will. I love you, Jimmy."

"I love you too. I'll see you. Bye."

Feeling better after his visit with Bobby, Jimmy went home and up to his room where he changed his thoughts to Hal and the house at Sale Creek. *I don't know if Hal is ready to be on his own yet, and I don't have the heart to run away and leave him hanging, but if I'm going, I need to go right away. I'll go to the farm in the morning and talk to him, and we'll see what happens. If he thinks he's ready to go to work on a regular job, I'll get the name of Dad's General Contractor and go talk to him. Tomorrow night I'm going to tell the folks in the group that I'm not going to be in the charity show.*

He went to bed, but slept fitfully. In his mind, even though there were a lot of problems, his thoughts all came down to one: Analisa. Not wanting to admit that he loved her, he tried to come up with anything that would substitute for thinking about her. He tried to think positive and tell himself that she would come around, but he was, by no means, sure that she would.

Stopping in Soddy-Daisy to pick up breakfast had become a regular thing and that day was no different. After a stop at the bait and tackle shop to buy some minnows and night crawlers, he went by and picked up two huge trays of food and took them to the farm.

Although he was still feeling depressed, he tried to hide it by acting upbeat and happy when he reached Hal. After they ate, Hal took him over to the spot where he had his stringer tied and pulled up a large catch or Bream. "You want to have another fish fry tonight," he asked.

"That sounds good, but I can't tonight. I have to go to Chattanooga this afternoon, and there's something I have to do tonight; maybe tomorrow night."

All day, all he could think about was how his leaving would affect Hal, and he decided that he would wait until later to contact a contractor. He was doing great, and his demeanor was like that of any other regular person and not like an alcoholic, but still, it hadn't been that long since he was so drunk he couldn't stand up. About mid-morning, he told him that he had decided not to go to Chattanooga that afternoon, and he could stay and work until around four o'clock.

At four o'clock sharp, Jimmy got into his car and headed toward Chattanooga. He wanted to get to the Burger and Shake before Mary Ann left. He didn't much think that Analisa would be there that night, and he didn't want a confrontation, so his timing was important. He walked in at around six o'clock, and Mary Ann was still working. "Hi, Sis."

"Hi. What are you doing here so early?"

"I have to tell the group something, then, I'm leaving. Are any of them here yet?"

"No, it's a little too early, and Analisa called and said she wouldn't be here tonight. She doesn't want to leave Johnny."

"Why aren't you going to play tonight?"

"I'm just not."

"Come on, Big Brother, tell your little sister what's wrong."

"Nothing's wrong."

"Bull! I know you, and I can tell when something is wrong; now, tell me what it is."

"Oh, all right. I just stopped by to tell the gang that I'm not going to play in the charity show. I think I'm going to rejoin my old group and start traveling with them again. I've made such a mess of things here, that it will be best if I just leave."

"What on earth are you talking about? What mess have you made?"

"Did you not hear about me taking Johnny for a Nascar ride and wrecking?"

"Yes, I heard about it, but what does that have to do with your leaving? Don't you realize how many people you're going to hurt?"

"It won't hurt anybody."

"Yes it will. Are you feeling so sorry for yourself that you don't care who suffers the consequences?"

"What are you talking about?"

"Do you want me to make a list? First, there's Dad. He has thought of nothing else ever since you told him you were going to come into Shepherd Apparel. That's all he talks about. Are you willing to hurt him like that? Then, there's Johnny. He is sure the sun rises and sets in you. You can absolutely do nothing wrong in his eyes. And how about Analisa? I'm certain that she loves you, and I know you love her. Why would you ever think about leaving two people that love you as much as those two?

"And last, but certainly not least, what about me? I love you, Jimmy, and when Bill and I get married and have children, I want you to be a loving Uncle to them just the way you are to Johnny. Do I have to keep going?"

"No, I think you've said enough."

"Well, did it do any good?"

"I don't know. I just think it would be best if I leave."

"Is all this because Analisa's mad at you? If it is, then you've got a really thin skin. I thought you were a tough, no-nonsense, macho guy. I can't believe you would hurt all these people just because your girl is mad at you. You're pitiful; you know that? What if she is mad at you? It's not the end of the world."

"But Sis, she told me not to come around Johnny anymore, and when I tried to reason with her, she told me to get out of her sight. I don't think I can stay here, knowing I can't see Johnny."

"Look, it's still a while before you're scheduled to start work. Why don't you take a vacation and clear your mind? You could go to

Grandmother's place in Florida, and it would be good for you. Ask one of your buddies to go with you. You might have a different outlook on life when you get back."

"I'll think about it, Sis. You know, you call this joint the Burger and Shake. Can I get a burger and shake. I'm hungry."

As a result of Mary Ann's talk, Jimmy decided to wait to tell the group that he was not going to play in the charity show until he had time to think about it some more. While he was eating, some of the group came in, and he just said that he was not going to be able to play that night. When he finished, he left and went home, but Mary Ann didn't; she went straight to Analisa's.

When Analisa came to the door and saw that it was Mary Ann, she invited her in. She offered her something to drink, but Mary Ann refused. She said, "Analisa, did you know Jimmy is going to leave?"

Still mad, she asked, "So? What does that have to do with me?"

"It has to do with you because Johnny loves him, and he loves Johnny. And if the truth were known, I think you love him. He hasn't said it, but I'm pretty sure he loves you, too. I know that what he did about taking Johnny on that trip might not have been wise, but he was just trying to show him some of the things his Daddy liked and felt. I'm sure this has hurt him more than it has Johnny, and you're not letting him see Johnny has made a wreck out of him. He told me that he couldn't live here knowing he couldn't see him, and that's why he's leaving."

"Why are you telling me all this, Mary Ann?"

"Because you and I are not only sisters-in-law, we're friends, and I can talk to you, and because you're the key to Jimmy's staying or leaving, and I hope you'll get over your *mad-on* and tell him he can see Johnny."

Seeming to warm up a little, Analisa asked, "Where's he going?"

"He said he was going to rejoin his old group and start traveling and playing clubs. You know that if he does, we might not ever see him again because those people travel all the time. They play until the wee hours, and then they sleep all day. Jimmy has a built-in future here with the family's business, and if he leaves this time, all that will be gone because Dad wants to retire in a few years, and he has to have someone trained to step in.

"I just wanted to make you aware of this, and I hope you will reach out to him and ask him not to go. You're the only one who can keep him here. He loves you and will do anything you ask."

A hint of a smile came on her face when Mary Ann said that, and she said, "I think you're giving me too much power, but I'll think about it. You know, he could have caused Johnny to get killed in that car, and I've already lost one Johnny. It scares me to think about it, and then I get angry again."

"I've got to go, but think about this; Johnny didn't get seriously hurt, and his injury was sustained doing something he loved to do, so please don't be too hard on Jimmy."

"I said I'd think about it."

"Okay. That's all I can ask. I'll see you."

CHAPTER SIXTEEN

The next morning, Jimmy got up and went to the farm as usual. After he and Hal finished their breakfast, they walked up the hill and began framing on two of the bedrooms. There was a common wall, running from the front of the house to the back, and in the center, a wall running perpendicular to the common wall creating two rooms. That really gave the house some shape, and encouraged them to work harder to see more progress. They were having such a good day, they worked right on through sundown, and quit when they couldn't see any longer.

Walking down the hill to the boathouse, Hal asked, "Do you want to fry up some fish for supper?"

"That would be fine or if you want to, we can go down to Soddy-Daisy, and I'll treat you to a good meal. What would you rather do?"

"I'd rather go to Soddy-Daisy because I need to get away from this place for a while."

"Are you getting cabin fever, Hal?"

"Yeah, I guess so. I haven't set foot off this place but a couple of times since I got here almost two months ago."

"Okay. Do what you have to do to get ready, and we'll go. You know, we haven't been to Dayton to eat. Would you like to go up there?"

"Anywhere is fine with me."

When they were ready, they got into Jimmy's pickup and headed toward Dayton. It was just as close as Soddy-Daisy, and they hadn't been up there to eat, so they drove around until they found what looked like a good place.

They went in, and the place had a nice atmosphere and a good menu. After they ordered and were waiting for their food, Jimmy asked, "Hal, what's your honest evaluation of your condition right now?"

Hal answered, "Honestly?"

"Yes, I need to know what you're thinking."

"I'm thinking that I've got this thing licked, thanks to you."

"Do you think you're in good enough shape to get back in society?"

"I'm pretty sure I am."

"Hal, we don't need *pretty sure*; we need *darn sure*. I'm only going to be up here for another week or so, and I have to be sure that you're going to be okay."

"I'll be okay, Jimmy. You don't have to worry about me."

"But I do worry about you. I remember when I first saw you, and it wasn't pretty. Let me ask you this; do you think you're ready to hold down a regular job?"

"Yes, I think I am."

"If you will recall, I asked you to stay another month until you got the framing done on the house, and the month is only a couple of weeks away. You said you should be finished with the framing and would probably have the house under cover. It looks as if you're on schedule, so what's next in your life?"

I'm going to try to find a job, but it's going to be hard because I don't have anywhere to live, and I don't have any transportation, but I'll make it. Don't worry about that."

"Will you let me help you?"

"Jimmy, you've already done too much. I can do it on my own."

"I'm sure you can, but I've got a couple of ideas, and I'd like to try them out on you. Can I do that?"

"Yeah, I guess so. What are they?"

"Well first of all, I have a pretty good idea where we can get you a job. Once we get you the job, then, we'll get you in one of the many subsidized apartments in town, and finally, when you're through working on the house, I'll be pretty much through, too, and I won't need my pickup, so I can let you use it 'til you can get one of your own. That should take care of the three concerns that you have. What do you say?"?

"I don't know what to say. You know, you're as close as a son."

"Speaking of sons; I'd like to find Randy. Do you have any idea where I could start looking? I think you two need to mend your fences because life is too short for a father and son to be estranged. Would you like to see him?"

"You know I would, but the last words he said to me were, *I never want to see you again.*"

"Well, that was then, and this is now. If you don't mind, I'm going to try to find him."

As soon as he said that, their food came, and they focused their attention on eating. "I wish I had known about this place before," Jimmy said.

"It's really good, isn't it?"

"Yeah, we'll have to come back up here."

They were both worn out when they got back to the farm, and it wasn't long before they got ready for bed. Jimmy wanted to see the ten o'clock news on their little TV, and he only made it about a third of the way through before he was asleep. Hal got up and turned it off and then returned to bed.

Coffee and toast was what they had for breakfast Saturday morning because Jimmy didn't want to go down to Soddy-Daisy to the restaurant, but it satisfied them both, and they got an earlier start than usual on the house.

Around eleven o'clock, Jimmy heard a car coming up the gravel drive, and his heart jumped up in his throat because he thought it was Analisa and Johnny, but his anxiety was for naught. It turned out to be Mary Ann and Bill. Although he was glad to see them, it was not like seeing Analisa and Johnny.

"Hey Sis, hi, Bill. What are you guys doing up here," Jimmy asked.

Mary Ann answered, "We just wanted to come up and see how you're coming on the cabin. This is sure not like Granddaddy said it was going to be, is it?"

"It's sure not. Sis, do you remember when we first came up here with him, and he said he wanted to build a cabin? Well, this is the cabin; all twenty-three hundred square feet of it. What do you think this would be if he said he wanted to build a house instead of a cabin?"

"I don't know, but it looks as if it's going to be a really nice place."

"Come over here and let me introduce you to Hal." He introduced the couple to Hal, and after a couple of minutes of small-talk, he went back to work while Jimmy showed them around. He took them down to the boathouse, and Mary Ann was amazed, even though she had helped Jimmy clean it up before he and Hal moved in.

When they got back to the house, Mary Ann asked him, "Have you heard from Analisa?"

"Not a word."

"After you and I had our talk the other night I went to see her. I told her you said you might leave town, and I explained how many people would be hurt if you did, including her and Johnny, and she promised me that she would think about letting you see Johnny. She warmed up a little when I told her you loved her."

"You told her what?"

"I told her that you loved her, and I knew she loved you."

"Sis, you're meddling in something that's none of your business. You should not have told her that."

"Why? It's true isn't it?"

With a half-smile he said, "Bill, will you take this girl somewhere and beat her?"

"Well, I would, Jimmy, but I think she speaks the truth."

"Oh, so she's got you on her side now, hunh?"

"No, I'm on your side."

"I can't believe that I'm the victim of a conspiracy conducted by my own sister."

"Well, get used to it, Big Boy. I'm not going to let up until you start making some sense."

Bill changed the subject by asking some questions about the house and boathouse, and in a few minutes, they said they had to go."

Mary Ann went over and kissed Jimmy on the cheek, and he and Bill shook hands. Mary Ann said, "Keep your chin up, Bro.; things will work out," and they got into Bill's car and left.

After they left, Jimmy and Hal finished the wall they were working on, and Jimmy said, "Why don't we quit for the day?" and Hal agreed. So much progress had been made, Hal thought that it might not take more than one more week to finish the framing and get the roof on. Getting the roof on was what Jimmy was waiting to hear because he was going to have to start work in a little over a week, and he wanted the house to be dry before they quit.

As with all construction jobs, a mess is created by all the cut-offs and scrap lumber, so when they quit working, they began to pick up some of the mess and burn it. While they were cleaning up, they heard another car driving up the driveway. That time, it was Joan and Monty.

"Hi Mom. Hi Dad. I'm glad to see y'all. What are y'all doing up in this neck of the woods?"

"We wanted to see how you were coming with your project. It looks like you're really coming up with it."

"We are. It should be under roof in another week. Oh, Mom, Dad, this is Hal Long. I've told you about Hal. He's the expert that has put all this together," Hal told them that it was nice to meet them, and he and Monty shook hands.

"You weren't kidding when you said this is a lot bigger job than what your Granddaddy had talked about. What's the exterior going to be; brick?"

"No sir, I don't think so. I'm toying with the idea of having Crab Orchard stone up to the windows and then redwood siding the rest of the way. Don't you think that would look nice?"

"Yeah, I didn't think about Crab Orchard. That will be pretty."

"You all come on down to the lake and let me show you the boathouse."

They walked down the path, and when they got there, Monty said, "Wow! This is incredible. Whose idea was this; yours or your Granddaddy's?"

"Both. Granddaddy came up with the idea of having a room and bathroom, and the air conditioning was his idea, but the rest of it was mine."

"What air-conditioner? I don't see one."

Jimmy closed the door and moved him over to the large grate, and then he flipped the fan switch. A large volume of cool air came up through the grate and out the back wall, and Monty said, "Well I'll be darn. That's the beatenest thing I ever saw."

Joan was a little repulsed by the dirty dishes in the sink and the un-made beds, so like a good mother, she spread up the beds and found some dishwashing liquid and washed the dishes. She did all that while Jimmy and Monty talked and went outside to look around.

In a few minutes they went back up the hill, and Monty said, "Well, I guess we had better be going. It's looking good, Son. I know you're proud of it."

"I am. I'm glad y'all came up. I've been wondering if you were ever going to come."

"I know. I'm embarrassed that we haven't been here before now, but I've been so busy, I have hardly had time to turn around. Maybe when you start helping me, I can do some things."

"At least you came, and I appreciate it. Dad, there's something I need to talk to you about sometime this weekend. Maybe tomorrow, after Church."

"Monty's heart sank when Jimmy said that, and he said, "You're not going to back out of coming to work, are you?"

"Oh no. I told you I would be there after Labor Day, and I will. I need to talk to you about something else."

"Okay, I don't have any plans for tomorrow afternoon, so whenever you're ready."

"Thanks Dad. It's something that's important to me."

Joan asked, "Darling, are you coming home tonight?"

"Yes ma'am. I'll be there tonight and tomorrow night."

"Good. Why don't I invite some of your friends over tomorrow afternoon for an impromptu pool party? Would you like that?"

Yes ma'am, that would be nice. Thank you. Who do you think you will invite?"

"Oh, I don't know. We can have some of your old school buddies and maybe Bobby and Sue Joyner. You all used to be so close. Maybe I'll call Analisa and see if she and Johnny would like to come, too. Do you have any other friends you would like to invite?"

"I don't know, Mom. A lot of them are married now. Do you know if Shirley Batson is? She would be a good one to invite if she's still single. I haven't seen her since college, and I'd like to see her."

"All right. I'll try to find out. Now, what do you want to have to eat?"

"Anything. Maybe Dad could grill some hamburgers and hot dogs, or we could just order pizza. We need to keep it simple."

After they left, Jimmy went back to picking up scrap boards, and it didn't take him long because Hal had continue to pick up while they talked, and he had it almost done by the time Jimmy joined him.

"Hal, if I spend the night at Mom and Dad's tonight and tomorrow night, will you be alright?"

"Of course I will. You go on and have a nice weekend."

"Do I need to get some groceries before I leave?"

"No, there's plenty here to eat. I'm going to fish some of the time, and if I catch any I'll fry them up and have as the English say, "*Some fish and chips, old boy*."

Jimmy could sense a new, self-assured attitude on the part of Hal, and he was thankful. Maybe things were going to be alright.

When he got ready to leave, he told Hal that he would be back sometime Monday, but he didn't know exactly when. It might be Monday afternoon because he had some things to do in town before he came.

Before he got into the pickup, Hal asked, "Jimmy, would you have time to help me get some plywood on the roof before you leave? If you can, I can start on it before you get here Monday."

"Sure. Let's do it," and they put ten pieces of plywood sheets up there.

Jimmy was ready for the week to be over because it had been a rough one, and he looked forward to having friends over the next day. He wondered if Analisa would be there. His Mom had said she was going to invite her, but he doubted she would come.

After Church the next day, Monty and his family went home and changed into swimsuits and cover-ups, getting ready for the pool party. Joan had invited about ten people plus Liz and Ben which was plenty. Jimmy and Monty went to the kitchen and fixed themselves a sandwich to tide them over until they had pizza, later. While they were in the kitchen, Monty asked Jimmy if it was a good time for them to talk, and Jimmy said no. It would be better to wait until everybody had left. At two-thirty, people began showing up.

Liz, Ben, Sue, and Bobby were the first ones there, and Jimmy was really glad to see them. Some more of his friends followed, and finally, Shirley Batson. He played the perfect host, and everyone seemed to be having a good time, but Jimmy caught himself looking toward the door, constantly, in hopes that Analisa was just running late. He, at last, realized she wasn't coming when it got to be four o'clock.

Shirley Batson was looking amazingly good, and during the course of the afternoon he began to notice her more and more. Shirley had gotten her degree in nursing and was one of the Emergency Room nurses at Erlanger hospital. The only thing Jimmy hated about that was the fact that she worked nights, and if he should decide that he wanted to date her, and her him, it would have to be during the day or on her day off.

Her working hours allowed her to be outside during the day, and she had a beautiful tan, emphasized by a red, red bikini. She had always had a good figure, and Jimmy thought she looked like a million dollars. He didn't bother her, other than speak, while she was lying in the sun, but when the pizza came, and everybody started to eat, he sat down at a table with her. She had put on a white cover-up, which disappointed Jimmy, but she still looked beautiful.

"Shirley, it's great to see you. I'm glad you came."

"It's good to see you too, Jimmy. It has been a long time. I don't think we've seen each other since college, have we?"

"That's what I was thinking. I'm glad you came."

"Me too. What have you been up to?"

"I guess you knew that I started playing professional baseball when I graduated."

"Yeah, I heard that. I stayed in touch with Analisa for a while after graduation, and she kept me up to date on what was happening with your family. Did you do good playing baseball?"

"Yeah, I did real good. In fact; it looked as if I was going to the *big show* when I ruptured my Achilles tendon, and that ended my career. Along with the baseball, some of my team members and I formed a musical group, and we played everything from county fairs to night clubs. Then, one night when we were playing a club, I had an emotional encounter with my conscience, and I walked off the stage and swore that I wouldn't get back on one."

"Man, that's some story. What have you been doing since you quit playing music?"

"Well, I came home, and Dad wanted me to go to work for Shepherd Apparel, but I wasn't ready to do that. My Grandfather left me some property on the lake up at Sale Creek, and I've been building a house on it. Do you remember Randy Long?"

"Yes, I remember Randy."

"His daddy has been helping me build the house."

"His daddy? I heard he was a lush."

"Was is the keyword. He was a lush, but not anymore. He has been helping me for about two months now, and he has not had one drink. I'm praying that he's going to stay sober. Well, to get back on the subject, the house is to the point now where I'm going to have to have a real builder come in and finish it, and I'm supposed to start working at Shepherd Apparel the day after Labor Day. Now, that's my story; let me hear yours."

"I don't have much to tell. After I got my nurse degree, I went to work at Erlanger, and I've been there ever since."

"Do you have a boyfriend?"

"No; no boyfriend."

"Why? A good-looking girl like you with no husband or boyfriend? I don't understand."

"I've dated a little, but Mr. Right hasn't come along, and I'm not actively looking, so if he comes along, fine, and if he doesn't, fine. I'm perfectly happy with my life just the way it is. Have you been dating anyone?"

"No. I've been spending some time with Analisa, but we're not dating. Right now, she's mad at me, so I don't know when I'll see her again. Her little boy, Johnny, is my buddy. He loves me, and I love him, and while I'm not his father, I try to give him a feeling of having a man in his life. He's a great kid."

Shirley said, "I'm disappointed in Analisa. You know, we were best friends in high school, and we roomed together for four years in college, and now she acts as if she doesn't want to see me. I've called her a few times and left messages, but she doesn't call me back. I talked to her a couple of times, and it was as if she couldn't wait to get off the phone, so I just quit calling. I don't know what's wrong with her. She has my number if she wants to talk."

"Shirley, since neither of us is dating anyone, would you like to maybe go out sometime?"

"I'd love to. Your Mom apparently has my number, so call me."

"Okay, I will. What's your schedule?"

"I work three, twelve hour shifts per week, all on weekends and all at night from seven to seven. When your Mom called and invited me over here, I got someone to swap a day with me so I could come, so now, I'm off 'til Friday night."

"How about we do something tomorrow night?"

"That sounds wonderful. What do you want to do, so I'll know how to dress?"

"I don't know. Maybe catch a movie and grab a bite to eat. I don't care. We can do whatever suits you. It's been so long since I've been to a movie, I probably won't know how to act, but I'd like to go to one. I don't even know what's playing."

"Me either. We'll have to look in the paper."

As they were setting up their date, Mary Ann walked by and said, "I didn't mean to eavesdrop, but I heard you guys setting up a movie date, and I think that's wonderful. Shirley, I don't know what you've been doing, but my big brother here has zero social life, and it would be great if you could help him out with it. Don't let me interfere with your conversation. I just had to tell you how great I think it is for you two to go out."

Before long, the guests began to leave, and Jimmy had to tell them bye and how glad he was that they came. They all promised to stay in touch a little better as they left. Soon, the crowd was down to Sue, Bobby, and Shirley. Bobby was in no hurry to leave because he wanted to spend some more time with Jimmy, and Sue was riding with Liz and

Ben, so there was no-telling how long they would stay. Jimmy was just getting comfortable with Shirley, and she appeared to be comfortable with him. He hated to divert his attention away from her, but good manners dictated that he pay attention to Bobby.

Mary Ann took care of entertaining Sue, so it turned into a three way conversation between, Shirley, Bobby, and Jimmy. Finally, Bobby said he had a date and had to go, so he and Jimmy said a long goodbye, and he left, leaving Jimmy and Shirley alone. They had had pizza so late, it was unlikely that there would be any dinner, so Jimmy couldn't think of a good reason to ask Shirley to stay. Soon, an idea popped into his head, and he asked, "Do you like ice cream?"

And she said, "I love ice cream. Are we having some?"

"No, not here, but I thought that we might go get some after a while, if you want to."

"I can't go anywhere like this. I'll have to go home and change into something that I can get out in. Would that be alright?"

"That will be fine. You'll have to give me your address. I don't even know where you live."

"Okay," and she gave him her address and described the directions how to get there. They talked for a while longer, and then she left to go home and change clothes. After she left, Jimmy went in to change also when he remembered the talk he was to have with his Dad. He thought about putting it off, but he knew Monty would probably be too busy to talk to him the next day, and what he wanted to talk about was important. He didn't know anything to do but call Shirley and explain the situation.

She acted disappointed and asked, "How long do you think you will be with your Dad?"

"I don't know. Probably a long time."

"If it's not too late, you can come over when you get through. Do you want to do that?"

"I'd like to, but I don't know how long this is going to take."

"Call me when you finish. I'd like for you to come."

"Okay, I will, but if we don't do anything tonight, we're still on for tomorrow aren't we?"

"Yes, but let's don't give up on tonight."

"All right. I'll call you."

He went in and changed out of his swimsuit into a pair of Jeans and a tee shirt with a picture of an eagle on the front. In the den, Monty was sitting in his recliner in front of the TV showing a pre-season football game, and he was sound asleep. Jimmy hated to wake him up, but he thought that maybe, if he shuffled some newspapers and made some other noises like that, that Monty would wake up, which he did.

"Dad, whenever you're ready, I'd like to talk to you."

"All right. I'm ready now. What's on your mind?"

"Dad, you saw Hal up at the house yesterday; did you ever know him before?"

"No, I never did."

"Well, I went to high school with his son, Randy, and he used to be a carpenter with a large construction company. He had a fine reputation in the community and was well thought of by everybody. Then, one day, he went somewhere to a meeting or something where people were drinking, socially. Hal had never had a drink before that, but not to be conspicuous, he took a drink like everyone else, and Dad, that drink proved to be his downfall. He liked it so much that he had another and then another, and he wound up drunk that night.

"The next morning, he woke up wanting a drink, and before long he was a hopeless drunk. His family left him, and he was homeless until I found him."

"Until you found him? How did you find him," Monty asked.

"One night, I went to the Dinner Party to eat, and when I finished eating I went to the Burger and Shake, you know, where Mary Ann works. Well sir, on the way to the Burger and Shake, this drunk approached me asking for money. I recognized him and tried to talk to him, but he didn't acknowledge anything I said. I offered to take him somewhere and feed him, but he was too drunk to understand, so he left me and staggered up the street. I watched him, and he went into the old Willard house.

"I went into the Burger and Shake and visited with Mary Ann and with the group that plays music in the back twice a week, and it began to storm. I tried to wait until it slacked up a little, but it just kept storming, and one bolt of lightning sounded as if it had hit just a few feet from us. The rain kept up. So I decided to run to the car, anyway. When I got outside, I looked and the Willard house was on fire; the lightning had struck it, and I remembered that Hal was in there. I ran up the street to the house and went in to try and find him. The smoke was so thick I could hardly see and had about given up on finding him, but then, I found him and dragged him outside. The emergency people came and took him to the hospital, and he stayed in there three or four days.

"I stayed in close touch while he was in the hospital, and then I checked him out. After three or four days, he was sober, but still in bad shape, so I talked to him and took him to Sale Creek, where he's been ever since. It's been almost two months now since he's had a drink, and he and I are both confident that he can make it now without drinking.

"Now, he's a framing carpenter, and the framing on my house will be finished later this week. I want to find him a job, and I was wondering if you would help me. I thought maybe Bob Martin might be able to use a good carpenter. Dad, you know I wouldn't ask this unless I was sure that he was in shape both mentally and physically to handle a job. I'm going to try to find him an apartment in one of the subsidized projects, but he needs to show that he has a job. I'll vouch for him, if you'll just help me."

Monty asked, "What do you want me to do?"

"I'd like for you to call Bob Martin, and if he'll agree to talk to him, I'll take him over there Tuesday or whenever he can see him. I thought a call from you would open the door for Hal to get in for an interview. Once he gets in to see him, he's on his own, but I feel strongly that he can make it. I'm going to look for his son while I'm in town tomorrow, and if I can find him, hopefully they will make amends and get back together.

"Also Dad, on a lighter note, I'm going to have to have a contractor finish my house. Do you think Bob would be interested in doing it, or is he strictly commercial?"

"I think he does some residential work. I'll ask him when I talk to him."

"Does that mean you'll talk to him for Hal?"

"I have to. You're so sure that he's going to be okay, how can I refuse? Besides, I'm afraid that if I don't, you'll decide to stay up there and work on the house yourself instead of coming in to the business."

"You know what, Dad? If Bob is interested in finishing the house, he'll have to see it, and if he goes up there, he can talk to Hal then. What do you think?"

"That may work. Let me talk to Bob in the morning, and we'll see what happens."

"Thanks, Dad. I knew I could count on you."

When they finished talking, it was after nine o'clock, but he told Shirley he would call, so he did. "Hey, Shirl, I just got through. What do you want to do?"

"I don't care. It's a little late to go out, so why don't you come over here? I can fix some hot-chocolate, and we can just visit."

"That will be great. I'd rather have hot-chocolate that ice cream, anyway. Do you want me to come now?"

"Yeah, just as soon as you can get here."

When he hung up and thought about her answer, he said to himself, *Wow! I'm on my way.*

Shirley gave him a warm welcome when he arrived at her apartment and invited him to come in and have a seat. She sat across from him, and they made small talk for a while. In a few minutes, she asked, "Are you ready for some hot chocolate?"

"I sure am," and she got up and disappeared into the kitchen. In a minute, she returned with a tray holding two mugs and a plate of home-made chocolate chip and raisin cookies. After his first bite of cookie, he said, "These are great, Shirl. Did you make them?"

"Yes I did. You see, when you're a spinster, you learn how to do a lot of things."

"Well, they're delicious, and you're definitely not a spinster. I think you're a beautiful and vibrant young lady," he said.

"Thank you, Sir," she replied. "How about another cookie?"

"Okay, one more; now that I'm not playing ball, I have to watch my figure."

"A cookie is not going to hurt that figure," she said. "Take two or three."

"Alright, I'll take two." Looking her square in the eyes, he said, "You're a temptress; did you know that?"

She said, "Yeah, right." Then, she put the plate of cookies on the coffee table and picked up the tray and took it back into the kitchen. When she returned, she sat down on the sofa next to him and said, "I'm really interested in what you've been doing since college. A professional baseball career sounds so exciting; and a music career, too. I wish you'd tell me about both of them."

"There's not much to tell. You saw me play in high school and college, and the pros is no different except all the players are better, and you have to work your butt off, or else, they'll replace you with somebody else.

“Playing music is a different animal, and I could go on about a musical career, but not tonight. I have a very full day tomorrow, and I need to leave. I don’t want to get so tired that I can’t enjoy your company tomorrow night. If you want to see a movie, be thinking about what you want to see. I thought we might eat at the Town and Country, if that’s alright with you.” When he was walking to the door, he said, “I enjoyed the hot-chocolate and cookies, and I enjoyed being with you.”

And with that, she put her arms around him and gave him a kiss that he wouldn’t forget. She said, “I’m glad you came over, and I look forward to tomorrow night.” She lifted his hand and kissed it and said, “Goodnight.”

CHAPTER SEVENTEEN

Monday morning, Jimmy was ready to take care of things for Hal. The first thing he did was to try to find Randy. He had no idea where to start, so he looked in the phone book, and to his surprise, there was an *H. Randall Long* listed. *Could that be Randy? The H could stand for Howard or Hal. I won't know until I call.* He dialed the number and got an answering machine, but the voice said Randy, and even though it had been years since Jimmy had seen him, he thought the voice sounded the way he remembered Randy sounding. He left word and hoped he would call him back.

Then, he looked for the address and phone number for the housing authority. He decided that it would be best if he went to their office instead of calling, so he spent the rest of the morning there.

When he finished there, he called his Dad's office to see if he had talked to Bob Martin yet, but he was in a meeting, so he went to Sale Creek before it got any later. Hal had all ten of the plywood sheets that they put up Saturday in place and was trying to get more up there by himself when he got there. A Four by eight sheet of plywood is heavy and too much for one person to handle alone. Jimmy immediately went to help him, and they got twenty-five sheets up before they wore out. After resting for a little while, they started again, and that time they put up another twenty. If their math was right, it was going to take around ninety sheets, so they had ten sheets over half of what they would eventually have to have.

Hal figured it would take him until lunchtime the next day to put the forty five sheets down, if he started right then, but Jimmy wanted to talk to him first. He told him what he had been doing that morning, and he asked him what Randy's full name was. When he said *Howard Randall Long,* Jimmy knew he was on the right track to find Randy. He didn't stay long because he wanted to get back to Chattanooga to get ready for his date.

He went by the Burger and Shake to tell the group that he wouldn't be there that night. Everyone was there except Analisa and nobody knew whether or not she would be there. Mary Ann had to work that night, so he went out front and talked to her for a few minutes. It was almost time for him to go pick up Shirley, so he told Mary Ann goodbye, and as he was leaving, Analisa came in. Jimmy stopped and said, "Hi Analisa," and she said "Hello," and kept walking, and that was all she said.

When she got to Mary Ann, she asked, "Where's he going all dressed up?"

And Mary Ann answered, "He has a date tonight," and when she said that, the expression on Analisa's face was indescribable; a mixture of shock and hurt. She went on to the back and unpacked her guitar and half-heartedly tried to play. She finished one tune, but before they could start the second, she told them that she didn't feel well and was going home. She packed up her guitar and left the back-room, and when she passed Mary Ann, Mary Ann asked, "You leaving so soon?"

Analisa replied, "Yeah, I don't feel well. I shouldn't have come tonight. I'll see you, Mary Ann."

"Okay. I hope you get to feeling better. Bye."

Before she even got to the door, Mary Ann was all smiles and thought; *I wouldn't take a million dollars for that look on your face when I told you that Jimmy had a date. That's what you get, Miss Ana, for being so unreasonable. I'd like for you and Jimmy to get together, but I like Shirley, too. She might make just as good a sister-in-law as you.*

Jimmy had told Shirley that he would pick her up at seven, so they would have time for a leisurely dinner before the movie. Since Shirley wouldn't say what movie she would like to see, he decided they would go to the Bijou to see Titantic, and afterwards they would go to Ellis' for coffee and dessert. When he told Shirley of those plans, she agreed wholeheartedly.

Dinner was a very pleasant experience. Not only was the atmosphere warm and inviting, but the conversation was equally as nice, and the dinner was wonderful. The movie was just as they both had expected, and they enjoyed it a lot.

To cap off the evening, they went to Ellis's restaurant for coffee and dessert. It, too, had a great atmosphere, and they both ordered sinful sweets to go with their coffee. They talked about what a great time they had had, and at one point Shirley asked Jimmy, "Can I tell you something?"

"Yeah, what?"

"Ever since we were in high school, I've had a crush on you, but you never seemed to notice me. I know a couple of times we would be together when Johnny and Analisa wanted to go somewhere and needed another guy for me, but that wasn't like tonight. Tonight, you actually wanted to be with me, for me, and I'm thrilled about that. Did you know that I had that crush on you?"

"No, I never did."

"I don't know how you didn't know. I thought it was so obvious."

"Well, I've never been accused of being real smart, especially around girls. Look, it's getting late. Do you think we should go?"

"Whatever you think. I hate to see the night end."

"I do, too, but I've got a hard, full day ahead tomorrow."

Jimmy paid the check, and they went towards Shirley's. When they got there, Shirley said, "You've got time. Come in for a few minutes."

Jimmy said, "Okay, but just for a few minutes. It's after mid-night, and I have to get up early in the morning."

Shirley held his hand on the walk from the parking lot, and when they got to her door, she handed him the key. He unlocked the door and opened it. As soon as they got inside, she turned to him and put her arms around him and gave him a passionate kiss. He put his arms around her and kissed her back, and they made their way over to the sofa. She was all over him, and in a few minutes, Jimmy's better judgment took over, and he said, "I think I had better go," and she responded with, "Why don't you stay here with me tonight? I'll be sure you get up early in the morning."

"That sounds wonderful, but no, I need to go. I've sure had a good time tonight, Shirl."

Disappointed, she said, "Me too. Do you think we can do this again?"

"I'm sure of it, that is, if you want to."

"I want to, Jimmy Shepherd, now, kiss me goodnight."

They embraced and kissed. Then Jimmy left, feeling good that he had not yielded to such obvious temptation.

He woke up the next morning thinking about the opportunity he turned down the night before. He thought, *I must have been crazy.* When he got up, Joan was already up, and she asked if he wanted any breakfast. He said he would like some, and while she was fixing it, she told him, "A Randy Long called you, and said he was returning your call. He gave me a number where he could be reached during the day if you want to call him."

He took the note and put it in his pocket, and said, "I'll call him later. Is Dad up yet?"

"Yes he left early; he has an early meeting."

"I guess I'll be doing that before long."

"I know, and your Dad is so excited. You two are going to be really good together."

"Mom, what time is Dad's meeting? I need to talk to him."

"Eight o'clock. He said it was going to be a short meeting, and it was important that they have it early. I think he should be through by eight-thirty or nine o'clock."

"Fine, I'll wait and leave after I talk to him."

Jimmy was finally able to reach Monty around nine-fifteen. Monty told him, "Jimmy, I talked to Bob Martin yesterday, and he would like to meet with you. It just so happens that he is building a house in Soddy-Daisy, and he said he could come up to Sale Creek to see your house."

"I told him about Hal, and he said he would talk to you about him when he comes up there. That way, he could get a good look at Hal without Hal knowing what he was doing."

"Did he say when he would be up there?"

"He talked like it would be Wednesday, but you had better call him to work out the particulars. Here's his number." Being slightly facetious, he asked Jimmy, "Now, what else can I do for you?"

Jimmy answered, "Nothing, Dad. Thank you for calling him, and I'll call him right now."

He spoke to Bob, and they set a time for Bob to come to Sale Creek the next day, Wednesday. Jimmy gave him the directions to the property and thanked him.

Next, he called Randy Long. "Randy, this is Jimmy Shepherd. How are you doing, Buddy?"

"Just fine, Jimmy. I was shocked when I got home yesterday and saw where you had called. What's up?"

"Randy, it's kind of complicated over the phone. Is there a time we can meet for coffee of maybe have lunch?"

"How about lunch today?"

"That would be great. Where and when?"

"I'm downtown. Do you like Tomlinsons?"

"Yeah, I do."

"How about eleven forty-five at Tomlinsons?"

"Great. I'll see you there. I'm looking forward to seeing you."

He and Randy arrived at Tomlinson's at the same time. They went in, and Jimmy asked for a table in the back. When they sat down, they talked about what each other had been doing since high school, and Randy said he was a textile engineer. Jimmy told him about playing baseball and music and brought him completely up to date on his life. He then led into the beginning of his relationship with Randy's father.

Randy sat there and listened to Jimmy and didn't say a word while he talked, and when he was through, Randy asked, "Did he tell you why I said I didn't want to see him again?"

"He did, but Randy, I'd sure like to see you give him another chance. This is likely the longest he's been without a drink since he started drinking, and I know he really wants to conquer the demons. It would mean so much to him if you would just go see him, even if it is for just a few minutes. He doesn't know I'm talking to you, so if you decide not to see him, he won't be any worse off, but if you do go see him, it would raise his life to a new level. What do you say?"

"Wow! This was the last thing I would have thought of. When you called, I thought that maybe you wanted to talk to me about going to work for Shepherd Apparel, or something having to do with textiles, but not this. Jimmy, I've gone so many years without my father being in my life that I don't know what I would do if he came back into it. When our relationship was ruptured, I had an extremely hard time, and I'm not prepared to get hurt like that again. Give me some time to think about it, and I'll call you."

"That'll be fine, but let me mention something before we go. Hal's going to finish at my place Saturday, and it would be great if you could go see him while he's there. It looks as if he's going to get a job, maybe tomorrow, and he will be leaving Sale Creek."

"Okay, I'll call you after I think about it."

The day was over half gone and Jimmy was still in Chattanooga, and he thought that if he was going to salvage any of it he had better get going, so he got in the truck and took off in a hurry.

Hal only had three sheets of plywood left that had not been put down when Jimmy got there, and the first thing they did was to put more sheets on the roof. If they had figured correctly, they would need only thirty five more sheets to completely cover the house. When they had finished putting up the sheets, Jimmy got his hammer, and went back up to help Hal. He had never put plywood on a roof before, but how hard could it be? Just butt a sheet up against the last one and put some nails in it.

"What do you want to do for dinner, "Jimmy asked.

"How about Largemouth Bass? I caught a nice one last night. We could have it with some Bream and fries, or if you would rather go out, we can do that, too. It's your call."

"I'm not really in the mood for fish. Why don't we go to that restaurant we found up in Dayton? We both liked it. Do you want to go up there?"

"That's fine. Let's take the minnow bucket and get some minnows while we're up there. I used the last one on that big Bass last night."

When they got back to the farm, they went down to the boathouse, and Hal immediately baited up two lines and cast them into the lake.

Jimmy had planned to stay at the farm overnight, but he was expecting the call from Randy, so he had to go home. When he got there, Joan said that there was no call from Randy, but Shirley had called, and wanted him to call her. He really didn't want to call her and he was disappointed that Randy hadn't called.

"Mom, what did Shirley say?"

"She said she wanted you to call her, that's all."

"When did you tell her I'd be home?"

"I didn't. I told her I didn't know; that you might spend the night at the lake."

It was getting late, and since he didn't know what time Bob Martin would be at the lake the next day, he thought he had better get to bed if he was going to get up the next morning.

He didn't call Shirley, and Randy didn't call him, so he went to sleep, hoping Randy would call before he left the next morning.

Coffee was all he had the next morning because he was going to stop in Soddy-Daisy and get breakfast for himself and Hal. When he got to the farm, Hal was already working and had to come down from the roof to eat. There was still some coffee in the boathouse, so they finished off the pot with breakfast. By that time it was nine o'clock, and they both went to work on the plywood sheets. Jimmy's mind was on Bob Martin's upcoming visit, and he was also thinking about Shirley' call. He thought he might call her when he got home after work.

At ten-thirty they heard a car coming, and it was Bob. Jimmy climbed down and greeted him, but Hal remained on the roof.

"Hi Bob. I'm Jim Shepherd. It's nice to see you."

"I'm glad to meet you, too. I knew your Grandfather, and I know your Dad, and I'm glad to meet you. For the last few years, whenever I would see your Dad, you were either at school or playing baseball, so I never had the chance to meet you."

"Yeah, well all that is getting ready to change; I'm going to work for Shepherd Apparel in about another week, so maybe we'll have a chance to do some things together. Bob, this is my quote *cabin*. My Grandfather bought this place before he died, and we talked about building a cabin before I left to go to school. He did some things after I left, such as the boathouse down there and the foundation for this building. When I came up here after being gone all those years and saw the size of the *cabin*, I didn't know whether to start over or build it to match the foundation, and that's where we are now.

"The fellow on the roof is Hal Long, and he's the one my Dad talked to you about. Hal is mainly a framing carpenter, although he has done some finishing work, and it looks as if the framing on this place is about to be finished. I'm excited about getting it done now, and I thought about you. I didn't know if you did residential building or if you were strictly commercial. Now that you see it, are you interested in taking it from here and finishing it up?"

"Yeah, Jimmy, I think I would be interested, but I'd like to see the plans first."

"Well, that's a problem. There are no plans. Granddaddy drew a sketch, and that's what we have being going by."

"Unh. That makes it rough, and there's not any way that I can give you a cost without having something to go by. I don't know what you want in the interior or whether you want brick or something else on the exterior, and those are things that I'll have to know before I can tell you what it's going to cost. Can I take your Granddaddy's sketch with me? If you'll come to my office tomorrow and tell me what you want in this house, maybe I can complete the drawing and come up with something for you. Can you do that?"

"Yes sir, I'll be there. Just tell me when."

"How about nine o'clock?"

"That sounds good. I'll be there."

"All right now, your Dad was telling me about your man, Hal, and I'd like to talk to him. Can you call him down?"

"Hal, this is Bob Martin. He owns the Bob Martin Construction Company, and he would like to talk to you. Bob, this is Hal Long. I'm going to leave you two to talk, and holler when you're through.

Jimmy left Hal with Bob, and he went down to the boathouse. He laid down on his bed while he waited on them to get through talking and wrestled with some thoughts he had in his mind. Waiting to hear from Randy was foremost, but Shirley was on his mind, too. *I wonder if Analisa is ever going to warm up to me, or should I devote my attention to Shirley? Shirley must like me or she wouldn't have called, and Analisa was pretty cool toward me when I saw her at the Burger and Shake the other night.* He laid there thinking until he nearly dozed off, but before he got totally asleep, he heard Hal call him.

He jumped up and went up to the house where Bob and Hal were. Bob was the first to speak. "Jimmy, I'm going to take Hal away from you. He has agreed to come to work for us on a trial basis. Hal, do you want to tell Jimmy what we discussed?"

"Jimmy, as Bob said, I'm going to work for him on a trial basis, and guess what I'll be doing."

"What?"

"Since he is going to finish this place for you, he says that he will assign me a job here, so I can work on your house while I'm on trial."

"Really? That's great. Bob, thank you so much."

"I should thank you. Hal looks as if he's just the person we need. He said he wanted to finish what he was doing up here, and that he should be through by Saturday. He's going to be here Tuesday, but he'll be working for me then."

"That's wonderful. Now, Hal, we can find you a place to live. I've already talked to some people, and I think it will work out."

"Thank you, Jimmy. I don't know what I'd do without you."

Bob said, "I've got to go, fellows. Jim, it was good to meet you, and Hal, I'll see you Tuesday."

"Okay, Bob. Bye."

After Bob left, Jimmy and Hal went back up on the roof, but didn't get too much done before they heard another car coming in. They both looked at it when it got into sight, but neither of them recognized it. The driver got out, and Hal asked Jimmy if he knew who it was, and he didn't, so he got down off the roof. When he got close to the man, he recognized him. Before even speaking, he turned around and yelled, "Hal, come here."

It was Randy, Hal's son. "How did you know where we were?" Jimmy asked.

"I called your parents' and your Mom gave me the directions. I'm sorry I didn't get back to you sooner, but I had a lot of thinking to do."

About that time, Hal reached them. "Hello, Dad," Randy said.

"Randy? Boy, am I glad to see you," and they grabbed each other and hugged for what seemed like forever. "How did you know I was here?"

"Our friend, Jimmy, here called me yesterday and said we needed to talk. We had lunch together, and he told me about you. I was unsure at first, but after thinking about it, I wanted to see you, and I would hope that maybe we can catch up on some things that we missed by being apart for so long. Would you like to go get some lunch?"

"I really would. Jimmy, would you like to go?"

"You two go on, and I'll see you both later. I might go on back to Chattanooga; I have several things to do. Hal, I might stay down there tonight, so if I don't get back, I'll see you in the morning, and Hal, tell Randy what else happened this morning. This has been a great, great day."

On his way down highway twenty-seven, he thought, *how could this day get any better? Hal got a job and a Son, and I found someone to finish my house without me having to work on it every day. Lord, I'm very grateful. Thank you, and thank you for all your blessings. Now, Lord, please help me work things out regarding Analisa and Shirley. I like them both and want to do what you want me to, so please help me. These things I ask you in Jesus' name.*

After he got home, he decided to return Shirley's call. When she answered, he said, "Hi Shirl. What are you doing?"

"Nothing, how about you?"

"I just got home. Sorry I didn't get back to you last night, but it was late when I got in, and I left early this morning. What did you need?"

"I didn't need anything. I just wanted to talk to you and thought we might go get that ice cream we talked about. What are you doing tonight?"

He said, "I'm supposed to go back to the lake. A lot is happening up there that has to be finished by Saturday, and I'm swamped."

"So you can't do anything tonight, either?"

"I'm sorry. It's just that there is so much going on right now. I'm going to start at Shepherd Apparel in about a week, and I can't leave things undone at the house."

Sounding a little peeved, she said, "Well, when you get all your projects caught up, give me a call, will you?"

"I sure will. I'm sorry, Shirl."

"I'll talk to you later, Jimmy. Bye."

As he was driving to the lake the next morning, he thought, *Yesterday was such a good day, I wonder what's going to happen today. I hope today is good as well.* The pair got off to a good start after they had their breakfast, and they were down to the last few sheets, when once again, they heard a car coming. Jimmy couldn't believe his eyes. It was Analisa.

He scrambled down the ladder and nearly ran to her and said, "Hey, Gal. This is a pleasant surprise. What are you doing up here?"

"I have to go to the doctor this afternoon, and I asked Charlotte if I could take the day off. I thought I would have time to come up here first. I need to talk to you, Jimmy."

"What about?"

She stopped, looked around, cleared her throat, and finally said, "I didn't know this would be so hard."

Jimmy said, "Just take it easy, and tell me what you want to talk to me about."

"Jimmy, Johnny is dying to see his Uncle Jim"

"What about Johnny's Mother? Is she dying to see his Uncle Jim too?"

She broke into a small smile when he asked that and said, "I over reacted when he broke his collarbone, and I'm sorry. I should have known you wouldn't do anything on purpose that would hurt him. He told me that you were trying to show him some of the things his Dad felt and liked. I guess I just never dreamed that he would get into a race car and ride around the track at a high speed, but when thinking about it, that sounds just like something his Dad would do. Slapping you was about the worst thing I could have done, and I've been miserable ever since it happened. I hope you'll forgive me. What can I do to make up for it?"

"You didn't answer my question. "Was Johnny's Mother dying to see me too?"

She answered, "I don't know about dying, but I've missed you, and yes, I desperately wanted to see you."

"I've missed you too, now, when can I see Johnny?"

"What about Saturday?"

"I'll be up here Saturday. We're going to try and finish the framing this weekend because I have a contractor coming in Monday to start doing the rest of the house. Why don't you come up here the way you did before?"

"Maybe we can. How about I bring us a picnic?"

"That sounds wonderful."

"I've got to go. I don't want to miss my doctor's appointment."

"Is something wrong?"

"No, it's just my regular checkup."

He walked her to the car, and they stopped at the door before she got in. He opened the door for her, and she put her arms around him and gave him a huge bear hug, and he hugged her back. Before she turned loose, she kissed him on the cheek, and when Hal looked down and saw it, he just shook his head.

"I'm glad you came up, and I appreciate you telling me how you feel. I'm anxious to start seeing you two on a regular basis again, and by the way; I'm starting work at Shepherd Apparel next week. I can't tell you how glad I am that you and Johnny are back."

"I'm glad, too. Call me. I've gotta go. See ya."

Jimmy picked up her hand and kissed it, and said, "Bye."

She started out the driveway and then stopped and rolled her window down. Smiling, she said, "I forgot to ask you, did you have a good time with Shirley the other night?" She rolled up the window and left, still smiling the whole time.

To say that Jimmy was in a state of euphoria after she left would be an understatement. He climbed back up the ladder and nailed plywood like never before. By the end of the day, they had only about a half-day's work left to do, and he wanted to knock off a little early so he could talk to Hal, one on one, instead of trying to make conversation while they worked. He told Hal, "So much happened yesterday that we didn't have much of a chance to talk, and I need to know some things, but first, are you and Randy going to be okay?"

"I hope so. I'm going over to his house for supper tomorrow night. He's going to drive up here to get me. Did you know he has a little girl?"

"No, I didn't know."

"Yep. That makes me a grandpa."

"That's wonderful. I know you all will become a close family. Now, here's something I need to know; the other day I went to see the people at the Housing Authority about getting you an apartment, and they said they didn't see any reason why you couldn't get one. Now that you have a job, you can afford one, but I was thinking last night that since you're going to be working up here for a while, you might want to keep staying in the boathouse until the job is finished. It would save you some money, and it would also let you save some to buy furniture and other things you are going to need. It's whatever you want to do; I don't care, but if you want to get an apartment, we need to go see the Housing Authority tomorrow because I can't go with you next week."

"Jimmy, does your offer to use your pickup still stand?"

"Yes, of course."

"Then, I think I would like to stay up here. With the pickup I can go to the store or out to eat or where ever else I might want to go, and besides, the boathouse is like home."

"Okay then; we're all set. Listen, I just had a thought; tomorrow, instead of Randy having to drive all the way up here, why don't you let me take you to his house as I go, and then he can bring you home."

"That will be fine, but I don't know how to get in touch with him to tell him."

"I know how to reach him. I'll call him tonight and tell him that's what we're going to do."

Some people were starting to get telephones in their cars, and Jimmy wished he had one as he drove to Chattanooga. He was anxious to talk to Analisa and thought he would see if he could go over there after dinner, but when he got home and called, there was no answer. After calling every half-hour without an answer, until nine o'clock, he finally gave up and wondered where she was.

The next morning he got up and left early, excited that they should finish the plywood by early afternoon. Still disappointed by not reaching Analisa the night before, he thought that maybe he could get back early enough to go see her and Johnny that afternoon, but he was in for another disappointment.

He and Hal finished covering the roof with plywood around lunchtime and cleaned up much of the cut offs and scrap lumber. They left the lake around two, and since it was so early, he took Hal to his house until time to go to Randy's. As soon as he got home, he called Analisa at work. "Hi, it's me. How're you doing?"

"I'm fine, but real busy. Can I call you back?"

"You don't have to do that. Just let me ask you one quick question; would you like to go out somewhere tonight?"

"Jimmy, I'd love to, but I already have plans. I'm sorry."

His heart sunk, and he said, "That's okay. Are you still coming to Sale Creek tomorrow?"

"Yes, I'm planning to."

"Great. I'll see you then."

After they hung up, the thought of her going out with someone else was eating him up. *Who could it be? I don't know of anyone she's ever gone out with except Johnny, and he's been gone for a long time now, so maybe she found someone at work. I need to find out.*

CHAPTER EIGHTEEN

At six o'clock, he delivered Hal to Randy's, and decided that he would go to the Burger and Shake and play for a while. Maybe Mary Ann would know who Analisa's going out with, but when he got there, Mary Ann had already left for the day. *Darn! I'm losing all the way around today.*

As he was unpacking his guitar, he casually asked, "Does anybody know if Analisa's going to be here?"

Bill said, "I think I heard that a friend of hers was coming in from out of town."

Trying not to show his desperation, he said, "I wonder where he's coming from."

"I think from Columbus, Georgia. Isn't that where your brother, Johnny, was stationed?

Not thinking about the friend being a woman, he said, "Yeah. He must be a friend of his."

They played and sang the songs they would be doing in the charity show, and they all agreed that there was more work to be done before they would be ready to go out in public. When they were through, Jimmy went home and watched TV in the den while Monty slept in his recliner. Mary Ann came in about ten o'clock, and Jimmy asked her, "Where have you been, Sis?"

"I've been at Analisa's staying with Johnny. She went out with a friend."

Determined not to show that he cared, he didn't pursue it any further, and he got up and went to his room to watch TV, and the whole time his stomach was in a knot.

Saturday was not starting out to be anything special the way he had hoped it would. He had been looking so forward to his visit from Analisa and Johnny, but his excitement was severely dampened by the thought of her going out with someone else. He was still excited about the prospect of seeing Johnny, but he wasn't sure about Analisa. The drive to Sale Creek would be the last time he would go up there to work, and he told the people at the restaurant when he stopped to get breakfast that he wouldn't be coming in anymore.

Hal was already there when he arrived and was working on the steps leading down from the deck. Jimmy joined him, and they talked as they worked. Jimmy asked, "How did it go last night?"

"It was wonderful. Randy has a beautiful family, and they made me feel right at home. His little girl, Belinda, took up with me, and we had a great time. We all agreed that we would stay in close touch. Randy brought me home, and we didn't get here until after midnight, and then he had to drive back to Chattanooga. I'll bet he's a tired puppy this morning.

"How was your night?" Jimmy said, "Nothing out of the ordinary. I went to the Burger and Shake and played some music, then, I went home and watched TV for a while."

Hal said, "I thought you might go over to Analisa's."

"Well, I wanted to, but she had already made other plans."

"She had a date, hunh? Well, that's too bad."

"Oh well, she and Johnny are supposed to come up here and bring a picnic after while, and we'll see what she says."

A little before noon they heard a car, and it was her and Johnny.

The second she stopped, Johnny was out of the car, running to see his Uncle Jim. "Hey, Uncle Jim, I sure am glad to see you."

"I'm glad to see you, too. Tell me what you've been doing. I see you've still got your arm in a sling."

"I have to keep it in the sling for two more weeks, and then I can get rid of it. What have you been doing; working on the house?"

"Yeah, and that's about all. I've missed seeing you and didn't have anything else to do but work."

"I know, but my Mom says she's not mad at you anymore, so we can do things together now."

"That's great. What do you think, Mom?"

"I think y'all can be buddies again. I'm sorry that I couldn't be with you last night, but I had this other thing that I had to do."

"That's alright. I can understand how a pretty girl like you is in demand by other guys. Maybe next time I can get to you before you plan another date."

"Another date? I didn't have another date. My friend, Amanda, was on her way to Virginia and stopped in Chattanooga to spend the night. Did you ever hear Johnny talk about his best buddy, Pat Shumate?"

"I think I did."

“Well, Amanda is his wife, and we became close friends when we were in Columbus. I don’t know what I would have done without her when Johnny died. No, I didn’t have a date.”

“That makes me feel better.”

“Why, were you jealous?

He blushed and didn’t answer.

“Well, were you?”

Still no answer; instead he said something to Johnny while the red left his face.

“Are you hungry?” she asked.

“I’m starved. What did you bring to eat?”

“Fried chicken and all the fixin’s.”

“Hal, this lady has got us all fixed up. Are you hungry?”

“Yep, I’m hungry.”

She spread the food on a cutoff piece of plywood, and they sat on a stack of roofing shingles while they ate. “Ana, this is great. Thanks for bringing it. Johnny, do you want some more?”

“Yes sir, I’ll get me some.”

After lunch, they walked around the house while Jimmy pointed out the different rooms and other features, and after that, Analisa said she had to go. Johnny asked, “Mom, can I stay with Uncle Jim?”

“Uncle Jim is busy, you go home with me.”

“Please, Mom,” and Jimmy said, “I don’t mind, if you don’t care. I’ll bring him home when I leave here.”

“Okay, if he won’t be in your way.”

He walked her to her car and opened the door for her. She got in, closed the door, and rolled the window down. “I like your house, and I can’t wait to see it when it’s finished. Thanks for letting Johnny stay with you this afternoon. I’ve got to go to the store and do some other things, and that will be a big help.”

“What are you doing tonight?” Then he smiled and said, “You don’t have a date do you?”

“One of these days, I might tell you yes when you ask me that.”

“I hope not.”

“How would y’all like to go to the Cracker Barrel?”

“I’d like that, and I know Johnny would.”

“Good, it’s a date.” He put his hand on her arm, and just as serious as he knew how, he said, “I’m glad you didn’t have a date last night, Ana.”

"Jim, there's no one that I want to date."

"Great, I may just keep you for myself." As before, he lifted her hand and kissed it, then patted her on her arm and said, "I'll see you later."

Hal had made a fire ring out of rocks and had built a fire to burn the cutoffs and other scraps, and he enlisted Johnny's help to keep the fire going. By the time everything was done that afternoon, they were all tired. Jimmy went down to the boathouse and gathered up everything he had taken down there in the way of sheets and towels and other things. When he got back up to the house, he asked Hal, "Do you want to take me home, and then bring the truck back."

Surprised, Hal said, "Yeah Boy, I'll take you." The three of them piled in the pickup, and Johnny laid his head on Jimmy's shoulder and went right to sleep. They went to Analisa's first, to drop Johnny off and then to Monty's. Jimmy told Hal before he left, "Take good care of old Betsy here. My Granddaddy left me this truck and I wouldn't take anything for it. Enjoy it like I have, and Hal, I want you to make me a promise. I want you to promise me that if you should ever get out of sorts and feel like you need to do something that you shouldn't, that you'll call me. Will you promise me that?"

"I promise, Jimmy. I don't know how to thank you for all you've done, and I won't let you down."

"I know you won't. Have a good day tomorrow and Labor Day and good luck on your new job. I'll be keeping check on you to see how you're doing, and I know you're going to do great. I'll see you later."

As soon as he got into the house he called Analisa. "Hello."

"What are you doing?"

"Nothing. I just laid down for a few minutes, and Johnny's down the street, playing. What are you doing?"

"I just got home. Do you still want to go to the Cracker Barrel?"

"Yeah, and when I told Johnny, he said, "Oh Boy."

"Is seven o'clock alright?"

"Perfect."

"I'll see you then. Bye."

They had a great dinner, and afterwards they went to Analisa's. Johnny talked non-stop, and Jimmy and Analisa could hardly talk at all. It was close to nine when they got home, and Analisa made Johnny go up and get his PJ's on soon after they got there, and Jimmy was thankful for that because he wanted to talk seriously to Johnny's Mom.

At nine-thirty, she told Johnny that it was bedtime, and he didn't argue. He was tired from all the work Hal had him do at the lake that afternoon. "Would you like for me to make a pot of coffee." She asked.

"It's a little late for coffee, but I could sure use some."

"Okay. It won't take but a few minutes. Come in the kitchen with me," and he got up and went with her.

They talked while the coffee brewed, and when it was finished, she poured each one of them a mug, and they went into the living room. She sat down on the sofa, and Jimmy sat down beside her. A college football game was on TV, and they watched it for a little while, and then, out of the blue, Jimmy reached over and took her free hand and asked her, "Ana, do you think this is going anywhere?"

"Is what going anywhere?"

"This; you and me. Is this as far as it's going, or do you think it might develop into something more?"

She answered with a question; "What do you want to happen?"

"Ana, when we were in high school and college, and you were dating my brother, I used to get so aggravated with you because Johnny never wanted to do anything except be with you, and now, I know how he felt. You know, it might not be supposed to happen, since you're my sister-in-law, now, but we're both single and neither one of us is tied to anyone, so we should be able to do whatever we want to do. I guess what I'm clumsily trying to say is, I'm crazy about you, and I'd like for us to become a dating couple. Any time that I'm not with you, I miss you. Those days, after Johnny got hurt, and you wouldn't let me come around were pure torture. I don't want to lose you, and I hope you feel the same way."

"Wow! I wasn't expecting that, but yes, I feel the same way," and they kissed; not a smack, but a full-fledged kiss. After the kiss, they sat back a little and looked at each other, and then they kissed again. "You know, that night, when you took Shirley out, I thought I would die. I don't think I slept over an hour that night, I was so torn up. Now, let me ask you something; how far do you want this to go?"

"I want it to go just as far as it can go. How about you?"

"I feel the same way," and she leaned over and kissed him again, but not as passionately as the first time.

Jimmy said, smiling, "Now that we've got that settled, what do we do now?"

Analisa was smiling by that time, and she said, “I don’t know, but there’s one thing I’m glad of.”

“What’s that?”

“I’m glad you won’t be going out with Shirley again.”

He took his forefinger and tapped her lightly on her nose, and said, “I’m glad we did this, aren’t you?”

She replied, “I never would have dreamed it would happen, but yes, I’m glad.”

“It’s getting late, and I guess I had better go. Do you want to come over and lay around the pool tomorrow afternoon? Dad always closes it after Labor Day and that’s Monday, so if we’re going to take advantage of it, we’ll have to do it tomorrow and Monday.”

“What time?”

“Well, we usually just fix a sandwich or something when we get home from Church, and you’re welcome to come for that. If not, just come whenever you want to.”

She and Johnny got there around two o’clock, and the first thing Johnny wanted to do was to go in the pool with his Uncle Jim. He loved his grandparents dearly, but there was just something about his Uncle Jim that was special. They splashed and dunked each other, and played until Jimmy was tired, and he said, “You’ve about worn me out, Big Guy. I’m going to get out and rest a while.”

Johnny answered, “What’s the matter? Are you a sissy?”

“Let me rest a minute, and I’ll show you who’s a sissy.”

It went on like that for most of the afternoon, and finally, Johnny tired out and got out of the water and laid down on a chaise lounge.

Analisa, Jimmy, Joan, and Monty were all relaxed in lounges, when Analisa asked Jimmy, “Is it Tuesday when you start to work?”

And before he could answer, Monty said, “Yep. He’s starting Tuesday. His vacation’s over.”

They laid there a while longer and Joan threw out a question to anyone that was listening, “Did you notice that the Rogers’ house next door is for sale?”

Jimmy immediately perked up. “Really? That’s a nice house. I wonder what they’re asking for it.”

Monty said, “I don’t know, but it will probably be a good deal for someone. Matt has been transferred to upstate New York, and the cost of living up there is a lot higher than it is down here, so I’m sure he will want to sell it as soon as possible in order to not have two house payments. Jimmy, you might want to think about buying it."

"Dad, I couldn't buy it even if I wanted to. I don't have the money to buy a house like that."

"Well, remember, you're going to be working."

"I know, but you haven't told me what I'll be making."

"Tell you what. I think Matt's already gone, but you can call Laura, and she can show you the house. Then, if you're interested, maybe I can help you make the deal."

"Are you serious?"

"I'm as serious as a heart attack. Why don't you go inside and call her?"

He called and Laura said it would be fine for them to come over then, so the five of them got up to go. Joan and Analisa put on a cover-up, and Jimmy and Monty put on shirts, and they went next door.

Everybody but Analisa had been in the house several times, but had not noticed it the way one would notice it if interested in owning it.

The house was large, and it was built around the same time as Monty's. The downstairs had an up-dated kitchen, dining room, laundry room, master bedroom, two baths, and a large den with a twelve-foot sliding door opening out to the pool. The upstairs contained four bedrooms and three baths. The pool was about the same size as Monty's, and it had a two-car attached garage.

After they had seen it all, they thanked Laura for showing it to them and went back to Monty's.

When they had all resumed their original places, Monty asked, "Jimmy, what did you think about the house?"

"I loved it, but Dad, I don't see how I could swing something like that."

"You might be surprised. We'll talk about it later."

Then, Jimmy asked Analisa, "Did you like it Ana?"

"Oh yeah, I loved it."

"Do you think you could live in a house like that?"

"You know I could, and she smiled when she said it."

She and Jimmy looked at each other during the questions and answers, and Monty and Joan also looked at each other, but with more seriousness.

In a little bit, they decided it was time to go in, so they got up, and

Jimmy suggested that they go somewhere to eat, but Analisa said she didn't bring any clothes, so she couldn't. He offered to take her home to change, but she said she was tired and would just drive home and stay.

He walked her to her car, but didn't kiss her goodbye. He didn't know if he should kiss Johnny's Mom in front of him, so he didn't. They did make a date for the next day, however, because it was going to be Labor Day, and cooking burgers and dogs was a tradition with Monty's family.

She left for home, and Jimmy went into the house and changed out of his swimsuit into some clothes. Monty asked them if they would like to go to the Greystone to eat, and they both said "Yes."

While they were eating, Monty wanted to talk about the Rogers' house, and when they left, Jimmy was pretty sure that he was going to buy a house. After they got home and were seated before the TV in the den, he said, "Mom, Dad, I want to tell you something."

"Joan asked, "What is it, Darling?"

Jimmy continued, "I don't know if you've noticed or not, but Analisa and Johnny and I have been spending a lot of time together. Well, Analisa and I are crazy about each other, and last night, we decided that we would start dating. I hope you all are okay with it, because I'm very happy right now."

"I think that's wonderful, Jimmy. Do you all have any plans?"

"Not yet, Dad. We only decided to start dating last night, but I've got to tell you; I could spend my life with her."

Joan piped in, "Darling, are you sure you're ready to take on a ready-made family?"

"Mom, she's already family, and Johnny has my blood in him. Next to his Mother, he has more of my blood in him than anybody else's, and he loves me."

Monty said, "Well, whatever happens, I want you to be happy, and if you two decide you want to get married, I can't think of anyone I would rather have as a daughter-in-law than Analisa." Then, joking, he asked, "Now, since she's already our daughter-in-law, if you two get married, what will she be to us? Double daughter-in-law?"

They watched the ball game until they got sleepy, and Jimmy got up and went upstairs. He looked at his watch and decided it wasn't too late, so he called Analisa. "Hello."

"Are you in bed?"

"No, just watching TV. What are you doing?"

"We went to the Greystone and then came back here. Ana, I told Mom and Dad about us, and they're okay with it. Dad even went so far as to say that if we ever decided to get married, that he couldn't think of anybody else that he would rather have as a daughter-in-law than you. How about that?"

"I'll keep that in mind."

"You're a wise-guy; did you know that?"

"When do you want me to come over tomorrow?"

"Whenever you all get up and get ready. Since tomorrow's the last day of freedom, we need to make every minute count."

"Okay, I'll be there around eleven."

As an afterthought, Jimmy said, "Listen, sit tight, and I'll come get you. I might want to come to your place when we leave here tomorrow night. Will that be alright?"

"That'll be just about perfect."

Labor Day was a fun time. Not only did Analisa and Johnny come, but so did Liz, Ben, Sue, Bobby and his girlfriend, Marilyn, and Bill, Mary Ann's boyfriend. Everyone had a good time, and Monty out did himself on the burgers and dogs. The pool area looked like a picture of seals lying on the beach after stuffing themselves. Everybody had eaten so much, they just wanted to lie down and take a nap.

Around six o'clock Liz and Ben said they were leaving, and soon after, Bobby and Marilyn left. In a little bit, Jimmy asked Analisa, "Are you hungry?"

"Are you kidding? No, I'm not."

"Well, I am. Let's go get a milkshake. Johnny and I can get one, and you can sit with us."

"Okay. A milkshake does sound pretty good. Let's go."

They told the others they were leaving, and Monty said, "Are you riding with me in the morning, or are you going to drive?"

"I'll drive. What time do I need to be there?"

"Eight o'clock. Come to my office, and I'll get you started."

"Okay. Good night."

CHAPTER NINETEEN

Jimmy had a few butterflies when he walked in the front entrance to Shepherd Apparel, but probably not as many as he would have if he were to be starting a new job at another company. He already knew most of the people, and that made his first day a little easier.

Driving, one behind the other, he and Monty arrived at the same time and walked in together. At Monty's suggestion, they went to the break room to get a cup of coffee before going to his office to begin work.

Once seated, Monty started out by saying, "Son, you can't imagine how glad I am that you're finally here. I've dreamed of this day for a long time, and I hope that one day you'll become as *gung-ho* about Shepherd Apparel as I am because at some point, all this will be yours and Mary Ann's."

"Dad, as you know, for a long time I was hesitant about coming to work here, but now, I'm really anxious to *get my feet wet* in the clothing business."

"That's good. Now, do to your starting so late in your life I'm still going to train you into every aspect of the business, but at times, it might seem to be backwards to you. Dad started me the same way your Granddaddy and Great Granddaddy started them; by beginning with the very first steps in manufacturing clothing. I started in the cutting room; spreading cloth. Then, I was moved to the pattern department to learn how to make patterns, and so forth. In your case, I'm going to by-pass those jobs for you and start you off in sales. Now, that's not to say that you won't have to learn those other jobs, but they'll have to be done at times when you're not out selling.

"I think I told you a few days ago that I'm going to depend on you to develop the country of Italy, and that's still my plan, but you've got to learn what to do in order to successfully develop it. The New York Fall Market will be the first full week in November, and there will be a whole lot of work that needs to be done to get ready for it, and I want you to be involved.

"I had another thought, the other day, and that's the *Fin* line. I think I'm going to turn that account over to you. You may have heard me talk about it before, but the *Fin* trademark is owned by All Conference Sports, and their President and CEO is a fellow by the name of David

Brownlee. David is a former All-American football player, and he loves sports figures. When he found out that I made All-Conference at Tennessee Tech, our getting his business was made much easier. I think with your personality and by you being an All-Conference football player and an All-American baseball player that you're going to wow him. I think you and I will make a trip out there next week so you can meet him. *Fin* is one of our most important brands, and I want to keep it that way, and I think you're just the one to do it.

"Even though you're not going to have to work in cutting and those other departments, I want you to at least get an idea of what they do, so today, I want you to spend a couple of hours in each one of them to get a small glimpse of what goes on. I'll have the head of each department take you under their wing and show you around.

"Tomorrow, when you come in, you'll go to the sales department and work with Jeff Ellis. He will be coordinating styles with the sample department, so you should be able to learn quite a bit there. Any questions?"

"No sir. I'll do my best, Dad."

"I know you will."

Monty called the Human Resources Manager, and when he got to his office, he told him, "Sam, this is my son, Jimmy. Jimmy's going to be working with us, and I'd like for you to take him with you and do whatever you have to do to sign him up as a new employee. When you're through, how about calling Charlie Owens in cutting, and turn him over to him. I'll call Charlie and tell him to be expecting to hear from you, okay?"

"Yes sir. I'll take care of it."

Human Resources was located in an area where the employees entered when coming to work, away from the offices. It was necessary to pass by the computer department when going from the office to the HR department, and when they passed it, Jimmy looked for Analisa, but didn't see her.

He spent a couple of hours in cutting and then moved to patterns. From there, he went to the dye house, and finally the shipping department. Feeling that he had learned something in each department, he was glad the day was over, and he was ready to talk to Analisa. Going to the computer department at five o'clock, he caught up with her as she was leaving.

She asked, “How was your day?”

“Good; I spent time in nearly every department, and I think I will go to sales tomorrow.”

“Did you enjoy it?”

“Yeah, it was good. Are you coming over tonight?”

“Do you want me to?”

“Of course. I always want you to come.”

“Well, maybe for a little while. Dad has got so much for me to do and learn, I’m going to have to have all my wits, just to keep up. I’m going to Seattle with him next week to meet the CEO of All Conference Sports. He said he’s going to turn that account over to me.”

“That’s great; they’re an important account. You know what? I’m glad you’re working here because I can see you occasionally. Well, I’ve got to go get Johnny. Come over anytime you want to.”

“I’ll give you all time to eat. I promised Mom I would eat there tonight or else I would take you all out, but I’ll see you before it gets late.”

At dinner, Monty told Jimmy, “Jonco Aviation called from Greensboro this afternoon and said the MD-11 is finished and ready to pick up. I’m going over there tomorrow. Do you want to go with me?”

“You bet I do. I can’t wait to ride in that jewel.”

“Did you think any more about the Rogers’ house?”

“Yes sir, I did, but I don’t understand how I can swing it. You said you would help work it out, and I’m sure you can, but I don’t understand how.”

“Well, do you want it?”

“More than anything.”

“Well then, go in there and call Laura, and tell her you’ll take it, and tell her that we will see her Wednesday and sign the Offer to Purchase papers and give her some earnest money. Also, ask her if she’s going to leave any of the furniture. You’re going to have to get some, you know.”

“I know. Thank you, Dad. I’m still not sure how we’re going to work it out, but I’m trusting you to do it. I love you, Dad.”

After the dishes were done, with Jimmy’s help, and Monty was settled and nearly asleep in his recliner, Jimmy told Joan, “I’m going to Analisa’s for a little while. I won’t be gone long.”

“Okay, Darling.”

On the way, he thought and prayed, *How good can a day get? First, I go to work for a billion dollar company that will be mine someday, and tonight, I bought a house. Thank you, Lord, and Lord, please help Analisa and me to do right in your sight. I love her, Lord, and I think she loves me, so if you will, please let it work out for us to get married sometime. Thank you again, Lord, and thank you for all your other blessings.*

When he pulled up to Analisa's, he was all smiles. He rang the doorbell, and when she answered it, he picked her up and swung her around and said, "You won't believe what just happened."

Her eyes sparkling, she asked, "What happened?"

"I just bought a house. Can you believe that?"

"The Rogers' house?"

"Yeah, I called Laura and told her I'd take it, and I would be over Wednesday to sign some papers and give her some money."

"That's wonderful, Jimmy, but why Wednesday. Why don't you go tomorrow?"

"Because Dad and I are going to North Carolina to pick up the MD-11 tomorrow. I can't believe all these good things are happening."

"I'm excited for you. I sure hope I will fit into some of these good-times."

"Ana, you're going to be a part of all of them if you want to be."

"What did you say?"

"I said that you're going to be a part of all the good things that are happening if you want to be a part."

"I look at you and Johnny as if you two are a part of me, and I want you to share all these things with me."

"Jimmy, I appreciate all that, but what happens if you get mad at me sometime and don't want me around anymore?"

"Are you serious? That would never happen."

"It could. We're both single and not tied to each other, so what would keep you from moving on to a different crowd where you would be free to live a single guy's life? It's different for me; I have a child, so it would be much harder for me to get out in the single scene."

"What are you saying, Ana? Don't you want to be a part of these good things?"

"Of course I do. I'm just afraid to get too involved in them for the reasons I said."

"Can I ask you a very serious question?"

"Yes, you can."

"Ana, do you think you could love another Shepherd?"

"Man, you just cut right to it, don't you?

"Well, what's your answer? Do you think you could?"

"You know what, Jimmy? I think I could.

"You think? You're not sure?"

"Yeah, I'm sure. I could. Why are you asking the question?"

"Because I want to say something, and I needed to know that answer first."

"What is it that you want to say?"

"Before I answer, let me ask you another question; Ana, do you love me?"

"You know, I never thought about it until that couple of weeks when I kept you away from us. Those were the most miserable days I could remember, and I realized then that I must love you, or else I wouldn't feel so bad. The answer is YES, I love you. Do you love me?"

"You bet I do. I love you more than anything."

"Well, we both love each other, so what do we do now, move in together?"

"You know better than that. I could never live with someone without being married to them, and I hope that you couldn't either."

"Let me ask you this," and he knelt down to one knee and said, "Analisa, I love you so much. Will you marry me?"

Tears came to her eyes, and she said, "YES, YES, I'll marry you. I really do love you, Jimmy."

As soon as he stood up, they hugged and kissed, and Jimmy asked, "Why don't we wake Johnny up and tell him?"

"He'll never go back to sleep if we wake him up and tell him something like that. Come over tomorrow night and we'll tell him together."

"Okay, that's probably better. When are we going to buy you a ring?"

"Whenever you say. We can wait 'til the weekend if you want to."

"Are there any nice jewelry stores at Hamilton Place?"

"I think so, but I'm not sure."

"We can decide later. The main thing is that we are going to get married."

They sat on the sofa after the proposal and talked, and during the conversation Jimmy asked, “Ana, can I ask you something? It’s something that’s bothered me for a long time.”

“Yeah, you can ask me anything, anytime.”

“Do you remember that first time when I came to the Burger and Shake, when you all were playing?”

“Yes, I remember, why?”

“Well, everybody back there was so friendly except you, and you acted as if I was a monster or something. Why did you act like that?”

“It’s hard to explain, and I’m over it now, but when you walked in, that was the first time I had seen you in a long time. You look so much like Johnny; he was gone and you weren’t, and I think there was a touch of resentment there. I’m sorry. I didn’t mean to hurt your feelings.”

“It’s okay; I have just been wondering since that night. Do you still resent me?”

“Oh no, I love you. Now, when are we going to tell your Mother and Daddy about us?”

“I’d like to wait until at least Wednesday night. Dad is so excited about getting his new plane tomorrow; I hate to distract him from his excitement. Is that alright with you?”

“Yeah, that’s fine. I think I’ll go ahead and call my Dad and tell him. He’ll be so happy. He thinks the world of you.”

****

Eleven o’clock was the time when Monty chose to takeoff for Greensboro. The veteran crew that had been with Shepherd Apparel so long was going, along with a pilot and co-pilot that Monty had interviewed for the MD-11 job. Although the flying time from Greensboro to Chattanooga was just a little over an hour, Chuck, his longtime pilot felt that that would be enough to tell how they would handle the new plane.

When they arrived at Jonco Aviation, they flew over the MD-11 as they approached the airstrip, and it was a sight to behold. In addition to customizing the interior, Monty had them paint and letter the plane like the 707, and unless told that it had some age on it, one would think it was new. It was so beautiful.

None of them knew what to expect before they saw the interior, but they were blown away when the door opened, and they went inside. No one would have believed that the Sheik's taste could be improved on, on the 707, but Monty's taste on the MD-11 rivaled it hands down.

When he stepped inside, his face just beamed. Chuck Jacobs compared his mood to that of becoming a new father. After the Jonco rep finished showing them the different features on the plane, Monty told his Gulfstream pilots they could go on back to Chattanooga, and he went inside and signed whatever papers he had to sign. When he finished that, they boarded and took off. Even though he had ridden in the plane in Dallas before he bought it, he could swear that it rode much better since it was fixed up, He couldn't keep his seat after they took off. He was up and checking out everything about the plane. The master bedroom was something; it was long and wide and tastefully appointed the way a five-star hotel would be.

He couldn't wait to get to Chattanooga to show it to Joan. He told Jimmy to call and see if Charlotte would let Analisa off early, so she could go see it, too. When they landed, Monty didn't want to get off, and said he was going to stay on board until Joan and Analisa got there. Of course, there was nothing to eat on board, but when he checked out the galley, he found enough equipment to cook a full meal, and enough refrigeration equipment to keep a lot of food for several days.

Joan arrived before Analisa, and she was just as excited as Monty. The first thing she said was something about taking a trip somewhere. Analisa got there soon after Joan, and she could hardly believe what she was seeing. She caught Jimmy with his back to the others and whispered, maybe we can go somewhere in it sometime, and he smiled and nodded.

After a while, Monty said, "Listen, it's close to dinner time. Would you all like to go somewhere and get something to eat?"

Joan and Jimmy said they would, but Analisa said, "I'm afraid I can't. I've got to pick up Johnny."

"Why don't you go get him and meet us?"

"I can do that. Where are you going?"

"How about the Town and Country?"

"That sounds good. I'll go get him and see you there as soon as I can get there."

Jimmy said, "I'll go with you."

On the way, Jimmy asked, "Are we still going to tell Johnny about us tonight?"

"I think we will. Don't you think we should?"

"Yeah, I just wouldn't want it to get back to Mom and Dad before we tell them. Just make sure he doesn't call them. Do you think he'll beat us to the draw tomorrow night before we can tell them?"

"I'll make sure he doesn't."

They all had a nice dinner, and afterwards, Joan and Monty went home while Jimmy and Analisa went to her place. As it worked out, the four people drove four cars. When Analisa and Jimmy got inside, Analisa offered to fix a pot coffee which Jimmy readily accepted. While they waited on it to get ready, Analisa went into her bedroom and changed out of her uncomfortable work clothes into a pair of jeans and a sweatshirt, and then returned to the living room and sat down on the sofa next to Jimmy.

Johnny had turned on the TV and was watching it when Jimmy said, "Johnny, could we turn that down? I want to talk to you."

Johnny, looking puzzled at that, got up and turned the TV down. "What do you want to talk to me about, Uncle Jim?"

"Well, Johnny, you know I've been spending a lot of time with you and your Mom, and I think you know how much I love you both, don't you?"

"Yes sir, and we love you, too."

"You know, when people love each other, they want to be together, and that's what your Mom and I want to do. Johnny, would you mind if I married your Mom?"

"You want to marry my Mom? Wow! No! I wouldn't mind at all. Does that mean you'll be coming here to live?"

"I'll be moving in with you all, but not here. You see, I'm getting ready to buy a house and the three of us will move there, after your Mom and I are married."

"Will you be my Dad?"

"I'll be what's called your step-dad, and I'll love you just like you're my real son. We can do lots of things together, and it'll be fun. Now, there's something I have to ask you to do for me. Your Mom and I haven't told my Mom and Dad about us getting married yet, and we're going to tell them tomorrow night. I want you to promise me that you won't say anything about it until after I tell them. Will you promise me that?"

"I promise."

Johnny turned and walked away, and as he left them, Jimmy heard him say to himself, "Oh Boy, I'm getting a Dad. Now I can be like all the other kids," and it broke his heart to think that Johnny felt like he wasn't like the other kids because he didn't have a Daddy.

Jimmy stayed for a few more minutes and then said he had to go. He hugged Johnny and kissed Analisa goodnight and left to go home.

As he was having coffee and a piece of toast the next morning, he was joined by Monty. Jimmy asked what he would be doing that day and was told that he would be working with Jeff Ellis in the sales department.

Then, Monty asked, "Son, are you still sure you want to buy the Rogers' house? If you are, we need to go to the bank today and arrange financing. I'll go with you."

"Dad, I really appreciate it, but what will I do when they ask me to fill out a credit application. I don't even know what I'm making."

"Well, I'll be darned. I never did tell you, did I?"

"No sir, you didn't."

When Monty told him what his salary was going to be, he nearly fell over because he had no idea that he would be making that much. He was just going to trust his Dad to take care of him, and he did.

They finished their breakfast at the same time and left for work at the same time. Monty walked him back to Jeff Ellis' office and turned him over to Jeff. He said, "I'll call you when I get that appointment set up."

"Okay, Dad. Thanks."

While Jeff was going over some of the styles, part of Jimmy was thinking, *Dad didn't have to pay me what he's paying me, so I'm going to prove to him that I'm worth every penny of it. I'm going to be the best representative this company has ever had,* and then he settled in and concentrated on everything Jeff told him.

At eleven-thirty Monty called. "Jimmy, we have an appointment with the bank at one o'clock. Why don't you and I have lunch together, and then we can go to the bank from the restaurant?"

"Okay, Dad. That sounds good."

"Be at my office at ten 'til twelve, and we'll take my car."

"Okay, I'll see you in a few minutes."

Jimmy was very impressed at the bank by the clout his Dad had. He must have told them what he wanted over the phone because they had everything ready when they got there. They didn't even ask him to fill out a credit report. They gave him a form and told him to take it home and fill it out and bring it back later. They did have him sign a note for the money he was getting then to be used for the earnest money, and Monty signed it as well as co-signer. Jimmy thought, *so this is what he meant when he said we could work it out. He's going to co-sign for my loan. Wow! Now I've really got to work hard. I can't let him down.*

On the way back to the office, they talked about the house, and Jimmy commented, "You know, Dad, with three of us having three houses next to each other, it's like having a Shepherd Compound,"

Monty laughed and said, "Yeah, I guess it is."

It was two-thirty when they got back to the office, and Jimmy went back to Jeff's, but before he started to work, he called Joan. "Hi Mom, what are you doing?"

She said, "You sound just like Liz. She always asks me that when she calls. What are you doing?"

"Just working. Listen, the reason I called is to ask you if you're cooking tonight, and if you are, do you think we could ask Analisa and Johnny to eat with us?"

"Absolutely. You don't ever have to ask that. They're always welcome. Tell them to come, by all means."

"Thanks, Mom. I'll see you later. Love you."

When he hung up, he asked Jeff if it would be alright if he went to the computer department for a minute, and, of course, Jeff said it would be. When he got over there, he went to Analisa's desk and asked her if she and Johnny would come to dinner, and that's when they would make the engagement announcement. Kidding, Jimmy said, "I'm afraid to tell them. I'm going to let you tell them."

"Yeah, right. I'm not going to tell them. If you're such a scaredey cat, then we just won't get married, Mister Macho."

"Alright, you talked me into it. I've got to get back to work. Try to be there around six or six-thirty. See you." He went back to Jeff's office and finished out the day there, staying until five o'clock.

Joan had prepared a feast of salad and spaghetti with meat balls because she knew that was Johnny's favorite. Monty, Jimmy, and Johnny stuffed themselves, but Joan and Analisa were more reserved, trying to watch their weight. After everybody was through eating, Joan started to get up and clear the table, but Jimmy said, "Mom, sit there a minute; I want to tell you something," Both she and Monty had strange looks on their faces, and Jimmy began.

"Mom, Dad, you all know I told you that Analisa and I are dating.

Well, we've decided that we love each other too much to just date, and we want to get married, so night before last, I proposed and she said "Yes". We haven't made any plans of any kind yet, and we hope we have your all's blessings."

Monty reached over the table and shook Jimmy's hand, then got up and walked over to Analisa and gave her a kiss on the forehead and a hug. He said, "I think that's wonderful. It's about time you two got together. Johnny, what do you think about this?"

"I think it's great. I'm going to be like the other kids now because I'm going to have a Daddy."

When he said that, Joan said, "Come here, Big Boy," and when he did, she gave him a big hug and kiss. Then, she did the same to Analisa and said, "I'm so glad, Analisa. I've prayed many times that Jimmy would find a good woman to marry, and now he has. I just didn't dream it would be someone so close. I'm absolutely thrilled, and oh yeah; he's going to have a nice house to move you into. That's perfect timing, isn't it?"

"It really is. I just hope he'll let me help him decorate it."

After the newsbreak, Joan and Analisa cleared the table and went into the kitchen to do the dishes, and the conversation was non-stop.

Jimmy and Monty went to the den and sat down. "Jimmy, you made a wise decision when you chose Analisa. She's a good woman. You know, we've known her for most of her life, and I couldn't be happier about you all getting married. When do you think it will be?"

"Dad, we haven't talked about it yet. If you noticed at dinner, I haven't even bought her a ring, and that's something I've got to do. I'm just grateful that you and Mom are okay with it because we didn't know how you'd feel because of her and Johnny. Then, we decided it was okay for her to remarry because it has been nine years since Johnny died. We're not going to rush it because I want to get my job moving, and I also want to get settled in my new house. I want her to have a say in furnishing it, but there's no rush in that either."

Changing the subject, Monty asked, "You haven't been at the company long enough to really tell, but do you have a feel of how you're going to like it?"

"I already like it a lot. I didn't have any idea that there are as many styles as there are, and Jeff says I haven't seen all of them yet. What I'm anxious to see is the David's Staff line. Anything with Granddaddy's name on it has got to be outstanding."

About that time Joan and Analisa came in and sat down. They talked for maybe an hour, and then, Analisa said she needed to go home. Johnny started to argue, but she was firm, and said she had to iron some things to wear the next day, so he hushed up and didn't say anything else. As she was leaving, both Monty and Joan reassured her of how happy they were that she and Jimmy were going to get married. Jimmy got up and walked her to her car, and when they got outside, he asked her, "Well, how do you think that went?"

"I think it went well. They both seem to be very happy about it."

"Are you happy?"

"Yes, I'm very happy, too. Are you?"

"I'm ecstatic. Look, tomorrow when we get off, let's go to Hamilton Place and see if we can find you a ring. Do you want to?"

"I'd like to, but what will I do about Johnny?"

"Wait here. I'll go in and ask Mom if she will get him." He went in and Joan said she would be glad to get him and feed him dinner. Running back outside, he said, "All set. I'll see you tomorrow. Give me a kiss before you leave." They kissed, and she and Johnny left, after Johnny hugged him."

After work the next day, they drove both cars to Hamilton Place, so Analisa wouldn't have to drive all the way back to Shepherd Apparel when they finished. They looked in two or three jewelry stores and finally found the ring they both agreed on. They bought it, but had to leave it to be sized for her finger. There were so many restaurants at Hamilton Place, they had a lot to choose from, and they decided to go Mexican. Having a hard time choosing, they both decided on the chicken chimichanga. After dinner, they shopped for a while, and then Analisa said she was tired and wanted to go home. Jimmy walked her to her car, kissed her goodnight, and watched her drive off.

Friday night was football night, and they went and watched Ashland beat Hixson fourteen to seven. On Saturday, they went to Hamilton Place and picked up Analisa's engagement ring, and then each one of them went home. Analisa had some things she needed to do in her apartment, and Jimmy wanted to wash and wax his car. After dinner, Jimmy went over to her place for a little while, but they were both tired, and he didn't stay long. On Sunday, neither one of them did anything except go to Church. Jimmy watched football, and Analisa slept most of the afternoon.

CHAPTER TWENTY

When Monty woke up from his nap, he asked, "Where's Mary Ann?"

"Joan said, "She's with Bill. Why?"

"Honey, I just had a dream. Actually it was more of a command than just a dream, and it involves Bill. See if you can find them and ask them to come over here just as soon as they can, will you?"

"They're probably at Bill's. I'll try there first," and sure enough, they were there. When Bill answered, Joan said, "Bill, may I speak to Mary Ann, please?" Monty didn't understand why she didn't just talk to Bill, but he learned a long time ago not to try and figure her out.

Mary Ann took the phone from Bill and said, "Hi Mom."

"Mary Ann, your Dad wanted me to call and ask Bill to come out here if he could. What are you all doing?"

"Just watching the ball game. What does Dad want with Bill?"

"I don't know. He just woke up from a nap a few minutes ago and said he had a dream that involves Bill, and wants to see him. Can you all come?"

Mary Ann held the phone down while she asked Bill and then said, "Mom, Bill said we could come. We'll be there in about a half-hour."

When Mary Ann and Bill arrived, Monty didn't beat around the bush; he asked them to sit down, and when they were seated, he began.

"Bill, since you and Mary Ann are dating, she has probably told you of some of the things I try to do for the Lord. I travel around the country, speaking at various meetings, and my most recent project was the Wauhatchie Farms ministry. I'm always keeping my eyes open for an opportunity to serve Him, and just a little while ago I had a dream that involves you. Rather, I had a command.

"Bill, I've heard Mary Ann talk about a fund-raiser that's coming up to raise money for your Church. After I heard about the fund-raiser, I rode by your Church one day, and Bill, it looks to me that it will take a lot more than a fund-raiser to get you a building suitable to worship in. Do you agree?"

"Yes sir. I wholeheartedly agree. Rather than a fund-raiser, we need a miracle."

"That's what I wanted to talk to you about. Do you think if you had better facilities, your congregation would grow?"

"I know it would, but we're held back because of the physical condition of the building. We have no air conditioning, for one thing, and in the summer, it's almost unbearable. We've lost a few families already due to that, and I'm afraid we're going to lose more, but at the same time, we're gaining new members faster than the ones were losing." Bill was thinking, *I wonder why he's asking these questions. It's strange since he's not a member of our Church.*

"Bill, this will probably shock you, but I believe God has told me to build you a Church."

"You're kidding. I don't know what to say, Mr. Shepherd except, praise the Lord."

"Now, here's the deal; I want this to be anonymous as far as your members are concerned, and I will be the one making the decisions on the building of it. Of course, you'll be involved, and I hope you will make many contributions in terms of suggestions, promotions, and other things.

"Now, if we put the new building where the parking lot is now, where will your members park?"

"I was thinking about that while you were talking. Several can park on the street, and I think I can get permission for a lot of them to park at the strip-mall next door. They're not open on Sunday morning, so there shouldn't be a problem.

"Do you own your present Church?"

"Yes sir."

"Is there a mortgage on it?"

"No sir, it's paid off."

"That's good. Bill, I'm going to call the contractor that does all of Shepherd Apparel's construction, and we'll come out to your Church one day this week. I want Bob to see the size of your property so we can decide how large to make the building. What I have in mind is to build the Church in your present parking lot, and when it's finished, tear down the old building, and make a parking lot of it.

"Now, I hope you will continue as pastor, and if you disagree with anything we do, I want you to tell me. I have some pretty definite ideas about the interior, and I hope you will like them."

"Can I ask, what kind of ideas do you have?"

"I would like theater seats rather than benches, for one, and I would also like two grand pianos."

Bill asked, "What about an organ?"

"No organ. Bill, I want the Church building to be very nice, but when people walk in I want there to be no mistake as to why they are there; I want them to feel God's presence, and when they leave, I hope they will take a worship experience with them. I know the Church already has a name, but with the new building, I suggest we give it a new one."

"What do think it should be?"

"I would like to see it called *CHRIST' COMMUNITY CHURCH.* Do you like it?"

"Yes sir, I do. Do you like it, Mary Ann?"

"Yeah, I like everything about this conversation. Dad, I'm so proud of you."

"Thanks, Honey, but it's not my idea."

Joan remained quiet during the entire conversation, and thought, *this man continues to amaze me. I wonder what he'll do next. Thank you, Lord, for letting me be a part of his life.*

"What do you think, Bill? Is this something that you think you would be interested in?"

"Mr. Shepherd, I'm speechless."

"The first rule is, you have to call me Monty. Is that a problem?"

"No sir, Monty."

When the conversation wore down, Joan asked, "Bill, would you like to stay for a sandwich?"

Before he could answer, Mary Ann said, "Yeah, he would like a sandwich, wouldn't you, Bill?"

Bill smiled and said, "Yes ma'am, I'd love a sandwich."

After they got on another subject, Monty turned on the ball game, and they watched it until Joan called them to come and eat.

Mary Ann and Bill left pretty soon after they ate, and later, as Monty and Jimmy were watching football, Monty said, "I'm going to try and set up a time for you and I to see David Brownlee on Tuesday."

"Good, I'm anxious to meet him."

"He's going to love you. He loves athletes."

"What are we going in, the new plane?"

"No, no, that's too expensive. We'll take the Gulfstream."

Jimmy spent Monday in the sales department, and at lunch he met

Analisa, and they went to a little neighborhood diner and had a hamburger. They had both missed several nights playing music in the back of the Burger and Shake, and they thought they would go that night, since it was Monday. Jimmy said he couldn't stay late because of his trip to Seattle early Tuesday morning. He told her he would pick her up and they would go to the B & S together.

At nine o'clock Jimmy said it was time for him to go, so he and Analisa put their guitars in the cases and left. When they got to Analisa's, Jimmy didn't get out of the car. He just kissed her and told her bye.

Wheels were up at six o'clock Tuesday morning, and Mike estimated that they would land in Seattle at one-ten that afternoon, Chattanooga time. An extra pilot was on board because if Mike flew the entire roundtrip, it would be too many hours to be within the law. Monty just wanted David and Jimmy to get acquainted, and whatever else David wanted to do, and he estimated that they would takeoff for the return trip to Chattanooga at two o'clock, Seattle time. That should put them back home around midnight.

When they first got to David's office, Monty introduced him to Jimmy. Then, he said, "David, I know how much you like all kinds of sports and athletes, and Jimmy won't tell you this, but I will. Jimmy made All-Conference twice in football at Tennessee Tech, and then in his senior year, he was named to the first team All-America in baseball."

David looked at Monty and asked, "Are you serious? I don't remember ever meeting anyone that had so many high honors. Congratulations, Jim."

"Thank you, sir."

"You'll have to tell me about some of your experiences sometime."

"I'll be happy to; anytime."

The time spent in Seattle was very pleasant, and it seemed the time went by too fast. Four hours was not a very long visit, considering the round trip took almost fifteen hours flying time, but it was a *get acquainted* trip, and it served its purpose. Jimmy liked David and David liked him, and Monty was satisfied that he was making the right move, putting Jimmy in charge of the account. On future trips, he would probably spend the night.

Mike had had plenty of food catered for the trip, and by the time they got back to Chattanooga, most of it was gone. Most of the trip was spent at thirty-three-thousand feet and the ride was super-smooth. Jimmy spent quite a bit of time napping, as did Monty.

At one point, when they were somewhere between North Platte and Kansas City, Monty looked over at Jimmy and said, "Son, what would you think about making some trips with me to speak at some of the FCA meetings? Your commitment to the Lord and your athletic background makes you a natural, and I guarantee you that you would be a hit, not to mention the influence you would have on them. Have you ever thought about doing something like that?"

"I've thought a little about maybe seeing if I could speak to Tech's club, but never serious enough to actually do it. Yeah, Dad, I'd like to go with you sometime."

"Good, I'm scheduled to go to Central Kentucky University in about two weeks. How about going with me to that?"

"Okay, I'll go, but I don't know what to say."

"I'll help you. Mainly, you just talk about the influence Jesus has had in your life, and some of the things He has done for you." David Brownlee will be pleased to know that you're going to speak at some FCA meetings. He used to be the head of the West Coast chapters.

Jimmy laid back in his seat and thought, *this is a completely new life from what I was doing. Instead of playing ball and playing night clubs, I've got a good job, I'm about to get married, and now, I'll be talking to young people about Jesus. God, you're truly a good God. Thank you for all these blessings.* Then, he dozed off and slept for about thirty minutes.

It was twelve-thirty when they got home, and even though it was late, Jimmy called Analisa. In a sleepy voice, she answered after four rings. "Hello."

"Hi, Sweetie. I hate to call so late, but I just had to talk to you. Are you doing okay?"

""Yeah, I'm fine. Did you have a good trip?"

"Yeah, it was a tiring trip. We have just this minute got home, and I wanted to call you. Go back to bed and try to go to sleep. I'll see you in the morning. I love you."

"I love you, too. Goodnight."

By the time they settled down from the flight and got to bed, it was a little after one- thirty. They were both really tired and went right to sleep. At four-fifteen, the phone rang. Monty got up and answered it. "Hello, Monty Shepherd."

On the other end, a voice said, "Hello, Monty. This is Myron Hober."

"Who?"

"Myron, in Tel Aviv. Monty, we have just been hit with a Palestinian rocket."

"What?"

"We have been hit with a rocket. The office and warehouse suffered considerable damage, but thank God, no one was hurt. We had closed for lunch, and there was nobody here when the rocket came. I thought I should call and let you know because I don't know what to do."

"What time is it there, Myron?"

"It's twelve-fifteen."

"In the afternoon?"

"Yes sir."

"Myron, I'll call my pilot, and we'll get there as soon as we can. Is there somewhere I can call you, and let you know when we'll be there?"

"Call this number," and he gave Monty two numbers; one to call first, and one to call in case there was no answer to the first one.

"I'll try to call you back within the next hour or two. Putting together a trip like this is a lot different than getting into your car and driving to the store, and it may take a little while, but I'll call when I know something. Is Tel Aviv damaged very much?"

"No, just our place and two more, next to us. You see, there are rocket attacks nearly every day. Sometimes there is only one rocket, and sometimes there are several, and many times, they don't hit anything; they just fall out in the desert. Unfortunately, this one hit us."

"Alright, Myron, let me get busy, and I'll call you back."

Monty looked up Chuck Jacobs number and dialed it. Amy answered, and Monty said, "Hi, Amy. This is Monty. Sorry to call so early, but I need to speak to Chuck, please."

Chuck groggily answered, and Monty told him about Myron's call, and said he needed to get ready ASAP to fly to Israel. He told him to get the MD-11 ready, as that's the one they would take. He told him to call Pat to co-pilot, and to call the new pilots they had on the trip from Greensboro. Flying non-stop was going to take over thirteen hours, one way, so they needed the extra men.

"Chuck, when you figure out when we can takeoff, let me know. I don't know if you have to gas up or not or what else you have to do. Be sure we have plenty of food. I'm going to take Jimmy with us, and he eats like a horse."

Chuck laughed and said, "It shouldn't take too long to get everything ready. I'll call you back."

"Do you have a sense of when we will leave? I have to call Myron back and tell him when we'll be there."

"Monty, off hand I'll say that we should be able to takeoff by seven-thirty or quarter of eight."

"Okay, let me know when you get closer to having everything ready."

When he hung up from Chuck, he went in and woke Jimmy up. "Jimmy, get up; our facility in Tel Aviv was hit by a rocket, and I've got to go over there, and I want you to go with me. Put two or three changes of clothes together in case you need them. I hope we can get everything done that we need to do early, or else we'll get caught up in the Sabbath, and that will cost us the whole weekend."

By that time, Joan was up, and she said she would go downstairs and fix some coffee. In about thirty minutes Chuck called back and said he hoped to be ready for takeoff at eight thirty. Monty then called Myron.

"Myron, we're going to be leaving Chattanooga in a little while, and we should be in Tel Aviv around five-thirty or six o'clock, Thursday morning, Tel Aviv time. We'll need to get a hotel when we get there

"Do you want me to make you a reservation?"

"That would be good. There will be six of us, so get three rooms with twin queens in each. Are you going to do that now?"

"Yes, I'll make your reservations when we hang up."

"Good. Tell the hotel that we'll be checking in around six a.m. when we get there. I'll call you back in about a half-hour to see where we'll be staying."

Jimmy wanted to call Analisa to tell her about their trip, but he wanted to wait as long as he could, so he wouldn't have to wake her up so early. After all, he had already interrupted her sleep one time that morning.

They took off at eight thirty-eight and Chuck estimated that they would land in Tel Aviv at nine-fifty-three, Chattanooga time, that night, but with the time difference, their arrival time would be five-fifty-three, Thursday morning, Tel Aviv time.

The MD-11 was really an enjoyable plane to ride in. Leveling off at thirty-six thousand feet was like floating on a silent cloud. The three huge engines were so quiet, and with every mile, Monty was happier with his purchase.

Ben-Gurion airport was relatively quiet when they landed at six-ten. Myron had made reservations for them at the Tel Aviv Hilton, so they took the limo to the hotel and checked in. As soon as they got to their room, Monty called Myron and told him they were there. They didn't eat breakfast on the plane, so he invited Myron to come eat with them.

After they finished eating, Monty and Jimmy got into Myron's car and rode with him to the burned out building that used to be Shepherd Global Apparel. It was sickening when they walked in. Myron had ordered and received thousands of dozens of Shepherd goods, and the rocket had destroyed most of it when it exploded.

Monty asked, "Myron, were you able to salvage anything in the office? Is your computer still usable?"

"Yeah, I think so. It looks okay, but I haven't tried it. The rocket knocked out the power."

"Did you have your inventory on it? I hope you did because it will be next to impossible to get an accurate inventory of this mess. Is there somewhere close by that we could take the computer to see if it works?"

"There's a building about a half-block down the street that's for rent. Maybe we could get permission to use it for a while."

"How about calling somebody about it, and if we can use the building, we need to rent a pickup or a van or something to carry the computer in. I'm anxious to see if we can salvage the inventory figures from it."

"Alright. Monty if you'll excuse me, I'll go and see if I can take care of those things. Are you and Jimmy going to stay here?"

"Yeah, we'll stay here and see if there's anything that can be saved. Have you found anything?"

"I found a few things. They're in that area over there," and he pointed to a section of the building that had relatively little damage. "The only thing is, any goods that weren't burned up were damaged by the water from the fire hoses. I feel like the insurance company is going to declare this a total loss."

"I agree, and that's why we need the inventory."

While Myron was gone, Yiska Goren, the office girl and two warehouse men came in to see if there was anything they could do. When

Monty told them he didn't know of anything at that point, they just stood around and talked. They were interested in just about anything American. Yiska was very attractive and looked to be about Jimmy's age, and Jimmy definitely noticed. She spoke very good English, so there was no problem carrying on a conversation.

In about an hour, Myron returned, driving a pickup truck. He told Monty that the building owner down the street said they could use his building until the Sabbath, and then he wanted rent after that. The two men who came in were pressed into action, and they loaded the computer on the truck, and rode with Myron down the street to the other building and unloaded it. Monty, Jimmy, and Yiska followed on foot, and when they got to the building, Myron had the computer plugged in.

Yiska was familiar with it, and when she turned it on, everyone was happy to see that it worked. "How about the printer; does it work?" Monty asked.

Myron answered, "I didn't think about the printer. I'll go back up to the office and see if it has been damaged." He told one of his men to go with him, and a short time later, they were back with the printer and a package of paper.

"Good," Monty said. "At least a few things were saved. Jimmy, do you know anything about computers?"

"A little bit, but not very much."

"A little bit is better than none at all. Tell you what; you and Yiska see what you can get off the computer. The inventory is the main thing and sales records would be very helpful. You all just see what has been saved, and I'll be working with Myron."

Yiska was more familiar with a computer than Jimmy, so she sat down to try to get what they needed from it. Two or three times, she would get to a snag, and Jimmy would have to sit down to try and solve the problem. Each time he did that, Yiska would be standing off his right shoulder, and would have to lean over him to show him something. Each time she leaned over him, her long, black, sweet-smelling hair would brush against his face, and he loved it. He thought, *I'd like to stay here and do this all day.*

At lunchtime, all six went to eat at a place that had not only kosher food, but western-style entrees as well. To sort of *meet in the middle*, Monty and Jimmy both ordered Ruben sandwiches and potato salad. Yiska had a hamburger, and Myron and the other two guys had something that neither Monty nor Jimmy had ever heard of. They talked business all through lunch, and Monty decided that he, Jimmy, and Myron would go out later and try to find a building to replace the one that was damaged.

In a couple of hours, Connie and the others would be going to work, and Monty needed to call her. Shepherd Global had insurance on the Tel Aviv installation, but every location was covered by one blanket policy, and his agent lived in Chattanooga. He had Joan call Connie the day they left to notify the agent, and he wanted to see what the situation was from the insurance's point of view.

They went back to their temporary, make-shift office, and before they left to look at buildings, Monty asked Myron to help him find a telephone he could use, and Myron offered to let him use the phone at his house, and he took him up on his offer. He told Jimmy, "Son, you stay here and see if there is anything else you all can find on that computer, and we'll be back soon. Then, we'll go building shopping, and I'll want you to go with us."

After Monty and Myron left, Yiska got a little bolder when she was next to Jimmy; nothing out of bounds, just a touch here and there, or maybe her hand on his arm or shoulder. If he had not been engaged, he would more than likely have responded to it in a more active way.

When they returned, they were ready to go look at buildings. While they were at Myron's house, Myron called a good friend who was a commercial realtor and asked him to meet them and show them some buildings. He told the two warehouse men they could go, and then, Myron told Yiska she could go home or if she wanted to, she could go with them. Of course, she and Jimmy had to sit next to each other in the back seat. Occasionally, Jimmy would catch her staring at him, and when he looked at her, she would smile a seductive smile. One time, she winked. The flirt was definitely on.

Harry Shapiro, the realtor, showed Monty three buildings, and he was definitely interested in one of them. He told Harry he would talk to Myron about it and get back to him the next day, and then they went back and let Yiska out so she could go home. She said she would see them the next day. Then, Myron took Monty and Jimmy to their hotel, and they talked for a long time about leasing one of the buildings before they got out of the car.

Monty told him, "Myron, look, you're the one who will be working in the building; not me, and I want you to pick the one that you think you'll be most comfortable in. According to Harry, there's not that much difference in the costs, so you should decide which one would be the most advantageous for you to do the best job for Shepherd Global."

"Okay, Monty. I appreciate the confidence you have in me, and any decision I make will be in Shepherd's best interest. Look, I know you guys are tired, so why don't you go get a good dinner, and I'll pick you up in the morning.

CHAPTER TWENTY ONE

When they finally went into the hotel, it was almost six o'clock, and Monty said he was going to take a shower before dinner. Jimmy asked him, "Dad, I haven't seen Analisa since before we went to Seattle, and I'd sure like to talk to her. Do you think it would be alright if I call her?"

"Do you know how to make a call from here?"

"No sir. Is it hard?"

"Not really. Here; these are the numbers you have to dial," and he showed him the order in which they had to be used.

"Thanks, Dad. I won't talk long."

"Okay, I'm going to get in the shower."

Jimmy dialed all the numbers that Monty had given him, and finally the Shepherd receptionist answered. "Jennifer, this is Monty Shepherd. Will you please ring the computer department and connect me with Analisa Shepherd?"

She hesitated, and then asked, "Analisa? I don't know if I'm supposed to or not."

Aggravated, Jimmy said, "Jennifer, give me Connie, will you?"

"Just one moment."

"Hello, this is Connie."

"Connie, hi, this is Jimmy. I'm trying to get in touch with Analisa and that alleged operator that answered didn't want to connect me. Will you do your magic and get me Analisa?"

"Of course I will. Just a minute, Jimmy."

"Thanks, Connie."

In a minute, "Hello."

"Hi Sweet Thing, how're you doing?"

"Jimmy, hi. I sure am glad to hear your voice. When are you coming home?"

"I'm not sure. I hope we're going to leave tomorrow, but if not, it'll be the first of the week. There's a lot to do before we can leave."

"What happened over there?"

"A Palestinian rocket hit our office and warehouse and the fire destroyed nearly everything we had. We have to find another warehouse and get things set up to resume business before we can leave. I miss you,

Sweetie. How's Johnny?"

"He's fine. He misses his Uncle Jim a lot, and his Mother does, too."

"Ana, you should see this place. It's beautiful, and they have a beach that's out of this world. I'll probably be coming over here from time to time, and after we're married, I'm going to bring you with me sometime. Well, I have to hang up now. We're cleaning up and getting ready to go to dinner."

"Dinner! What time is it there?"

"It's six-twenty-five."

"Oh, I didn't know there was that much difference in the time."

"Yep, eight hours. I've got to go, Hon. You can check with Connie for updates on when we will be home. If we don't leave tomorrow, I'll call you again. I love you. Have a good day."

"I love you, too. Your call has already made my day good. Hurry home. Bye."

When Monty got out of the shower, he called Chuck and invited him and the others to have dinner with him and Jimmy, and he readily accepted. On past trips he had learned of some good restaurants, so they went to one of them.

Friday was a day of hard work; not physical labor, but work none-the-less. A building had to be leased; office furniture and equipment bought, racks and many other items had to be bought for the warehouse. Monty was trying to squeeze several months work into just one day, and he didn't know if he could do it or not, but he was sure going to try.

Leasing a building had to be the first thing done before anything else, and fortunately, they were able to get the one they had zeroed in on the day before. Myron knew just where to look for the office stuff as well as the warehouse equipment, and they had made arrangements to get it by shortly after noon.

He had Yiska call the electric company and the telephone company to resume their service as quickly as possible. She also called the company that sold them their computer, and ordered a service technician to come out and go over it. Unfortunately, none of those things were going to happen until next Monday. Myron and Monty also found that none of the things they ordered would be delivered until Monday, as well.

They kept going, and at every turn they found that nothing was going to happen until at least Monday and possibly Tuesday. Soon, Monty resigned himself to the fact that if they didn't go home that night, it would possibly be the middle of the following week before they could leave, and he couldn't wait that long. He had important meetings scheduled for next week, so he explained all that to Myron and asked for suggestions.

"Monty, as you know, Ulrich Steen and I set up the original office here, and through the years there have been many changes, and I have been here to make those things happen. I see no reason for you to stay any longer on this trip. I can take care of things, so go on home. I don't mean to sound arrogant, but Monty, I can handle it. Okay?"

"Okay, I'll go. Myron, I didn't mean to make you think I couldn't depend on you to handle things. I can't think of anyone I would trust more than you. I'm sorry. That being said, let's go to my hotel and go over what has been and what is to be done, and we'll get out of your hair. I'll tell my pilot to be ready to take off first thing in the morning." Being slightly facetious, he said, "They don't close the airport on the Sabbath over here, do they?"

Myron laughed and said, "No, Monty, they don't close the airport on the Sabbath." Then he got serious and said, "But according to God's law, everything is supposed to be closed on the Sabbath. Today's society puts more emphasis on Things other than God's Commandments, and I'm afraid we're going to have to pay for it one day."

"I totally agree, Myron."

They said their goodbyes, and Myron left. Monty and Jimmy went upstairs to their room, and Monty called Chuck. "Chuck, we're going to leave first thing in the morning, so do what you have to do to make it happen. Listen, you had better call the caterer right now because the Sabbath starts at sundown, and I want us to have plenty of food on the flight. Call me back and let me know what time we can takeoff, will you?"

When he hung up, he said, "I think I'll take a shower and have a short nap before dinner."

Jimmy said, "I think I'll do the same thing when you get out."

Monty went into the bathroom and turned the water on, and as soon as he stepped in the shower, the phone rang. Jimmy answered it, and the voice on the other end said, "Is this Jimmy?"

"Yes, it is. Who's calling?"

"Jimmy, this is Yiska. I just wanted to tell you how much I enjoyed meeting you and working with you. I'm sorry you're leaving so soon. I was hoping that we might get together and have a drink(pause) or two one evening while you were here, but maybe we can when you come back. Myron said that you would be coming over here occasionally, is that right?"

"Possibly."

"I just wanted you to know how much I enjoyed being with you, and maybe we can get together sometime in the future. Goodbye, Jimmy."

"Goodbye."

Jimmy had to stop and think after that call. *Wow! She sure comes on strong. I guess it's a good thing that I'm leaving tomorrow. She's really good-looking and seems to have a great personality, but I'm committed to Analisa. If I wasn't, I would sure be tempted. Man!*

Monty finished his shower, and Jimmy went in to take his when the phone rang again. Jimmy's heart stopped because he didn't want his Dad to know about Yiska's call, and he was afraid the second call might be from her, too, but he was relieved when Monty said Chuck's name.

"Okay, that sounds good. We'll be ready. Listen, Jimmy and I are going to have dinner here in the hotel tonight, if you guys would like to join us. I've got some paperwork to do, and I want to hit the sack early since we're getting up early in the morning. Will seven o'clock be good for you? Okay, we'll meet you in the lobby then. See ya."

Hotel restaurants are usually just fair, at best, but the one at the Hilton was excellent. They all had a great meal and returned to their rooms by nine o'clock.

Chuck had set it up to takeoff at eight o'clock the next morning, which meant the crew would probably be up at five, and Monty and Jimmy at six. Breakfast would be on the plane, so they would just have coffee before they left for the airport.

Takeoff was right on schedule, and breakfast was served when they reached altitude. Instead of it being just Jimmy and Monty, Chuck and Pat joined them. Fred Vanhoy and Scott Shelton, the two new pilots, were flying the plane, so they could relax on the first half of the trip. With the addition of Chuck and Pat, breakfast was even more enjoyable. After the mess was cleaned up, the quartet went back and relaxed on the plush, luxurious furniture that Monty had picked out.

When they had been flying for a couple of hours, Chuck told Monty he had something he wanted to talk to him about. Monty said, "Shoot.

What is it? Are you wanting a raise?"

"No, no, it's nothing like that. Monty, as you know, the three of us came to work for your Dad when he first bought the DC-8, and then, we moved into the 707 where we are now. Monty, it has been a lot of years, and we have enjoyed every minute of it, but we've been talking, and all three of us feel that we want to retire."

"Retire? You can't retire. Who will fly me around when I want to go somewhere? You're my crew. I don't want another one. You can't retire."

Acting as if Monty hadn't said anything, Chuck continued, "We want to give you plenty of time to find a new crew, so we think if we work for you until the first of the year that should give you enough time. I can probably help you find someone. I know a couple of people that are not real happy with the companies that they are with now, and they would kill to be able to work for somebody like you."

"Well, guys, I sure hate to see you go, but I understand completely. You need to have some time to enjoy life before it gets too late, and I will appreciate it if you will help me find your replacements."

They talked a little bit more about the pilot situation, and then Monty began talking to Jimmy. "Son, when we get to Chattanooga, I need to go to the office. Bryce and I have got to order replacement goods for Tel Aviv, and it's going to take a long time. I'm very thankful that you and Yiska could get the inventory. That will save a tremendous amount of time, but there's still a lot to do, and you can help me with it.

The rest of the trip was pleasant and uneventful, and they landed at Lovell Field at one-fifteen, Chattanooga time.

Monty was in a hurry to get to the office, so he and Jimmy didn't tarry long, once they were on the ground. Jimmy's car was at home so he rode with Monty, and they got to the office around two o'clock. When they got there, Jimmy said, "Dad, I'll be right back. I want to go down to the computer room and see Analisa. I'll just be a couple of minutes."

"Alright, but don't stay too long."

"I won't. I'll be right back," and he hurried down to where Analisa worked. He said, "Hi, Pretty Lady," and she turned around and grabbed his hand. She thought it would be better if she didn't hug him in front of the other employees. They walked outside into the hall and told each other how glad they were that he was back. He said, "I'm going to be working with Dad the rest of the day, so when you get off, come by his office, and if I'm about through, you can give me a ride since I don't have my car. Do you want to do something tonight?"

"I'd love to. What do you want to do?"

"I don't care. We can go out for dinner and catch a flick, or we can just go back to your place. Whatever you would like to do."

"You know, this is Burger and Shake night. Do you not want to go there?"

"Gosh, I forgot about that. Yeah, we can do that if you want to. Is that what you want to do?"

"Why don't we? We can go back to my place afterwards. Instead of going out to eat, we can get a sandwich there."

"Sounds like a plan. If we're going to do that, I'll just ride home with Dad and then pick you up. Alright?"

Jimmy took another new song with him, and they practiced it until it sounded good. Most of the regular tunes were played, and the session ended with everyone upbeat.

Back at Analisa's, Johnny was trying to make up for the time they lost while Jimmy was gone, and Jimmy hardly had enough time to do anything with Analisa except say a few words now and then. At last, it was time for him to go to bed, and while Jimmy really loved him, he was ready to have some one on one time with his mother.

Analisa made the customary pot of coffee, and she and Jimmy stayed in the kitchen until it was ready. Finally, she poured each one of them a cup, and they went into the living room and sat down.

"When are you going to be ready to set a date for the wedding?" she asked.

"I've been ready. I thought you were going to decide on the date."

"Honey, that's not the way it's done; we both decide on the date, together."

"Oh, do you have one in mind?"

"No, I don't, but I think we should get married before the end of the year, don't you?"

"Yeah, I do. Are we going to have a big wedding?"

"I don't think so. Since this is my second one, I wouldn't feel right having a big Church wedding. I'd like to just have our family and good friends, and then, we can go to someplace real nice and have dinner for our reception. What do you think about that?"

"Where will we have it? I know you said you didn't want a big wedding, and I don't especially want one either, but I'd really like for God to be a part of it." And then he said, "I've got it!!! Why don't we have it in the *Bride's Room* at your Church? There's plenty of room for the people we'll have, it's a really pretty room, and it's in God's house. What do you think?"

"That's a good idea, Sweetheart, and we can have Doug Luffman marry us. Let's do that. Now when?"

"Here's a thought; what would you think about the Saturday before Thanksgiving? That way, we would have eight days to go somewhere, but we would only miss three days of work."

"If that's when you want it, it's okay with me. That's a strange way of deciding on a wedding date, though."

"It's just a suggestion. If you would rather do it another time that will be fine with me."

"No, the Saturday before Thanksgiving is good. Boy, that's not long, is it?"

"It can't come too soon. That's less than two months, and then you will be Analisa Shepherd."

Without thinking, she blurted out, "I'm already Analisa Shepherd."

With a funny look on his face, Jimmy said, "That's right. You are."

She could see that her remark disturbed him, so she went over and put her arms around him and said, "I'm sorry. That was insensitive of me. It just came out. I'm sorry."

"That's alright."

On Saturday, Jimmy went by and picked her and Johnny up, and they went to Sale Creek to see the progress on the house, and when they got there, he was shocked at how much had been done since he left up there. He looked down toward the boathouse and saw Hal looking up his way, trying to figure out who the intruders were.

Jimmy held his breath as he walked down the hill because he wasn't exactly confident that Hal was *out of the woods* with his drinking, but he was very pleased when he got down there. Hal was in good shape and seemed to be very happy. He said his job was going great, and he and Randy talked every couple of days, in fact; he was going to his house for burgers that very night.

Jimmy told him, "Man, I'm glad to hear that. That has made my trip up here worthwhile." They stayed for a while longer, and then they went back to Chattanooga.

When they got back, they went down to the riverfront and messed around. They got a hot dog and messed around some more, and then Jimmy took them home around two or two-thirty.

Joan said she would keep Johnny that night, so Jimmy and Analisa had dinner at the Town and Country and then went to a movie.

Monty had closed the pool for the year, but Sunday was such a pretty day, Analisa and Johnny went over to sit in the sun with Jimmy's family.

While they were at poolside Jimmy asked Joan, "Mom, has Laura said anything about when they're moving? I'm getting anxious to get into my house."

"I saw her the other day, and she said they hoped to be out by October first. Is that when you're going to leave me?"

"Mom, don't sound like that. I'm just going to be next door for crying out loud, and yes ma'am, I would like to move as soon as I can."

"Ana, I'm going to have to buy some furniture. When can you help me?"

"How about next Saturday?"

"Next Saturday's good. We'll do it."

First thing Monday morning, Monty called Bill Mason and asked him to come by his office when he could. Bill got there around nine-thirty and went into Monty's office. After the greetings, Monty told Bill, "Bill, I'm going to call my contractor this morning, and I just wanted to be sure we're on the same page concerning the new Church. I feel that God told me to build one, and I think He wants me to build yours, but I need to be sure before we go too far. Have you been praying about this?"

"Yes sir, I sure have, and I told my congregation that we might be getting an anonymous gift to build a new Church, and I believe every one of our members has been praying, too."

"Well, I know I'm supposed to build one, but after I got to thinking about it, I thought that maybe I came on too strong and overwhelmed you."

"No, no, you didn't at all. We have been praying that we could find a way to upgrade our building, and then, you came along with this. Mr. Shepherd, I truly believe you and your gift is the answer to those prayers."

"Good. You've relieved my reservations. Now, do you and your group have any particular style of architecture in mind?

"No sir. Whatever style you want to make it."

“Okay, sit tight, and let me see if I can get in touch with my man.” He looked in his directory for Bob Martin’s number and dialed it.

“Hello.”

“Hi, Bob; Monty.”

“Hi Monty. What’s up?”

“Bob, I think I’m going to have a job for you. Are you interested?”

“You bet I am. What are you thinking about; an addition to one of your plants?”

“Oh no. This is the farthest thing from a plant. Bob, I want to build a Church. Are you still interested?”

“Even more so. When do we start, and where will it be?”

“When could you meet me? There’s an existing Church building there now, and the new building will be built in the parking lot, and then, the old building will be razed when the new one is completed.”

“I’m free pretty much anytime today. Just tell me when and where.”

Monty conferred with Bill and then gave Bob the time and directions. They were to meet at the site in one hour.

When they met, Bob had several good ideas about the architecture as well as the building itself, so he and Monty shook hands on the deal, and Bob went to his office to start planning, and Monty went to his bank to make arrangements for the financing.

CHAPTER TWENTY TWO

After he got back to the office, Monty called Jimmy and asked if he would like to have lunch with him. Jimmy accepted the invitation, and at noon they went to Sweeney's for some of their scrumptious barbecue. While they were eating and talking, Jimmy said, "Dad, Analisa and I set the date for our wedding."

"Really? When is it?"

"The Saturday before Thanksgiving. It will just be a small wedding with our families and a few close friends. We think we want to get married in the Bride's Room at Analisa's Church. After the ceremony, we think we will take everyone to the Read House for dinner, instead of having a reception. What do you think?"

"I think it sounds wonderful. Your Mom may not agree, but I think you're wise not to have such a large deal. You can take the money you'll save and come pretty close to paying for the furniture in your house, and you'll be just as married. Is Analisa okay with having a small wedding?"

"Yes sir. It was her idea."

"Well, that's great. Now, let me change the subject. Son, do you remember when we were first talking about what you'd be doing once you started, and I told you that I thought I would give you the country of Italy to develop?"

"Yes sir. I remember."

"Well, I think the time is right for you to *get your feet wet* and start working on it. I have been talking with a sales agency in Rome, and I'm pretty sure Shepherd Apparel is going to go with them. The name of their company is Ricci-Moretti Sales. It is operated by Adriano Ricci and Cosimo Moretti. They both speak very good English, and from talking to them over the phone, they sound very sharp and very nice. They will both be at the New York Market in a few weeks, so you can meet them then. If we definitely decide to go with them, after we talk at the show, then I want you to make a trip over there to work with them for a few days."

"Will I go by myself?"

"Probably not for your first trip. I'll have to see how busy Bryce is. If he's too busy or if he's somewhere else in the world, I may go with you."

"It sounds as if I'm going to be on the go, doesn't it?

"Is that a problem?"

"No sir. I'm only wondering how it's going to be when I have to go out of the country for a week, right after I get married. It won't be a problem for me; I just hope it won't be for Analisa."

"Do you think it would smooth things out if she went with you?"

"Are you serious?

"I'm just thinking; I don't think your Mother has ever been to Rome, and I'm sure she would love to go. Maybe the four of us can go, and you and I can work while the girls do whatever they want to do."

"Gosh, that sounds wonderful, Dad."

"If Analisa goes with us, who will Johnny stay with?"

"I don't know. He has a friend down the street from where they live now, and maybe he can stay there. What about Grandma Thil? Do you think she would let him stay there?"

"I don't see why not. You can ask her. She would probably love it.

"Have you all thought about where you're going on your honeymoon?"

"It hasn't been mentioned yet."

"How would you like it if your Mom and I treat you to your honeymoon?"

"Wow! Where do you want to send us?"

"I don't know. My Dad sent your Mom and me to Hawaii, and it was great. If you and Analisa would like to go over there, I'll swing for it."

"Dad, you can't imagine how much I appreciate that."

"Yes I can because I felt the same way when my Dad did it for us. Now, what's the exact date when you're getting married? I'll have to be sure the plane will be here."

"Saturday, November twenty-second. Which plane will we take?"

"Probably the MD-11. You know, you're making plans, and your bride doesn't even know about them. What if she doesn't want to go to paradise?"

"Are you kidding? I'm going to go tell her the minute we get back to the office. Don't be surprised if she comes up to your office and gives you a kiss."

****

On Saturday morning, November first, Monty, Jimmy, Jeff Ellis, Bryce Coleman, and some of Shepherd's sales reps took off for the New York Mid-season Market. They spent Saturday afternoon and all day Sunday setting up the space to be ready for what Monty hoped would be a flood of customers the next morning. Monty was missing Charles Crawford and his expertise in setting up the space. That was his first market since Charles retired. He didn't want to say too much because it was so early in his tenure, but he was already counting on Jimmy to do many of the things that Charley did. Jimmy had that *knack* for getting things to fall in place without having to use an extra amount of effort. Monty thought, *I can't wait for the show to start and see how Jimmy does with the customers.*

He got his wish the next morning. The space filled up in a hurry when the doors opened at eight o'clock, and he was glad to see that there was so much interest in the David's Staff line. When he added more footage to the space a couple of markets ago, he tried to separate the men's goods from the ladies. Each group had its own sales force, but Jimmy was going to work with both, the same way Monty did. Although he hadn't had time to get really familiar with either one, Monty had so much confidence in him that he was sure he would pull it off.

Around ten o'clock the buyers from one of the larger group of stores in the United States came in, and Monty was busy with another customer. Both ladies were known to be very hard to deal with, and since he was tied up with another customer, Jimmy waited on them, and Monty thought, *uh-oh; I'm afraid those gals are going to eat him up.* He continued working with his customer, and they moved to another part of the space. In a few minutes, they worked their way back to the area where Jimmy and his buyers were working, and he couldn't believe his eyes. That six-foot-three, well-proportioned frame of Jimmy's, and his extremely handsome face had the buyers eating out of his hand. Jimmy and the two women were laughing and joking, and the best part of it all; Jimmy was writing an order.

When Monty was finished with his customer, and Jimmy and his ladies were about to conclude, the ladies went over to Monty and said, "You may not believe this, Monty, but we gave your son an order. Normally, we don't place orders at the show, but we liked him so much we made an exception. We want to compliment both you and Jimmy on your ability to be warm and yet, professional. One of the women said,

"That Jimmy is a charmer. I wish I was twenty years younger."

And the other one asked, "What would you do if you were twenty years younger?"

"You might be surprised at what I would do." Jimmy just stood there, smiling, trying to be cool.

One of them looked in her market directory and said, "We need to go, and she looked at Jimmy and said, "Thank you, Jimmy. I can't tell you when I've enjoyed placing an order as much as I've enjoyed this. Take care and make Monty let you come see us."

He said, "Thank you, ladies. I've really enjoyed working with you. You've made my day."

Monty looked at him and smiled. "It looks like you made some fans; good job."

By then it was lunchtime, and they went downstairs and grabbed a sandwich.

After they ate, they went back upstairs, and the afternoon was extremely busy. Once, about two o'clock, Monty noticed Jimmy working with a lady, and when they finished, he heard Jimmy say, "Thank you so much, Ms. Ledford. I've really enjoyed working with you. You've made my day."

Then, he walked over to where Monty was and Monty, said, "Hello Mr. Suave. I heard you tell Ms. Ledford the same thing you told those ladies this morning. Are you going to tell that to all the women?"

"It all depends; I might."

The rest of Monday was a very busy and very profitable day. Many orders were written, both in ladies' and men's goods, and when they got to their hotel they were so tired they didn't want to go anywhere to eat, so they went downstairs at the hotel and got a *so-so* meal.

After they got back to their room, Monty said, "You know, we could have our sales meeting here in New York instead of bringing everybody to Chattanooga. I think I can get a room downstairs, and maybe we'll have one Thursday night."

"Will all the reps still be here?"

"They should be. No one is supposed to leave until after three o'clock Friday afternoon. Yes sir, we'll have a meeting Thursday. That way, we'll save thousands of dollars by not having to bring them to Chattanooga."

Soon after they got back to the room, Monty called Joan, and when he hung up, Jimmy called Analisa. He hoped to move into his new house the week after they got back from New York, and they talked at length about that.

The first order of business Tuesday morning was to go around and tell each rep about the sales meeting Thursday night. The day was very busy and time flew by. Monty thought the guys from Italy would be by, but so far, they haven't shown up.

As soon as the doors opened Wednesday morning, the two fellows were there. They handed a card to one of the Shepherd salesmen and asked to see Monty. When Monty went up front, he said, "I'm Monty Shepherd."

One of the men said, "I'm Cosimo Moretti," and the other one introduced himself, and said, "And I'm Adriano Ricci."

"Won't you gentlemen come with me back to my office?"

When they got there, Monty said, "Will you excuse me for a minute, please?" and he walked a couple of steps out of the office and told someone to find Jimmy and have him come back there. In a couple of minutes, Jimmy came in, and Monty introduced him as the one who would be representing Shepherd Global Apparel if they were to get together.

After the two Italians went over, in detail, their operation in Rome, Monty took the floor. He explained how Shepherd worked with sales representation companies throughout the world, and he indicated that he would like for Ricci-Moretti Sales to represent him in Italy and the islands of Sicily and Sardinia. They met until about noon and then told Monty they had a lunch meeting with someone, and as they were leaving, Monty told them that he and Jimmy would more than likely come to Rome sometime in December and would let them know when.

After they left, Monty asked Jimmy, "What do you think?"

"They seem to be awfully sharp, and according to the figures they showed us, they're apparently good salesmen. I'd say that all their reps are equally as good, so I think we'd be foolish not to go with them."

"That's what I was thinking, and we can get a better picture when we go to Rome and work with them. By the way, did you remember that Saturday is when we go to speak at the Central Kentucky FCA?"

"This Saturday?"

"Yeah, did you forget?"

"Yes sir, I sure did. We won't get home 'til Friday night, and then we have to leave again Saturday?"

"That's right. We won't be gone very long, though. Dinner is at six o'clock, and the program is at six-forty-five. If we get out of there by eight o'clock, we'll be home before ten. Say, do you think Johnny would like to go? He would get a kick out of being around all those athletes."

"He probably would. I'll ask him when I call Analisa tonight."

The sales meeting was a huge success Thursday night. The new styles along with the carry-over groups enabled all the reps to write a lot of business, and that's why they were there. Monty reviewed the year up to that point, and the figures were great. He announced that Shepherd Global Apparel Group had made an agreement with a large sales representation company in Rome that would cover the entire country of Italy plus the islands of Sardinia and Sicily. When he said Sicily, one wise guy in the back cracked, "Monty, did you have to join the Mafia to get them?"

Monty wisecracked back. Borrowing a line from the *Godfather* he said, "Yeah, I made them an offer they couldn't refuse."

Everybody laughed, and others made wise cracks until finally, Monty called the meeting back to order. He thanked everyone for their contributions to the success of Shepherd Apparel and after challenging them to do even better next year, he closed the meeting with a prayer.

The Gulfstream picked the group up at five-thirty, Friday afternoon, and everyone was very happy to be going home. Before they landed at Lovell Field, Monty went up front and told Mike Taylor to refuel when they landed, and do anything else that would be required to fly to Campbellsville, Kentucky the next day.

Joan met Monty, and Analisa and Johnny were there to meet Jimmy when they landed. The whole group went to Monty's, first, and then, Jimmy, Analisa and Johnny went to Analisa's. Analisa asked Jimmy when they got to her place, "Do you realize that two weeks from tomorrow we will be married?"

"I know, and I can't wait. Are you getting excited?"

"Yeah, I am. Come in here and let me show you some of things we got at the shower last Sunday," and she led him into her bedroom where she had everything stored until they could move it into their house.

"Honey, I forgot until Dad reminded me that we have to go to speak at the Central Kentucky FCA tomorrow night. Did you forget it too?"

"No, I remembered, but it's fine if you go because I have a shower tomorrow night."

"We won't be gone long. We don't have to leave until three o'clock, and we'll be back tomorrow night. Then, I won't have to go anywhere for two weeks, and you'll be going with me. We're going to paradise on that trip. Then, back home for two weeks, and here's a surprise. On the fifteenth of December, you and I and Mom and Dad are going to Rome. How does that sound?"

"It sounds wonderful, but what am I going to do with Johnny?"

"I don't know. I thought about my Grandmother, and I also thought about his friend down the street. Here's something I just this minute thought about; He goes to school until the afternoon, right? Well, what if the bus lets him off at the Burger and Shake, and he could ride home with Mary Ann when she gets off. She and Grandmother can split up the babysitting duties. Will that work?"

"I don't know. Let me think about it, and I'll come up with something. I'm going to take a pocketful of coins to throw in the fountain."

"What fountain?"

"The Trevi fountain, silly, but there are a lot of fountains in Rome, and I may just throw a coin or two in every one of them."

"Whatever floats your boat."

"Ana, I'm going home. I'm tired after this week at the market."

"Will I see you tomorrow?"

"If you want to. I'm going to be at my house most of the morning, and you can come over there if you would like. They're supposed to deliver the furniture next week, and then I can start staying there. It won't be long until you can stay there with me. Do you need for me to do anything to help you plan for the wedding?"

"No, thank you. I think I have everything pretty much set. I'm just waiting until I hear your nervous self say "I do."

"Well, don't worry your pretty little head; I'll say it. I've gotta go. See you in the morning?"

"Maybe."

"If I don't, I'll see you Sunday," and he kissed her. "Good night."

"Good night."

Coach Kevin Johnson met the plane Saturday afternoon and took the pair to the Student Center, where the dinner and meeting was to be held. The dinner was a pleasant surprise; so many times a banquet will have ham with raisin sauce and undercooked mixed vegetable, but that night they had steak and baked potato and pecan pie.

Jimmy had a serious case of butterflies during dinner and thought he might back out of his part in the program. He was expecting to be the *lead-off hitter* with Monty closing out the program with his always wise words, but the organizer tricked him; he was to be the main speaker, and he wasn't prepared for that.

Unbeknownst to him, Monty had set him up because not only was he confident about what Jimmy would say, but he thought it would help him in future appearances.

As always, Monty was impressive and enjoyable, and everyone there was left with several things to think about. Monty introduced Jimmy, not only as his son, but as someone who was a great athlete with something to say about what Jesus had done in his life.

Jimmy did just that. He told a couple of sports stories, and then he told how Jesus had done so many good things in his life. As it turned out, he was the hit of the meeting, and Monty couldn't have been prouder of him. When the program was over, they stayed around for a while, talking to a lot of the members and answering many questions. When the crowd thinned out, Coach Johnson drove them back to the airport, and the impression of the beautiful Gulfstream was not lost on him. They took off and were back in Chattanooga before midnight.

Furniture was to be delivered by two furniture stores Monday, and Jimmy asked Joan if she would let the delivery men in. He told her basically what would go where and asked her to tell the men. That evening, Analisa went over, and they rearranged some things from his original plan, and thought about what they still needed. The Rogers' had left all the appliances, so they didn't have to worry about the kitchen. He had bought two bedroom suites, one king for the master bedroom and a queen-size for one of the others, but he had not bought any linens. He asked Joan if she would please go out and buy some the next day, and she not only went out and bought the stuff, she made up the beds. As an added bonus, she went to the store and bought a mega-size buggy full of groceries and loaded up the pantry for him.

Jimmy had been given a tremendous amount to learn about construction, styling, sales, and shipping apparel, and he was trying really hard to learn it, but the fact that he was getting married the next week made it extremely hard to concentrate. He was very grateful to anyone who came in and distracted him from what he was doing. Monty included him in some of his meetings, and that helped a lot.

Finally, on Thursday before the wedding, Monty told him he could be off that day and the next. The rehearsal was to be on Friday, and even though he tried to act very cool, his stomach was in knots. More furniture was being delivered Thursday afternoon, among which was a new bedroom suite for Johnny.

Analisa was going over with some of her things because when they got back from Hawaii they would go to the house and not her apartment. She had to make two trips in order to deliver all her clothes. That evening, after working hard all day, she, Johnny, and Jimmy went to Mickey-Dees and ate. When they finished, they went back to their house so Analisa could get her car and go home.

Jimmy went into Monty's and sat down with his Mom and Dad and talked about his soon to end bachelorhood and his upcoming marriage. Monty wanted to make sure that he had his shuttle tickets, his credit cards, and plenty of money. After he was satisfied that all the preparations had been taken care of, he and Joan shared some of their honeymoon experiences when they went to Hawaii.

Based on their high endorsement of Lanai, Jimmy and Analisa had decided to go there first when they got to Hawaii, and Jimmy got excited just talking about it.

CHAPTER TWENTY THREE

Jimmy didn't see Analisa Friday until everyone assembled at the Church. Since the ceremony was to be so small there wasn't much rehearsing to do. They went through the movements a couple of times, and then everybody went out to eat. Jimmy and Analisa went to their house when they left the restaurant. There was nothing left to do before the ceremony, so they just sat and talked about their dreams for the future.

"Honey, I want us to be sure that we include God in our marriage. If we do, I believe He will bless us and our marriage. Mom and Dad have done that, and look at their lives."

Analisa said, "I think I need to leave now. Where will you be tomorrow?"

"I don't know; why?"

"Well, I'm not supposed to see you since it's our wedding day, and I have to bring my suitcase over here, so your Dad can put it on the plane for me."

"Come anytime you want to; just call first in case I'm here. If I am, I'll go to my room and stay until you leave."

Six o'clock was the time of the wedding, and the small group began showing up a little after five-fifteen. Jimmy was outside the Church greeting the people and talking, trying to keep himself as relaxed as possible, when he saw one lady that he didn't recognize. When he went over and introduced himself, she said she was Amanda Shumate. "You look exactly like Johnny," she said.

"I know; we were identical twins."

"Johnny used to talk about you a lot. He was very proud of you."

"I was very proud of him, too. Did you drive up from Columbus today?"

"Yeah, I just got here. I didn't tell Analisa that I was coming. I hope it's alright."

"It absolutely is. It's great to have you. Would you like to go back and see her?"

"Yes, I would love to, but I don't think you're supposed to take me."

"Oh, I know. I'll get someone else to take you."

"Jimmy, it was sure nice to meet you. You're getting a great gal."

At a quarter 'til six, Doug Luffman stuck his head out the door and said it was time to come in. Monty was Jimmy's best man, and they went to stand in front of Doug. All the guests took a seat, and in a minute, Analisa and Mary Ann, her maid of honor came in accompanied by Eddie Phillips, one of their B & S group. When they reached Jimmy and Monty, the music stopped and Doug began the ceremony.

It was a simple, standard wedding the way Analisa wanted, and in about ten or fifteen minutes it was over. A photographer took some pictures, and then everyone got into their cars and went to the Read House, where they had a room reserved. Jimmy and Analisa didn't have their cars, so they rode with Joan and Monty, and since Analisa's Dad and Amanda were alone, she rode with him.

The meal was one fit for a king, and everyone really enjoyed it. The plane wasn't going to take off until ten-thirty, so there was plenty of time to visit after they finished eating. At one point, Analisa excused herself and went into the rest room and changed into her traveling clothes. Monty was going to wait and change on the plane.

At nine-thirty, Monty told Jimmy that he and Analisa needed to start telling everybody good bye because they needed to leave for the airport in about a half-hour. They stood at the door to the banquet room and hugged and shook hands with everybody as they left. Without exception, each person congratulated them and wished them good luck.

Getting to the airport at ten-fifteen, they hugged and kissed Joan, Monty, Thil and Johnny and told them they would see them next Sunday. Analisa's Dad and Amanda also went to the airport and told them goodbye. Before she left, Amanda pulled Analisa aside and said, "I'm not believing this airplane. You're a lucky girl, Analisa Shepherd."

"I know I am, and my family is wonderful. Amanda, come back up and spend some time with me soon. Jimmy and I just bought a big house and we have plenty of room. When you come, bring Pat if you can. I think he would like Jimmy. Will you do that?"

"You can count on it. I'll call you when you get back. Have a great time, and I'll see you soon."

Fred and Scott were standing at the door of the plane waiting on the newlyweds when they drove up. As soon as they saw them, they went inside and prepared to take off. When all the good byes were said, Analisa kissed Johnny one more time, and then, she and Jimmy climbed the stairs, turned around and waved and said "Bye", and went aboard. Fred told them to take a seat and to fasten their seatbelts because they were ready to take off.

Instantly, the big engines started, and in a couple of minutes they began to taxi down the runway to the spot where they would gun the engines, and then, roar down the runway and lift off. They held hands in anticipation of the takeoff, and then relaxed once they were airborne.

Monty and Joan remembered what Don did when they got married and thought it would be nice if they did the same thing for Jimmy and Analisa, so Joan picked up three, one dozen bouquets of roses and a bottle of good wine. Don had bought French Champagne, but Joan didn't like it and thought wine would be better. She put a dozen roses on the dresser in the bedroom and one dozen in the lounge and another dozen in the dining area with the wine.

Analisa had been on board the 707 and was still in awe of its luxury and beauty, but the MD-11 absolutely blew her away. When they got aboard, she told Jimmy, "Honey, if you don't want to go all the way to Hawaii, I would be happy to just stay here on the plane for a week. It's so beautiful; I can't imagine Hawaii having anything any prettier."

When they reached altitude, Jimmy said, "Come on, Honey, I want to show you the rest of the plane." First, they went to the dining area and poured themselves a glass of wine, and then, holding hands, Jimmy led her all through the plane and into the bedroom last.

When Analisa saw the king size bed and dressing room, she commented in a kidding way, "Boy, this is some playground, isn't it?"

"You bet it is, and we're going to see how much fun it is in a little while."

"I can hardly wait."

When they finished the tour of the plane, they went up to the flight deck. "Fred, are we going to refuel at LAX?"

"Yeah, your Dad said we should to save money. You can't believe the difference in the cost of fuel in Hawaii and California. If we fill up in L.A., we'll be able to get to Honolulu and back without having to buy any in Hawaii."

"Okay, now we've got tickets for the nine o'clock Commuter to Lanai when we land in Honolulu. Do you still plan to land around five A.M.? Dad suggested that we sleep until almost time to catch our flight. Did he talk to you about that?"

"Yes, he did. He told me to wake you up around seven for some coffee and breakfast. A golf cart will pick you up at the foot of the steps and take you to the gate where you will catch the plane. Have you got your tickets?"

"Yeah, we've got 'em."

"Good. We've got this all under control, so y'all go on to bed, and we'll take it from here. Good night, Jimmy, and pleasant dreams."

The newlyweds went back to the bedroom to get ready for bed. The 707 had a nice bedroom and a bath, but the MD-11 not only had a bedroom almost twice the size of the 707 and a bath, it had a nice size dressing room as well.

When they were ready to get ready for bed, Jimmy told Analisa to use the dressing room first. She did, and when she came out, she looked like a vision in a lilac peignoir set with slippers to match. Her long hair cascading over her shoulder made Jimmy declare, "Ana, you're the most beautiful thing I have ever seen. I think I've died and gone to heaven."

"Well, thank you. Hurry and get ready so we can go to bed."

Jimmy went into the dressing room and put on his short pajamas. The pajama pants came to a little above his knees. He came out with his shirt unbuttoned, exposing his six-pack, and he looked like something out of Esquire magazine and Analisa couldn't take her eyes off of him. They met at the foot of the bed and embraced. With each kiss the hormones sped up some more, and in a couple of minutes the peignoir was lying in the floor next to Jimmy's shirt, and they turned down the spread and top sheet and got into bed.

They hugged and kissed for a while, and then melted into each other's arms for the night. They burnt quite a bit of energy and soon they were both asleep. Around three o'clock, Jimmy woke up and then woke Analisa, and they had a replay of the night before. They went to sleep again and slept until Fred woke them up at seven o'clock.

Bleary eyed, but smiling, they went to the table and had a cup of delicious coffee along with a breakfast that Fred had had catered for the occasion. At eight thirty-five a cart arrived at the foot of the steps and loaded up their luggage and took them to the gate where they would board the Commuter plane.

When they landed in Lanai, they went to their Four Star hotel and checked in, and after talking to Monty before they left home, Jimmy wanted to begin his marriage the same way his Mom and Dad had done.

He had talked to Analisa about it and she agreed, so before they did anything, Jimmy got the Bible out and read a Scripture from the book of Ephesians, Chapter five, verses twenty five through thirty-one. Then he took Analisa's hand and said a prayer; thanking God for all His blessings and asking Him to bless his marriage. He also asked God to bless him and Analisa.

They spent the next three days in Lanai, and Monty was right; it was paradise. They went on picnics, rented a jeep and toured the island, rode bicycles, lay on the beach, and made love every day, right after lunch.

On Wednesday they caught the shuttle back to Honolulu and checked into a hotel over there; the same hotel where Fred and Scott were staying. They spent the next four days sight-seeing, lying on the beach, eating, and all the things tourists do in Hawaii. On Saturday night, they invited Fred and Scott to join them for a luau. They went to a good one; one where they roasted a pig in the ground, had hula dancers and guys dancing with knives and swords. None of them drank, so other than being sleepy from the late night, there was no problem getting up Sunday morning. They took off at seven-thirty (Honolulu time) on their way back to Chattanooga.

The long trip allowed them to watch a movie, read, and to talk about things they had never talked about. At one point, Jimmy asked, "Ana, do you want to keep working?"

"Yeah, I have to work don't I?"

"No, not if you don't want to. I make enough to support the three of us, and if you'd rather stay home and be a homemaker, you can certainly do it."

"Wow! Let me think about that. I want to have some money of my own without having to ask you for it."

"You'll never have to ask me for money. We'll set up a joint bank account, and anytime you need something, you can get it. We'll also get you a couple of credit cards, so you shouldn't want for anything, but if you would rather keep working, that's up to you." He could feel the plane changing its attitude and begin its descent, and they stopped talking.

When they landed in Chattanooga at eleven-thirty that night (Chattanooga time), Joan and Mary Ann were there to meet them in Mary Ann's car. An airport porter helped unload and load their luggage, and after saying good bye to Fred and Scott, they began the ride home.

It felt strange when Mary Ann pulled into Jimmy's driveway instead of Monty's. Jimmy had lived in Monty's house since he was born, and not to go there when coming in from a trip was just not right. Joan and Mary Ann didn't get out; they left just as soon as Jimmy got their things out of the trunk. Johnny was sleeping next door with Monty, and Analisa didn't want to wake him, so she decided to leave him there until morning.

When they got to the front door, Jimmy put the suitcase down and unlocked the door and told Analisa, when she started in to "Wait a minute; come here." When she did, he picked her up and carried her over the threshold and put her down on the other side of the room. He said, "Welcome home, Mrs. Shepherd," and then, they both went out and brought in the suitcases. They carried them to the master bedroom, and when they got in there, Analisa said, "Honey, I love your house, and I'm look…."

Jimmy interrupted her in mid-sentence and said, "Hold on there, Lady. This is not my house; it's our house. Okay?"

"Okay. Now, as I started to say, I'm looking forward to living here with you in *our* beautiful home."

Jimmy said, "I'm looking forward to living here with you, too, now Kiddo, it's after midnight. Let's go to bed."

Each opened their suitcase and got their gown and pajamas and put them on, and then got into bed. They wondered why they went to the trouble of putting their things on because just as soon as they got in bed, the gown and pajamas were lying on the floor. Both of them were tired after the trip and didn't wait too long before getting re-dressed and going to sleep. Before they got to sleep, Analisa said, "I wish we didn't have to get up and go to work in the morning, don't you?"

"Yeah, I do, but all good things have to come to an end I guess."

Music from the clock-radio woke them up at six o'clock the next morning, and Analisa got out of bed first and went into the kitchen to make coffee. Soon, Jimmy got up and went in to join her. As they were sitting at the table enjoying their coffee, they heard a banging on the door and a high-pitched voice yelling, "Uncle Jim, Mom, open up."

Analisa went to open the door, and Johnny, still in his pajamas, ran in and put his arms around her. Then, he ran into the kitchen and threw his arms around Jimmy and said, "Hi, Uncle Jim. Boy, am I glad your home."

"I'm glad I'm home, too. I've missed you."

Not being used to where everything was, it was a little un-handy trying to fix breakfast and get ready for school and work, but they managed, and once they got there, it was the *same old same old* just as if they had not been gone.

While Jimmy and Jeff Ellis were in the break-room, Monty came in and sat down with them. He asked Jimmy if he was getting back into the swing of things, and then said, "You need to work hard this week and next because we leave for Rome two weeks from today. If you're not sure about anything, ask Jeff, and he'll enlighten you." Then, Monty asked some questions about the Hawaiian trip and wanted to know if he and Analisa had done some of the things that he and Joan did years ago. As they got up to leave the break-room, Monty said to Jimmy, "I've got to go meet Bob Martin. He started work on the Church last week."

"Okay, I'll see you. Oh, would you ask Bob to call me when he has a chance? I want to see how he's coming on my lake house."

Two weeks later

Joan and Analisa were like two teen aged girls as they prepared for their trip to Rome. Joan wanted to see the Pope and the Coliseum, while Analisa wanted to throw coins in Trevi Fountain. Monty and Jimmy wanted to write some good business.

Fourteen hours was the scheduled flying time to Rome the next day, and in order for them to arrive in time for work, Tuesday morning, Monty wanted to leave Chattanooga at eleven A.M.. Due to the time difference and the fourteen hour flying time, if they left at eleven they would be in Rome at seven A.M. Tuesday morning. That would give them time to have breakfast, check into their hotel, and meet Adriano and Cosimo in time to work a full day.

Things worked out just as he had planned and they left Lovell Field right on time. At seven-sixteen, Tuesday morning, they landed at Rome's Fiumicino Airport. After breakfast on the plane, they went to the Hassler Roma Hotel and checked in. Monty went ahead and registered for Fred and Scott and told the desk clerk to remember them when they came in. He pulled the business cards that Adriano and Cosimo had given him and called their office. When Adriano answered and Monty told him who it was, Adriano said one of them would be right over to pick him and Jimmy up.

In about thirty minutes Adriano drove up in a big Mercedes and took the pair back to the Ricci-Moretti Sales office. Once inside, Cosimo came out of his office and greeted Monty and Jimmy. Then, Adriano took them around the office and introduced them to the various employees and told them what their jobs were at the company. After their tour of the office, they went into Adriano's office, and Cosimo came in and joined them. They told Monty that they would like to spend the day familiarizing themselves with the Shepherd line and not go see customers until the next day. That didn't sit well with him, but he figured that they knew what they were doing, so he went along with it. A little later, he found out that the buyers at both stores they were going to call on were out of town and would be back that day.

The rest of the morning was spent going over the ladies' line until they broke for lunch. After lunch, Monty finished reviewing the ladies' styles and moved into the David's Staff groups. Jimmy had been with the company for almost three months and had been studying all the styles ever since he came to work, but in the entire three months, he thought that he had not learned as much as he did in the few short hours of that day when Monty went over everything. In fact; he felt as if he had learned so much that afternoon and was so confident, he wanted to make the presentation to at least one of the accounts they were to see the next day.

At four o'clock, they knocked off, and Adriano took them back to their hotel. Joan and Analisa weren't there when they got there, so they decided that that would be a good time for a nap. After a while, the women came in and said they had been having a grand time. The hotel directed them to a sightseeing tour company, and they saw a lot of the sights in Rome. There was still much to see, and they bought tickets for another tour the next morning that would take in the Coliseum, and a walking tour in the afternoon.

Analisa told Jimmy, "Honey, this place is incredible. I just wish you could go with us to some of the places we are going to."

"I know, Baby, but I'll be coming over here on a regular basis, and I can do all that later. I'll bring you with me some of the times, and we can see Rome together, but this trip has to be a working trip. We can still be together every evening, though."

"I know, but I still wish you could go with me."

"Maybe next trip."

The next morning, the four of them had breakfast together downstairs in the hotel restaurant while they waited on Adriano. At eight forty-five, he arrived, and he said he had a full day planned for them. They went back to Adriano's office first to pick up Cosimo and to discuss how they planned to work with the accounts they would be seeing that day.

Their first appointment was with the buyers at La Rinascente Department Store. La Rinascente was the largest Department Store chain in Italy. The first buyer they saw was the men's' buyer, named Gavino Conti, and when they walked in, Jimmy noticed a large picture of Mickey Mantle on the wall, and on one of the credenzas were baseball items, including a Louisville Slugger bat.

He didn't say anything about them until Adriano introduced him and Monty and while they were getting acquainted, Mr. Conti asked them about their backgrounds and so forth, and when Jimmy said he had been a professional baseball player, the conversation quickly switched from apparel to baseball.

Gavino was such a fan that he became involved in the Italian Baseball League as a part-owner. He explained that baseball over there was nothing like baseball in the states. The current IBL consists of eight teams, each playing forty-two games; a team plays two, three game series against every other team The four teams that finish with the best regular season record qualify for a round-robin playoff. The first and second place finishers of the round-robin are cast into the best of seven Italian Baseball Series and compete for the championship, referred to as the Scudetto.

After Jimmy told him all about his baseball career, he was so impressed that Monty could have probably written an order for whatever and how much he wanted to. Gavino was thrilled to know that Jimmy would be coming back to work with Adriano and Cosimo in the future, and he promised that La Rinascente would push David's Staff as much as they could.

Next, they went to the ladies' sportswear department and talked with Damiano Rossi, the buyer. The visit there was not as enthusiastic as the call on the men's department was, but it was enthusiastic, and Damiano said they would do their best for Shepherd Global.

After they left the store, Adriano asked, "Are you fellows hungry?"

Monty answered, "We can eat anytime. I feel sure Jimmy is hungry."

"Do you like Pizza?"

Monty and Jimmy both said in unison, "We love it."

They went to a restaurant that was famous for its pizza and split two large ones. Monty and Jimmy agreed that it was the best pizza they had ever eaten and they said they would like to come back there sometime.

After lunch, they called on the buyers at the Coin Department Store, and they were received very well by both buyers, Fino Fraccari, men's, and Enrico Fusselli, ladies.

When they finished at the Coin, Adriano took them back to the hotel and invited them, along with Joan and Analisa to have dinner with them and their wives. They readily accepted, and that night they took them to a very nice, high dollar restaurant. All the Shepherds liked Italian food, but what they had that night was something far above anything they had ever had.

Wednesday and Thursday were replays of Tuesday, except they called on different accounts and were not taken out to eat at night. Even though Monty and Jimmy were busy every day with business, they did take some long walks with their wives at night.

Monty had told Fred and Scott that he wanted to leave around eight o'clock, Friday morning, and when they ordered food from the caterer, to have them bring food for breakfast as they would not eat before they left. Fred did exactly as Monty told him, and they took off from Fiumicino Airport right on time.

The weather was beautiful, and the flight was uneventful. Monty and Jimmy sat on one of the plush sofas while Monty explained a lot of things about the way Shepherd Apparel did business. Joan and Analisa each sat in an easy-chair talking and reading. Finally, after fourteen hours in the air, they landed at Lovell Field at four o'clock that afternoon and were very glad to be back on the ground.

Jimmy and Monty went to the office Saturday morning, but only stayed until around noon. Monty told Jimmy while they were still at the office, "Well, Son, it looks like we're going to be able to stay at home for a while. With Christmas and New Year's coming up, I think we'll be here until the January show in New York."

"I'm glad, Dad. I need to get used to living with my new wife, don't you think?"

"You're probably right. Now, let's go home."

On the way back from Rome, while they were talking, Jimmy told Monty, "Dad, when we get back to work, I wish you would let me shadow you most of the time instead of doing the way I've been doing.

Jeff is a good teacher, but, you know what? I've learned more in the last three days than I've learned in the last three months the way I've been doing. You keep saying that you want me to learn the business; well, I believe I can learn it in a fraction of the time if I can watch you and learn from you."

"Are you not learning from Jeff?"

"Yes sir, Jeff's good, and I'm learning, but not the way I learned from you this week."

"We'll see."

When they got home, Jimmy asked Analisa and Johnny if they would like to ride up to Sale Creek to see what had been done on the house. They pulled into the driveway, and the house looked very different than the way it looked the last time Jimmy was there. It was nowhere near finished, but that time, they had started putting the Crab Orchard stone and Redwood on the front.

Analisa commented, "Oh, I like this."

And Jimmy said, "I do too, and it's not costing nearly as much as the house we're living in." Kidding, he asked, "Do you want to move up here?"

Kidding back, she said, "Yeah, let's do."

Johnny, with his child's naivety' asked, "Are we really going to move up here?"

They kidded around for a few minutes, and then Jimmy said, "No, Pal, we're not going to move up here. We're just going to come up here when we want to come to the lake."

Then, Jimmy looked around to see if Hal was there, but he didn't see him. He looked for his pickup, and it was gone, too, so he figured that maybe he had gone to Randy's. Then, he thought, *I wonder if he has moved into an apartment. The house is almost finished and it would be foolish for him to stay way up here if he's not working up here. I'll call Randy and see.*

On the way back to Chattanooga, they stopped in Soddy-Daisy for an ice cream cone, and then, they went home.

That night, as they were just relaxing, a potential problem came up; where were they going to go to Church? Jimmy had always loved his, but was gone from it for the years that he was in college and playing baseball, and now that he was back, he felt as if that was where he belonged.

Analisa, on the other hand, loved her Church as well. That's where they got married, and her pastor was the one who married them, but her attachment was not as strong as Jimmy's, so after some discussion they decided to go to Jimmy's, and Analisa would move her letter.

Monty was very pleased with their decision, and to celebrate, he and Joan took them out to lunch the next day, after Church. "Dad, has Bob Martin said when the new Church will be finished?"

"Yeah, he thinks he can have it completed by July or August if he doesn't lose too much time because of weather this winter. We've decided to use a metal building and dress it up. When it's finished, you won't be able to tell it's metal. That will speed up the building process, and at the same time it will save quite a bit of money. Bob showed me some pictures of other metal building Churches, and you can absolutely not tell that they're metal.

"Well, if everybody's finished, let's get outa here. We're missing the football game."

That afternoon, Mary Ann called Analisa and said she and Bill were going to be at her Mom and Dad's later in the afternoon, and she said she wished that the two of them would be over there, and Analisa told her they would.

They watched for their car to pull in the driveway, and then they went over. Analisa sensed something by the way Mary Ann was acting so giddy, and in a little bit she said, "Everybody, I want to show you my ring; at lunch, Bill asked me to marry him, and I said yes."

Everybody congratulated them and went on about how pretty her ring was, and Joan asked, "When's the big day?"

Bill chimed in and said, "We don't know exactly. We want to be the first couple to get married in our new Church, so it will depend on when it gets finished before we will know."

"Praise the Lord," Monty said, almost yelling. "What a year! Both of my children have found soul mates, the Lord is letting us build Him a new place to worship, Jimmy has come into the company, and the company just keeps on growing. Thank you Lord. This is going to be a fantastic Christmas. Joan, do you have any of that spiced cider? If you do, break it out and let's have a toast to the newlyweds and the newly engaged. It's just hard for me to fathom how good God is."

CHAPTER TWENTY FOUR

The next day was the start of Christmas week. Christmas was on Thursday, and that meant Shepherd Apparel would only be open two days. They would close Tuesday afternoon and not reopen until January fifth. Of course, Monty and Jimmy would work while the plants and office were closed. Everybody was getting excited, especially Johnny, and some of them said they weren't through with their shopping.

Tuesday was pretty much a loss, production-wise. Each department had their own Christmas Dinner, and each person brought a covered dish. The company gave everybody a bonus, and those were handed out at the dinners.

On Wednesday morning, Jimmy wanted to go to Sale Creek to see if Hal was there and to see the progress on the house. Analisa had some things to do, so he and Johnny went up. He was wondering what Hal was going to do for Christmas and decided that he would invite him to their house if he didn't have other plans.

The Crab Orchard and paneling was finished when he pulled up to the house, and it really looked good. He pointed to the lake and asked Johnny, "Padna, do you see that spot right there?"

"Yes sir, why?"

"Because that's the spot where I'm going to dunk you next summer when we come up here."

"Yeah, right. I'll be the one doing the dunking."

About that time, Hal yelled at them from the boathouse. They walked down there, and Jimmy said, "Hi Hal. I was hoping you wouldn't be here. I don't want you to have to spend Christmas alone. Do you have any plans?"

"Oh yes, I'm going down to Randy's this afternoon and spend Christmas with them and stay 'til Saturday. I can't tell you how much I appreciate what you did to get us back together, Jimmy. Ever since I've been back in Randy's life, my demons have stayed away, and I have you to thank for that."

"Well, we're not going to stay; we just wanted to come up and see what was going on, and it looks as if everything is lovely. Am I right?"

"You're absolutely right."

“Okay then, I may come back up one day next week. I want to talk to Bob Martin about some things. I’ll see you, Hal; Merry Christmas.”

“Merry Christmas to you. Bye.”

On Wednesday evening, Christmas Eve, all the Shepherds went to Church, and afterwards, Joan had everybody over to her and Monty’s house for dinner. She had begun planning it before they went to Rome, and everything turned out to be perfect. In addition to the immediate Shepherd family, she invited Liz and Ben. When she called Liz, Liz wanted to know if it would be alright if Sue and Mark, her boyfriend and Bobby and Marilyn, his girlfriend came. Of course Joan said it would be, and everybody came early enough to go to Church for an inspiring service.

Bill had to conduct a service at his Church, so he and Mary Ann were unable to make it to Monty’s service, but they were able to get there in time for dinner.

Christmas Day was a super day. Everyone got nice presents, especially Johnny, and Monty made sure that nobody forgot what Christmas was all about. He not only asked God to bless the food at lunch, he asked everybody to stop what they were doing after the gifts were opened, and he said another prayer, thanking God for the gifts, and asking God to help them remember the purpose of the day and the season.

The week after Christmas was just another week at work for Monty, and although he didn’t have to do it, Jimmy went in every morning and tried to help. It was just part of his learning process. Around nine o’clock, Monday morning, Jimmy got a phone call.

“Hello, Jimmy, this is Randy Long. How are you doing?”

Jimmy’s heart sunk when the voice said it was Randy, and he answered, “Hey, Randy, I’m doing great. Hope you are.”

“Yeah, I’m fine. Listen, Jimmy, is there any way that I could come to your office and talk to you, or maybe we could have lunch somewhere?”

“Sure, why don’t you come over here? I’ll probably be here until around three o’clock.”

“Okay, if it’s alright, I’ll just come on now. I should be there in about a half-hour.”

Alright, I’ll be up front in a half-hour and look for you. The doors are locked, and I’ll have to let you in.” He was very uneasy after talking to Randy. He figured there was a problem with Hal.

When he got there, they went to the break-room and got a Coke, and then, went to Jimmy's office. They sat down, and Jimmy said, "Okay, Randy, what can I do for you this morning? Is something wrong with Hal?"

"Oh no, he's doing great, thanks to you. Listen Jimmy, the reason I wanted to talk to you is this; do you remember me telling you that I'm a textile engineer now?

"Yes, I remember."

"Well, I have been working at Mountain Textiles for the last five years, and now, it looks as if they are going to have to down-size, and since I'm one of the newest, I'm afraid I might be cut. Shepherd Apparel is large, and the word is it's getting larger, and I wonder if there might be a place where I could fit in as an engineer."

"Gosh, Randy, I don't know. I don't have anything to do with hiring, but I'll be glad to get your name before someone who does."

"That would be great, Jimmy. I brought a resume with me, so if it's alright, I'll leave it with you."

"Tell you what, Randy; Dad's here. Let's go see if he can help."

They walked into Monty's office, and Jimmy said, "Dad, do you remember Randy Long from High School? Randy played left tackle on my side of the line."

"Yeah, I remember you, Randy. How have you been?"

"Dad, Randy is a textile engineer and he works for Mountain Textiles. He says Mountain Textiles is going to down-size, and he's afraid he's going to be cut. He's wondering if Shepherd Apparel might have something for him. Here's his resume."

"Randy, I don't know what to tell you. There's a good chance we can use you, but the head of our engineering department is the one you'll have to talk to. He does all the hiring for his department, and he won't be back to work until the fifth of January. I'll give him your resume, and we'll see what happens."

"I will appreciate that, Mr. Shepherd. I've heard so much about Shepherd Apparel, that I'd love to work for you. It would be good to work with my old wide receiver again, too."

Jimmy let Randy out and told him that he would follow up with Jack when he came back to work, and hopefully something could be worked out. And then, he returned to Monty's office."

"Jimmy, wasn't that Hal Long's son?"

"Yes sir."

"Well, he seems like a nice young man. Maybe Jack can use him."

March, three months later

Jimmy had just returned from a trip to Seattle, and was playing *catch-up* in his office when the phone rang. "Hello."

It was Analisa. "Hey, Big Boy, I want your body."

"Well, you can have it. Are you wanting it right this minute?"

"No, I'll just wait and capture you when you get home."

"That sounds like my kind of deal. What are you up to?"

"I thought I would call and tell you that that body of yours has gotten you in trouble."

"What kind of trouble?"

"Have you ever heard of John Dodd?"

"No, I can't say that I have. Why?"

"Well, his full name is John Dodd, M.D., and I went to see him today, and do you know what he told me?"

"I hope he told you why you're feeling so bad all the time."

"He did, and he also told me that we're going to have a baby. Can you believe it?"

Silence…After about ten seconds, Jimmy said, "You're not kidding, are you?"

"No, you're going to be a daddy, and that's why I've been feeling so bad." And then, kidding, she said, "I hope you're worth all this."

"Don't worry; I'm worth that and a lot more. When is it due? Did he say?"

"As near as he can tell, it should be September nineteenth."

"Wow! That's great news, Sweetheart. When are we going to tell people?"

"I don't know. We can tell your parents now, but why don't we wait a little while before we tell anybody else."

"Whatever you say, but I'm going to have a hard time keeping the secret."

Later, that evening, after dinner, he and Analisa went over to see Joan because he hadn't seen her since he got back from Seattle. They let Johnny stay home to do his homework. After visiting for a little while, they were getting ready to tell about the baby, but before they could, Joan asked, "Guess what?"

Monty and Jimmy both asked, "What?"

"I talked to Liz this afternoon, and she said Sue and Mark are going to get married in late June."

Monty said, "That's quick, isn't it?"

"Yeah, but that's what they want to do, and you know how June is supposed to be Bride's month."

"Yeah, I know, but it's still quick."

After the wedding conversation died down, Jimmy said, "Well, in case anybody is interested, the doctor told Analisa today that she's going to have a baby."

Joan squealed and got up and went over and hugged both Analisa and Jimmy. Monty got up and shook Jimmy's hand, and then he went over and put his arms around Analisa and told her how happy he was for her.

Joan asked, "When is it due, Ana?"

"The doctor said as near as he can tell, it will be September 19."

When she said that Monty began to count on his fingers, and a few seconds later, he looked at Analisa and smiled, and then, looking straight into her eyes, he said, "I knew we shouldn't have left you two alone that last night in Rome. See what happened?"

Analisa blushed and said, "I know; I guess you just need to keep a closer watch on us."

"I guess so; somebody needs to keep you out of trouble."

April second marked the six-month anniversary for when Jimmy went to work for Shepherd Apparel, and Monty was amazed by how much he had learned, and how well he could do things. It was also very gratifying to Monty to know that Jimmy was getting to be in demand as a speaker. Surprisingly, Jimmy began taking it upon himself to go to different places and speak to groups about Jesus, and he just loved it. Monty felt as if he could finally see a little light at the end of the tunnel when it came to thinking about retirement because he knew the company would be in good hands when he left, however, there was still much training to do.

Morning sickness had begun to ease up a little on Analisa, and since she was feeling better she was devoting a lot of her time to decorating their home. She unselfishly involved Joan and Thil in her projects and every week, the house looked a little bit better. Sometimes it was only Analisa and Thil because Joan was helping Liz get things done for Sue's upcoming wedding.

June 24, Sue's wedding day

After a cloudy start, the sun came out, and it became a beautiful day for a wedding. Ever since Sue and Bobby went to live with Sue and Ben, they had been attending the Tiftonia Community Church, and that's where the wedding was going to be.

Sue wanted a Church wedding, but not a huge one. Ben and Sue were helping out with the expenses; however, she didn't want to create a burden for them, so she and Mark pitched in and helped out with the costs. Around two-hundred were invited, and they hoped that maybe a hundred would come.

The Church was decorated with simple decorations. There was some greenery and a few flowers around the alter, but other than that, there were no decorations.

The wedding party consisted of the bride and groom, of course, and Sue had four attendants, including Mary Ann as her Maid of Honor. Mark had three ushers plus his Dad as his Best Man.

Three o'clock in the afternoon was when the ceremony was scheduled, and people began coming in around two-thirty. Their estimate of one hundred came pretty close.

After reciting the standard vows, the preacher declared them man and wife, and they walked back up the aisle to the outer hall. Both Sue and Mark were all-smiles until they reached the fifth row of pews from the back of the sanctuary. Mark kept smiling, but Sue's happy look left her instantly when she reached that point. When she looked at the person sitting on that row, she was shocked to see her Mother sitting there. She had not seen her Mother since she left her and Scott Tate and moved in with Liz and Ben; about ten or twelve years ago.

After everyone got out of the sanctuary, the wedding party went back in for pictures, and Sue couldn't get her mind off her Mother. She whispered to Bobby, "Did you see Mama?" "Yeah, I saw her. I wonder what she wants."

"I don't know, but I'm sure we'll find out."

When the pictures were finished, they started out the back door to walk around the building to the Fellowship Hall where the reception was to be held. The outer vestibule was empty by then except for one person; Sue and Bobby's Mother.

She and Mark stopped, and she said, "Mama, what are you doing here?"

"Honey, I saw your picture in the paper announcing your wedding, and I knew I had to come."

"Mama, I haven't seen you in years. Where have you been?"

"I live in Rome now. Darling, do you think it would be possible for us to get together and talk?"

"When, Mama? Don't you understand that this is my wedding day? Tell you what; come on in to the reception, and maybe a little later we can talk for a minute before I leave for my honeymoon. Oh, Mark, this is my Mother."

As is the case with most Christian weddings, there was no drinking, and without that the reception didn't last too long. In a little while, Sue went over to her Mother, but Bobby didn't, and her Mother said, "Sue, you're a beautiful bride. I'm very happy for you."

"Mama, is Scott with you?"

"Oh no, I haven't been with Scott for nearly ten years. I finally got sense enough to leave him. The last I heard, he was in prison. Did you live with the people at Wauhatchie Farms after you left us?"

"Yes, Mama, and they were and are wonderful. They raised Bobby and I the way people are supposed to raise children, and we had a very happy childhood after we left you all."

"Did you ever miss me?"

"I'll have to be honest and say that I did at first, but you were so messed up, and Scott was so mean, I never wanted to come back. Bobby and I look to Ben and Liz as our parents now because they love us, and you know what, Mama? They never hit us one time. Can you believe that?"

"Darling, thank you for seeing me. I hope I didn't mess up your big day, but when I saw your picture in the paper, I knew I had to see you. If you don't hate me too much do you think it would be possible for us to meet for lunch sometime when you get back and talk some more? I'm not the same person that you knew twelve years ago. Now, I have a good job in Rome, and I'm married to a good man. If you will just let me see you again, I think you'll be pleased with your Mama. I don't know if Bobby will ever want to see me again, but I hope he will."

"Mama, yes, I'll meet you for lunch. Give me your number, and I'll call you when we get back, and Mama, I don't hate you, and I'll talk to Bobby." They hugged and said goodbye, and both women had tears in their eyes.

After Linda left, Bobby went over to Sue and asked, "What did she want?"

"She wants to meet me for lunch sometime when I get back so we can talk. She said she would like to get together with you, too, but thinks you hate her too much."

"Do you hate her, Bobby?"

"No, I don't hate her. I just can't forget how she and Scott treated us when we lived with them, and I don't want to be reminded of it by meeting with her."

About that time, Mark came over to them and asked. "Mrs. Hammond, are you ready to head down to the sunshine state?"

"Yes I am, Mr. Hammond. Bye, Bobby; I'll see you in about a week. Love ya."

After they left, Liz went over to Bobby and asked, "Wasn't that your Mother that Sue was talking to?"

"Yes ma'am that was her."

"What did she want? Did Sue invite her?"

"No, she didn't invite her; she saw Sue's picture in the paper, and I don't know what she wants except she wants to meet Sue for lunch when she gets back from her honeymoon."

"Does she want to meet with you too?"

"I don't know; I didn't speak to her."

Liz didn't say anything else; she just pondered the purpose of Linda's presence at the wedding.

A little after noon on Monday, before he went to lunch, Jimmy's phone rang, and when he answered, he was surprised by who it was. "Hello, Jim, David Brownlee here. How are you doing?"

"I'm fine thank you. How are you, Mr. Brownlee?"

"I'm doing well. Listen, Jim, I want to ask a favor."

"Anything, Mr. Brownlee. What do you need?"

"I guess the short answer is I need you. Jim, I know you're familiar with the FCA because you used to belong to the organization, and you have spoken at some of their meetings; right?"

"Yes sir. That's right."

"Well Jim, I have been working really hard setting up a new organization that will help keep the athletes involved when they age out of the FCA, and I call it Former Athletes for Jesus or FAJ for short. We're going to have several chapters out here on the west coast before we spread to the east, and the first chapter is here in Seattle, and this brings me to the favor. If I send my plane to pick you up, will you consider being the keynote speaker at our kickoff event?"

"Wow! What an honor. When is it, Mr. Brownlee?"

"It's on the evening of August sixteenth. Are you free then?"

"I'll make it a point to be. Thank you, Mr. Brownlee."

"No; thank you, Jim. I feel privileged to have you on board. Look, the sixteenth is on Friday, so I'll have my plane in Chattanooga to pick you up on Thursday and then take you back on Saturday. Does that sound alright?"

"That sounds perfect. My Dad's going to be very happy about this. I can't wait to tell him."

"Jim, that reminds me; do you think he would consider coming for the kickoff? We could sure use his celebrity to add to the event."

"I don't know, but I'll ask him. He's out of town right now, so I can't ask him until tomorrow. Will that be alright?"

"Yeah, no rush. Just let me know or have him give me a call. Jim, thank you so much. I know you're going to be a big hit. Most of the guys are around your age, so I know you can relate. I'll call you when it gets closer to time to reconfirm everything, okay? Oh, and keep those *Fins* coming, will you?"

"We sure will. Thanks again, Mr. Brownlee. Goodbye."

At first, Monty said he wasn't going to Seattle, but after thinking about it for several days, he decided to go. The All-Conference plane was there to pick him and Jimmy up at noon on Thursday, and it took until four o'clock Seattle time to get there. David Brownlee and his wife treated the two to dinner, and Monty and Jim thoroughly enjoyed spending time with them.

Jimmy usually just spoke from the heart without the use of notes, but for that important event, he made some to use in case he needed them. Eight o'clock was the scheduled time for the meeting to start, but people began showing up a little after seven. David had done a remarkable job of promoting it by advertising that the FAJ was an organization where former athletes could continue their roles as examples to others by showing what God had done in their lives.

Finally, eight o'clock arrived and David acted as host and emcee. He made a short talk and then introduced several well-known former athletes, including Monty Shepherd. Then he introduced Jimmy, using more superlatives than Jimmy even knew existed. The crowd enthusiastically welcomed him, and he began to speak. He was so into what he wanted to say that he didn't use any of his notes, and the crowd was spellbound. After twenty minutes, he concluded his speech and was given a standing ovation. Before the meeting ended, David Brownlee presented him with a beautiful plaque indicating that he was the featured speaker at the inaugural meeting of the Former Athletes for Jesus.

David could not have been more gracious and couldn't do enough for Jimmy and Monty. By the time they got back to their hotel it was ten o'clock, and they were both tired and wanted to go to bed. Their ride was to takeoff at seven the next morning, and they said their goodbyes before they went up to their room.

David's pilot had had food catered the way Monty's pilots did, and they had a snack for breakfast on the plane. Monty wanted to tell Jimmy several things during the seven hour flight. One of them was how proud he was of him by the way he conducted himself at the FAJ meeting the night before. The rest of the things he wanted to talk about were business related. During the flight, Jimmy asked, "Dad, do you realize that it's only four weeks before you're going to be a Granddad again?"

"Really? I knew it was soon, but I didn't realize it was only four weeks. Wow!"

The plane landed at Lovell Field at eleven o'clock, and Joan, Analisa, and Johnny were there to meet them. When they got home, both of them crashed and rested all Saturday afternoon.

CHAPTER TWENTY FIVE

September 18, four weeks later

Around five a.m. Analisa woke Jimmy up and said, "Jimmy, wake up. I think it's time to go."

"It can't be time. It's not due 'til tomorrow."

"Get up, Sleepyhead; the baby doesn't know that. We've got to go. Call your Mom and tell her so she can come over and get Johnny up when it's time."

Arriving at Erlanger Hospital at five forty-five, Analisa was put on a gurney and taken upstairs to the floor where the delivery room and nursery were located. Jimmy parked the car and ran into the hospital. Finding out where Analisa had been taken, he rushed up there. A nurse was with her when he got there, and the doctor came in a little later. After examining her, based on how much she was dilated, he concluded that it would probably be three to four hours before the baby was born.

Jimmy was beside himself with a major case of nerves, and in about an hour, he looked up and saw his Mom coming into the waiting room. "Mom, what are you doing here? Where's Johnny?"

"Just calm down. Your Dad and Grandmother are looking after him. They'll be here after Johnny leaves for school. Have you heard anything yet?"

"The doctor said it will probably be three or four hours."

"Why don't we go downstairs and get a cup of coffee while we wait; do you want to?"

"No ma'am. I don't think I want to leave. You go and get you one."

He tried reading magazines; he watched TV and did everything he could to get his mind off of Analisa. Finally, a nurse came and told him he should go back to room six and be with his wife because it looked as if the baby would come shortly.

In the meantime, Monty and Thil had come, and they were in the waiting room with Joan. Joan woke Mary Ann as she was leaving home, and she got to the hospital just after Jimmy went to be with Analisa. Everyone perked up when the nurse came to get Jimmy, and they began trying to guess whether it would be a boy or a girl. There were four guesses and the count was two for a boy and two for a girl. Each had reasons why their guess was right, and one of them said, “It seems as if we’ve done this before.”

At nine-eighteen a.m. a new baby Shepherd boy greeted the world. After cleaning him up and examining him, he was declared to be healthy, with ten fingers and ten toes. Before they took Analisa to her room, they invited the rest of the family to come see the baby. Each of them got to hold him for a minute, and then they handed him to Analisa. She was really a proud Mom.

Mary Ann asked, “Do you have a name picked out?”

“I think so, but we’ll have to talk about it some more. More than likely, he will be named after his Daddy.”

Monty said, “Boy, that would be great. If you do name him after Jimmy, you all will have a Jimmy and Johnny just like Joan and I did.”

In a few minutes they came to get the baby and take Analisa to her room. Everyone followed and continued the gaiety until Analisa fell asleep after her ordeal. Whoever named it *labor* had the right word. Having a baby was very hard work.

After dinner, most of the family returned to the hospital, and the baby was already in the room. Jimmy was holding it, and when Monty and Joan walked in, he said, “Mimi and Granddad, I want to introduce you to James Montgomery Shepherd, Jr.. Say hi, Jimmy.”

Analisa rested most of the afternoon and was feeling good that night. She was told that she could go home the next day, and that made her happy.

Jimmy took the next day off from work to take Analisa and the baby home, but returned the following day. He didn’t have to worry about Analisa because there was a steady stream of her friends going in to visit, and when the friends left, there was Joan and Thil. Johnny was happy to meet his little brother, but Jimmy thought he sensed that all the attention he had been given was going to have to be shared, and he didn’t know about that.

Two and one-half years later

Over the last three years, Jimmy had learned nearly every job in the Shepherd Apparel Group. His real expertise was in handling people, but he could almost tell the manufacturing cost of a garment just be looking at it. Monty had become so dependent on him that he didn’t have to worry about sales anymore because Jimmy could see to it that everything was handled. Then, one day Monty called him into his office right after the regular Monday morning staff meeting and told him to sit down. When he was seated, Monty came around his desk and sat down beside him and began talking.

"Son, ever since my Dad turned Shepherd Apparel over to me I have been working my fingers to the bone trying to make it the best company, making the best product, using the best people in the world, and I think we've accomplished that now. Over the last three years you have been a large part of that process, and I want to thank you for that. In fact; I think the time has come for you to step into a bigger job. Do you want to know what that job is?"

"Yes sir. What is it?"

"Jimmy, this is the day I've dreamed of for many years. Today, I'm promoting you to the position of President of Shepherd Global Apparel Group, and you will have full responsibility for the day to day operations of the company. I will retain the position of CEO and Chairman of the Board, but the company is yours for the most part.

"As you know, your Mom and I fixed up and enlarged the Florida house, and now, we hope to enjoy it. We will be splitting our time between here and there. I won't dump all this in your lap at once; I'll stick around to help you for a while, but I don't think it will take too long before you can handle things."

He got up and walked back to the credenza behind his desk and picked up the Shepherd's staff. "Son, this Shepherd's staff is the symbol of our company. It has two meanings; first, the Lord is our shepherd, and this represents His staff, and second; we are the shepherds of our employees, operating with integrity and guidance. My granddaddy handed this staff down to my Dad and Dad handed it down to me. Today, I'm handing it down to you, and I pray that you will handle it with the reverence your Fathers have. Any questions?"

"No sir; I don't have any questions. I'm too stunned to be able to think of any, but I'm sure that after the shock wears off I'll have plenty. Thank you, Dad. I had no idea you were thinking about this."

Monty went to the door and told Connie to call everyone who had attended the staff meeting to come back to the meeting room for a minute. He wanted to tell them something.

When everyone was there, he made the announcement that Jimmy was the new President of Shepherd Global Apparel Group, and he hoped they would give him their wholehearted support and cooperation. He explained that he would still be the CEO, but Jimmy would be in charge of the day to day operations of the company. Everybody applauded, because they all liked Jimmy, and they pledged their support.

As soon as that meeting was over, Jimmy excused himself and went to his office and called Analisa. She picked up on the third ring. "Hello."

"Hi Sweet Thing, what's happening?"

"Have you ever heard the term *terrible twos?"*

"Yeah, I've heard it, why?"

"Well, your little boy gives that term new meaning, and I'm about to spank his little butt. What are you doing?"

"I thought I'd call and tell you that I got a promotion today."

"Really? What kind of promotion?"

"Would you believe that I'm the new President of Shepherd Apparel?"

"You're kidding. You are kidding, aren't you?"

"No, I'm dead serious."

"That's wonderful. I'm happy for you. You deserve it."

"How about we go out to eat tonight to celebrate? Can you get a baby-sitter?"

"I'll try. What time?"

"Around six-thirty. Look, I've got to go. See you tonight."

After the announcement and Monty was alone in his office, he began to reflect on his life, and he thanked God at the same time. *Lord, with your help, I have been successful at many things, and I'm eternally grateful to you for that. First, you let me be born to good parents, and then, you gave me a really good wife. We were blessed with three great children and now two wonderful grandchildren, and during all this, Shepherd Apparel continued to grow, again with your help.*

Lord, life is good right now. Jimmy is now the head of our company. Mary Ann has a good man and is apparently doing good things for you in his new Church. And Lord, please be with Mary Ann as she prepares to have the baby. Bobby is now head of our accounting department, and he and Marilyn seem to be doing well. Sue and Mark are very happy with their new little girl. And Lord, thank you for helping Linda Tate regain her life after the rough time she had with Scott. I'm grateful that she and Sue are once again mother and daughter.

Father, thank you for all these things and all your other blessings. In looking back at my life and coming forward, it is now truly serendipity.

www.ingramcontent.com/pod-product-compliance
Lightning Source LLC
Chambersburg PA
CBHW060916250626
47159CB00008B/3026

9781630662073